BREAK THE

Jenny W

For Peter... For always believing in me and inspiring me to reach for the stars...

A creature so simple as the dog can teach us so many of the skills we need in life; slow to anger and quick to forgive. How do they practice patience so well? Why do they never get angry? Why are they beyond joyful when we re-enter a room we merely left five minutes ago? Humans spend their entire lives attempting to master mindfulness, our canine friends were born with it.

Prologue

Jane was hiding under her bed; they were coming for her. Her body shook with fear, she placed a hand over her mouth to stifle her cries, she couldn't let them hear her, couldn't let them discover her hiding place.

"Jane." *She* was calling her, the voice drawled with sick, low malice. "Jane, please come downstairs and see us." The voice feigned sweetness that made Jane shudder with terror.

Seven year old Jane continued to lie under the bed, her body clenched, frozen in fright, eyes wide open in search of feet that might approach.

She heard the creaking of the floor boards on the stairs, they were coming for her; they would find her. Her sister, Tess, was in her own room, sleeping peacefully, no doubt.

Jane watched from her open bedroom door as the size eleven, dirty boots came tramping from the hallway in to her bedroom, searching, sniffing her out. Jane's heart thudded violently against her chest, did he know where she was hidden?

Then, as quick as lightning, a large, spade of a hand grabbed at her arm, Jane shrieked a high pitch scream in panic and horror and tried to pull away out of his grasp. He managed to clutch at the material of Jane's pyjama top and dragged her out from the under the bed.

His expression was manic, he reeked of alcohol, he had her lifted above his head. Jane's body went limp, submitting to what had to be done. There was no escape.

Chapter 1

"Jane, there's a work night out next weekend if you're interested? Plenty of doctors to feast your eyes on!" Millie announced eagerly one afternoon in work as they sat completing paperwork; Millie was Jane's closest friend and fellow midwife.

"No, I'm ok, I'm just going to relax next weekend. Thanks anyway." Jane replied indifferently, keeping her head down, focusing on her writing task.

"Oh, come on, Jane! You can't spend your whole life with those dogs, you need to live a little. Go out, meet people, let your hair down." Cried Millie excitedly, nudging Jane with her elbow encouragingly.

"I'll think about it." Jane replied ambiguously, having no intention, whatsoever, of going out with pretty much an entire group of strangers. What could be worse?

"I'm going to hound you until you agree to go." Millie said, with a devilish twinkle in her eye.

"Alright, but I'm only going to please you!" Jane puffed, giving in, thinking she could text Millie later to cancel.

"I'm happy enough with that." Replied Millie. "Let's meet at mine beforehand and get ready together!"

Jane hated these social etiquettes, why can girls not just get ready on their own? Why all this fuss just to *'get ready'*.

Jane was single. *Very* single. Having had an exceptionally unsuccessful dating record to date, she had given up putting any more effort in to finding a man and despaired at the thought of nights out with friends, pathetically drooling over the same vile, pub going men each week. At thirty years old, Jane lived a quiet, independent life, she had a budding career in midwifery, and lived alone in a small, two bedroom house with her two beautiful dogs. Jane felt satisfied with her simple life.

Being alone did not bother Jane, having spent all of her childhood and much of her adulthood feeling as though she could not relate to anyone on a deep, personal level. She was uncomfortable and awkward in social situations and she had a small group of friends who she felt did not truly know the *real* Jane, as she lacked the ability to trust another and feared the rejection if she was to give away too much of her true thoughts, feelings, and most importantly, her dark background.

The truth was, Jane had a troubled past, a skeleton in the closet she could not reveal to anyone. This hindered her ability to maintain friendships and procure a long term relationship as her guard was always raised and she pushed people away. No one could ever completely understand how her disastrous past had affected her, and because of this, she felt disconnected to everyone that she met and envious of the people who felt secure to divulge their biggest secrets to people whom they barely knew.

Jane knew that these people had never truly been faced with any genuine hardship or tragedy in their lives. They had also never been given a reason not to trust any person they ever met. Jane's circumspection in the human race was not unjust, therefore, she put all her energy, warmth and love in to her dogs and her career.

After her shift, Jane returned to her house, it was a two bedroom, semi-detached house with a pebble dash render, situated not far from the seafront, she was greeted frantically by her two dogs; Jack and Ruby. Jack, her first born, as Jane liked to refer to him, was a golden Cocker Spaniel, full of energy and kisses and lived for the tennis ball. Ruby, her Cavalier King Charles Spaniel, was a nervous, clingy little dog, who lived for cuddles on her Mummy's knee.

Jane stepped through in to the hallway, pacifying the dogs with enthusiastic strokes and words of reassurance that she was home. She threw her coat over the stair banister and went through the living room in to the kitchen to make herself a cup of tea. The living room was small with only enough room for a two seater sofa and a chair, despite the small space, Jane had stylishly accessorised the walls with contemporary art and hanging plants. Her bargain sofas were artfully draped with thick, knitted throws and plush, pink cushions. An electric fire was situated on the main wall giving warmth to the small space.

The kitchen was typical of a turnkey home; not offensive but not particularly stylish either with wood effect door panels and marble effect laminate worktops. The kitchen was nowhere near big enough for a kitchen table so Jane had bought a collapsable table and two chairs and placed them squished in to a corner.

Jane sat on one of the chairs and sipped hot tea poured from her teapot before taking the dogs out for their walk. Jane classed herself as somewhat of a tea connoisseur, her favourite blend was Nilgiri, she loved it for its intense, bold zest with subtle hints of fruity, flowery flavour.

Jane was horrified that people would think to even use teabags, in Jane's modest opinion there was a process to making tea, it should be enjoyed and savoured and appreciated. She topped up her cup from a porcelain infuser teapot, adding only a dash of milk so as not to dim the flavour.

Jane savoured her Nilgiri contemplating Millie's offer. What harm could it do? On the other hand, it could be painfully boring, or worse, she might actually have to *talk* to people. Jane hated small talk, especially with people she knew she would never see again

However, against her wishes, Jane did go to Millie's house that following Saturday to 'get ready'. Jane arrived at a charming, detached house ten minutes from her. Jane let herself in as she knew she was always welcome at Millie's. The house was grand and much bigger than Jane's, it was artfully and elegantly decorated. Her heart sank when she heard the shrieks of excitable girls, she didn't have the energy or enthusiasm to feign that level of joy. Jane entered in to the living room where the commotion was coming from and was temporarily blinded by a face full of hair. One of the girls had jumped up to hug her.

Jane blinked through the mane of hair to see Martha, who was a slim, tall girl with hazel eyes, and dark brown hair that flowed gracefully down her back, she stood before her, beaming brightly. Jane always thought she had a model type quality to her look. She had a bubbly and somewhat immature personality. She was Millie's school friend who had subsequently become Jane's friend. She was a receptionist in a health centre and loved nothing more than a night out socialising on her weekends off. Jane surmised that Martha was most likely trying to get away from her loveless marriage to her husband, Lucas, as she was an insatiable flirt.

"Hey Jane!" Said a slightly rounder and shorter girl, waving in her direction. Jennifer, who was sat on one of the sofas, was very pretty with blue eyes and blonde hair, she was single but being only twenty three this did not cause Jennifer too much worry. They had met Jennifer on a night out a few years previous and had maintained a consistent friendship. Jennifer worked for a travel agency, she had chosen her career based purely on her love of holidays.

"Hey!" Jane squeaked, standing awkwardly in the doorway, clutching tightly on to the bottle of white wine she had brought with her.

"Long time no see, Jane! Where have you been hiding?" Martha screeched, her eyebrows raised.

"Oh, you know, busy working away." Jane replied sheepishly. "Where's Millie?"

"She's in the kitchen." Said Jennifer.

Jane walked through the living room in to the kitchen, it was large and spacious with navy blue kitchen cupboards and a stylish grey island. Millie stood with her back to her, preparing drinks and snacks.

"Hey Millie." Jane said brightly, Jane always felt most comfortable in Millie's company, she understood her the best out of anyone she knew.

Millie spun on the spot, her face lit up when she saw Jane and she dashed over and draped her arms around her warmly.

"I'm so glad you came, Jane!"

Millie was a vibrant redhead; beautiful and freckled, confident but not cocky, graceful but not posh. Jane admired Millie and longed to look and behave like her. Millie had a long term, live in boyfriend called Oliver. He was friendly and kind and Jane greatly approved.

They moved in to the living room again and Jane sat sheepishly on to the sofa next to Jennifer, with a glass of her white wine. Jane took a generous gulp and felt the wine coarse through her veins immediately, settling her nerves only slightly, she took another large swig. Jane felt as though she was the ugly duckling of the group, but that could not be farther from the truth, being of medium height and slim build, she had a small face with electrifying, green eyes and long, blonde hair. She had a striking appearance to most that saw her and girls often displayed envy towards her obvious good looks.

Jane was unsure of how to interact with the highly vivacious girls. She guzzled some more wine until the glass was finished, hoping that it would help and quickly topping it back up again.

The girls were chattering away in their usual hysterical manner, they loved that they were allowed to gatecrash the hospital work night out and spoke excitedly of the calibre of doctor that would be there.

"James, one of the doctors in the unit, is always checking you out, Jane!" Millie beamed excitedly, as they sat drinking wine and spirits and applying extra layers of make up.

"Of course he is, most men are checking Jane out, she is so gorgeous." Jennifer smiled sweetly towards her friends.

"I'm sure he wasn't, I don't think I'm his type." Jane replied evasively, clutching her glass firmly, feeling uncomfortable that she had been so suddenly thrust in to the spotlight.

"You are always so modest, Jane." Scorned Millie, as she delicately brushed rouge across her cheeks.

"Well, if you don't want him, Jane, he is up for grabs tonight, then?" Cried Martha, winking at Jane and flashing her a mischievous smile.

Martha and Jane were friends, but, Martha was exceedingly jealous of Jane's effortless good looks, Martha always caked her make up on too heavily in a desperate attempt to look more attractive to the opposite sex, whereas, Jane chose to wear minimal amounts of make up with a more profound effect.

"Yes, Martha, I have no interest in James, or any man. But don't forget that you are married!" Jane tutted jokingly.

"I don't think Lucas would notice me even if I came home straddling James." She said sadly, her head bowed slightly.

"Things are no better?" Jennifer asked softly.

"Worse. He pays the kitchen tap more interest than he does me. I don't know where to go from here." She admitted, her head hung depressively between large gulps of a fruity cocktail she had skillfully created.

"Well, let's have a fun night tonight and forget all about our troubles!" Millie suggested, trying to turn the ever depressing tone of the evening back around again.

Jane and the girls lived in Clovelly, a small seaside village in Devon, renowned for its natural beauty. The pub they were headed for was set right on the water's edge, looking out on to the Bristol Channel.

16

The local pub was, as you would expect, small and cramped and full of the same people who went every week, this weekend was a bit of an exception because of the thirty or so doctors, nurses and midwives who were there for their monthly work get together. What Jane observed straight away was, that despite everyone letting their hair down and getting a break from work, they were all talking about work.

"How dull." Thought Jane. It was going to be a long night.

Jane was lingering in a corner with a glass of red wine whilst the other girls mingled and chatted with the crowd. Millie had no interest in flirting, as she was dating Ollie, but she was a social being and enjoyed fraternising and getting to know people. Martha and Jennifer were enjoying the attention they were receiving from a couple of male nurses.

Jane became aware of James after her discussion with the girls earlier in the evening; he was making a particular effort to catch her eye which she had never noticed before. Once they had made eye contact James must have felt that it was his opportunity to pounce, because, just then, he started to approach her. Jane panicked. Despite his good looks, she had no interest in making small talk with the stranger.

"Hi there." Were James' first words as he saddled up beside her with a smug expression on his face, whipping his overly long, fair hair out of his eyes.

"Hello." Replied Jane, a little too quietly.

"You're one of the midwives in the maternity unit aren't you? Jane Abbott?" Asked James, his hazel eyes alight with excitement.

"Yes, I am. You're one of the new doctors?" Jane tried to act indifferent so as to discourage him, but she also didn't want to be rude either.

"James Dunbar. Can I get you a drink?" James asked in a confident manner.

"No, thank you, I'll probably be leaving soon. Parties aren't really my thing." Replied Jane, scanning the bar for an escape.

"Come on, let me get you a drink, I think I could change your mind on parties. I won't take no for an answer." Said James, a little too forcefully. Jane was put off by his eagerness and over confident attitude but agreed to the drink because it didn't seem as though he was going to give in too easily.

"So, how long have you been a midwife?" James asked, leaning his arm up against the bar and appearing far too self satisfied.

"Nine years. I qualified when I was twenty one." Jane replied in a bored tone, not reciprocating the question.

"Ah, you've just given away your age. Don't worry, I don't mind older women." Jane looked at him incredulously.

"Anyway." Said James. "Didn't fancy being a doctor instead?" This was just getting worse.

"No, I think a doctor and a midwife are very different professions." Replied Jane rather coldly, staring him down in mock shock. Was this guy serious?

"Sorry, that was rude of me. I'm sure midwives are valuable to the hospital, too." He smirked.

"I don't think the maternity unit could run without midwives." Said Jane, even more incredulously. "Do you think the babies just come out all by themselves? And what about the antenatal and postnatal care? And if there is an emergency, we are the first on hand to provide any treatment needed." Jane was angered and gobsmacked, not only had she been coerced in to having a drink with this man, she was now having her entire career insulted. It was totally ridiculous. She needed out of there.

Then, Jane spotted *him*, over the top of James' shoulder. A dark haired, dark eyed, handsome man with the most bright, expressive eyes she had ever seen, a mixture of coffee and caramel in colour and a contagious smile, sitting in a corner booth.

Jane was transfixed, she had never felt so drawn to someone before, so attracted to someone at first sight. He looked up and caught her staring. She glanced away quickly, feeling horrified. He definitely noticed. He definitely noticed her ogling at him like a fifteen year girl. She didn't dare look over at him again for a long time to be sure he wasn't still looking.

She carried on pretending she was listening to what James was saying, something about haemorrhaging. Clearly talking about work, "how interesting," she thought sarcastically to herself. She dared a glance over again at the handsome stranger but he was chatting diligently to the girl next to him. Probably his girlfriend. Typical.

Meanwhile, James was still talking away enthusiastically about his achievements and goals for the future, Jane had lost interest, her mind was elsewhere. She politely said to James, "I'm sorry to be so rude but I have to head home now."

"I can't encourage you to stay?" James said, looking quite surprised. "I thought we were just getting started." He winked at the same time, making Jane feel slightly queasy.

"Sorry, as tempting as that sounds I'd really better be off. Just going to say to my friends I'm leaving. Bye. Nice to meet you". She quickly stalked away, relief flooded her insides, glad to be away from the excruciating, painful encounter, leaving a bewildered James standing alone at the bar.

As Jane walked away she took one last glance at the mysterious stranger in the corner, he was looking directly at her. His piercing gaze shot through her like a dagger, rendering her completely entranced and captivated.

Their gaze lingered upon one another for a moment until he looked away to talk to the attractive female beside him again. Her stomach had been doing back flips until she remembered he was there with a woman. She desperately wanted to go over to him and tell him to ditch the girl and come home with her instead. Had she lost her mind?

Jane dragged her eyes away once the alluring stranger's attention had been drawn back to the girl beside him. She approached Millie who was chatting with a couple of the doctors.

"Millie, I'm leaving." She stated firmly, preparing herself for the resistant comments.

"Oh, Jane, please don't go! The fun is only getting started and it looked like you and James were getting on very well!" Millie squealed excitedly, bouncing up and down, clutching her glass with both hands.

"He's vile and stuck up, I wouldn't touch him if my life depended on it." Jane shot back, rolling her eyes in disgust at the memory.

"Jane, you always do this with every guy you meet, you find the fatal flaw as to why it would never work out between the two of you!" Millie shot back even more forcibly.

"Millie, do you know who that man in the corner is over there?" Jane pointed to the mysterious, attractive stranger who had captivated most of her evening.

"No, I don't think he's with us. Why? Do you like him?!" Millie exclaimed, her brown eyes brightening.

"No, I just thought he looked familiar, that was all. Anyway, can you tell Martha and Jennifer that I am away home?"

"No problem, you are missing out on all the fun though, Jane!"

"I'm sure I'll survive." She replied derisively.

"Text me when you get home safe, please!" Millie urged.

"I will."

Jane left and hailed a taxi. Just as she suspected, another highly unsuccessful night with one very pompous, leering man. But, the mysterious stranger was at the forefront of her mind. Who was he? And why had he the ability to completely hypnotise her mind, to take away all thoughts of anything else other than him?

Chapter 2

The next day, Jane woke up feeling rather refreshed. She drank Assam tea, an Indian blend with a strong, bold tang. She savoured the rich, malty flavour before heading out to walk the dogs. She enjoyed the quiet life and found the solitude of a brisk walk a remedy to life's stresses. Jane's favourite dog walking spot was the beach, which was just a short car journey from her house. It was mid June, therefore, it was perfect weather for a nice, breezy walk by the sea.

Ruby, always loyal, stayed by Jane's side, ready and willing to bark at anyone who got too close. Jack played fetch with his ball for the full hour as though his life depended on it and greeted any passersby happily, sniffing out pockets for hidden treats.

Jane was nearly finished her walk for the day when she noticed that Jack was getting in to bother near the water, the tide was on its way out and this meant the sand was water logged and treacherous. Jane normally checked the tide times before going out, but hadn't that day. Jane could see Jack struggling, his paws were sinking in to the sand and he couldn't get them lifted out to proceed further, he began to yelp frantically.

Jane ran, with all her might, but she was slowed down significantly by the sinking sand. Her heavy welly boots were being sucked under by the watery quick sand. Jane tore off her welly boots and waded, as fast as she could, through the perilous sand, but she wasn't getting there quick enough, she saw Jack's body rapidly being sucked under.

Jane screamed hysterically, wailing uncontrollably as she witnessed the horrendous loss of her adored pet, powerless to help in any way. Ruby was stood back, barking wildly, as she watched the events unfold. Jack's head was still brimming the surface, his tongue was pointing out in a contorted shape, Jane knew he was desperately clawing underneath to get back out, but to no avail. Jane continued to try to traverse through the sand but Jack was so far away from her.

Just then, a sprinting figure darted across the sinking quick sand, almost on tip toes, and managed to reach Jack, their feet were sinking, the person grabbed Jack roughly by the head and trailed him out violently in one dramatic swoop. The figure hauled her precious dog over their shoulder and dashed quickly out of the sinking hole, knee deep in sand and water.

Jane trundled quickly out of the sinking sand when she knew Jack was safe. The figure approached, Jane's eyes were blinded by ferocious tears, her body heaved laboriously in huge, great sobs. She grabbed Jack forcefully out of the strangers arms and clutched him tightly, bawling furiously in to his shoulder as they both lay sprawled in the sand.

Jane looked up to thank the mysterious person who had come to her rescue, it was the handsome stranger from the night before. How could she bump in to him two days in a row? There he was, the magnetising stranger she had been drawn to the night before, somehow coming to her rescue that day. He seemed to recognise her as well, he studied her face. He stood with an air of power and self assurance and he had a mean look in his eyes that made Jane feel weak at the knees. Jane's heart was pounding, she thought she was going to be sick, he was so tragically beautiful.

He was stopped in front of her, slightly breathless and windswept, he looked breathtakingly attractive.

Jane continued to sit on the sand bed with Jack shaking her lap. "I don't know how to thank you, you saved him, he was about to die!" Fresh tears sprung from her eyes as she stroked Jack frantically.

"It's no problem at all, I was out for a run and saw you guys were in trouble so I ran over as quick as I could." He breathed, still slightly out of breath from the rescue mission.

"I don't know what I would have done if anything would have happened to him." The thought sent shivers through Jane's spine, she had almost witnessed the slow death of her beloved pet, she felt traumatised and shook up.

"Don't I know you from somewhere?" He asked, hands on his hips, the sun peaking out from behind him, Jane could make out the silhouette of his muscular frame.

"Yes, I was at a work party last night, I saw you there." She admitted. It was hard for Jane to look him in the eye, his intense gaze seemed to burn a hole right through her, she was mesmerised.

"Fancy meeting today again." He smiled. "Wish it could have been under better circumstances." He smiled sadly down at Jack.

"Could have been much worse." Jane sighed, hiccoughing through tears.

He nodded in agreement. "I'm Matthew Carson. I'm not the local stalker or anything." He laughed.

"Jane Abbott. You don't seem the type." She giggled nervously. "Nice to meet you."

Matthew reached his hand out to help Jane stand up, Jane's heart gave a flutter and she felt the hairs rise on the back of her neck when his skin had touched hers. Could he notice how nervous she was? She felt completely foolish becoming so nervous in front of this man. Maybe he would think it was shock from the ordeal. This was Jane; opposed to all forms of romance and ridiculous, amorous displays of affection in public. What was he doing to her?

"Nice to meet you too, Jane." Matthew ran his hand through his hair, looking tremendous. "Do you have far to get home?"

"No, I live about a five minute drive away, Errings Way." She explained, trying to hide the shaking in her voice.

"Do you really? I live in the development next to you, Cottings Hill. Small world." He said incredulously.

"It really is." Replied Jane, a little dumbly and somewhat lost for words that this beautiful stranger could have been living so close to her all this time. She merely stared at him in awe, mesmerised by his intense, dark eyes and strong physique.

She was dumbstruck, barely able to string a sentence together under his critical gaze that seemed to scan her over like an X-ray, as though he could see right through her, see how powerful a hold his charm had on her, rendering her almost speechless. Jane was mortified by her lack of words. Why was she being such an idiot? She needed to pull herself together, he's just a man. Nothing to get so excited about.

She tried to appear cool and nonchalant on the outside, knowing that she was completely failing. Her mouth felt as dry as sandpaper. As he made to reply she licked her lips to try to moisten the ever drying desert of her mouth.

"Is this other one yours, too?" He pointed to Ruby who was stood firmly at Jane's side, eyeing up Matthew carefully.

"Yes, she's mine." Jane smiled down at her beloved animals.

Jane and Matthew chatted for a long time, it turned out Matthew was a paramedic, it all felt right to Jane, he had a great career and they could both relate to each other in that respect. She couldn't believe she hadn't bumped in to him before now.

"Well, I had better get home and get cleaned up." He smiled, staring down at his sand covered trainers and legs.

Jane's heart sank, was he trying to get away? Was he bored of the conversation and put off by her idiotic staring?

"Oh, yes, so am I." She said, trying to save face and play it cool. Momentarily she had forgotten that there was a world outside of this encounter with Matthew, the mysterious dog rescuing, bar attending stranger.

"Well, nice to meet you." He said, smiling in that cheeky, boyish, grin type way that made Jane catch her breath.

"Nice to meet you, too." Jane lingered, hoping that at any moment he was going to ask her for her number. She felt pathetic, she was sure that he was bound to see the desperate longing in her eyes. What had gotten in to her? He didn't ask for her number.

Jane felt tremendously disappointed. He merely smiled at her and turned and went for the direction of his car. Jane was devastated. They might never see each other again and there was this man, the first man she had ever met, that on first sight she was so struck dumb by lust and longing that she was lucky if she could just about remember her name.

Later that day, Jane had given Jack a hot bath and wrapped him in blankets, she lay on the sofa and stroked him tenderly as he fell in to an exhausted sleep. Jane's thoughts drifted off to Matthew. She couldn't believe it; this beautiful specimen of a man who had ignited the fire inside of her that had been dormant all of her adult life, was living in the development just next to hers. *And* he was a paramedic. What were the chances?

But Jane was consumed with thoughts of why he had not asked for her number. Maybe he was just making polite conversation. He probably wasn't interested at all and Jane was being nonsensical, thinking that he had felt the same spark of electricity between them. Yes, that's probably it; he was just a polite stranger.

It was best for her to forget about him. It was nothing more than polite conversation after noticing each other from the night before. But he *had* noticed her. Could that mean something? Jane's head was going round in circles, torturing herself, wondering if he liked her back. Jane went to bed that night with only one person on her mind.

Jane returned to the beach every day for a week, ensuring that she went when the tide was in to avoid another disaster, but never bumping in to Matthew again, had she dreamed it all? Had she fabricated in her mind the man who had come to her rescue and softened her hardy exterior? Jane returned to the beach that same day also, she couldn't lie to herself that she was going there to see if she would see Matthew again,

27

because she was, there was something about that man that had surprised Jane, she was intrigued and desperate to know more.

But, alas, he was not to be seen on that day either, Jane was loading Jack and Ruby in to the boot of her car when she heard someone say; "Fancy meeting you here again." Jane spun around, it was Matthew. *Hallelujah*. Jane's heart skipped a beat; she couldn't help but look happy to see him.

He stood in running shorts and a T shirt and the same trainers he had worn the day they had met, he had clearly just finished another run as his swarthy skin glistened in the sunlight. His appearance took Jane's breath away. She smiled goofily at him and felt positively giddy with delight. Then her nerves kicked in, she stumbled over her words slightly and managed a reply; "I know, we need to stop meeting like this," Jane noticed that she had flirted and felt incredibly self conscious.

"Well, rather than bumping in to each other every so often, how about we arrange to go out some time?" He asked, a little nervously.

"I would like that." Jane replied quickly, trying to keep her excited voice steady and attempting to appear cool and indifferent to this proposal but inwardly wanting to scream at the top of her lungs in delight.

Matthew looked equally delighted when Jane had agreed.

"It might be a little short notice for you, but I am actually free tonight. I know, no plans for a Saturday night." He laughed, he looked down at his feet sheepishly then glanced back up at her again with one eyebrow raised and an apprehensive grin, looking magnificent. Was he as nervous as she was?

"That would be great, I'm free tonight, too. No Saturday night plans either." She exhaled, surprising herself at how available she was making herself look, why did she not say she had plans in order to play hard to get? He was going to think she was so dull having no weekend plans, but, then again, he had no plans either and Jane was very eager to go on a date with him that she couldn't possibly play hard to get because what if she lost her chance?

"Great!" Exclaimed Matthew and he smiled brightly at her, a smile that reached his eyes and made them come alive. "I'll book us a table at the Goat's Inn for around eight o'clock if that suits you? I can pick you up if you want?"

"That would be great! See you then." Jane went to walk away, wanting to burst with excitement, trying to resist doing a victory dance in the middle of the beach car park, when Matthew called out to her;

"How will I get in contact with you?" He smirked at her.

"Oh, yes, right." Said Jane, rather dumbly and somewhat embarrassed, fidgeting to find her phone. Matthew smiled at her nervousness, she was making it too easy for him. "I'll give you my number." Matthew took out his phone casually and handed it to her so she could type in her number. She noticed his screensaver was a little boy. Was Matthew a dad?

"Cute kid." She said to him, hoping he would reveal the connection, handing his phone back to him.

"My nephew." Jane breathed a sigh of relief. "See you tonight."

"See you then."

Jane returned home and bathed the dogs after their very sandy walk, she felt completely distracted. She was ecstatic, she could hardly believe it. Just over a week ago, Jane was chronically single and overly critical, judging others for being unduly romantic and wearing their hearts on their sleeves, feeling sick at the thought of people's public displays of affection, and now Jane was one of them. Positively gleeful and feeling giddy and excited. She dried off Jack and Ruby and then phoned Millie to relay this new and strange information.

"Millie, I have a date tonight."

"You have a *what*?!" Gasped Millie in excited shock.

"I have a date." Jane laughed.

"Oh, is it James?! I knew you would come around to him!" Millie said in a know it all type of voice.

"No! *God* no! It's not James." She scoffed. "It's another man, he was actually at the party, the one I had asked you about. Turns out he lives just around the corner from me and we bumped in to each other a couple of times at the beach and he asked me on a date!"

"Oh, my goodness, Jane! How romantic! On a dog walk! I can't believe this. This must be your first date since David!" Millie replied excitedly.

Oh, yes. *David.* The ex boyfriend. Jane had broken up with David a year previous. He had wanted marriage and children and some form of commitment, Jane wanted none of it. How ordinary, how dull. How *predictable*. David was not happy, he harassed her for months, told her that she had wasted his time and led him on. He sent abusive messages, phoned her countless times a day and would appear at her house unexpectedly demanding that she take him back.

Jane was afraid of David during this time, never had he appeared to have these stalker tendencies while they were dating, but rejection can turn people sour and reveal a nasty side. Eventually, Jane's dad, Gary, intervened and threatened David, saying that he would phone the police if he didn't leave Jane alone.

This seemed to deter David for a while, but then he seemed to gain momentum again. Martha, to Jane's surprise, had stepped in also to tell David to back off. This show of loyalty seemed to strengthen her friendship with Martha.

After many months Jane had finally phoned the police, David eventually gave up and left Jane alone, the fear of having to spend a night in a prison cell seemed to be the encouragement he needed to finally give up and leave her alone. Jane always remained nervous and wary that David would some day make a reappearance in to her life.

Along with Jane's lack of interest in a real commitment or to ever have any children, this one experience of a long term relationship was enough to put Jane off men altogether. Until now. Matthew was the first man that she felt differently towards, a new sensation of lust and allure filled Jane up, and she wanted more.

That evening, Millie came over to help Jane get ready for her first date with Matthew. They popped a bottle of Prosecco and poured two flutes, Jane felt she needed alcohol to ease her ever spiralling nerves. Jane was not much of a wine connoisseur, her passion for liquid drinks being countless flavours of tea leaves, perfectly blended and brewed with just the right amount of milk, or no milk at all, depending on the blend. But Prosecco was an alcoholic drink that Jane could handle, enjoying the soft bubbles and warm feeling spreading over her skin, giving her that false sense of confidence she needed for a first date.

"Jane! So, who is this mystery man you are seeing tonight?!" Millie gushed at her friend.

"He's called Matthew Carson and he's a paramedic." Jane couldn't deny she was enjoying the interesting new version of herself, her friends would finally be able to relate to her now.

"You are not wearing *that*, are you?" Asked Millie, looking scandalised.

They were in Jane's bedroom, Jane was trying on clothes and they were sipping greedily on the Italian sparkling wine while the dogs lounged on her king size bed.

"Yes, why what's wrong with it?" Jane asked, looking perplexed, staring at her reflection in the mirror.

"Jane, you're wearing jeans and a T shirt for your first date in a year! You need to show some skin, tease the guy! Show him that you are mildly interested by wearing something sexy!" Shrieked Millie, rolling her eyes exhaustively.

"But I feel comfortable in these clothes. I don't need to show off my body just to get a guy to like me." Remarked Jane rather smartly, Jane had always been renowned for having a feminist attitude, why did she have to show off her skin to get a man's attention?

"Of course you don't, but it definitely helps if you want to get him feeling even more interested." Replied Millie, equally as smart. "You are super hot with a banging figure, show some of it off from time to time. I'm not asking you to go out in a mini skirt and boob tube, but maybe something just a bit sexier than a T shirt." She raised her eyebrows at Jane.

"Ok, ok. I get your point." Jane laughed, finally submitting to her.

Jane eventually agreed upon a knee length dress ("Not too much leg on a first date please, Millie!") that accentuated her attractive curves and showed only a small amount of cleavage. She wore her hair curled and down by her shoulders which framed her face rather well, she donned a simple pair of earrings and some eyeliner to set off the look. Jane thought she looked quite pretty for someone she would have described before as a 'Plain Jane'.

"Jane, you look amazing! Matthew's getting lucky tonight!" Millie squealed excitedly. Jane rolled her eyes and felt the nervous flutter in her belly again, she washed it away with more helpings of Prosecco.

Chapter 3

Matthew had arranged to pick Jane up in his car to take them to dinner, he arrived early which surprised Jane as she wasn't ready. She ran to the door to let him in, hair askew and make up half done. Not the great first impression she was hoping for.

She opened the door to him and was taken aback by his striking good looks, he looked breathtaking in an open collared shirt, boat shoes and tight jeans that she inwardly thanked the lord for.

"Hi Jane." He smiled that boyish grin that made Jane's stomach flip over, he had one shoulder leaned up against the house with his legs crossed, this confident stance seemed to ooze charisma and self assurance. Jane was doomed, she knew Matthew was a bad boy; too charming and sexy for his own good, she knew she could never resist his appeal.

"Hi Matthew," she smiled goofily, "Sorry, I'm not quite ready yet, but you can come in and wait?"

"Thanks. Sorry, I know I'm a little early." He walked in. Jane felt nauseous, Matthew was standing in her house. She hadn't even vacuumed that day, she could see sprinklings of Jack's hair scattered everywhere. She inwardly kicked herself for not cleaning up earlier.

"The dogs are in the kitchen, I can let them out if you want?" She hoped that they would create a distraction from the disarray of her house.

"Absolutely, I never say no to a dog cuddling opportunity." He smiled and sat down on the sofa.

Oh stop. He was just too damn perfect.

When she came back downstairs she was delighted to see that Matthew was kneeled down on the living room floor playing with Jack and Ruby. Jane was relieved to see that Matthew liked dogs, she wondered why he didn't have any.

"Sorry, couldn't resist, I love dogs," he said cheerfully, "and now I'm all covered in dog hair." He stood up and brushed himself down.

"No need to apologise, I spend most of my life covered in dog hair," she smiled. "It's great that you like my dogs, some people aren't really in to them." She said awkwardly.

"I love dogs, I never got one, though, as I thought it was unfair with the long shifts that I do." He smiled down at her. Ah, that made sense. She smiled back in relief.

Dinner went exceptionally well in Jane's opinion, Matthew was interesting and funny and passionate about his job and a true dog lover. The conversation flowed easily after Jane managed to get control over her nerves, and with copious amounts of alcohol this prohibited her mouth from becoming too dry and helped to calm her nerves and steady the, now seemingly, permanent shake in her hands.

"Do you like being a paramedic?" Jane asked, as she sipped generous mouthfuls of vodka and coke, she needed the hard liquor, no fancy, watered down cocktails were going to ease her nerves.

"I love it, don't get me wrong, it definitely has its moments, the stress is unrelenting and there are some very ungrateful people out there. But the feeling I get when I have helped someone, well, it's hard to explain. You probably get it with your job." He tipped back his glass of whiskey and coke. Jane loved his enthusiasm, loved that he cared about others. It was a wonderful trait.

"Definitely, sometimes there's just no pleasing people, I think there are people who are just born to find fault in every little thing. Then there's the others who can't be more thankful." She contemplated as she circled her fingers along the rim of her glass.

He nodded in agreement. Jane couldn't help feeling overcome by her attraction to Matthew; he was outrageously handsome and very charming. They were both sat at the back of the restaurant in a hidden away booth; Jane felt flutters of butterflies in her stomach. He was sitting very close to her and she could smell his intoxicating scent of sandalwood, spices and notes of lavender, it was like a drug, she wanted so much more.

Matthew looked at her, she felt overwhelmed by his extreme stare, boring in to her, she could feel the fire swelling up inside of her. Those eyes. He leaned over and put his arm around her, he was touching her; how good it felt to have his skin touching hers.

She felt tingles spreading all over, she suddenly felt chilly and cold despite the restaurant being suitably warm. He seemed to notice this and he squeezed tighter. Jane didn't know how to react; she sat there stock still, unable to move a muscle in case he retracted the arm, realising he had made a terrible mistake.

"You are very beautiful, Jane." He eyed her seductively. Jane felt her face flush outrageously.

"Thanks." She squeaked, it was all she could manage to get out, she didn't know where to look, his gaze penetrated her very core. She could feel his hand caressing her arm. She leaned in to him. Was he going to kiss her?

He leaned in, all the saliva in Jane's mouth seemed to make a drastic run for it, could she quickly nab a drink of water to moisten her mouth? Too late, he had planted his mouth on hers. It was better than she had been expecting. *Much better.*

Those lips, so soft, brushing against hers, a little hint of his tongue made the tingling throughout her even stronger. Jane forgot about her sweaty palms and dry mouth and felt absolutely, wholeheartedly, thrillingly transported to a different planet in those few minutes.

Who would've thought that Jane Abbott would be snogging a perfect stranger in the middle of a restaurant? Jane was unsure of how much time had passed but she knew they had been kissing for a long time. The restaurant was virtually empty.

They broke free from each other, the blood had drained from Jane's brain and she was feeling lightheaded and giddy. She was high on Matthew's kiss.

"I don't want to be forward but would you like to come back to my place?" Matthew asked tentatively, brushing her hand with his, the effect was seductive.

Damn. She knew it. He was only interested in one thing. Jane's feelings of euphoria were quickly replaced by feelings of disappointment and frustration, she thought they had been going somewhere, that he had been genuinely interested in her, but it had all been an elaborate hoax to get her back to his place.

"I had really better get home to the dogs, sorry." Jane replied rather bluntly and with an air of finality to her tone.

"That's no problem, sure we can share a taxi to yours, I want to make sure you get home safe." He said, looking confusingly at her.

"Ok, thank you." Her tone was clipped, she gave him a suspicious glance, was he going to try it on when he got back to hers?

They pulled up outside Jane's house and Matthew walked her to her door, Jane was feeling sullen and depressed, what a waste of time. Just another bloke trying to rapidly gain entry in to her underwear. How boring. How unoriginal.

They stopped at the front door and Matthew gave her a come hither expression but Jane was having none of it. She was feeling wary and on guard, was this just gentlemanly behaviour or was he wanting an invitation in to her house?

Then he unexpectedly leaned in and kissed her again. Despite her best efforts at restraint, Jane felt herself being caught up again. "Did kissing always feel this good?" She thought to herself, "maybe I should just invite him in, this is too good to stop. No, I must be sensible, I don't want a one night stand."

They must have been kissing at the door for a while, because when they eventually parted the dogs were standing at the front door staring up at them. Ruby was clawing at the door to get to 'Mummy'. Jane had reluctantly stopped kissing him.

"I have to go." She breathed, pulling her keys out of her bag.

"I really don't want to stop." He said, looking at her with a yearning gleam in his eye that was hard to say no to.

"We really should, though." She rasped, as he clutched her side and drew her in closer.

"I'll walk away now, just say the word." He breathed in her ear, sending shivers down her neck.

"Go. You need to go, now." She leaned her head on to his chest, already regretting each and every word she had just said.

"Ok, I'll text you tomorrow." He kissed her on the cheek and he was away.

Jane knew she wouldn't hear from again, he was just looking for a one night thing. He was too well practised on the date, too comfortable and confident. She had been hoodwinked by his modest charm. No, she had to think positively, she always thought the worst of people. Maybe he was genuinely interested and hid his nervousness very well. But, on the other hand, he was very good on a date, too good. Those lips, that tongue…

Jane woke up the next morning feeling exhilarated but disappointed at the same time and generally confused. How could one date create so much emotion? One thing was for sure, Matthew was sexy and Jane wanted to see him again. She longed for a message from him, but it got to twelve o'clock and there was no sign of an after date text. Maybe he had just been looking for something easy and it hadn't transpired.

Two o'clock came and Jane had given up hope, why had Matthew not text her? Was the date not as good for him as it had been for her? "Oh, for goodness sake, Jane. Would you wise up and move on with your life!" Jane thought angrily to herself.

But, just then, Jane heard the *bing!* of her phone. Had he text? She snatched desperately at her phone to check the incoming message, nerves elevating inside of her along with apprehension and excitement. But, no. It was her mother. She loved her mother dearly but she was sorely disappointed that it hadn't been Matthew. Jane thought it typical of all the times her mother could text that it would be at that crucial moment, but then she did like to keep in frequent contact with her

Mother daughter relationships, were they ever straightforward? Jane went to throw her phone away when she glanced in to her messages and noticed a new message she had not read or seen before. There sitting, was a message from Matthew from eight o'clock that morning! How had she not seen it? She opened it up, trying to contain her excitement and control her shaking hands;

"Hi Jane, I know I am messaging very early this morning but just wanted to let you know that I had a great time last night and would really like to see you again some time. PS. Nice lips x"

Jane could hardly control herself, of course she wanted a second date, but how was she to control the lusty demon inside of her for a second time? Surely putting out on a second date was just as bad as putting out on a first? Jane replied;

"Hi Matthew, sorry I'm only getting back to you now, just seeing this message. I'd like to see you again too. PS. Thanks, yours aren't bad either x"

They agreed to meet for drinks at a nearby bar on the Wednesday during the week as they were both off on the Thursday, one of the benefits of shift work, Jane had thought.

40

The night went as expected for Jane, with a lot of touching and kissing and laughing. At the end of the night Jane had to forbid Matthew entry in to her house again in an attempt to appear coy and ladylike.

"Jane, you are an enigma." He breathed in to her neck longingly, as they stood by her front door kissing again, before he released her. What must her neighbours be thinking? She chuckled inwardly to herself. This was a new Jane, a happier, more spontaneous and fun Jane, and she loved it.

"I'll be worth the wait." She promised. She pecked him on the lips and dived in to her house, leaving him stranded and wanting more.

Matthew and Jane dated for the next foreseeable weeks, some times out for dinner, some times at each others' houses, but Jane was adamant that the longer she abstained, the longer she would have Matthew's interest.

Jane was perky and happy, her colleagues and friends had noticed the change in her. She was more accepting of invitations out and met with her three closest friends more often.

"A good man was all she needed to get her to come out of her shell." Stated Martha, one afternoon. Martha and Jennifer had met for coffee and were generally gossiping about life.

"She's been living on her own too long, she probably forgot how fun it was to get out and socialise." Jennifer nodded.

"Yes, she was becoming a bit strange, always staying in the house with those dogs." Martha said with an air of superiority.

"Now, Martha, no bitchiness. Jane is one of our best friends. She had a really rough time with David last year, she needed some time to herself to reset." Jennifer was always very kind and caring, she always saw the good in people. Whereas, Martha nearly always took a negative viewpoint on life, much to her own punishment than anyone else's.

"Jennifer, you are always so nice, do you never just feel the need to have a rant about someone?" Martha mocked.

Jane had always described Jennifer as a golden retriever type person, always in such pleasant form and an immense amount of effort would be needed to make her angry or upset. Martha, on the other hand, was more in line with a feisty Jack Russell.

"Maybe people I don't like, or people who have been unkind to me or my friends or family but certainly not my best friends. It doesn't show good character if you always have a snide comment to say about people." Jennifer was bored of gossiping and bad mouthing people; it brought her no happiness and generally always put her in an aggravated mood.

"You are always so diplomatic, Jennifer. I'm not trying to be horrible about Jane; I'm merely stating that a boyfriend has been a long time coming!" She snapped defensively.

"I'm happy for her, I really hope it works out this time."

"Finger crossed she hasn't attracted another psycho like David."

"Martha!"

"What?! Come on, David was a nutcase. I just hope that he is not the 'type' that she attracts from here on out."

"No, I suppose you're right. That wouldn't be great." She admitted.

A week later and the fateful night came where Jane could hold off no longer, Matthew had gone over to Jane's house that evening where they cuddled up on the sofa, drank red wine and put a movie on.

Earlier in the day, Jane had met up with Millie for lunch at the local cafe on the seafront.

"So... I'm dying to know, Jane! How are things going between you and Matthew?" Millie asked excitedly, sipping on a hot, frothy cappuccino.

"Really well. I've never felt like this, Millie. I feel like a teenager." Jane couldn't help smile an embarrassed smile, she hid her blushing face behind her coffee mug, Jane opted for coffee rather than tea, the big conglomerate companies normally butchered the tea making process, in her opinion.

"Who would have thought, my Jane, blushing over a boy." Millie beamed proudly.

Jane laughed, "I really like him." She admitted. "I'm scared."

"Why on earth are you scared?" Cried Millie, confusion furrowed her brow.

"What if he turns out to be completely crazy like David or he breaks my heart? I've never let anyone in before, this is brand new territory for me." She whispered anxiously, her face contorted with worry, lines forming across her forehead.

"Jane, you can't live your whole life in fear of getting hurt, you will end up alone forever. I say take the chance, fall head over heels in love and if you get hurt, then, so what? At least you tried, at least you can say to yourself; well I gave it a shot."

"Millie, you are so sensible. How are you so sensible?"

"Just born that way." She mocked. "Well, I've been dying to ask... How is he?"

"How do you mean?" Jane asked innocently, staring blankly back at Millie.

"How is he in bed!' Shrieked Millie, laughing at Jane's naivety.

"Oh, right, well, we haven't really got that far, yet. I didn't want anything to happen until I knew for sure he liked me." Jane explained, furiously blushing and staring at her hands.

"It's been six weeks, Jane, I think he likes you." Millie replied sardonically, tilting one eyebrow.

"I suppose he does. It's been very hard to resist if I'm being honest, he's very good looking." She gazed pensively out the window, thinking of Matthew's lean stature and magnetising stare.

"He is indeed." Admitted Millie, winking cheekily at her, Jane giggled sheepishly.

"Look at you, Jane. Succumbing to the inner fiery woman in you! I say do it tonight!"

"Millie! You are wild!" Jane gasped, blushing further.

"You only live once, Jane. And guys like Matthew only come around once in a life time, take the chance, take his clothes off." And Jane laughed herself sore.

Maybe Jane was being too standoffish, maybe she should let her hair down and throw caution to the wind. God knows she deserved a good time; it had been a rough year.

That evening, before Matthew and Jane met up, Matthew was feeling at his wits end, he had himself convinced that this girl thought they were in some form of relationship where you only kissed each other. He didn't want to pressure her, but he also wanted to know if this was more than a kissing friendship. At the end of the day, there was only so long a guy could wait until he had to move on.

Matthew was due to leave for Jane's house in the next ten minutes and he was feeling apprehensive, was the night going to go the way he hoped or was he going to have to have a discussion about where things was headed?

Jane had made rump steaks, mediterranean vegetables and baby boiled potatoes. After dinner, they sat close together on the sofa, arms brushing off one another, sparks flying between them. The dogs snoozed in their beds. Matthew sensed how Jane was looking at him, surely that was a sultry look she was throwing his way? He felt so confused, she was giving him all the signals that she was attracted to him, but absolutely nothing had transpired. Any time he had gone to make his move his hand had been batted away like a naughty child.

She looked very attractive to Matthew that night. She was wearing a knee length skirt and a stringy vest top. He decided to try again, to make his move. One more attempt and then he would call it a day.

Matthew kissed her passionately, Jane sunk in to him, completely consumed by the kiss. "God she smells great." He thought to himself. But kissing was not out of the ordinary between them. Matthew decided it was now or never, his hand slipped down on to Jane's bare thigh, but this time, Jane didn't stop it.

Chapter 4

J ane was in heaven, she delved between that dreamy state of not quite awake and not quite asleep. She woke up beside Matthew the next morning, he was still asleep and naked. Jane lay admiring the shape of his body, his broad shoulders and muscular arms. She reminisced back to when those strong arms had picked her up so effortlessly the night before. It had felt so natural, so easy, so satisfying, not at all awkward like it usually was.

They were in tune with each other's mind and body, as though they had known each other for years. But, at the same time it had been so wonderfully exhilarating it had felt like the very first time, they had both wondered what they had been doing all this time without one another. Jane thought wistfully to herself, whilst lying in bed next to him; how was he so good at it? He was exceptionally talented and gifted. Then Jane started to worry again, was he too good at it? He must be well practiced, honing his skills on the female body. Yes, he was far too good at it; he probably had a different girl every week.

Jane had to stop herself, her mind reverting to that terrible habit of drifting off to a darker place. She had to be positive. Why was that so hard? She knew the answer to that. It all stemmed from her past. A past that she had kept close to her chest in the fear that she would be viewed as 'damaged' or 'broken' or would come with too many issues for anyone to have to handle.

Not even Jane's best friend, Millie, knew anything about her past. Her friends knew that it hadn't been completely straightforward but they didn't know any of the appalling details. Jane had been thinking very seriously about revealing her past to Matthew. He was different from the other men she had met, he was someone she felt comfortable around, as though she could talk about anything and never be judged, this was a revelation to Jane, she had never revealed anything remotely close to the truth in her whole thirty years on Earth. Matthew was different. Was it only fair then to pre warn him in order for him to know what he was getting in to? The thought terrified her, what if he ran away, her baggage too much for him to have to take on board?

Matthew woke up with a broad smile on his face, he leaned in to kiss her. Jane savoured the kiss, wondering should she hold off divulging her life to him, maintaining their cosy bubble for now. He still had that powerful hold over her, Jane wondered if he had enjoyed himself the night before. Terrible scenarios formed in her mind of him comparing her performance to all his previous lovers, where did she rank amongst them? How many had there been? Was she just a drop in the ocean for him, amongst a sea of beautiful, skilled lovers.

Jane noticed that he even looked good first thing in the morning. What must she look like? She hadn't even bothered taking off her make up from the night before.

"Well, good morning." He said with an over exaggerated, wide grin.

"Could you look anymore happy with yourself?" She chuckled nervously, her mouth felt parched from too much alcohol and too little water. Did she have terrible morning breath?

"I don't think so." He poked her affectionately in the side. "I have just spent the best night with the most amazing girl; I had a fantastic time, Jane." He kissed her softly. Jane felt woozy and light headed again; she stared at his beauty, taking in his topless form.

"I'm glad you had a nice time." She smiled, feeling very aware that she didn't want to come across as the clingy girl the day after the night before.

"Did you have a good time?" He asked, with a hint of apprehension in his tone.

"I really did! It was great." How awkward, how could she tell someone she barely knew that they were the best she had ever had and that she was falling head over heels for them, without coming across too strong?

"I'm glad. I would definitely like to make *that* a regular occurrence." He laughed, taking her hand and caressing it softly, Jane felt temporarily distracted and lost her train of thought.

"I'm sure you would!" She teased, bringing herself back round to reality.

"Don't act all coy now, Miss Abbott. I know you had as good a time as I did." He mocked playfully.

"Maybe." Her eyes twinkled mysteriously at him.

They got out of bed and were greeted by two very excited dogs when they opened the bedroom door. To Jane, it just felt right, they both worked in health care and they both had a passion for the outdoors, it all fit nicely in to place. But could he see that too?

Jane made Matthew eggs on toast and one of her most favourite tea blends, Darjeeling. They were sat at the small kitchen table. Matthew had requested coffee but Jane insisted he try her tea blend. He sipped tentatively on the hot liquid once Jane had carefully poured and then added the smallest dash of milk.

"That is lovely, Jane!"

"I told you." She smirked.

"What got you in to tea then?" He asked as he took another sip.

"My granny, or 'Nanny' as we called her." Jane's heart twinged at the mention of her beloved Nanny. "She loved tea, she could identify a type of tea just by tasting it, she hated those big profit, conglomerate companies that massacre tea in our opinion. I guess I just found a passion for it from her."

Matthew stared at her sympathetically, "And where is your Nanny now?"

"She passed away last year." The memory broke Jane's heart all over again, she swallowed back tears. Her Nanny was the one person who got her, understood who she was and accepted all of it, and now she was gone. Jane couldn't comprehend the loneliness that her Nanny had left behind.

"I'm so sorry." Matthew said sincerely and placed a hand on top of hers.

"Thank you." Jane squeezed his hand. "So, yeah, my Nanny was big in to tea and I guess I loved that about her, her passion for it. It's not just the drinking of the tea that's

49

enjoyable, it's the whole experience of making it and savouring the experience." Jane chuckled nervously.

"Yeah I get it, it's good to be passionate about something. Most girls are too interested in their make up and Instagram profile to notice an actual world out there with real experiences. You have a passion for dogs and tea, that's pretty awesome." Jane couldn't be more delighted with this response, she beamed up at him, unable to take the ridiculous grin off her face. This guy was perfect.

Just then, the doorbell rang. Jane jumped up, wondering who would be at her house so early in the morning.

Jane walked to the door and drew the curtains. There standing, was none other than her *dad*. She panicked, what was he doing at her house, and so early in the morning! What would she say to him? How could she get rid of him? This was all new to Jane, never had she been faced with a situation where she had been caught with a man, bedsheets still warm, from where he had just vacated them.

Jane swung open the door, she was dressed only in a pyjama set of short shorts and a string vest top;

"Hi dad!" Jane screeched unnaturally, in an attempt to feign casualness. "What are you doing here?!"

"Just called over for a cuppa and to see how you're doing, it has been a few days since I last saw you." He stepped through in to the hallway. Jane and her dad were close, he knew he was always welcome to just drop over whenever he wanted but the timing could not have been be any worse that day.

"Oh, right, ok. Well, right now isn't actually a good time, dad, sorry." Her dad stared at her confusedly.

"How come?" He asked curiously, suspicion glinting in his eyes.

Just then, Matthew appeared in the doorway from the living room. Jane's heart fell to the ground. She was caught out. She put her face in her hands in absolute exasperation. Matthew stared at her dad, unaware of who he was. Jane's dad glared at him, he stood completely still, his shoulders hunched slightly and his fists clenched.

Jane broke the horrendous silence; "Dad, this is Matthew. Matthew, this is my dad." Realisation dawned on Matthew's face as he stood there barefoot with shorts and a T shirt on. They both reached out and shook hands stiffly.

"I think I'll be heading, Jane, sorry to disturb." He coughed uncomfortably and glanced sideways at Matthew, scrutiny in his eyes.

"No problem, dad. I'll chat to you soon!" Jane ushered him out the door and kissed him on the cheek, closing the door behind him and drawing the curtains back again.

"Oh, my god! I can't believe that just happened!" Jane squawked. "I'm absolutely mortified!"

"How do you think I feel?!" He chuckled, looking completely unfazed by the materialisation of her father.

"You don't understand, this never happens to *me*! How will I ever face my dad again! This is awful!" She put her face back in her hands again, wishing the last five minutes had not just happened.

"Just don't bring it up to him and I promise, he won't be rushing to bring it up with you either. You're an adult, it's no big deal." Jane contemplated this for a moment and accepted his reasoning. "Anyway, I'd better head on." He explained, his expression stoney.

Jane felt crestfallen, was he ditching her?

"Ok, thanks for coming over." Matthew's quick getaway and lack of effort to make plans that day despite them both being off together, confirmed in Jane's mind that he had got what he had wanted and was done with her. The added humiliation of her dad's appearance hadn't helped either.

She knew it, and this was confirmation. He was just being well mannered when he had accepted breakfast, but he had ultimately wanted to leave because he had already achieved his goal.

Jane sat at home that afternoon, feeling a mixture of elation at the events that had transpired, and worry that it might have been the last time she ever saw him again.

"Oh, the frustration of it all!" She thought out loud to her self, making the dogs jump. Now it was the wait to see if Matthew contacted her again. Jane was worried. She felt herself becoming emotionally connected to Matthew already, and that was never a good thing, emotional girls got hurt, fact.

Jane's phoned pinged an hour later as she lay sprawled across the sofa with the television on and Ruby and Jack snuggled in to her side.

"Hope you don't think I'm being too forward, I didn't want to scare you off earlier, but I'm free for a walk today if you are?" It was Matthew. Hallelujah. He must like her. He must *really* like her.

"Yeah, that would be great. I could meet you in an hour. At the beach?" She replied.

"Perfect. See you then x"

Jane arrived at the beach, Matthew was already there waiting for her, leaning against his car looking suave and sexy. Why do men who lean on things look so great?

"Hey there." He said as she approached, with a broad smile on his face.

"Hey you, again." She smiled coyly.

They set off at a leisurely pace along the beach, Matthew and Jane's opposite hands dangled at their sides, Jane longed for him to grab a hold of it, once or twice their skin had brushed off one another, but Matthew hadn't clung to the connection. Jane laughed to herself, it felt so nerve racking to know if she should or should not hold his hand despite the level of intimacy they had reached the night before.

"So, I've been thinking." Matthew started.

"Yes?" Jane implored, slightly apprehensive as to what he had been thinking about.

"Well, I was thinking earlier when I was texting you that I'm not even really sure what we are or what we are doing."

Oh dear god, was he dumping her before they had even started?

"Ok, what does that mean?" She asked, not sure if she really wanted to know the answer.

"I guess what I'm trying to ask is… do you think you would like to, em, be my girlfriend?" Jane stared at him quite speechless. She could have jumped up and high-fived him in absolute, ecstatic delight. However, she kept her cool and replied; "Yeah, I would really like that!"

Matthew grabbed her hand and squeezed it tightly. They spent the rest of the walk hand in hand, every so often glancing at one another with ridiculous smiles on their faces.

As they were nearing the end of their walk, Matthew turned to Jane. "I guess I should probably tell you that I've already told my parents about you."

"Matthew Carson, I think you are smitten." She laughed, glancing up at him sideways above hooded eyelids.

"I think I am," he smiled and gave her cheeky poke in the ribs. Jane loved their playfulness and touching. "The thing is, they would really like to meet you." He continued.

"Oh, dear goodness, that is serious." She said, without thinking, fidgeting her hands nervously, thinking of all the things she could end up saying wrong in front of these people.

"If it's too soon for you I completely understand." He replied quickly, peering at her nervously.

"Well, you have already met my dad, so I guess it's only right I meet your parents." She winked cheekily at him. He gave her a devilish smile and a raised eyebrow.

"Would you like me to meet your parents?" She continued.

"I really would, I'd like to show you off at every opportunity, you're some catch, Miss Abbott." She gazed at him. She was a catch?

"I'd be delighted to meet them. Oh, gosh, now I'm all worried." She laughed nervously, twiddling her fingers, heart pounding. She wasn't exactly an ideal candidate for a social situation where she had to excel exceedingly.

"Don't be. They will love you." Had he just dropped the L word already?

"Hopefully."

Jane got home from the walk and was preparing dinner, she finally felt relaxed in the knowledge that she was now Matthew Carson's girlfriend. Matthew really liked her and wanted to spend time with her. Jane's inner demon, the ability to self destruct, raised its ugly head. "Why me? Out of all the girls he could be with, why me?"

Jane shook off the negative notion and thought to herself, "Because you are a great catch, as Matthew said. Have some faith in yourself."

Matthew had arranged for Jane to meet his parents a week later. Jane was extremely apprehensive; she hadn't met with a boyfriend's parents in a long time. How should she behave? What would she talk about? She wanted to make a good first impression in front of them and, of course, in front of Matthew. She would look even more desirable, in his eyes, if his parents liked her, too.

Jane met at Matthew's at seven o'clock the following Tuesday evening, they were meeting his parents at a steakhouse nearby at half past seven. Matthew had given Jane a back story of his parents before they were to meet. His mum, Jessica, and dad, Bill, were still together after thirty five years of marriage which was quite unheard of in modern times; Matthew had arrived shortly after, when they had been married for five years. He had a younger brother called George that he was very close with. It sounded like a completely normal, happy childhood with no dramatic hiccups or lasting, painful scars. Jane couldn't help but feel a mild streak of envy.

His mother was a radiologist which was a relief to Jane, at least they would have a bit of common ground. His father was an accountant, not so much to talk about there, but dad's were generally easier to please.

When they arrived, Jane could hardly control her nerves, her hands were shaking and she had become very quiet.

"You will be fine!" He hugged her and laughed. "They will love you!" There was that L word again.

They arrived at the restaurant and Matthew's parents waved them over. His mother radiated happiness with a broad smile; she was beautiful and brunette with the same dark eyes as Matthew. His father was tall and handsome, with kind, chestnut eyes and salt and pepper hair.

They all hit it off right away; Matthew's parents put Jane at ease immediately. They were very chatty and interested, she found them easy to talk to. Jessica shared her experiences as a radiologist, Jane was in awe of her. Jane explained what it was like to be a midwife and Jessica appeared equally as awed.

"Matthew has been telling us all about you." Jessica smiled, creases reaching twinkling eyes. "He tells us that you are quite the girl!"

"Oh, does he now?" Jane chortled and flashed an affectionate smile at Matthew in appreciation.

"Mum!" Cried Matthew, "yes, well of course it's true." He threw them all his cheekiest grin and broke out in laughter. Jane was delighted with his public announcement of affection towards her. She couldn't peel the smile off her face.

"What was Matthew like as a little boy?" Jane asked, feeling quite comfortable after having had their main meal and conversation flowed favourably.

"Oh, Matthew was the angel child." Replied Jessica, glancing at her son lovingly.

"It was George who encouraged us to not have any more children!" Bill yelled with laughter. "He was a terror, cried all night, temper tantrums by day. Matthew slept all night and always did as he was told."

Jane smiled, "so what changed?" Matthew's parents laughed hard at this joke and gave Matthew an approving look.

"Hey!" Matthew mocked offence.

"I'm kidding, of course, you are very agreeable as an adult, too." She smiled sweetly at him, he smiled back. Jessica and Bill noted the exchange and smiled at each other.

"So, what did Matthew have to do to get a lovely girl like yourself?" Bill asked, Jane could see where Matthew got his charm from.

"Well, your son was quite the charmer. He pretty much had me at 'Hello'." She admitted, biting her lower lip. Wondering had she divulged too much information.

"That's my boy!" Roared Bill.

After dessert they all said their goodbyes, Jessica gave Jane a tight hug and Jane shook Bill's hand. Then they all went their separate ways. Jane got in to Matthew's car.

"That went so much better than I expected." She sighed a breath of relief.

"I told you they would like you! You were great!" He beamed at her.

"Thanks, your family are really lovely; I had such a nice time with them." She reflected back over the lovely evening they had shared together.

"I'm glad to hear it. I guess it will be my turn to meet your family at some point." He raised his eyebrows comically.

"Very presumptuous, aren't you?' She poked at him.

But Jane felt panicked, meeting Jane's family would be like walking in to an active war. Dysfunctional was a mild word to use to describe her family. How was she going to explain to him the dynamics of her family?

"Of course, you are all mine now, Jane Abbott, and your family comes with that package."

"My, oh, my. Are you marking your ownership over me?" She teased.

"Of course." He smirked.

"Well, I am happy for you to meet my family, but remember, you haven't met my mother yet." She half joked, feeling concerned and biting her lip at the thought.

Jane's parents had divorced when she was eleven years old, an awkward age when puberty is on the horizon and you have to move schools. They had both remarried some time ago and Jane was very fond of her step parents.

"Well, I'm happy to meet them, officially that is," he winked, "whenever you are. Just name the date."

"I feel bad for you because I have two sets of parents, makes it a bit more awkward, adds to the pressure." She bit nervously at the skin around her nails.

"I'm fine with it, Jane. I'll look forward to meeting both of them." He exhorted.

They got back to Matthew's house where Jack and Ruby lay snoozing on the sofas, Jane was planning on staying the night so they had brought the dogs over earlier. Matthew went to the fridge and lifted out a chilled bottle of Prosecco and poured two glasses.

Matthew's house was typical of a man's, the interior was simplistic and lacked clutter. There were no fancy furnishings or decorative plants, just the bare essentials, but it was homely and warm. Jane felt comfortable there.

He walked back in to the living room and handed Jane a glass and sat down beside her on the sofa.

"I think we should have a chat before you meet my family." Jane said, staring at him seriously, swigging a large mouthful of Prosecco, feeling the buzz of alcohol soar through her veins, easing her nerves slightly. Was she really going to get in to this?

"Ok. Is there something wrong?" He asked, sensing the tone and shifting in his seat uncomfortably.

"My family isn't straightforward and I kind of just want you to be pre warned before you meet them." Jane's heart thudded rapidly against her chest, her mouth suddenly lost all traces of saliva and she gulped back the nervous lump in her throat.

"What, are they serial killers or something?" He joked, but looked apprehensive all the same, sipping his Prosecco but not taking his eyes off her.

"No, they're not, cheeky!" She nudged him with her shoulder.

"I haven't really told anyone this before; I'm not even really sure why I am telling you. I guess I just want to start off as I mean to go on. By being honest." She explained, staring at him sternly, feeling determined.

Chapter 5

M atthew stared at Jane, looking perturbed and waiting in anticipation of what was to be said next; "Ok, you have me a bit worried if I'm being honest, Jane."

Jane took a deep, steadying breath and decided to get stuck straight in. She took in his entire, beautiful appearance, wondering would she ever see him again after she had revealed everything.

"My aunt, my mum's sister, and my uncle, started hitting me when I was four up until I was about eighteen, I guess when I decided to leave home-" Matthew stood up quickly, making Jane jump, he looked completely outraged. Jane thought he might walk out the door. Had she made a terrible mistake?

"Dear god, Jane! Did they do prison time? Please tell me you told the police and they went to prison?!" Matthew shouted, looking conflicted. Jane was taken aback by this display of anger; she hadn't expected him to get so mad so quickly.

"You're the first person I've ever told. Apart from my sister, Tess, obviously, and a counsellor as a child." She admitted, staring at him warily, trying to gauge his out of control reaction.

"What the hell, Jane?! What about your parents? Did you not tell them?" He demanded, hands on his hips and a crease in his brow.

Jane let Matthew calm down slightly before she started, he sat back down beside her but his face still emanated anger; "Well, I always wondered did they know, deep down. You know, because it was my mum's sister after all. There used to be a lot of friction between me and my parents, because they were supposed to protect me and I felt they were just letting this happen." Jane took a long gulp from her glass, the bubbles helped to steady her nerves. The truth was out there, there was no turning back.

"But if your aunt and uncle didn't live with you then how were they able to do it?" He asked, with trepidation in his voice.

"We stayed with my aunt and uncle once a week, at the weekends mainly, to give my parents a break. If I misbehaved I would be sent over earlier because they knew I hated being there." Matthew looked horrified, his mouth parted. To think that any parent would knowingly send their child off in to that environment.

"You should've told your parents, Jane. They could have stopped it from happening." He looked at her with deep pity in his face, Jane hated it. Hated him feeling sorry for her. Did he view her completely differently now?

"Maybe. But my mother is very persuasive; she convinced my dad that it was good for their relationship to send us away. When I came home crying at the end of every weekend she would tell him that I just missed being at home. That was partly true." She stared fixedly at the ground.

"How come?" He asked, deeply enthralled and emotionally invested in the confession.

"I hated being at home too, I felt resentful towards them, I thought they knew what was happening but were letting it go on ahead anyway." Jane's head remained down, she stared intensely at a small speck of dirt on her shoe rather than looking him directly in the eye.

"Did you ever bring it up with either of them?"

"Never." Matthew stared at her wide eyed.

"I'm afraid to ask, but what did your aunt and uncle do to you?" He sat back down and held her hand tightly, Jane was sure it must be uncomfortable doing so because she was sweating profusely.

"Well, if they weren't physically beating me, then it would be mental torture instead, some times this felt worse than the physical torture. The degrading comments of how worthless, stupid and fat I was. To have your whole life broken apart and humiliated right in front of you every single weekend for most of your childhood. I was a degenerate in their eyes." She breathed deeply, there was no going back, she had to be brave. Jane could feel panic rise at the thought of what she had been subjected to as a small child.

"What sort of things did they say to you?" He asked gently.

"It was mainly my aunt who made the demeaning comments, my uncle barely spoke to me, he reserved his energies for the beatings. My aunt would tell me that I deserved what was happening to me, that I didn't deserve to be happy. This made it so much more difficult to comprehend because my aunt obviously knew that what her husband was doing to me was wrong." Jane's voice shook, she felt her emotions rise; she swallowed them down, trying to remain strong.

"That must have been so hard." He breathed, staring at her pityingly.

"Of course, the eating disorders set in from an early age, mum and dad used to go crazy because I wouldn't eat any of the food they made, they couldn't understand why. They decided to put it down to peer pressure in school. All my dreams in my life were quashed by my aunt and uncle; I was too stupid and untalented and ugly to do anything."

"I'm so sorry this happened to you, Jane. But I don't understand why they wanted to hurt you so much? Did Tess get the same treatment?" He looked at her grimly, his eyes were sad and Jane was sure she could see tears.

"Oh, no, definitely not. She missed out on it all. But I did a lot of research in to it as I got older because you tend to blame yourself. Apparently people who commit domestic violence upon children normally have a *favourite* child that they prey upon, I would say I was the unfortunate one, but I would never have wished a fate like that upon my sister."

"Does Tess know?"

"Yes, she witnessed most of it. She would come home screaming on a Sunday when we got home. Telling my parents to never send us back there and explained what all had happened to me. I would be black and blue, but Aunt Margaret and Uncle Thomas would just say that I fell off my bike or fell down the stairs." Tears prickled the corners of Jane's eyes, she tried her best to keep them at bay, she couldn't look at him.

"How did your mum and dad not figure out what was going on? If you came home with injuries and Tess had none? And especially when Tess had outright told them what was going on!" He looked furious, his eyes ablaze with anger and injustice.

"I don't know, I was torn; sometimes I thought they definitely knew what was going on and just chose to ignore it and other times I figured they just thought we hated being there and that I must be a very accident prone child. They worked an awful lot and they were probably distracted with their failing marriage, as well. Mum and dad were always fighting, they would scream at each other right in to the night. All Tess and I could do would be to cry in to each other's arms until we fell in to an exhausted sleep." Jane examined his face for a sign of revulsion, she saw only pity.

"But if you weren't accident prone in your own house and you were at your aunt and uncle's, then how did they not just put two and two together and believe what Tess was telling them?!" He demanded angrily, shoving his hand through his hair, looking exasperated.

Jane merely looked at him, he knew the answer deep down, he knew that Jane's parents had not been stupid and knew exactly what was happening but chose to completely ignore it and allowed the abuse to continue for fourteen years, right under their noses.

Jane let out a deep breath and gave him a; 'I don't know what to tell you' look.

"Jesus. Jane. This is crazy." He stared at her furiously, completely baffled at the injustice and lost for words.

He finally spoke; "And how is your relationship with Tess now?"

"Fantastic. I held a lot of jealousy and resentment towards her for a long time, I hated her in fact. Why was she the perfect one and I was the failure? Tess got married a few years ago and I was the subject of humiliation. Of course Jane wasn't married because who in their right mind would marry me? This was just one of the delightful things my aunt would say via text message. I've blocked her numbers multiple times." Jane breathed dejectedly.

"That's so unfair." He said sadly.

"My entire childhood was unfair. I went to school and got bullied; being a child for me was horrendous. There was never a single, solitary moment of solace. I think that's why I lived on my own for so long. I was finally free." She let out a trembling breath, overwhelmed that she had told him so much, there was no taking it back.

"You got bullied at school, *too?*" His eyes, if possible, grew even wider.

"Yes, quite badly, for years I spent my lunch break in my teacher's classroom because the kids would through food at me, shove me in the hallway, or sometimes punch me. The talking about me right in front of my face was the worst, laughing and pointing at me like I was some kind of circus freak." Jane gulped back her nerves.

"Please tell me there was something done about the bullies, Jane?" Jane stared back at him, silent.

"So your teachers and parents did nothing about the bullies?" He looked incredulous.

"The teachers phoned my parents from time to time but they told me to stop creating so much hassle and asked why was it always me causing the trouble. Sometimes they didn't even believe I was getting bullied. I'm so grateful my childhood is over, it's hard to grasp on to any good memories when I look back."

"Yeah, I can get that." He stared at her unblinking, lost for words at this huge revelation, overwhelmed with feeling of injustice and unfairness. "So, what about your aunt and uncle now?" He finally said.

"Well, I never have any contact with them. After I moved out I never saw them again. My mum still sees *her* sometimes, which aggravates me a lot. I always get a little flashback of hell when I think of my aunt or uncle. Which, unfortunately, means I get a little flashback of hell any time I see my mum, if I'm being honest." She looked up at him, admiring his handsome face, hoping it wouldn't be the last time she laid eyes on it.

"I am so sorry this has happened to you, Jane. But, I'm glad that you felt you could share this with me. I want you to feel as though you can talk to me about anything." He explained earnestly, grabbing her hand and squeezing it tightly. His mouth curved in to a small, sympathetic smile.

"I really just wanted to give you a little head's up. I didn't expect to divulge everything when I first started; it all just kind of seemed to splurge out. The last thing I want is your pity." She said seriously, still staring at her feet, feeling exposed.

"You probably needed it off your chest after all those years," he said understandingly, "and I don't pity you, I guess I feel angry. Angry that all of this happened to you and nothing was done about it. Nobody protected you." He continued to stroke her hand.

"Well, I thought telling you would be helpful, just in case my aunt or uncle's name ever comes up in conversation, which is highly likely, and I suddenly change in behaviour." She said, glancing up at him quickly, her hands trembling.

"How do you mean?" He asked curiously, the crease in his brow seemed to be a permanent fixture now.

"Well, my aunt or uncle's names are sort of triggers for me; some times I can have a panic attack at just the mention of them. I will most likely seize up and become fidgety and anxious." She dared a brief look at him to try to gauge where his head was at, then darted her head back down to her hands again. She bit her lip nervously.

"Jesus, Jane." He stared at her for a moment, studying her face with severe consternation. "Can I ask you a serious question?"

"Yes, of course." She replied.

"Why did you never say anything to your parents about this? Even now?" He stared at her adamantly.

"Because my mum and dad's lives were difficult at the time, I didn't want to make things even more complicated for them. And now I just feel as though too much time as passed to start digging up the past and upsetting everyone. It wouldn't get me anywhere." Her hands fidgeted in her lap.

"It's not really a good enough excuse though is it? To ship you off to your aunt and uncle's house every week even when they knew what you were in for. It's totally unfathomable to think about and with the bullies on top of it all and they still did nothing to protect you, you were just a child." Matthew could feel himself becoming very angry, he clutched her hand tightly, steadying the tremble. Jane wondered had she made a mistake, was Matthew's view of her parents tainted forever?

"It's difficult to comprehend when you really think about it. I guess I got my head around it by telling myself that my parents didn't know about my aunt and uncle." She squeezed his hand.

"What about your Nanny? Did you tell her?" Jane's heart squeezed at the mention of her beloved Nanny.

"I never told her, how could I tell an elderly woman what was happening? It would destroy her. Going to Nanny's was my sanctuary, I could learn about different types of tea and why each one was individual and amazing in its own way, all the while being fed cake and biscuits. Why ruin that with reality?"

Matthew lowered his gaze solemnly, "I'm glad you had her."

"So am I." Jane's bottom lip trembled.

"Did your aunt and uncle ever have any of their own children?"

"No, they couldn't have any. I think that's why my mum and dad sent Tess and I to see them every week, to fill that void in their life I guess." She exhaled.

"And how do you think this all has affected you as an adult?" He asked warily.

"Are you worried I'm some violent nutcase or something?" She laughed nervously.

"Definitely not. You are the most laid back person I've ever met but all that hurt is bound to leave a few scars." He said genuinely, staring at her intently.

"It definitely did, I won't deny that. When I was in my late teens and early twenties I found it difficult to control and interpret my emotions. I was angry and outraged with the world. My dad sent me to anger management counselling because of my intense rage.

"I just didn't have an outlet for all the built up fury. I couldn't understand why I had been subjected to so much torture at the hands of these people who were supposed to care about me.

"I was let down by the most important people in my life. Of course, that has a ripple effect throughout your future relationships. I was reluctant to trust anyone; I had some very aggressive and intense relationships. I treated men whatever way I pleased, never taking in to account that these were human beings that I was using and hurting." She spoke quickly, her voice shaking.

"Did the counselling help?" He stroked her face gently, wiping away a tear.

"It really did, it was a channel for my unresolved anger; my counsellor allowed me to scream and shout in my sessions. It was a real vent of frustration. What really helped me, though, was my sheer determination that I would never allow myself to turn in to *them*. I could never let that happen. So the best way to get around that was to be alone." She said sadly.

"And how do you feel you are now?"

"Although I resented them for a long time I do feel grateful to have my mum and dad, I don't know what I would have done without them. After their divorce, when I was eleven, I noticed my mum become increasingly more protective and controlling. She has to know where I am at all times. I think she feels guilty for allowing it all to happen right under her nose." She breathed exhaustively, frowning at the thought.

Matthew nodded understandingly. "And how is your relationship with your mum now? With the controlling aspect?" He asked pensively.

"We have a really close bond, we are best friends. Yes, she can be suffocating and always at the end of the phone but I don't know what I would do without her. I can't blame her for something other people did to me." She breathed.

"And what about your dad?" He asked, listening intently, eyes focused on her.

"I'm really close with him too, he's a bit more relaxed than my mum, doesn't need to know my whereabouts at all times but he is very protective, very wary of new boyfriends." She laughed and gave him a wink.

"Oh dear, I'm done for!" He managed a chuckle despite the circumstances. Jane smirked at him.

"Were things different for you after your mum and dad broke up?"

"When my parents broke up life actually got a bit easier for me. I was able to stay at my dad's half the week and my mum the other half, which meant I visited my aunt and uncle a lot less often, it was total bliss. The only problem then was that I still had to go to school and face the bullies." She said depressingly, resting her face on the palm of her hand, reflecting on the fact that she was grateful the horrific chapter of her life was behind her.

Matthew let out a long, whistling sigh, "Jesus, Jane. That's about the worst upbringing I've ever heard of from someone."

"I'm sure there are a lot of less fortunate people out there. The only thing I can say is that I always had a roof over my head, I never wanted for any toys. In fact, I think my parents overcompensated out of guilt and got me all the toys that money could buy."

"Doesn't make up for it, though." He said strongly.

"No, unfortunately it doesn't. I need you to know, when you meet my mum, that is, that she isn't all bad, I think she just holds a lot of guilt and wants to look out for me. It can be quite overbearing but she means well." She admitted.

"I'm sure it can be, I'm glad you have a good relationship with her despite everything that went on. Do you hold any resentment towards your dad? Surely he must have had as much of an inkling as your mother did?" He asked, he curled his lip in a grimace.

"Maybe. I guess I forgave my dad a bit more quickly because he wasn't blood related to my aunt. I think I blamed my mum for my aunt's behaviour just as much as I actually blamed my aunt." He looked at her accusingly. "I know, I never told her so how could she know?" She popped a shoulder in a shrug.

"Yeah, I can get that." He put one arm around her and drew her in tightly. "I'm proud of you for sharing this with me, thank you. I want to be able to support you in anyway possible. I've grown to care about you a lot, Jane." He repeated.

Jane looked up at him with tears in her eyes, he kissed her softly and he stroked her cheek with the back of his hand. It seemed to sweep all the pain away that Jane had been feeling, the all encompassing love for this man was overwhelming and now she had divulged the biggest secret of her entire life to him. The emotion got all a bit too much, she could feel it rising up inside of her; she didn't stop it. Matthew cradled her head in to his shoulder and she weeped quietly until she could cry no more.

Jane awoke abruptly the next morning with a fuzzy head from the Prosecco and a nauseous feeling as the memory returned of her confession to Matthew. Should she have revealed so much to him? She was second guessing herself. She was placing a lot of trust in a person that she barely knew. But Matthew had opened up a whole new world to Jane, a world where she didn't have to be a recluse and a cynic, one where she could break the chains of her past that were dragging her down, one where she could have love and trust and stability.

The memories of her childhood stabbed painfully as she recalled recounting them to Matthew. Obviously he had only been given a taster of what had actually happened, the graphic images of what went on fully would have been too much for him to deal with. Flashing images of metal belt buckles, her aunt's heeled stilettos and large, clenched fists swam in to Jane's memory. She could still taste her fear. The fear of being dragged out from under the bed by her drunk uncle, the all encompassing terror of what was to happen next.

Jane remembered her uncle banging her head off her bedroom wall repeatedly, causing severe pain and white spots to appear in her vision, all while her aunt stood nearby, throwing vicious comments at her. Jane never forgot what her aunt said to her on those occasions; her stupidity, her worthlessness, how pathetic and insignificant she was. While her uncle would whip the metal belt buckle against the back of her legs, making her stand up again each time she crumbled to the ground in agony.

Confessing to Matthew had awoken a memory that Jane had tried to keep dormant for many years, the thoughts were fresh in her mind as though they had happened yesterday. The injustice of it, the want to know why she deserved all that suffering over so many years. Her childhood torn away from her. Jane believed for a long time that she was as worthless as her aunt and uncle had made her out to be, that she had been asking for all the trouble, that was, until she got older and realisation set in. Jane was plagued with anxiety and frequent panic attacks. Her dreams turning to nightmares as she subconsciously dug out the torture she had endured.

The one lasting thought that Jane could never shake from her mind was, why had her parents never done anything? Why had they turned a blind eye? Tess had outright told them, she had injuries to back her story. Jane quickly became withdrawn, having no one to turn to, even at school when she was pushed and shoved and taunted for being strange. Jane contemplated many dark thoughts as a teenager, longing for it all to end, the suffering seemed to be never ending, no light at the end of the tunnel.

Jane broke out of her reverie and turned her head to see Matthew staring at her, his eyes wide and wary. Jane's fear had come true, he was looking at her differently now, it had changed everything. Matthew lifted a hand and stroked her cheek tenderly, his eyes glistening with wanting tears. Jane felt an unexpected tear roll down her cheek, Matthew wiped it away and pulled her in close, squeezing her so tight. Jane exhaled a deep, shaky breath. Everything was going to be ok.

Chapter 6

"Jane, I can't wait to meet this new boy in your life! This is so exciting!" Jane had asked her mum to meet Matthew over text the next day.

"Thanks mum, he's looking forward to meeting you too :-)"

"I really hope you find happiness with this one, but know that you always have your mum here for support if you ever need me. I love you so much."

Jane suddenly felt exceedingly guilty that she had revealed such a negative side to her mum before Matthew had even the chance to meet her. Had she jumped the gun a little too quickly? It wasn't actually her mum who had been the terrible person, just her sister and brother in law. Her mother had such genuine and kind qualities, she hoped Matthew could see that too.

Matthew was charming as always when he met Charlotte and her husband, Bob. Jane's mother was positively giddy at the idea of being introduced to Jane's boyfriend. Charlotte and Bob arrived with an impressive array of sandwiches, scones and buns for an afternoon tea at Jane's house. Charlotte was dressed in her best, donning an expensive pant suit and a beautiful diamond necklace. Bob looked equally expensive in an open shirt and slacks; he had silver hair and tasteful stubble on his face. Definitely her mother's usual type.

Charlotte appeared agitated and jittery and kept offering Matthew things to eat and touched his arm frequently. On arrival, Charlotte had immediately went for the fridge and poured herself a glass of Pinot Grigio. Jane had a bad feeling, her mother was absolutely wonderful without alcohol, but with it, she developed a motor mouth and some times said the wrong thing. Jane assumed she was drinking in the middle of the afternoon out of nervousness.

"Oh, Matthew, it's so nice to meet you! Oh, how I longed for Jane to meet someone!" Charlotte roared excitedly, as she sat on the sofa beside him, altogether too close, taking a large bite of a cream scone and a generous gulp of white wine.

Jane poured tea from one of her larger teapots in to everyone's cup, she had opted for a Assam blend, originating from India, Jane loved the strong, malty favours. She also enjoyed people trying a tea they had never had before.

"She has been on her own for so long I was beginning to give up hope!" She continued with her mouth full. "Well, at least I have grandchildren from my youngest girl, Tess is my saving grace!" She spoke very fast and without a break in between sentences and with absolutely no consideration of the words she had just spoken.

Jane gave her mother a '*stop talking*' look. Charlotte was completely oblivious to this and carried on chatting away excitedly about Jane's baron ovaries and her weird obsession with dogs. It was when Jane's mother started talking about her ex boyfriend, David, that Jane had to step in.

"I think that's quite enough on the history lesson, Mum!" Jane said harshly through her teeth.

75

"I'm just filling him in dear! No harm in that!" Her mum laughed hysterically and glanced for support from the room. She received none.

Matthew was quite lost for words, but smiled on anyway. Jane was glad she had told Matthew a fair bit of her upbringing; otherwise nothing could have prepared him for the ridiculous display of erratic behaviour. Jane supposed her mother was nervous, she was never normally as rude or excitable around others.

"So, Matthew, I believe you a paramedic." This wasn't a question.

"That's right." Matthew said, glad of the change of conversation.

"Didn't fancy being a doctor then?" She blurted out.

"*Mum!*"

"Charlotte!" Bob gasped at his wife, one of his few words spoken during the visit.

"What?" Cried Charlotte, in ignorant bliss. "It's just a question, no harm done." But Charlotte looked uneasily around the room, realising that she had spoken out of turn. She sunk back in to the sofa and sipped on her wine, quietly.

Jane noticed the quiet surrender and began to relax. She gave her mum a thumbs up in offer of reassurance.

"Charlotte, we need to get going, I said to John I would meet him at three o'clock to play nine holes of golf." Explained Bob.

"We had better get the dogs out." Jane announced as well. "They are starting to get antsy for a walk." Jane had put them in the kitchen whilst they were eating their food, she could hear them clawing ferociously at the door.

Charlotte looked devastated, she knew she had put her foot in it. Jane's heart bled for her, she knew her mother meant well and was just anxious to make a good impression.

"It was very nice to meet you both." Matthew said graciously, but quite clearly lying through his teeth, he was immensely relieved that the meeting was over.

"Nice to meet you too, Matthew." Bob said kindly, he reached over and shook his hand. Matthew smiled at him.

"It was so lovely to meet you Matthew." Charlotte shook his hand and gave him a sheepish smile along with an apologetic look.

Charlotte and Bob left.

"I am *so* sorry." Jane inhaled deeply, trying to steady herself mentally, as she closed the door behind them and they stood facing each other in the hallway. "Mum is never like that, that was really out of character for her, she actually is really nice."

"Don't worry about it, I think she seems nice, maybe just a bit overexcitable. I think she has high hopes for us." His lips curved up in to a delectable smile.

"Well, I have told her very good things about you." She smiled above hooded eyelids and approached him slowly, gently pressing her hands against his chest and her mouth against his.

"Oh really? You have high hopes for us, too?" He joked, placing his hands around the small of her back, linking his fingers.

Jane looked at him seriously from an arm's length. "Of course." He smiled and kissed her softly, Jane melted in to him.

"Bob's a quiet man." Matthew stated after they had broken apart.

"I guess my mum probably likes it that way" Jane contemplated amusingly.

"I guess you're right." Matthew sniggered. "Come on, let's get these pups out, the fresh air will do you good." He pulled her in tight again.

Later that night, Charlotte text Jane to apologise for her behaviour in the afternoon.

"Jane, I'm so sorry for my outburst earlier, I think the mixture of the wine and the excitement of meeting Matthew all just got a bit too much, I'm ashamed!"

"Don't be mum! You were fine. Matthew was just glad that he had made a good impression and he hopes that you like him!"

"Well of course I do and if I may say he is one fine looking dish too!"

"Mum! He is something alright ;-)" Jane was glad all was well with her mum again, she worried about her, Jane felt a lot of guilt that her mother was always so concerned for her safety and whereabouts. Jane thought it must have a detrimental effect on her quality of life.

"Jane if I can be so bold as to say I don't think I've ever seen you looking this happy before."

"He's different, I can't explain it. I feel different. Like I'm a better person when he's around."

"You were a great person before he came around, he has maybe just been able to shed light on the fact for you."

"When did you become so wise mum?" Jane's eyes glistened on reading the kind words her mum was sending her.

"I have been known to have my moments. If I'm not too valiant to say, I think I spied the look of love in your eye?"

Jane stared at the message, she was caught completely unawares. How to respond. Her mother text again quickly.

"Have I spoken out of turn?"

"No no. Not at all. It's just, we haven't said it yet."

"But you feel it?"

"Desperately!" Jane admitted in a single message, glad to finally tell someone. Jane continued; "I've never felt a feeling like it before! I feel as though I'm going crazy!"

"You're not going crazy, darling. You're in love."

Matthew and Jane dated for several more weeks; Jane felt the bond between them had grown even stronger ever since she had divulged the truth about her aunt and uncle. Matthew had not run away and this was monumental in Jane's mind. Although, this didn't stop Jane feeling insecure that Matthew might eventually become fatigued with the knowledge of bearing a '*damaged*' girlfriend and seek to move on.

Jane had to squash these negative feelings; they didn't do anyone any good. It was hard for Jane to combat pessimism, though, it was all she knew. Her entire childhood had been met with cynicism at every turn.

Matthew had not officially met Jane's father ever since the brief, but terrible, encounter they had all shared the day after Jane and Matthew had first had sex together. Jane was not complaining. Her father was highly protective and had annihilated boyfriends in the past with his overprotective ways and gruelling questioning. Jane's dad was also a dentist, therefore, his time was limited. Jane was proud of her dad and his ambitious work ethic, it was one of the reasons she had strove to be successful in life.

Jane met with Matthew one Sunday afternoon for one of their regular walks; it was one of the rare occasions they hadn't spent the night together. They had both been working late the night before and it made sense to go to their separate homes. Jane was glad to see him again, she felt anxious when they were apart. Worried that the time he had to think on his own would be spent on planning how to dump her, at least if she was with him she could convince him that it was a great idea to be with her.

This was one of the repercussions of her traumatic childhood, a horrendously low sense of self esteem, never feeling worthy of anyone's love and affection and when someone did show her interest or amity she would wonder why, and subsequently self destruct and destroy the relationship. And when it all ended, she could tell herself that she knew it would end all along. Millie was Jane's longest standing friend, there had been many occasions when Millie could have walked away, when Jane was being unbearable or causing an argument but she never left, Millie was always there, loyal through the good and the bad.

"I have a question to ask you," Matthew started, as they traipsed over rough terrain at a nearby forest as Jack and Ruby ran ahead. "It's completely fine if you say no." Jane couldn't imagine what the question might be.

"Ok..." She said tentatively.

He looked at her nervously before starting, what on earth could the question be? "Can I break up with you?" She thought to herself, laughing inwardly at her intense lack of self confidence.

"Well, I have this yearly work ball that we all go to and we are allowed to bring a date with us. It's usually a pretty nice event, black tie etc. I wondered if you might like to go as my date? If it's too soon, I understand, I don't want to scare you." He glanced sideways at her nervously, waiting for her to break the bad news.

"I would love to!" Jane gasped, completely relieved and beyond excited by the invitation.

"Really? That's great!" A broad smile appeared on his face, he looked like a Cheshire cat and the smile couldn't be wiped from his face.

"When is it?" Jane asked happily, trudging through a muddy puddle, clothes protected by knee high wellies.

"It's two Saturdays away, is that enough notice for you for work? They only just announced the date." He explained.

Jane checked her calendar of shifts on her phone.

"I'm off that weekend!" She screamed, a little too excitedly. Jane had to control her excitement; she still wanted to play it cool with Matthew. She didn't want to come across as desperate and needy, especially when he knew one of her most concealed secrets.

"Great!" He exclaimed. "You will be quite the trophy on my arm." He teased.

"Hey! I'm not a piece of meat." She elbowed him affectionately in the ribs.

The night of the paramedic ball had come around all too quickly. Jane was apprehensive and excited. She had gone to a lovely, little boutique in town with Millie the previous Saturday to pick an outfit. The shop was laden with long and expensive gowns for every shape and size, Jane was overwhelmed. Shopping was not really her thing and with so much choice it meant that the dress choosing would not be an expedited event.

Thankfully, Jane had brought Millie with her; her most stylish friend with brilliant taste and an eye for what suited Jane's figure best. Millie chose a champagne coloured dress with a deep, plunging neck line and a split up the length that went right up to Jane's hip.

"I cannot wear this!" Cried Jane, facing a full length mirror, Millie had presented her with a pair of gold stilettos to set off the look.

"Jane, you look absolutely breathtaking! This is the dress! Matthew is going to go nuts when he sees you in it and then he will be even more delighted that he gets to show you off on his arm to his friends!" Millie shrieked delightedly, clapping her hands together in applause.

"But Millie, it is so revealing, I'm showing leg and boob." She urged vigorously, her face contorted in disapproval.

"So what, you look elegant and sexy all at the same time. Look at yourself in the mirror... properly!" She pressed.

Jane stood, staring at herself. She did look good, the silky material clung to just the right areas of her body, accentuating her curved and full backside and nipping in at her waist, showing off her hourglass figure. The slit up the leg was actually quite appealing, especially when she walked, and she thought to herself that maybe not so much of her cleavage was on show as she had originally thought. The truth was, Jane looked hot, and she knew it.

Ten minutes later and the dress was bought, a lot more of an expense than Jane had intended on but Millie said that it would be worth it.

Chapter 7

It was the night of the ball and Jane had her hair pinned up by Martha who was very talented at up dos. Jane did her own make up, she didn't want anything too heavy; she hated the caked on look.

Jane slipped on the dress when she was ready and all three girls screamed excitedly. Millie, Martha and Jennifer never missed an opportunity to socialise together with Jane and this was a perfect excuse to pop the Prosecco.

"Jane! You look absolutely incredible!" Martha sank the glass of Prosecco and clapped excitedly.

"He's definitely going to think you are wife material after tonight!" Jennifer yelled deafeningly.

Jane couldn't deny that she was enjoying the attention, ever since she had met Matthew things in her life had begun to look up. She now had a closer bond of friendship with the three girls than she had ever had and her future was finally starting to look bright.

"Thanks girls." Jane answered appreciatively, feeling her confidence rise by the minute.

Matthew arrived at Jane's house to collect her just as the three girls were leaving, she could hear them chattering excitedly as she stayed up in her room, taunting Matthew with her big reveal. She heard the front door close and silence prevail, she heard the tip tap of paws on her wooden floor and knew the dogs were greeting Matthew happily.

Jane walked to the top of the stairs and started to descend. She saw Matthew standing in the hallway; he was dressed in an extremely well fitted and expensive looking suit, steel grey in colour with a sharp navy tie. It was doing a wonderful job of accentuating his strong back and shoulders and highlighting his strong, rugby player type legs. Men in suits, so simple but so amazingly satisfying to the eye. Matthew hadn't noticed her yet as he was too preoccupied stroking Ruby and Jack. He looked up as he heard a creak of a floor board and drank in her appearance greedily.

His mouth fell open comically and he stood stark still and completely speechless at the mirage standing before him.

"I look that good, then?" She asked breathily. He continued to stare with no words. "You look amazing Matthew." She eyed him up hungrily, too.

"I'm going to have to phone ahead and tell them we're going to be late." He said fiercely, with a rawness to his voice as he stepped over and pulled her slim body towards his. Feeling his ragged breath on her, she could smell his glorious hints of woody aftershave and citrus shower gel. Jane felt good, she loved having this power over him, to see him completely flabbergasted was a massive ego boost.

"We'd better go." She said, taunting him, turning on the spot so he could take in the whole spectacle.

"You are a damn tease, Jane Abbott. I've changed my mind, we're not going. No other man is allowed to see you like this." He said seriously, but then the sides of his mouth formed an upward curve.

"I'm glad you like what you see." She stroked his face softly.

"I think I love you." Jane nearly choked on her own saliva.

"What?!" She cried out.

"I love you, Jane. You are breathtaking; you have changed my life for the better." He stood holding her hands, willing her to feel the same way, shifting in his spot.

"Damn. This must be a good dress." She chuckled awkwardly.

"You don't feel the same way?" He asked, shock and disappointment flooded his expression.

"What?! Oh, no!" She had forgotten, over the shock of it all, that she hadn't actually responded to his comment. "Matthew, I loved you from the moment I first saw you, spending all this time with you has just confirmed it more and more each day."

He picked her up around the waist, lifting her feet easily off the ground and spinning her around quickly. Laughing happily and kissing her passionately.

Jane broke free. "Right, we really do need to go! And I need to fix my make up again. You have me all flustered." She giggled flirtatiously and turned to walk away, knowing that he was checking her out, and loving it.

He loved her, he really loved her. Jane couldn't comprehend it, this man knew everything about her, her skeletons in the closet, how she looked first thing in the morning, the good and the bad and still he loved her. The stable, functioning, no baggage Matthew, actually loved her. She couldn't understand it, he was so perfect and so wonderful and she was so... Well, not perfect, in any way. But, he still loved her. Jane's heart soared with happiness, high on ecstasy.

Jane returned, wearing a grin so wide that Matthew's face brightened as soon as he saw her. They clutched each other tightly, the unspoken connection between the two of them now stronger than ever before.

Matthew had ordered a limo to take them to the ball, Jane was impressed, he had gone all out to impress. She was grateful she had made the extra effort with her outfit. "Unless he does this every year with a different girl every time." She thought anxiously in to her self. She shook the negative thought from her mind, determined to enjoy the moment. There was no denying that Matthew had a sexual past, but what was the point in thinking about it all the time? She couldn't change it.

They arrived at the Ponty Hotel, a five star hotel in the centre of Clovelly. Matthew was a gentleman and opened the door for Jane. As she stepped out of the limo the slit in her dress opened up, revealing the entirety of her leg.

"Damn it, Jane. How am I going to survive this night without touching you?" He gasped.

"You can touch me." She explained naughtily, winking at him, taking his hand and stepping graciously out of the limo, feeling like a queen.

"Not in the way I'm thinking." His dark eyes bore in to her, igniting that spark that had been present throughout the entire limo journey.

Because of the darkened glass in the limo, the young couple had complete privacy in the back of the car, the sexual tension was tangible in the air. Matthew had his hand too far up Jane's thigh; he squeezed wantonly every so often.

"All in due course." She had teased.

"It's not soon enough." He breathed, kissing her neck.

They arrived in to the busy vestibule of the hotel, with Matthew's hand at the small of Jane's back. The touch was sensational; the energy between them was corporeal. On first impressions, the hotel looked outstanding; the vestibule had a very high ceiling, lined with huge chandeliers. There were lavish couches sporadically spread about the lobby with large vases filled with flowers lining the walls. Expensive art was hung around the walls adding to its grandeur, and the smell as she had entered had been divine.

Matthew was greeted by a couple of his male colleagues, they shook hands and quickly their eyes drifted towards Jane in sheer delight at her appearance. Matthew introduced them and she shook both their hands, their eyes lingered too long over her. Jane was pleased with herself; she was quite the asset to Matthew.

"Damn it. Every mans' eye is on you." He scolded. "You are far too hot in that dress." His hand ran down the bottom of her back, brushing against her buttocks, she inhaled sharply at the touch.

"Excuse me for looking nice." She taunted cheekily, removing his hand from her backside. He smiled, his face pained with want. He squeezed her round the waist and pulled her in tight, she could feel the sexual desire through his fingertips. She loved every moment of his torture.

They entered the main room where they would be having their meal, it was similar to the vestibule, grand and lavish but instead of couches in the room, large circular tables and chairs of a rich cream colour scattered the room. Each table had a large vase of flowers on it also and the ceilings were lined with similar looking chandeliers.

They approached the bar that was gold in colour and utterly breathtaking, it spanned the length of the room and had every type of alcoholic beverage stocked that you could ever dream of.

They placed their order of Prosecco for Jane and Whiskey and coke for Matthew. As they waited for their drinks, Matthew was approached by a very tall and attractive woman; Jane automatically drew out her hypothetical claws in anticipation of competition. Who the hell was this *bitch*? Jane noticed that she was equally as slim as Jane, but taller with long, flowing, dark brown hair that reached the middle of her back. It was perfectly straight and Jane couldn't deny that it looked amazing.

The woman was in a black, full length dress that accentuates all her good attributes. She appeared highly confident and was outrageously flirting with Matthew; she continually touched his arm and laughed at a simple joke. Jane was furious as she stood there, not once had the woman looked in Jane's direction or acknowledged her presence, and not once had Matthew turned to look at her or even introduce her to the beautiful woman.

Rather than standing and observing the torture unfold, Jane turned and stalked away. She breezed around the room and tried to feign an air of sophistication, as though she was taking in the beautiful room but she was utterly distracted by Matthew's behaviour and indifference towards her. Who was the vile woman who had grabbed the attention of her boyfriend?

Jane's mind had drifted off and she was staring in to space, maddened and frustrated by Matthew's incredulous behaviour. It had only been a mere hour ago that he had told her he loved her and now she had, unashamedly, been ditched for another, more attractive woman.

Jane's internal struggle was interrupted by an attractive looking man. He was tall, taller than Matthew and very broad, he was extremely masculine and Jane couldn't deny that he was attractive.

"I saw you standing on your own for a while, looking a bit lost, so I thought I would come over." He started, shuffling nervously.

"Sorry, I was kind of off on another planet." She explained, bringing herself back round to earth. A quick glance at the bar confirmed that Matthew was still at the bar with the woman. What the hell was going on?

"I could see that." He laughed, she smiled back meekly.

"I'm Thomas, I'm a paramedic. I don't think I've seen you before?"

"No, I don't think so. I'm Jane." Jane did not offer up who she was there with, why should she when an attractive man presented himself so readily to her and Matthew was quite happy in the company of another woman? The night was not going as Jane expected it to, she felt as though she could burst in to floods of tears at the injustice of it all.

"Can I get you a drink?" Jane noticed her empty glass.

"That would be great, I'll buy them." She thought it would be taking advantage if she made Thomas buy her drinks as well, at the end of the day he was merely a method to enrage Matthew, he shouldn't be out of pocket because of that.

Matthew and the woman were gone when she and Thomas approached the bar. Where were they? Was he actually cheating on her in plain sight? Jane's eyes darted frantically around the room in search of the pair. There was no sign of them.

Thomas and Jane ordered their respective drinks and Thomas chatted enthusiastically to her, Jane was not even pretending to listen, she felt sullen and depressed. Her boyfriend was off with another woman the very moment they had entered the room, her world felt as though it was crashing and crumbling around her.

Jane noticed Matthew re-enter the hall, before he could see her looking she turned her attention to Thomas and acted as though she were highly fascinated by his company.

Matthew approached the two of them; "Hi Thomas, I see you've met my girlfriend." He glowered at her disapprovingly. Jane glared back furiously, arms folded across her chest defensively.

"You didn't tell me Matt was your boyfriend." He said, looking shocked and aggravated.

"It never came up." She scowled even harder at Matthew.

"I'll leave you two to it." Thomas grabbed his drink and stormed off, enraged at the loss of opportunity.

"So, you've come here to flirt with my friends and deny that I'm your boyfriend?" He said in such a low voice that it actually instilled fear in Jane.

"Well, I could see that you were preoccupied so I didn't want to stand in your way any longer." She spat.

"What are you talking about?!" He looked dumbfounded.

"Don't treat me as though I'm stupid, you couldn't take your eyes off that woman!" Jane snapped viciously in a low voice, trying her best not to make a scene, but she could feel her eyes welling up and her emotions rise to the surface.

"Are you serious? She's just a work friend!" He cried adamantly, staring her down with an incredulous expression.

"So why did you not introduce me to her? Why did you completely ignore me when you spoke to her? You didn't even notice when I walked away from you because you were so distracted by her!" She could feel her temper soar, her voice had gone up a decibel.

"Don't be ridiculous, Jane! I must've forgotten to introduce you both!" He confessed, his eyes wide with frustration.

"Convenient that, wasn't it?" She shrieked, feeling mental and becoming hysterical.

"Don't be like that, Jane!"

"Don't tell me how I should be, we are here five minutes and you are already sauntering off with another woman and I'm completely forgotten about. You are a joke, Matthew. I never should have come. How would you feel if the tables were turned and I had done this to you?!" She demanded, her eyes wide with accusation, tears prickling the corners, threatening to break free.

"Well, you kind of did, you were flirting with Thomas." He suggested, but somewhat sheepishly.

"Not exactly the same is it, I don't even know him. I didn't choose him over you and this is not my function that I invited you to!"

"I'm sorry, Jane. I see it now, I was silly. She's an old friend and I guess we had a lot to catch up on." He explained apologetically, trying to take her hand but she snatched it away.

"What do you mean she's an old friend? I thought she was a work colleague?!" Jane thought her head might explode with anger.

91

"She's a colleague, too, we go way back." He admitted, staring down at his feet then back up to her.

"Oh my god, please don't tell me you both have *that* kind of history together!" She screeched manically, her blood pounding in her temple.

"You are making a scene, Jane. And no, we don't have *that* kind of history. She's just a friend." He glanced round the room to see if anyone was staring.

"Oh, I'm sorry, am I embarrassing you?" She spat derisively, narrowing her eyes in fury at him.

Matthew took Jane by the arm to pull her away. Jane shrugged off his arm and ran to the toilets, she had been crying, she wanted to fix her face and then leave with what little dignity she felt she had left.

Jane entered the bathrooms, tears invading her face freely, she hiccoughed through sobs, trying to understand how the night had nosedived so spectacularly. She took out her powder and mascara from her clutch. She started to dab at her face in an attempt to hide the streaks of mascara tracking down her face, when someone exited one of the toilet cubicles. It was Matthew's mystery *friend*. Jesus.

The woman smiled a knowing smile at her and proceeded to stare at her beautiful reflection in the mirror. Jane could taste the disgust the woman emanated towards her. The woman washed her hands and proceeded to freshen her make up also. Jane wished she hadn't looked so dishevelled. The tension was as thick as ice between them, the woman seemed to radiate hatred, confidence and beauty all at once. Jane couldn't deny that her appearance was mesmerising. Her gut flipped, her heart ached painfully. How could Matthew do this to her? Had Matthew been seeing this transfixing woman behind her back? From the very beginning?

"He's good in bed, isn't he?" The woman suddenly spoke.

"Excuse me?" She did not just say what Jane thought she said. Jane thought she might throw up.

"Matthew. He's great in bed. We used to sleep around for a while, just for fun, he wanted something more serious but I just wasn't ready. Now, though, I feel as though I am." The malevolence in her eyes shred Jane in to pieces. She was speechless. Her world came crashing down around her.

"Why are you telling me this?" Jane asked quietly, fury deepening, she had to resist the urge to punch the woman repeatedly in the face.

"Because, I know you two are sleeping together, Matthew tells me it's nothing serious so I wanted you to know that he's mine. Keep your hands off." She snapped and threw her a vicious look.

Jane stared at her in disbelief. Matthew had said that they were nothing serious? How could he say that? Jane felt her world shatter.

"You can have him." And she stormed out of the bathroom.

Chapter 8

J ane was met by Matthew as she ran out of the bathrooms, she tore past him with fresh tear stains splotched down her face again.

"Jane!" He shouted. "Where are you going?!"

Jane ignored him and jumped in to the waiting limo. She asked the driver to lock the doors and drive as she saw Matthew running towards her. The limo driver obeyed and took off at speed, leaving Matthew stranded at the kerb.

Jane climbed in to bed with Jack and Ruby when she got home, still fully dressed, make up and hair intact. She cried hard in to her pillow. She knew Matthew was too good to be true, she knew it would all end somehow and at some time. She had just hoped beyond hope that it wouldn't.

What a waste of money on an expensive dress. What a waste of her emotions over the last few weeks. To think he had said he loved her at the start of the evening, how it had all changed so drastically in the flip of a moment.

Jane jumped up with a start when she heard banging on her front door. The dogs barked hysterically at the break of the silence. She tried to 'shush' them so she could hear what was happening. Was it an intruder trying to break in? The banging was so loud.

She closed the disturbed dogs in to her room and slowly crept down the stairs, afraid to see who would be at her door.

She pulled back the curtains, slowly, just a crack, so she could see.

It was Matthew, looking furious and banging violently on the door. He hadn't noticed that she was peaking round the corner. He looked upset and frustrated and was pacing up and down her driveway.

Jane went back upstairs and got in under the covers, the banging persisted relentlessly. She could listen to it no longer. She dialled Matthew's number and began ringing.

"Jane! Are you in the house? Please answer the door to me!" He said frantically.

"I'm just phoning you to say leave me alone, I don't want to speak to you." She answered coldly.

"Please, Jane, if you gave me a chance to explain you would understand." Jane couldn't resist his sweet voice, the sound of him crying and in pain was destroying for her.

"Can we not just talk in the morning? I'm very tired."

"No. Please let me in." He sounded harsh and firm and exasperated.

Jane went back downstairs and opened the door to let him in; he stormed in like a whirlwind and grabbed her tightly, she stumbled under the loss of balance.

"What the *hell* are you doing, Matthew? Get off me!" She shoved him off.

His expression was that of utter heartbreak. Jane scolded herself inwardly for being so cold.

"Jane, you have it all wrong with me and Alessandra!" *Damn.* Even her name was beautiful.

"Oh, I *really* don't think I do!" She snapped at him. "See, your precious *Alessandra* filled me in on the two of you whilst we were in the bathroom."

Matthew looked horrified. Jane felt an element of smugness. He had definitely been caught red handed.

"What did she say to you?" He said in a low, measured tone that made Jane's skin crawl.

"She told me that you both used to have sex regularly, like some kind of 'friends with benefits'. How dare you ignore me all night for some cheap bit on the side you used to sleep with, and how dare you then have the audacity to lie to me about it!" She screamed hysterically. "There is nothing else to talk about; you clearly have unresolved feelings for her. You couldn't take your eyes off her for god's sake!"

"I never slept with her."

Jane was out of breath and misty eyed from all the screaming. It took her a moment to comprehend what Matthew had just said to her. He stared at her resolutely, unblinking. She couldn't tell if he was lying or not.

"What?" She asked when she had got her breath back.

"She lied to you. I never slept with her." He was completely calm and stared at her unwaveringly, unperturbed by her screaming. Jane was speechless, she assumed he might try to deny it but the way he was denying it, the way he was so composed and not at all upset, was unnerving.

He continued, "Alessandra has been obsessed with me for years, she tries to follow me most places and she makes very good and sometimes successful attempts at destroying my relationships. She's stalking me, I have a restraining order against her. I notified the police when I saw her at the hotel. When she approached me I knew I had to try to get rid of her, I spoke quickly to her, trying to diffuse the situation. I obviously didn't introduce you to her because I didn't want her finding out who you were.

96

"I encouraged her to leave, told her that she shouldn't be there, that it was a private party. But when you try to push Alessandra away it only draws her closer, I was getting angry so I removed her from the room. I know that must have looked bad, but I had to get her away from you. The girl is unstable.

"So I told her I had to go to the bathroom and I guess she went to the bathroom too, I then went back to the party to find you and you were getting cosy with Thomas, that's when I intervened. You ran to the bathroom and that's obviously when you bumped in to Alessandra. I saw you run out, Alessandra not far behind you with a triumphant look on her face. I knew she had worked her magic." He breathed heavily, tears staining his face, his brow furrowed in obvious stress.

Jesus. Jane had no idea how to respond; she didn't know how to process all the information. Matthew had a stalker, a very beautiful stalker. The damaged Jane had scepticism about his story. Matthew's Jane wanted to run over and hold him so tight and scream with delight that he wasn't, in actual fact, cheating on her.

"How do I know you're telling the truth?" She asked tentatively, not feeling wholly convinced, eyeing him up warily with her arms folded firmly across her chest.

"If you had stayed any length of time you would have heard from all my friends and work colleagues first hand that she has been a major problem in my life for a long time." He looked at her pleadingly.

What had Jane done? She had ruined his work party, the ball of the year, the day he was to officially show her off to all his friends and colleagues. She felt devastated, annoyed at herself for acting so rashly.

"I don't know what to say. Matthew, I'm sorry. I'm so sorry I reacted so impetuously. I shouldn't have ran away like that, but you can't imagine how angry I was when she told me you both had slept together and you had this big history between the two of you. I was engulfed with jealousy and anger. I thought I'd been played."

Tears streamed violently down her face. Had she completely ruined it between her and Matthew? How could she rectify the state of affairs? At the same time, did she want to rectify it when he had a stalker after him?

"Look, it's still very early." He said, walking slowly towards her. "We still have time to go back to the ball and have a few hours of dancing and fun?"

"I don't know; did I not make a massive fool of myself in front of your friends?" She asked, feeling quite embarrassed now at her spectacle of a performance.

"To be honest, I think they only noticed your dress." He winked at her vivaciously. She laughed and he grabbed her towards him and held her tight, so tight that she thought he might never let go.

"I thought I'd lost you, Jane." She could feel his tears fall on to her back.

"I thought I'd lost you too." She cried.

"What do you say? Back to the party then? Try to cheer ourselves up." He smiled at her, studying her for a response.

"Ok." She glanced in her hall mirror, horrified by the reflection, she had mascara streaks all down her face. "But first, I really need to fix my make up."

"I think you look great." He nudged her teasingly.

Jane and Matthew returned to the party a half hour later, they had missed the dinner but it was only nine o'clock so they had plenty of time for drinks and dancing.

Thankfully, all of Matthew's friends had thought they had just nipped home for a bit of fun and had returned again. Jane was relieved to hear this. Second time around, Jane had a wonderful time. She got to meet all of Matthew's work colleagues and Matthew didn't leave her side once.

The next morning, Jane awoke abruptly to the memory of Alessandra, she had been so vicious and callous towards Jane, her desperate craving for Matthew was consuming Jane's thoughts, clouding her mind and judgement. She was stalking Matthew. She couldn't blame her really; Matthew was beautiful and charming and knew his way around a woman, but to be so madly infatuated with someone that you actually tried to tear down their entire life. It was terrifying just thinking about it.

Jane tried to forget about Alessandra, it was the rest of the evening that had gone splendidly. Matthew was charming and polite and was only too happy to show her off to everyone. When they had returned home, they had craved each other terribly. After the dramatic and emotional events and Jane's oh-so skimpy dress, Matthew couldn't keep his hands off her any longer.

Jane turned to face Matthew that morning, but he wasn't there. She sat up swiftly. Had he snuck out while she was sleeping? Had he actually been furious about her behaviour but had concealed it because he wanted to go back to the party? Why not just stay at the party without her? Why chase after her and then bring her back? Unless, he wanted her there so he looked as though he had a nice, little trophy girlfriend on his arm. Jane scolded herself inwardly for her incessantly pessimistic outlook.

Jane decided to get up and head downstairs, she was greeted happily by Jack and Ruby and breathed a sigh of relief when she saw Matthew sitting at the kitchen table drinking a cup of coffee.

"Hey you." He said cheerfully, as she walked in to the kitchen and approached the kitchen table. He was wearing nothing but boxer shorts, Jane eyed up his displayed body eagerly, the memory of their bodies clinging to each other the night before sprung fresh in to her memory. Her hardy exterior softened slightly.

"Hey. You're up early." She watched him pensively.

"Couldn't sleep." He flicked through his phone casually. Jane wondered was he reading messages from Alessandra.

"Things on your mind?" She asked nervously, grabbing a seat beside him.

"Always." He smirked. "But no, I normally can't sleep after a drinking session." He explained, setting down his phone and giving Jane his undivided attention.

"Ah, I thought you might be restless because of the Alessandra situation." She looked up at him quickly, his face had traces of concern and tension, Jane sensed this wasn't the first time that Alessandra had interfered in his relationships.

"That didn't help, I will admit." He sighed.

"Did the police get back to you?"

"Yes, she spent the night in police custody but she was released today." He scowled.

"How come?" Jane's brow furrowed in concern, was Alessandra going to be a problem for them?

"They told me it was because it's the first time she's breached the order, she was cautioned and sent home."

"That's so unfair!" Jane shrieked, slamming a fist on the work top, startling Matthew. Her eyes wide with anger. "She knew fine rightly what she was doing and she got away with it!"

"We both know what she was trying to do; she was trying to get between us, push us apart, but thankfully she hasn't succeeded." Matthew stared passionately at Jane, his eyes ablaze with fury at Alessandra and desire for Jane.

Jane crumbled under his smouldering gaze, "You know, I can completely understand why a woman would want to stalk you, you are completely irresistible." Jane stood up and sat on Matthew's lap, resting her hands against his strong chest, leaning in to him, he rested his hands at the bottom of her back, they sunk in to a luxurious kiss.

"Can you now?" He asked as they pulled away from each other, looking dewy eyed from the intimacy.

"Yes, I already felt crazy jealous about other girls looking at you. I don't blame them, they are only human," she laughed, "but last night was horrendously awful, I never get jealous, that's not me. But I thought I might actually attack her." She confessed, shuffling her feet nervously.

"I love that you're so jealous, Jane, it means you just can't get enough of my dashing good looks and tantalising charm!" He smirked in an appealing, captivating way.

"You're an idiot." She rolled her eyes mockingly.

"I get jealous, too. I went crazy when I saw you and Thomas together." This pleased Jane greatly. Although it hadn't been Matthew's intention to leave her stranded on her own at the start of the party, it felt good to know that he had suffered some feelings of jealousy also.

Jane sat silent for a moment, contemplating. "It's so unfair about Alessandra."

"Alas, such is life. Anyway, let's not talk about that anymore. We need to try to put the whole fiasco behind us and hope she doesn't make a reappearance in to our lives again." He shrugged his shoulders in a defeated sort of way. "I have more pressing matters to discuss with you." He said, quickly turning his frown in to a wicked smile.

"Oh?" Jane stared at him, waiting in anticipation at what he might want to discuss.

"See, I've been thinking about our living arrangements and they're just not working out." His facial expressions were not giving anything away.

Jane was confused, her brow knitted, she studied his face for an explanation. "What do you mean? Do you not like it here?"

"No, it's not that." He said with a mysterious and mischievous tone, raising his eyebrows in delight.

Jane was baffled. "What is it then?"

"It's *you* living here."

"Me?" Jane gawked at him in utter bewilderment. "Why would there be an issue with *me* living here?"

"Because, you should be living with me." He stated simply, a grin appearing wide on his face.

Chapter 9

Jane had to grab hold of the table to steady herself. She was completely and absolutely blindsided by Matthew's suggestion to move in together. She wasn't prepared for it. She straightened up and stared at his beautiful face, absolutely lost for words.

"I've freaked you out? It's too soon for you?" He was retracting quickly, his eyes wide with dejection.

"Matthew, I'm completely speechless. You want us to live together?" She breathed.

"Yes, but if you don't want to then it's totally fine. I'm sorry if I freaked you out. We can forget about it." His smile evaporated, quickly replaced by a frown and a look of sheer embarrassment. He looked down at his hands and shuffled nervously.

"I would love nothing more." She embraced him tightly, overwhelmed by her love for him.

"Ah! That's fantastic! For a minute there I thought you were going to do another runner!" She nudged him in the side then put her arms around him again, squeezing tightly. Never wanting to let go, feeling grateful to have him in her life.

Jane was very surprised at Matthew's suggestion to move in together, apart from the passion and laughter they both shared, Jane had been unsure if there had been any real depth to their relationship. Of course they had both told each other they loved one another, but Jane always reserved a little bit of scepticism when anyone said this to her, especially when they hadn't known each other that long. They were both exceptionally attracted to one another and their friends couldn't deny the chemistry between them, but was physical attraction enough to stand the test of time?

"Jane, he can't stop staring at you!" Cried Martha when the four girls were out for coffee with their respective partners. The girls had huddled together, away from the boys, for a private conversation. Or a gossiping session, as Jane knew to be true.

"Oh, stop." Scoffed Jane.

"Modest as always." Said Millie. "He really does look infatuated by you, Jane."

"He asked me to move in with him yesterday!" Jane divulged, rather excitedly, between sips of her coffee, looking up from her mug with a mischievous glint in her eye.

"He didn't!" Martha leaned in closely in order to hear better, only a mild hint of jealousy present in her tone.

"What did you say to him?!" Exclaimed Millie, setting down her coffee in order for her to listen more attentively.

"I said yes, of course, I was very surprised, though, we've only been dating a few months. I also have my own house to think about." Her brow furrowed.

"Yes, well that is easily sorted. Just rent your house out, it's in a good area, it will be popular." Said Millie, quite frankly.

"That's a good idea, I was thinking I might have to sell up." Intrigued by this new idea, it certainly sounded a lot more straightforward and quicker. As much as Jane was taken by surprise at Matthew's proposal of living together, she couldn't wait to get moved in.

"Yes, it's a great idea and that way if you guys break up you still have somewhere to live!"

"Now, Martha, that is not very nice, there is nothing to indicate, at all, that Jane and Matthew will ever break up. Look at how in love they are!" Millie scolded, eyeing up her friend disapprovingly.

"I used to be in love with my husband and have all that passion and longing for each other, now he comes in from work and barely looks at me, just turns on those stupid computer games and ignores me for the rest of the evening.

"I don't know how to get through to him or how to get our passion back again, and when I tell him all of this he just says that I am nagging him again and would I ever leave him alone!" Martha said fretfully, not looking any of the girls in the eye, but rather, fixing her stare down upon her wedding ring. Her eyes gleaming with tears.

She had not meant to reveal such a large portion of her marital problems to the girls, but seeing Jane and Matthew so happy had made Martha feel rather bitter and resentful towards her husband for not maintaining the spark and magic in their relationship.

"Oh, Martha, I am sorry to hear all of this, do you think suggesting marriage counselling to Lucas would help? He might then see that you are genuinely unhappy and that things have to change if the marriage is to continue?" Jane said softly, squeezing her friend's hand tightly.

"I have threatened divorce before, but he says my threats are empty and I would never go through with it. I feel like our marriage is over and I don't know how to salvage it and I don't know why he doesn't care. I long to have those early years back, to feel like you do now Jane, towards Matthew. I hope it doesn't all change for you the way it is has done for me." Martha clutched at Jane's hand and eyed her up sorrowfully.

Later that day, when they got back to Matthew's house, Jane explained to Matthew, Millie's suggestion. Matthew was happy with the idea of renting Jane's house out but they both agreed that their relationship would not turn sour like Martha's had done. Jane moved in with Matthew in the December, just in time for Christmas together.

"You know, we really should have had our first holiday together before moving in together. That way we would've known if we could stick each other or not." Jane teased one afternoon as they sat huddled together on Matthew's sofa.

"This is true, but you just couldn't get enough of me, Jane, so I had to give you what you wanted." He replied jokingly, giving her a wink and a nudge in the side.

"Don't be silly, you were practically begging me to move in!" Jane gasped in mock shock, nudging him back.

Jane recruited the help of Millie, Martha, Jennifer and Tess to help her move her things over to Matthew's house, the new tenant was moving in the following week. Jane walked around her empty house, tears streamed freely down her face. Her house had symbolised freedom, a new life, a new start from the horror of her past. She brushed the walls with her fingertips, taking in the detail, thanking the place for being the turning point in her life.

Jane drove her last run to Matthew's house with the last of her items, as soon as she arrived she immediately knew she had made the right decision, Ruby hopped over and greeted her enthusiastically, tail wagging frantically. Matthew sat on the sofa with Jack cuddled in tightly.

"We never really discussed the dogs moving in here as well." Jane observed, standing in the doorway, admiring her new life.

"Well, you guys are kind of a package deal." He smirked. "I guess I'll just have to put up with these guys." He nuzzled Jack affectionately, Jack lay his head on his lap.

"Yeah, seems like that's going to be really tough for you." The corner of her mouth curled up in to a smile. He winked back at her.

They spent their first Christmas alone together. They took full advantage of having Christmas Day off together. They enjoyed a small turkey dinner and gave the skins to the dogs.

Later in the day, they took the dogs out for a fresh, crisp walk along the beach, reminiscing on when they had met in the June. In the evening, they visited Matthew's mum and dad and then on to see Gary and Agnes for mulled wine and mince pies. This was the first official meeting of Matthew and her dad, he laughed at the cruelty of having to meet him on Christmas Day.

Jane felt quietly apprehensive about the meeting between the two men, Jane's dad was extremely overprotective, she knew Matthew was in for a grilling of questions about what his intentions were with his daughter. She knew her dad was making up for the lack of protection he offered whilst Jane had been a child, and she couldn't blame him for it. Jane only hoped that her dad could see the good, kind person in Matthew, the way she could.

Jane and Matthew were to meet at Gary and Agnes' house, if possible, Matthew seemed more nervous than when he had been meeting Charlotte and Bob.

"There is no need to be nervous." Jane looked at him curiously with a smirk on her face. Matthew's nerves were quite adorable. "My dad will love you!" Jane felt it best to try to reassure Matthew, for all she knew her dad might have reigned in the acquisition this time.

"I'm not nervous." He answered quickly, "Just want to make a good first impression." He said this with a male bravado tone to his voice.

"You will! I'm thirty, my dad will like you and if he doesn't then there is something seriously wrong with him!" She put a consoling arm around him and stroked his back.

"It just feels like there's a lot riding on this, you know, mum's are easier to impress. He'll have a lot of influence over your choices. It's important that he likes me." Jane felt an evil twist of delight at his suffering, she still hadn't fully forgiven him for the Alessandra fiasco at the night of the ball. Her jealousy and suspicion sat eagerly waiting in the background, she tried to qualm these feelings because she wanted to be able to trust Matthew, but the feelings of doubt were ultimately there.

He was stood in the hallway, looking in the mirror, fidgeting nervously with his tie. Jane grabbed his hands to calm them and proceeded to fix his tie properly.

"You are worrying over nothing." She pulled him in to her. "But, it's really sweet that you are, plus, my mum is overprotective, too, and you won her over." Jane looked up at him with a comforting smile and kissed him warmly on the cheek.

They arrived and were welcomed in by Jane's dad. Gary was a warm and pleasant man, with a welcoming smile, he had a thick head of sandy, brown hair and a tall stature. He shook Matthew's hand tightly and greeted him with a wide smile. Agnes was a petite blonde with a small face and just a slight amount of middle age spread, she was bubbly and fun and always had an ice breaker of a sentence that could break any silence.

Agnes loved a drink, so she wasn't long in cracking open a bottle or two of Prosecco and poured everyone an overfilled glass.

"Matthew, it is so good to meet you!" Agnes chuckled excitedly, raising her glass to him as they stood together in the kitchen.

"Thank you, Agnes. It's nice to meet you both, too." Matthew said graciously, taking a quick sip of his sparkling wine.

"Jane has told us so much about you!" She continued excitedly, her eyes alight with irrepressible delight.

"Has she now?" He glanced at Jane with a devilish twinkle in his eye and a cocked eyebrow.

"All good things mind you." Agnes chortled.

"I'm glad to hear it." He nudged Jane affectionately.

"I believe you're a paramedic, Matthew?" Gary asked.

"Yes, that's right. I believe you're a dentist." Matthew reciprocated.

"I am indeed. Fantastic job; paramedic. Don't get nearly enough credit for all you do." Gary said proudly.

"Thanks, that means a lot."

"So, what are we eating?" Jane asked happily, beyond relieved that her dad had been so kind and welcoming and not at all tyrannical.

"Get your priorities right!" Agnes yelled vivaciously.

"Too right. You think I'm here for the company?" Jane giggled.

"Well, tonight, I am serving up mince pies, cocktail sausages and volau-vents." Teased Agnes, putting on a posh accent.

"Sounds amazing." Said Matthew. "Thank you for going to so much bother."

"It's no bother at all." Said Gary. "Because I'm not making it!" He gave a big belly laugh and everyone joined in. Matthew relaxed instantly, Jane looked at her dad, lost for words.

"Lucky for some getting to sit on their backsides while I slave away in the kitchen." Said Agnes, mocking offence.

"Come off it, Aggie. We know your favourite place is in the kitchen! You wouldn't let dad near it even if he wanted to!" Jane sniggered, rolling her eyes melodramatically.

The four of them sat around the kitchen table, there were several bottles of Prosecco drank and conversation flowed easily.

It was getting late and they were all rather tipsy. Jane ordered them a taxi. They all said their goodbyes; they couldn't get away for Agnes talking excitedly, delighted at the new, budding relationship.

They got in to the taxi and waved goodbye.

"That was fantastic." Matthew blurted out quickly, breathing a sigh of relief as he sunk back in to the seat.

"I told you they would like you! I'm so glad you liked them, too!" Jane said enthusiastically.

"I felt as though I could talk to your dad forever, it was all so easy. They are such nice people." He said reminiscently.

"I'm so relieved my dad was on such good behaviour!" She sighed contentedly.

"Were you expecting it not to go as well tonight?" He asked, looking slightly betrayed.

"It just went better than I expected." She admitted, biting at her lip and looking up at him.

He gave her a smirk. "What were your mum and dad like when they were married?"

"Oh, they fought all the time, they are actually very similar people, so they always clashed with each other. They are both quite dominant and controlling and that just doesn't work in a relationship, I don't think it does anyway." She wondered to herself.

"Who do you think is dominant between us?" He gave her an unbelievably, breath taking smile and Jane was glad she was sitting down or she might have fallen over.

"Your mind is filthy!" She laughed loudly and glanced awkwardly at the taxi driver who appeared not to be hearing a word.

"You bring that side out in me." His eyes twinkled. Jane squeezed his thigh suggestively.

"You look like your dad." He said, staring at her face.

"Jesus, don't tell my mum that! You'll be extradited and never allowed back." Jane replied sardonically.

Jane had told her mum and Bob that she would see them on her own the next day as Matthew was working the Boxing

Day shift. Tess was visiting her husband's family so they and the children could not be there either. Jane went to her mum's, sad that Matthew could not come and enjoy another Christmas dinner. Charlotte had prepared a beautiful turkey dinner with all the trimmings.

"Thank you so much, mum. This looks incredible!" Jane smiled gratefully towards her mother.

"I know now, why I married you." Bob winked, as he lifted a heavily ladened forkful of food to his mouth.

Charlotte smiled warmly at them both, donned in an apron and oven mitts. "No bother for my favourite people." Jane loved the maternal warmth she felt around her mother, they had a close bond. Jane only wished her mother wouldn't worry as much about her.

Jane returned home in the evening and was greeted enthusiastically by Jack, Ruby and Matthew. She kissed Matthew when she arrived in to the living room and joined him on the sofa.

"How was your day?" Matthew asked, stroking Jane's thigh which distracted her thoughts somewhat.

"Great! Dinner was unbelievable, I'm so sorry you missed it." She placed a hand on top of his.

"Me too, would've definitely beat being in work." He shrugged. "Anyway, I was thinking, I have a suggestion." He looked at her with an unreadable expression, what could his suggestion be?

"Go for it." Hating the suspense.

"I was thinking, why don't we go away for a city break next month?" He suggested.

"I never say no to a holiday." She chuckled. "Where would we go?"

"Wherever you fancy, preferably somewhere that won't break the bank balance, I'm not a doctor you know!" He teased, referring back to Charlotte's one lapse in behaviour the first time they had met. Jane hoped that Matthew didn't forever hold this against her mum.

"Oh, you are so bad!" She giggled. "Well, what about Krakow, in Poland? It's supposed to be so beautiful over winter."

"That's it settled then." He smiled.

Chapter 10

T heir first holiday to Krakow went as well as they expected, they decided to go mid January in order to break up the long month. They spent the three nights sight seeing, drinking red wine and enjoying each other. They visited the concentration camp, Auschwitz, and spent the remainder of the day feeling sombre.

"What a dreadful place." Started Jane, as they returned back to their hotel and sat in the lobby, watching the people go about their day. "How could they do that to all those human beings? The torture, the starvation, the humiliation. I can't get my head around it."

"That's what happens when a total nutcase is in a very high place of power." Matthew replied solemnly.

"Let's go out for drinks somewhere." Jane suggested. "I could do with a distraction after that day." Jane felt distressed by the horrors that had taken place in the concentration camps.

"A day like today reminds us of how lucky we are, it is very humbling."

Jane looked up at the beautiful man and appreciated his wise words. She felt particularly grateful, that day, for her very fortunate life. Despite her difficult upbringing, it was nothing in comparison to what those people had endured during the Second World War.

Matthew and Jane spent the remainder of their holiday absorbing the culture and indulging in the food and wine. It was the holiday break they had needed after a busy Christmas period, in and out of work.

They got home after their long weekend, not quite ready for their bubble to burst, when they would have to go back to work on the Monday morning. Jane couldn't believe how much weight she had put on in the four days they had been away.

"What did we eat?" She laughed, as they sat on the sofa, she stroked her pot belly.

"You're just comfortable with me now and letting yourself go." He teased jokingly.

"I need to stop eating so much bread and cheese." She said, poking him in the side for his cheeky remark.

"But that's no fun." He retorted.

Jane had gone back to work on the Monday and had struggled to get her trousers zipped up before she left. She had really let herself go. She would go to the gym that night, burn off some of the holiday weight. Being a woman, Jane always tried to compensate for some pre-menstrual bloating. Her period would be coming any day. She got out the calendar on her phone to calculate her dates; her period normally came like clock work; every twenty eight days.

Jane checked and double checked her dates; sure that she had made a mistake. Her calendar was telling her that her period was late by one week.

"Pregnant. Oh, my good god, I *must* be pregnant." Jane had to sit down on the bed, taking sharp, shallow breaths. She thought she might faint, she knew she was about to experience a panic attack. She tried to use some of her medical knowledge, she began taking deep, steadying breaths. Her entire body shook from head to toe. "How the hell can I be pregnant?!" She shouted out loud to herself. She caught herself on, she didn't want Matthew to know of her concerns just yet.

Jane gathered her things together for work, shakily, and left the house quickly. Kissing Matthew goodbye, she didn't mention the missed period, but thought it better to take a pregnancy test first before panicking him, needlessly. She spent the day feeling completely distracted, time seemed to be going by more slowly than normal.

Millie, who was working the long day, noticed her facade and asked her if was she feeling alright. Jane said she was fine and carried on, keeping herself busy so as to make time move faster. She finished work that afternoon and hurried over to the local supermarket, not far from the hospital, for a pregnancy test. Hoping, beyond hope, that she wouldn't bump in to anyone that she knew.

Her heart was pounding when she got home, thankfully she had't ran in to anyone in the shop. This was going to ruin everything. They weren't ready for a baby. Did she even want children? She didn't know if she did, but she knew after seven months of dating, that she and Matthew were not ready for one. It was too big. It was too much. How could this have happened?

Jane wracked her brains desperately, wondering how this could have happened. She always took her pill religiously at the same time everyday. Unless, maybe she did take it late one of the days and had just forgotten?

Jane was waiting the three minutes for the test result to appear, why were those three minutes always the longest?

What would her parents say? What would Matthew's parents say? Could she and Matthew afford this? Were they a strong enough couple to face the challenges of parenthood? What if the baby came between her and Matthew and affected their ultimate happiness?

So many thoughts dashed viciously around her head, she felt as though her mind was swirling, she thought she might be sick.

The moment of truth, Jane was too scared to look. She had her eyes covered with her hand. She reached a hand out blindly to grab on to the urine stick. She thought her heart might actually burst through her chest, her legs had gone weak and her hands were shaking uncontrollably. She uncovered her eyes and looked down... The two deep blue lines confirmed it, she was *pregnant*.

"Oh, dear lord." She said out loud to herself. "Jane, you are an idiot."

Her mind felt like a whirlpool, tears were streaming down her face, so many thoughts and emotions were racing around her head. She was pregnant. She had the perfect relationship and now it was ruined forever because she must have missed a pill or taken a pill late.

How was she going to break it to Matthew? How would he take the news? Would he break it off with her for being so irresponsible and leave her as a single mother? Or, would he be happy or even excited at the prospect of being a father? Jane doubted the latter, it was too fast. They didn't know each other well enough, she didn't even know if this was something that he wanted out of life.

Matthew was downstairs. Jane had nipped in after work and said a quick "Hello" to Matthew and said she needed to run to the loo. Would she break it to him soon? Or wait until after dinner?

"Hey, honey." Jane nearly leapt off the toilet seat, completely startled by Matthew's voice through the door. He must have come upstairs to the bedroom to check on her. He was standing outside the en-suite door.

"Are you feeling ok, Jane?"

"I'm fine." She shouted through. "I'll be out in a minute."

Jane stashed the pregnancy test in to her back pocket and washed her hands. She opened the door, Matthew was sitting on their king size bed. Jane thought she might vomit at the thought of having to reveal to Matthew the result of her pregnancy test.

"Hey sweetie. Are you ok? You look a bit peaky." Matthew had stood up and cupped Jane's face in his hands, studying her features.

"I'm fine, honestly. How was your day?" She asked nervously.

"It was great, got some house work done and took the dogs to-"

"I'm pregnant."

There was a moments pause. "Sorry?" He had gone white and stared at her dumbly.

"I'm pregnant." She said again, she stood staring at him, her eyes danced over his face, trying to read his expression to the extremely unexpected news.

"Hhh, em. How?" He stuttered, "I mean, I thought you were taking the pill?" He asked accusatorially. Jane noticed most of the colour drain from his lips, his pupils were pin point and he fidgeted nervously. He was not happy.

118

"I was. I am. I don't know how this happened. I don't think I missed a day. I could have taken a pill late and that caused it, but I can't be sure, and I don't remember taking a pill late, it's not like me." She explained hurriedly, desperately willing him to be happy about it. Her bottom lip trembled as the angst of it all became too much.

Matthew stood silent for a moment, apparently taking it all in. It was a lot to digest so quickly.

"Holy crap. Pregnant." He shoved his hands through his hair, looking exasperated and obviously trying to choose his next words quite carefully.

"You're angry." Said Jane, after some time had passed and Matthew had not said a word. Tears trespassing on to her face.

"No, no, of course not. Just a little shocked. I wasn't expecting it, that's all." He coughed and straightened himself up. He looked at Jane and noticed her tears.

"Oh, honey, don't cry. It will all be ok." He brought her in to a tight hug.

"Really?" Asked Jane, feeling unconvinced, pressing her head against his chest.

"Of course it will." He chuckled, letting out a breath. "We will have a beautiful little baby to love as well as each other." He pulled her in closer and stroked her head soothingly.

"You're happy about it?" She asked in to his shoulder, tears flowing freely.

He stared at her from outstretched arms, hands resting on her shoulders. "I'm very shocked." He admitted. "It's not what I was expecting to hear from you today, but I think it will be really great. We will love this baby more than anything else in the world and we will be a great team, learning as we go along."

119

Jane smiled and cried even harder. Tears sprung from Matthew's eyes.

"I'm so relieved," she cried, "I thought you might want to run away."

"You really think I would do that?" He looked at her sternly.

"No, I don't. But, I wouldn't have blamed you if you did. It's all such a shock." She sighed, hiccoughing.

"How do you feel?" He asked, his eyes raking over her face, deep creases marked his brow.

"Do you mean mentally or physically?" She breathed a sigh.

"Both, I guess." He managed a smile.

"Physically, I don't feel any different; I just thought I was putting on weight. My breasts are maybe a bit sore but nothing dramatic. Mentally, I don't know. I'm feeling very overwhelmed. How will we manage? Will we be good parents? It isn't exactly great timing for us, we were only getting started." Her words tumbled out fast, tears streamed down her face again.

"Wow, Jane, it's all going to be ok. We're going to do this together. We will be fine." He put his arm around her and drew her in tightly again.

But, Matthew felt the same. He couldn't lie to himself that he wasn't terrified of the thought of becoming a father, he wasn't ready. Of course they would love the baby unconditionally, but he couldn't deny that it was poor timing when their relationship had only just begun. However, it was done and the life they had started to form together had taken a different path.

Matthew had taken the news with the grace and composure that Jane would have expected of him. They were a team and would face the new challenge head on.

Jane was eleven weeks pregnant and she had known for eight weeks that she was going to have baby. She had not only come to terms with the idea but felt overwhelming delight at the thought of introducing their precious creation in to the world.

No one can describe how it will feel to carry an unborn baby and feel the unconditional love formed for them without ever having met them. To know that you created that person and that they were growing inside of you was astonishing and magnificent to Jane.

She would only eat the best food and would not drink coffee or any caffeinated product. Jane's tea habit was reduced to the herbal kind, she wasn't bothered much by this as she indulged in delicious blends such as; Butterfly Pea Flower Tea or Burdock Root Tea or Chamomile Blossoms Organic Tea. She had tried to drink her favourite Elderflower Tea infusion but her pregnancy taste buds made her run to the bathroom to hurl any time she had tried this. She would go for regular walks with the dogs and drank plenty of water. Her colleagues and manager in work were very supportive and allowed her to run off the ward whenever she felt the need to throw up.

Matthew had been incredibly supportive, the initial shock and fear had worn off and he began to feel excited about the prospect of becoming a father. The bond between Matthew and Jane grew stronger, they even started to buy little outfits for him or her and had their pram picked out.

"I wonder how the dogs will react." Jane thought out loud, as she lay on the sofa one evening with Ruby cuddled in and cup of tea in hand. Jane stroked her belly protectively.

Matthew was sat on the other sofa with Jack, flicking through the television channels. "I think they will love them, I think Ruby will be the protector, she's such a mummy." He stroked Jack lovingly on the head.

"I worry that they will become jealous or feel neglected." Jane looked at them both anxiously, biting her lip.

"They won't feel neglected," Matthew stated plainly. "We will still walk them every day and cuddle them as much as we can and they will still have run of the house."

"But we won't have as much time for them, what if they are sad?" She asked worriedly, drawing Ruby even closer in to her.

"That's true, we won't have as much time to give them endless amounts of cuddles, but we will still take them out for long walks everyday, like we always do, we will just have the pram with us and we will be able to cuddle them as much as they want in the evening when the baby is asleep. They will be fine, Jane. We'll make sure we don't forget about them." He answered ambiguously, giving her a 'don't worry' expression. It maddened Jane.

"No, of course we won't forget about them! But, what if they become resentful toward the baby? We can't ever leave the baby unattended with them!" Jane crossed her arms, feeling irate and anxious. How could he be so calm?

"Of course we won't leave the baby unattended!" He laughed. "You need to worry less, it will all fall in to place."

"Yes, you say that, but it doesn't hurt to be prepared for every eventuality so we know how to deal with it when it arises." She snapped grumpily at being told to not worry about a massive, life changing situation. She scowled at him in an 'are you serious?' expression.

Matthew always had a laid back approach to most things, discussing how to manage two dogs and a baby seemed a perfectly reasonable suggestion to Jane, but, of course, she was always met with, 'Everything will be fine!' Or, 'Just don't worry about things as much!' But, she had to worry, they had to be organised if they were going to be good parents.

"We'll deal with it when it arises." He suggested, shrugging his shoulders and turning his attention back to the television.

"Would you not prefer to just be organised rather than just hope that everything works out for the best with minimal effort?" Jane was getting annoyed; this was why she had never wanted children. Men seemed to automatically take the back burner while the women did all the organising, and the caring, and the cleaning, and the cooking. Then women are labelled as 'nags' because they had the audacity to ask their lazy partners to actually help them out every once in a while.

"Jane, you are getting yourself worked up over something that has not even happened yet." He said impatiently.

"I just want to know that I have a supportive partner through all of this!" She said vehemently, crossing her arms more tightly and knitting her brow.

"Honey, this baby will be the most important thing in the world to me, you have nothing to worry about. Have you ever doubted me in the past? I promise I will feed them and change nappies and do laundry and get up in the middle of the night when they are crying. You have nothing to worry about." He moved over to sit beside her and kissed her softly on the forehead.

"I'm sorry, I just have so much going on in my head, I want us to be great at this." She explained, leaning her head in to him, feeling slightly embarrassed.

"We won't be perfect, Jane, but I think we will be brilliant parents together, we are a team." She smiled at him lovingly.

Chapter 11

J ane was getting ready for work the next morning, she went to the toilet when she noticed blood on her tissue paper. Jane gasped audibly, immediately panic coursed through every morsel of her body. Why was there *blood*?

Jane felt tears tumble heavily out of her eyes before she even knew she was crying, she fell to the ground and sobbed heavily. Shaking violently, knowing what this meant.

Jane, being a midwife, knew that bleeding so far in to a pregnancy was not a good sign, it was too late to have an implantation bleed. The other alternative was too difficult for her to bear the thought of. She gathered herself up from the bathroom floor and tried to stem the flow of tears and steady her shaking hands.

Matthew was already away to work early that morning so she was in the house on her own, should she phone her mum and tell her? Or maybe that would worry her too much. No, she would go in to work and see if anything more came of it over the course of the day, work would be a good distraction.

However, Jane went in to work, unable to control her pain and anguish and went straight to the ward sister's office. Pauline was a plump, kind woman, she ran the maternity unit well and was popular amongst her staff for being firm but fair.

Jane knew she wouldn't be able to concentrate all day in work, wondering what could possibly have caused the bleeding. In her line of work it was paramount that she was alert and focused. Jane explained her dilemma to Pauline, breaking down again, trying to inhale through drowning sobs.

"I'm bleeding." She sat down in the chair in front of Pauline's desk without invitation, her head in her hands as she leaned against the desk to steady herself.

Pauline, ran round the desk and over to Jane, looking concerned but trying to be consoling as she patted her soothingly on the back.

"You're sure it couldn't be an implantation bleed?" She smiled encouragingly, nodding her head enthusiastically as though Jane was a puppy receiving praise.

"I'm eleven weeks pregnant; it would be far too late for an implantation bleed, that happens two weeks in to a pregnancy." Jane was shaking violently.

Pauline obviously knew that bleeding so far in to a pregnancy was a bad sign, being the manager of a maternity unit, but she wanted to try to reassure Jane.

"Maybe it is just a one off, light bleed and everything will be ok?" But Jane could hear the doubt in her voice.

"Pauline, you know this is not a good sign. We know what this means!" Jane yelled fervently, her eyes wide, a deranged and desperate quality leaked from her every pore, scaring Pauline.

"I'll go and speak to one of the doctors and see what they can do. You stay here and rest, don't go out on to the ward in this state." Pauline patted her on the back again, worry furrowed her brow.

126

"But the ward will be short staffed, I'll be ok." Jane croaked unconvincingly.

"Don't be ridiculous!" Cried Pauline, "the others will manage, it's not too busy today anyway." She lied, glancing nervously at Jane.

Jane knew that Pauline would be away to find out if she could order an emergency ultra sound scan to check the viability of the pregnancy. At least Jane would be able to get some answers that day.

One of the benefits of working in a maternity unit was easy access to obstetricians and gynaecologists. Pauline returned half an hour later and informed Jane that she was booked in that afternoon for an ultrasound scan of the baby. Jane phoned Matthew, she felt sick with worry, how would she tell him? She was still in Pauline's office, Pauline had reassured her that she could stay there until she was going for her scan or until her boyfriend arrived.

"Hi, Matthew?" Her voice trembled as she spoke.

"Hi, sweetie. Is all ok?" His tone was laced with uneasiness to be hearing from her at work. Jane crumbled at the sound of his voice.

"Not really." Her voice broke, she didn't know if she could carry on telling him the rest.

"Jane, you're worrying me. What's going on?" He asked firmly.

"I'm bleeding!" She wailed, sobbing uncontrollably.
Silence.

"What does that mean?" He asked seriously, his voice low, cracking slightly.

"It. Em, Means. There's. Something. Em, Wrong. With. The. Baby!" She whispered through sobs. She then howled uncontrollably, taking deep, shuddering breaths.

"Do you know that for certain, Jane?" He asked earnestly, maintaining calm.

She sniffled, "Not yet. I'm going for a scan at three o'clock."

"I know it's really hard, honey, but let's not panic until then, it might not be anything. Are you still bleeding?" He shushed her soothingly. Matthew always had the magical ability to calm the most upsetting or stressful situation.

"No, I'm not, actually." She admitted, her mood lifting slightly.

"There you go, it may just be nothing, a bit of residual of what was in there. I'm not an expert on this, but let's not jump straight to the worst case scenario."

"You are so wise and level headed. How do you do it?" She asked in wonderment, it was one of the reasons why she loved him; he was her inbuilt counsellor. Always available for invaluable, accurate advice when she needed it most.

"You're right, of course you're right. Thank you." She sniffed again, although her sobs had ceased.

"Do you feel a bit better now?" Genuine concern heavily embedded in his voice.

"Yes, I do. Are you able to get out of work for the scan do you think?" She asked tentatively. What would she do if he couldn't and she had to face it alone?

"No question. I'll say to my supervisor and aim to get out of here as quickly as possible, they'll understand." He promised.

"Thank you. I really need you here with me right now."

"I know, I'll be there in no time to take care of you."

Matthew arrived a half an hour later, he was still donned in his paramedic uniform when he bounced in to the sister's office and pulled Jane in to a tight embrace.

"Are you ok?" He cupped her face in his hands and studied her with a concerned and serious expression.

"I'm much better now." She smiled weakly and snuggled in to his chest. She needed him there, he was her strength, she couldn't handle this on her own. She held him tightly against her, hoping against hope that the dreaded scan would be bring good news and she could put the horrific ordeal behind her.

She was trembling at the thought of the scan, but Matthew was right, there was no further bleeding so maybe it was just a false alarm?

Pauline directed them in to the relatives' room off the maternity unit to allow them more privacy.

The moment Pauline closed the door Jane fell to the floor in convulsions of tears, anxiety gripping her entire body. She couldn't breathe, she couldn't pretend to be strong anymore; she couldn't come to terms with what was likely facing her in the scanning room. She wanted to runaway to yesterday when she had a growing, healthy baby inside of her and the unbelievable prospect of becoming a mother. It was all slipping through her fingers.

"Sweetie, you need to calm down. Everything is probably fine." He tried to soothe her, kneeling down beside her and rubbing her back. "You haven't had any more bleeding, let's focus on that."

"I know, I'm just terrified, I've just seen this all too often, I just know it's not good. I have a gut feeling." She hiccoughed through tears.

He looked at her, lost for words. He couldn't deny the wisdom of a midwife in her own field of work.

"This will just be a routine check up, we will be laughing about this later." He said encouragingly, but feeling more and more unconvinced by the minute. Deep lines formed across his forehead.

"What if our baby is dead?!" She screamed wildly. "What will we do?!" She banged her fist on the ground in an uncontrolled rage. Matthew looked on in complete bewilderment, unsure of what to say or do. He pulled her in tight and stroked her head softly, unsure of how to console her or what to think. "Everything will be ok." He said.

They arrived at the ultrasound department a half hour early, unable to wait any longer in the relatives' room. Thankfully, they were called in early. Jane felt as though she was walking the Green Mile, only too aware of what the outcome was going to be when she was walking back through those doors again.

The obstetrician was a kind woman and had a warm smile and a tender expression, who appeared understanding of the situation.

"Jane, I'm Dr Magill. I believe you've had some bleeding today?" She asked softly, aware of the delicacy of the situation.

"That's right." Replied Jane, hands and voice trembling.

"And how many weeks are you?"

"Eleven weeks and six days, I thought I was nearly out of the danger zone." She wept, producing a tissue from her pocket.

Dr Magill looked at her, Jane could sense the doubt in her countenance.

"Was it a heavy bleed today?" She asked, a lot more clinically and professionally than previous, taking notes in a file as she spoke.

"No, it was just very light spotting, but I haven't had any of that throughout my pregnancy." She tried to urge the significance.

"And any further bleeding since that episode?"

"No." Jane thought she might be denied a scan because there wasn't enough evidence to warrant an apparent problem. Jane couldn't bear not knowing what was happening. She needed the scan.

"I think it would be wise to proceed with the scan, in light of the new bleeding today, so far in to your pregnancy. It will be a vaginal ultrasound scan. Is that ok with you?" She asked delicately.

"Yes, of course." Jane replied faintly, shock hitting her. The doctor wanted a scan, there was something wrong. Jane felt her bottom lip tremble.

Dr Magill set up the scanning trolley and ordered Jane to remove her trousers behind the curtain and put on a theatre gown. Jane then lay on top of the procedure bed and put her feet up on to the leg rests. Jane tried to relax herself as much as possible. Matthew was sat in a chair beside her, holding on to her cold, clammy hand tightly. Dr Magill began the procedure, the instrument was cold and intrusive and Jane wanted it all to stop. She squeezed Matthew's hands tightly, begging for it to be over.

After a few minutes, silence persisted.

Why was Dr Magill not saying anything? Jane and Matthew both tried to look at the ultrasound screen but it was tilted, inconveniently, out of their sight. Why was she not being told what was happening? Dr Magill looked at her solemnly and Jane knew.

"Jane, I'm so sorry, this is not a viable pregnancy, I'm sorry." Not a viable pregnancy. Jane couldn't take in the words, she sat silently, staring, in a daze.

"What exactly does that even mean?" Matthew asked, demanding an answer, was he just supposed to know what a non viable pregnancy was? Was she or was she not pregnant?

"Technically she is still pregnant, but we are only measuring the foetus in at five weeks. I would surmise then that this pregnancy will not be able to develop any further and that you will miscarry the baby in a number of days or weeks. I am so sorry." She repeated. Dr Magill looked devastated and heart felt, she squeezed Jane's hand, Jane retracted, wanting away from her. Panic rising again as the words set in.

"So, what you mean to say is, my baby died at five weeks and has been inside Jane ever since?" Matthew roared, venting uncontrolled anger.

"Technically, yes. I'm surprised there haven't been any signs of miscarriage before this. I'm just so sorry that you had to get so far along before finding out." Dr Magill replied solemnly.

Jane had not said a word, she knew what a non viable pregnancy was, she had delivered the same exact phrase to countless hysterical women, never thinking she would be on the receiving end of that line one day. She chose to stare off in to space, a practised method of protecting one's self from repeated trauma. She drifted in to the clouds, avoiding the catastrophe that was occurring precisely in front of her. Matthew then quickly thanked Dr Magill and helped Jane out of the bed and in to her clothes again.

132

Jane left the hospital in a haze of shock and bewilderment, surely she was dreaming? Surely this couldn't be *real*? Jane couldn't get to grips with her emotions. She felt so much anger and resentment and guilt towards herself, there had been a time when she had never wanted a baby, she had been so sure that she never wanted to have children. Until, that is, she fell pregnant and it had all changed, now she would have done absolutely anything to make it a reality again. She had ended up falling in love with this unknown human being inside of her, and now she was having them snatched out of her grasp in the blink of an eye. How cruel life can be.

Chapter 12

J ane and Matthew spent the car journey in silence. He kept his hand on Jane's hand the entire time, even when he had to awkwardly change gears.

They arrived back in to the house and were greeted warmly by the dogs, Jane lay on the ground and clutched at the dogs tightly, desperately craving their love.

"Jane, are you ok?" Matthew looked at her sombrely, his eyes red and puffy. She remained on the floor with the dogs.

"I'm fine." Was her only quiet response as Ruby licked her nose.

"Can I get you anything?" He asked cautiously, gazing down at her pitiful appearance, feeling wretchedly powerless that he couldn't help her.

"I just want to be on my own." She replied coldly, not looking at him.

"Let me look after you, Jane." He pleaded, he knelt down on the floor with her.

"No, I just need my own space." She snapped, standing up quickly and storming off with Ruby and Jack, slamming the bedroom door behind her.

Matthew was angry at her retort, he was distraught and upset about the miscarriage too, it wasn't just Jane who was suffering. He needed comfort as well, but Jane had shut him out.

The next morning came and Jane had only left her room to go to the toilet and let the dogs out, she hadn't eaten anything. She hadn't even had a cup pf tea. She was on one of her excursions out of the bedroom to get a drink of water when she crossed paths with Matthew;

"How are you today, honey?" He asked hesitantly, studying her warily. He leaned against the worktop, folding his arms.

"I'm fine." Was Jane's only reply, again. Her eyes were red and blood shot and her normally tamed golden hair was in every direction.

"Can I get you anything? You haven't eaten since yesterday."

"No, I'm fine, thank you."

"Are you sure you're holding up ok?" He prodded again, trying to connect with her.

"Fine." Jane didn't make eye contact with him, he could see the tears in her eyes.

"I would like it if you left your room and kept me company? I'm upset too." He admitted sadly, he stepped forward, approaching her warily, but Jane backed away quickly.

"I'm not very good company." She said quietly, tears streaming again.

"I don't mind." He pleaded, wounded by her rejection.

"I just need to be on my own." And she retreated to her bedroom.

Matthew stood frozen on the spot, dejected and devastated. How could she react so selfishly? They needed each other more than ever and she was shutting him out. Leaving him to deal with the grief on his own, offering him no support. He wanted to be there for her and he wanted her to be there for him.

Meanwhile, Jane lay in her bed with her dogs spooning up beside her. The dogs would never be able to comprehend the comfort they brought to her. Jane was numb, this was her reaction to pain, her self defence, survival mode, to block out everyone and pretend it wasn't happening. It was the much better alternative than having to actually face her emotions.

She couldn't come to terms with the loss, couldn't fathom it in her mind. She had suffered so much already in her young life and this was just another tragic blow, would she ever be happy? Or would catastrophic events just keep propping up against her will, destroying her chances of happiness.

A week had passed and Matthew and Jane had exchanged barely a few words with each other. Jane was struggling physically as well as mentally. Not only was the emotional strain of losing a baby catastrophically, earth shatteringly painful, there was the physical aspect of it also.

Jane had started to bleed heavily, the cramps were unbearable. She was lightheaded from the amount of blood and clots she was losing, she thought it couldn't be normal, so she went to her treatment room nurse who checked her bloods and gave her strong pain relief for the cramping.

The painful bleeding and excruciating cramps were horrific, Jane knew they were the contractions of her uterus expelling the once sought after baby. It was a constant, agonising reminder of the baby she had almost had, the baby she loved so dearly without even knowing who they were; being flushed from her body.

Her ward sister, Pauline, had been very understanding of Jane's circumstance and had given her an unlimited amount of time off work to recuperate. Jane had told her friends to leave her alone until she was ready to talk to them. Her family and friends were very concerned and kept in regular contact with Matthew to find out how she was.

Jane spent the next three weeks in bed. Matthew had tried to engage with her every day, but was met with clipped responses or no response at all. Matthew was devastated also, but being a man and having not physically carried the baby, he could not comprehend or appreciate the physical and emotional connection in which Jane had felt.

Jane's mum, dad and sister, Tess, contacted her daily. They had been round to the house delivering cooked meals and junk food for them both, Jane would acknowledge them and then go back to her room.

One afternoon, Jane was holed up in her bedroom, absentmindedly stroking Ruby's soft head. She heard the doorbell and thought it might be her family or friends again, Jane crept out of bed and opened her door slowly and quietly and put her ear to the door, listening through the crack.

Jane heard Matthew open the front door, a woman's voice travelled through immediately; shrill and commanding; "Hi there, I'm Jane's Aunt Margaret, can I see her?" Jane's knees went from beneath her, crashing hard to the ground. She gasped for air, clutching at the door handle as she lay sprawled on the ground, images of her childhood flashing back in large, crashing waves, sending Jane in to a frenzy of anxiety. Why was her aunt there? Had she found out about the miscarriage and come to torture her?

"Jane's not available right now, sorry." Matthew said in a cold, pointed tone. Matthew was probably as shocked as Jane, he knew all about Jane's abusive aunt and uncle.

"I heard the news about the miscarriage and only came to wish my niece well." She drawled in her condescending tone, sending shivers down Jane's spine.

"Thanks, but she's just not here at the moment."

"You know, I don't get what the big deal is. One in eight pregnancies end in miscarriage. It's a very common thing." She heard her aunt say, she could hear the superiority resonating in her voice. Jane could have twisted her aunt's neck. Once again, Margaret was the fountain of knowledge in a field where she had received absolutely no education.

"Oh, so you've experienced a miscarriage first hand then, Margaret?" The sarcasm in his voice reverberated through the house. Jane inwardly congratulated Matthew for his brilliant retort.

"Em, well, no. I haven't." She stuttered, shocked at Matthew's come back.

"Then you can have absolutely no say on the topic. Thanks for calling round. Bye, now."

Jane heard the door slam. Matthew had balls. To stand up to Margaret was very brave. Jane would have loved to have seen the expression on her aunt's face. Jane rolled over and cried in to her pillow, she had not heard from her aunt in years, Jane knew that Margaret had chosen that particular time in her life to make a reappearance purely to torture her. This sickened Jane, she was a good person and didn't deserve someone as malicious and evil as that hanging over her, waiting to reappear at any given moment. Jane ran to the the en suite and vomited at the thought of her aunt being so nearby, all those agonising memories, newly restored in her mind, taunting her at her most vulnerable and distressed moment.

Jane's three closest friends; Millie, Jennifer and Martha had visited the house, but Jane had refused to see them. She couldn't face it. The pity party as she saw it. Tilted heads in sympathy and wails of screams and emotions over the latest new drama. They resorted to texting her every day to check in on her and offer words of comfort. No one could seem to get through to Jane.

After the three weeks, Matthew had become more than impatient with Jane. They had got up that Monday morning, Matthew was getting ready for work, Jane was slouching around the house with her duvet draped around her.

"Jane, we need to talk." Matthew started as they stood in the living room, coffee mug in his hand. Jane merely stared at him, waiting for his next sentence.

"You need to get out of the house, have a shower, think about going back to work. This behaviour isn't healthy *or* normal." He said all at once, with a harshness to his voice, a determined and mean look in his eye.

"I'm not ready to do that." She replied grimly, sinking in to the sofa, arms folded.

"You need to figure out how to get over this so that we can move on with our lives." He said firmly, standing in the doorway, taking a sip from his mug.

"I'm sorry that my grief is causing you such inconvenience, I'm not some kind of robot that can just forget about my feelings and move on." She snapped, deeply offended by his lack of tact. Closing her eyes tightly, willing it all to stop.

"You are not an inconvenience. You heard the doctor, this was not a viable pregnancy, it probably never would have developed any further. It was nothing more than a gathering of cells." He regretted his last words when he saw the horrified expression etched upon her face.

"What the hell did you just say to me?" Jane's voice was low and dangerous; she narrowed her eyes threateningly at him. He stared on in bewilderment.

"How can you be so bloody heartless?!" She screamed vehemently, "and just forget about our baby like this? How can you talk about our baby as if they were nothing?!" Jane's voice had steadily rose, she had stood up and dropped the duvet and turned to face him. Rage in her eyes, her cheeks puffed, breathless with fury.

"I am not being heartless, I am being realistic, Jane. You have been in bed for three weeks, we can't sustain this any longer. We need to try to move on." Matthew stared at the ground solemnly, unable to meet her piercing gaze.

"I can't just flick a switch and move on, Matthew, how can you be so cold? I thought you were upset about this, too?" She stared determinedly at him, pointing her finger at him aggressively.

"I am upset, I didn't want this to happen to our child, but you have to admit, the timing of this pregnancy was not exactly ideal for us." He looked at her, realising his mistake, fear in his eyes as rage swelled within Jane.

Jane yelled at the top of her lungs, her face bright red with rage; "SO YOU WISHED OUR BABY DEAD?! YOU WANTED THIS TO HAPPEN TO OUR CHILD BECAUSE IT WASN'T *CONVENIENT* FOR YOUR SCHEDULE?! HOW *DARE* YOU!"

140

The dogs scrambled frantically towards Jane, Ruby barked wildly. They peered up at her curiously and anxiously, Ruby scratched madly at Jane's knees, Jack spun in circles.

"Jane, calm down, I'm not saying it wasn't convenient but you said yourself-"

"Don't you dare say that I wanted this, too, I was terrified about becoming a mother, but I was still happy about having this baby. I thought you felt the same, I thought you were as broken as I was, but turns out this is just one big relief for you!" Jane jumped from the spot she was standing and began to walk away, the two dogs hot on her tail.

"I am not relieved, Jane, I never said those words. I would much rather go back to a few weeks ago, before all this happened, but we can't. We can't change this, all we can do is try to get over it and be happy. And, most importantly, we need to be there for each other." Jane noticed his chin wobble, she looked in to his eyes and large tears were breaking the surface, threatening to fall.

Chapter 13

Things were never the same between Jane and Matthew after that fateful argument, Jane felt alone in her grief and misery. She didn't know of anyone who could relate to her suffering, she remained quiet and reclusive. Matthew struggled with the new, withdrawn Jane. He tried to reach out to her, but Jane cut him off and blocked him out. The pain of his words during that argument were too much for Jane to overcome, to think that he had been relieved!

Matthew couldn't continue any longer in the hostile atmosphere, he approached Jane the following week before he was going to work, to try to talk to her. Jane was sat on the sofa in the living room, Matthew stepped in, slowly, unsure of how to best approach the subject;

"Hey, honey, do you want to go out for dinner tonight? To the Goat's Inn like old times?" He stared cautiously, feigning a casual, warm tone, hoping she wouldn't go off the handle again.

"No, not tonight, I just want to stay in." She replied impassively, sitting in yesterday's pyjamas and a blanket draped around her, with Ruby and Jack up beside her. She hadn't bothered to look up at Matthew when he spoke, this blatant disrespect angered him further.

"You stay in every night." He stated the obvious, attempting to push down his ever growing ferocity towards Jane.

"I just don't feel like going out, what if we bump in to someone, I don't want to make small talk and pretend everything is ok." She continued to stare at the television, hoping that Matthew would walk away and give her head some peace.

Jane had subconsciously slipped in to a depressive type state. She remembered doing the same as a child when her uncle was giving her regular beatings. Jane believed that zoning out, drifting off in to an imaginary world, was what saved her, if she wasn't focused on what was actually happening then it couldn't hurt her. Jane, subsequently, was criticised by her mother for being an air head and always staring off in to space, as though she were some kind of idiot.

"Everything will go back to normal the more we start to act like it," Matthew urged. "You can't continue to hide away and not face reality."

"All I am asking from you is for is a little bit of time, Matthew. I can't just go back to normal as soon as you click your fingers and say it's so. Just give me space to breathe, I feel claustrophobic when you pressure me like this." She pulled anxiously at the clothes around her neck, feeling warm and closed in.

"I have tried giving you space for weeks," he shouted angrily, "I feel as though I've lived on my own over the last few weeks, but all the while cleaning up after some hidden tenant."

"Well, at least I know I have your support when I need it." She spat sarcastically, rolling her eyes at him.

143

"Look, Jane, we can't keep things up like this, home life is miserable now. Is this to be our future?" He asked sadly. "I never see you and when I do, all we do is fight." He stood staring at her, longing for her to snap out of it and be his girl again.

"Matthew, I know you might be over the death of our baby that occurred a mere *four* weeks ago but I am not. I'm sorry that my grieving process is affecting your quality of life, but what do you want me to do? Jump up and down in elation? Pretend to be happy just to benefit you? I can't do that."

"Well, then, I can't do this anymore, Jane. It's too hard. We can't carry on like this, there is such a hostile environment in this house now and I don't know how to help you when you just keep pushing me away any time I try to get close. We are caught in a terrible rut of grief and resentment and I feel we can't move on together because we will both be a reminder to each other of the loss of our baby." Matthew stared resolutely on the ground. Jane stared at him in disbelief, unable to comprehend what she was hearing.

"Are you seriously breaking up with me right now? After I have literally just miscarried our baby, are you seriously doing this right now?! After all we have been through, this is when you choose to ditch me?" Her voice steadily rose to a scream, sending the dogs in to another frenzy. She was shocked and beyond hysterical. The dogs were frantic and distressed at the new outburst. Jack stared inquisitively at Jane. Jane stroked him and apologised.

Matthew merely continued to stare at the ground, Jane continued; "You are a heartless asshole, I don't know how I could have ever loved you! I don't even know who you are right now, this isn't the man I fell in love with!"

144

Jane was crying and sobbing, unable to fathom how all this heartache could be happening at once. The loss of her baby and now the loss of the only man she ever truly loved, it was too much to endure.

"Jane, I don't want to end this, but, I don't know what else to do. I can't see how dragging things out will make things better for us. We shouldn't waste anymore time, we should just try to move on with our lives and deal with this grief separately." Tears trickled down his face as he eventually looked up at her. Her face streaked with pain, her lips had turned white and her eyes were furious.

"I'm sorry, I won't waste anymore of your time." She spat at him.

"You know what I mean, Jane, you can't be happy living like this either? A change will do us good, it will be refreshing and hopefully help us in the long run." He tried to explain, unsuccessfully.

"I could be happy again if you would just give me time to grieve, why can't you do that for me? I can't just become happy again over night, I need time. If you had ever loved me you would gladly have given me as much time as I needed. But, as soon as things aren't perfect, you just runaway and bury your head in the sand. You're just a spoilt child throwing your toys out of the pram because things aren't going your way." She left the room swiftly before he could come back with a retort.

Jane stormed off upstairs and began to viciously pack a bag, ferocious tears blinding her vision and dropping heavily to the ground. Matthew hadn't followed her, he remained downstairs. Had he ever loved her? He was making no effort to make amends, his mind was made up.

Jane walked downstairs with her back pack thrown over her right shoulder, Matthew was sitting in the living room, he wept silently;

"I'm taking my dogs with me." She stated matter-of-factly.

"Ok." Was his only clipped response. He didn't look at up at her.

Jane stared at him, boring a hole in to the side of his head, longing for him to get up and change his mind, to tell her he had made a terrible mistake. He didn't. He merely sat there, stock still, with his hands folded in his lap.

"Do you even care where I'm going to?" She eventually said, a little more forcefully than she had intended, regretting her words, they were hardly going to make him change his mind.

Matthew rolled his eyes and sighed heavily. "Tell me where you are going then." He asked with complete disinterest, turning his head away.

Jane's anger bubbled and the dejection stabbed her painfully in the chest, "You couldn't even care where I go, could you? Couldn't care less if I'm safe, couldn't care if I have anywhere to go." She gasped exasperatedly, fists clenched, her eyes narrowed, shooting him a malicious look full of hatred and disgust.

"Of course I care, Jane, but you have two parents, a sister and a lot of friends, I am guessing you are going to one of their houses. I'm not completely heartless." His voice broke slightly.

"Matthew, do you really want me to go? Do you really want to finish this altogether?" She looked at him pleadingly, desperately.

He replied only with; "Yes." Still not looking up at her.

Jane stared at him, speechless. How could he be so disdainful? How could he just throw her out? Throw her out at her most weak and vulnerable moment? Jane felt her world crumbling around her, she couldn't take it, couldn't cope with the all encompassing agony. She loved Matthew more than she had ever loved anyone. He had been the turning point in her life. Once cold and distant and indifferent to any form of emotional relationship, he had transformed her to someone loving and caring and most of all; trusting.

Apart from the brutal heart ache she felt, Jane also felt utterly betrayed. Matthew was the one person, other than Tess, who knew her deepest secret. And now he was just ditching her, like she was trash he was throwing away. How foolish she had been to think that she could trust another human being. It had taken all her confidence and courage to divulge her past to him, but, yet again, he was just another person who let her down. Jane contemplated to herself; why had she been surprised? Everyone disappointed and broke her trust, eventually.

She walked out without saying another word, taking Ruby and Jack with her. She would not lose her dignity and self respect, on top of everything, by begging him to reconsider.

Jane got in to her car, her hands trembled uncontrollably and she gulped back huge sobs causing her to hiccough. She was having a panic attack. She began to wail and scream and thrash about in the car, kicking off the rear view mirror and sending her travel mug flying. The dogs were in the boot of the car, barking hysterically, trying to fight their way through the iron dog gate in the back of the car to get to her. The

147

anger, frustration and unimaginable pain had built up inside her like a volcano and it was beginning to overflow.

She couldn't gain control of herself. She would steady herself for a moment and resume a normal breathing pattern, but when she tried to do anything functional, such as phone her sister, it sent her in to a frenzy of distress and violence again.

Jane sat in her car in the driveway for an hour, unable to make the phone call to her sister, she knew she wouldn't be able to string the words together in to a formed sentence. She decided to send her a quick text message to say she would be over that afternoon. That would give her some time to settle herself.

She looked round at the dogs, almost forgetting they were there and felt immensely guilty. They were probably worried and confused. Jane decided to take them to the beach, a bit of fresh air would do them all good.

She let the dogs off their leads when she arrived and stroked them all individually and apologised profusely for her violent outburst. They forgave her instantly when she threw the ball for them endless amounts of times. Jane stood by the water, the cold breeze stinging her face and cooling the tears that were permanently there.

She loaded the dogs back in to the car after an hour and a half of contemplation over the last four weeks' events. A miscarriage and the loss of Matthew, it was too unimaginable to conceive.

Jane arrived at Tess's house, looking dishevelled and distraught. She arrived at the front door with her back pack and two dogs in tow. Tess opened the door looking alarmed and concerned;

"What's going on, Jane?!" She shrieked, "Why do you have a backpack *and* the dogs?!" Eyes wide, darting madly from her to the two, excited dogs. Tails wagging hysterically, pulling against their restraints to get to Tess.

"Matthew dumped me." She stated simply, tears spilling heavily from her eyes.

"What?! How could he?!" She demanded, looking outraged and ready for war. "You've only just had this miscarriage! Why has he done this?" She insisted upon an answer.

"He said my grieving process was too difficult for him to deal with." Jane explained with a detached tone, unable to look directly at Tess.

"Jane, that is madness. He can't do this! Does he not know this is just a temporary measure?! You need time to heal from this!" She shrieked loudly, her voice echoing through the trees. Her maddened expression reminded Jane of the times Tess had fought her corner, with no success, after another cataclysmic visit to their aunt and uncle.

"I told him that. He said he couldn't stand the oppressive atmosphere any longer. Said that we needed to go our separate ways with a fresh start, that it would be good for us." Jane spoke in a monotone voice, reverting back to her self defensive, withdrawal mode.

"Jane, you need to snap out of that, I know what you're doing. You're not ten years old anymore. We need to figure this out." She commanded, pulling her sister in to a tight hold.

"I can't face it, Tess. I can't face anymore agony, I'm done." She said in to her sister's shoulder.

"What the hell does *that* mean?" She demanded, a frightened look streaked across her face. Tess examined Jane carefully, her eyes darting wildly over Jane's countenance.

149

Jane made no reply.

"I'm phoning Matthew, I'll find out exactly what the hell he is playing at!" She yelled viciously.

"No! Don't phone him, Tess. He'll think that I got you to phone him for me!" Tess studied Jane's face severely, her lips narrow and pale. Seeing the pleading look in her eyes, she put her phone away.

"Thank you, Tess."

Jane got herself settled in, Tess's three children were at school, thankfully, and her husband, Glenn, was at work.

"The dogs can sleep in the kitchen," Tess explained, "and you can sleep in our spare room at the back of the house." Tess was looking anxious and shoved her hand through her hair.

Tess's house was colossal in size, compared to Jane's modest two bedroom in town. It was a six bedroom, country cottage with high ceilings and wooden beams across the ceilings.

The house oozed warmth and country living with a wood burner in each of their three reception rooms, stone walls and a large range in the kitchen. The entire perimeter of the house was lined with decking, with a rocking chair out on the front porch. Glenn was a partner in a large IT firm, clearly earning himself a good wage.

This had obviously been very agreeable to their aunt. Tess had bagged a wealthy man, had the huge house out in the country and three beautiful children. Jane was the outcast, disappointment in comparison. But Jane had no resentment towards her sister, anymore. She was happy for her and was content as long as her sister was happy with her choices.

Chapter 14

"I really appreciate this, Tess." Jane embraced her sister tightly. Longing for warm, human connection.

"That's what sisters are for." Tess attempted a semblance of a small smile but it quickly reverted back to a profound gloominess. She smoothed the hair away from Jane's face, staring at her intently, worry etched in the lines of her face.

"Can the dogs sleep with me?" Jane asked tentatively.

"But… my sheets and mattress!" Tess began to object but then looked at her sister's puppy dog eyes. "But you know I could never say no to you." Tess laughed as she yielded so quickly.

"You're the best!" Jane smiled, hugging her sister again.

Jane left the dogs in the kitchen while she unpacked her things. She decided to send Matthew a message to tell him she was staying at her sister's house and that she would get her sister to call for some of her things in the coming days. She also thought it wise to phone the rental company that was overseeing the tenancy agreement of her house. Thankfully Jane was within her rights to evict the tenant if she wanted it for her own use again, but, she had to give the tenant one month's notice. A month living with Tess, Glenn and three young children, along with her and her two dogs. It would be cramped.

Jane was grateful, though, that Tess had put her up. She couldn't face living with her mum or dad and all the questions and never ending concern for her wellbeing that it would entail. At least with Tess, Jane knew she could hide away in her room and not face anyone for days at a time.

Later in the day, all Jane felt was numbness, the trauma and pain over the last four weeks was overwhelming. How could she get rid of the pain? Jane had felt like ending it altogether, the brief, dark thought was there and then was gone again as quickly as it had appeared. She would have to be strong, like she had been so many years previous.

Tess, was very worried about her; Jane had become very withdrawn and angry in a short space of time. She could never fully understand how Jane felt either, though, she was happily married with three children, all three who had come easily to her. Tess had very little experience of heart ache and she had definitely never suffered a miscarriage before.

In the afternoon, Tess left to pick the children up from school and preschool. Glenn would be home late, earning a good living came at a price, and he normally wasn't home from work until at least eight o'clock every evening; leaving child care duties predominantly to Tess. Tess didn't mind this as she was currently on a career break from her job as a teacher, in order to raise her children.

While Tess was out, Jane took the opportunity to phone her mum and dad to break the news to them both. She felt it better to rip the band aid off right away rather than dragging out the inevitable. She decided to phone her mother first, get that over and done with, and out of the way, as quickly as possible.

Her finger hovered over her mother's name in her contacts list on her phone, she breathed deep, steadying breaths. She

152

knew that by revealing the break up to her mother she would go in to an episode of panic, she detested upsetting her mum at the best of times, but she knew her mum would lose at least a few nights sleep thinking this over and worrying endlessly.

The phone began to ring, there was no turning back now.

"Hello?" Her mother's voice rang through.

"Hi mum." She said cautiously, trying to measure Charlotte's current mood, hoping that she wouldn't be catching her too off guard.

"What's wrong, Jane? Is everything ok?!" She asked worriedly, her voice elevated to a high pitch squeal on the last question. She was already worried just because of the phone call, how would she react when Jane revealed the news to her?

"Matthew and I broke up." She ripped the band aid off. Jane went in to convulsions, she needed her mum, needed her to be there for her. She let it all out in deep, heavy sobs.

Silence.

"Sweetie, I'm coming over right now. Where are you?" Her voice trembled and was carved with unease.

"I'm at Tess', but mum, you don't have to." She breathed, steadying her tears. But Jane hoped that her mum would come and put her protective arms around her and take all the pain away. Jane couldn't help but blame herself for Matthew bailing on her, he didn't want to know her, didn't want to touch her ever again. She would never feel his hands caress her skin or feel his lips brush against hers. The agony was too much, she couldn't handle it.

"I'm coming over, Jane, I need to be there for my little girl." Charlotte's words were soothing and reassuring, Jane was grateful for her.

"Ok, thank you, mum." Jane croaked. She hung up and let herself be submerged in a sea of tears and depression, telling each individual family member about Matthew was going to feel as though she was being stabbed in the chest each time.

Jane couldn't help but self destruct at a time like this, to blame all her problems in life on herself. Abused by a violent and psychotic aunt and uncle and having had no friends throughout school, victim to vicious bullying and now; as an adult, she finally fell in love and he didn't want her either, couldn't put up with her. What was wrong with her?

Jane pulled herself together and prepared to phone her dad. She knew he would be equally as concerned as her mum. She breathed deeply through shuddering tears and took a large drink of her water, preparing to relive the event all over again.

"Hi Jane, sweetie. How are you?" She could hear him smiling through the phone at the sound of her voice. Jane let her tears fall stupendously to the ground.

"Hi, dad." She rasped.

"Long time no see!" Gary had not heard her mewl.

"I know, it must've been about three days since our last get together." Jane scoffed, then viciously broke down over the phone. The warmth of her dad's voice cut through her emotions and she crumbled.

"Sweetie? What's wrong?!" His tone laced vigorously with concern.

"Matthew and I broke up!" She heaved through enormous sobs.

"What! Oh, no! Oh, sweetie! I'm so sorry, are you ok? Where are you right now?" He gasped.

"I'm at Tess's, she's letting me stay here for a while." Jane sniffed.

"Honey, you could have come to stay with us. We've always got room for you here!" He cried.

"I know, dad. I didn't want to put you and Agnes out, and I knew the kids would love to have the dogs to stay." She explained deftly, not wanting to hurt her father's feelings.

"Well, that's true." He sounded injured nonetheless, but attempted to hide it. "Tell me what happened, honey. Want me to go and kill the guy." He asked seriously.

Jane laughed, "No, I just think the stress of the miscarriage was too much for us. I wasn't coping well and he was getting fed up."

"Asshole! So, he just bails the first time things get rough! Bloody coward, you're better off without the likes of that." He yelled.

"I thought he loved me. I thought the two of us could get passed anything."

"He just wasn't the one, sweetie. You will find someone who's deserving of your sweet, beautiful, kind soul." Jane bawled at these comforting words, in desperate need of a dad hug.

"Thank you, dad."

"I'll call over later today, ok honey?"

"No, don't worry, I don't want to bother anyone, I'll see you through the week." She assured him.

"Don't be silly, I'm coming over to see my baby girl in her time of need." He explained.

"Thanks dad." Jane was grateful knowing that she had her parents' support.

Half an hour later and Jane was still weeping silently in to her pillow, she jumped when she heard the door open, it was her mum as promised. Charlotte couldn't hold back at the

155

sight of her daughter, pathetic and wretched in the bed. She burst in to tears and climbed in to bed beside Jane, squeezing her tightly. Jane held on for dear life, grateful to have comfort and support right at that moment. They lay there for a long time, Charlotte stroked Jane's hair softly and Jane fell in to a deep, exhausted sleep.

Jane awoke in the spare room, her mother was gone, she had no idea how long she had been asleep for. When she heard the children storming through the front door she knew she couldn't have been asleep for long as the children were just home from school. There were shrieks and yells of delight. Jane decided to go downstairs and greet them.

She crept down the stairs, Josh, the youngest, noticed Jane out of the corner of his eye and let out a yell at the sight of her.

"Auntie Jane! Auntie Jane!" He screeched, running over and throwing himself in to her arms. Jane let out a cry, her emotions could not handle the sweetness and innocence of such a young child.

The others ran in to see who their guest was and were equally delighted to see their Auntie Jane. Jane couldn't help picturing the fact that this was what she had been to her Aunt Margaret and Uncle Thomas all those years ago. It made it even more difficult to fathom how her aunt and uncle could have hurt her so badly, in so many ways. Jane looked at these children and could never imagine a moment or situation that she would feel the need to hurt them.

Jack and Ruby had followed Jane down the stairs and greeted the children with wagging tails and invasive kisses. Grace, the eldest, was seven years old, and took her position as older sibling very seriously. She was tall for her age with long, golden blonde hair and bright blue eyes; she was very inquisitive and loved to learn. She could be found in her room, playing very nicely with all of her dolls, or having pretend tea parties with her teddy bears.

Beth, the middle child, was five years old. Her hair was the similar golden colour to Grace's, but had not grown very long yet. It was normally parted in to pigtails on the top of her head, her eyes were equally as blue and sharp as her sister's. She did not have an interest in learning; instead she liked to spend her time playing in puddles and running around the house like a lunatic.

Josh, the youngest, at four years old, was a typical boy; loved getting up to mischief, never sat still for a moment and thought of the walls in the house as his very own colouring book. His hair was slightly darker and his blue eyes were as deep as the ocean; resembling his father much more than his mother.

"Auntie Jane, Auntie Jane! Come and see my tree house!" Yelled Beth, tugging at Jane's hand.

"No! Auntie Jane, come and see my toy trucks!" Screamed Josh, tugging at the other hand.

"Are you staying with us?" Asked sensible Grace, staring serenely at Jane, she was the calming influence over the other two.

"I am." Jane smiled down at her.

"What happened to your other house?" She asked inquisitively.

"It's getting some work done to it and won't be ready for a month." Beth and Josh continued to clutch at both her hands.

Grace considered this and accepted it as a reasonable excuse to stay.

"But, where is Uncle Matthew?" She asked, noticing there was someone missing.

Jane's stomach gave a lurch at the sound of his name. The pain came crashing back as though struck by a violent wave. She felt sick.

"Uncle Matthew is busy at the moment." Tess explained. She asked them to go to their playroom so that 'Mummy' and Auntie Jane could talk.

Jane left and retired to her room, taking Ruby and Jack with her, leaving a stranded Tess. Jane wasn't much in the mood for talking and the venture out to see the children had been quite enough excitement for one afternoon.

Jane's dad, Gary, called in for an hour to see Jane. He hugged her tightly. His embrace had always made Jane feel completely protected from all the dangers of the outside world. Jane didn't feel much like talking about anything and Gary left, not before giving her a kiss on the forehead and telling her he was always there if she needed him.

Glenn got home from work later that evening, when the children were already in their beds. Jane was still up in her room. She could hear Tess and Glenn talking as she had left her door open just a crack;

"Jane and Matthew broke up, she's staying with us for a little while." Tess was explaining tremulously.

"I'm sorry to hear that, I always liked Matthew. How is she holding up?" He asked.

"Not good, I haven't seen her this down since we were children." Tess's voice was laced heavily with strain and upset. Jane felt guilty for causing her beloved sister so much worry.

"Well, we'll take good care of her. I'm sure the kids are happy to see the dogs."

"They really were!"

Jane's heart warmed at the kind welcome from Glenn, despite trespassing in on their lives. He really was a nice man, Jane was glad Tess had found happiness. Tears trickled steadily down Jane's cheeks as she reflected on the day gone by; it had been long and exhausting. She would be glad when it was over.

Chapter 15

Two weeks later and Jane had not ventured much farther than the spare room in her sister's house. Having the dogs with her was what had kept her going, their constant companionship and affection was inconceivably comforting. They had been the encouragement to get her out of bed every day as they needed their daily walk and trips to the toilet.

Jane had delved in to a profound state of melancholy that she feared she might never return from. She couldn't envisage a life without Matthew, she couldn't process it, couldn't rationally deal with her emotions. She knew that what she had with Matthew, she would never find again. It had been a once in a life time, momentous, devastating, earth shattering moment in time that was now gone forever.

She missed everything about him; his hand caressing her face, the sound of his voice, the protective way he took care of her. The way he made her feel, that magical spark of chemistry that cannot be explained by words. It was a feeling, a most wonderful feeling, gone forever.

Jane cried for long periods of the day, her eyes permanently red and blotchy, she tortured herself by staring at photos of her and Matthew when they had been together. Was he thinking about her? Was he as devastated as she was? Or, was he relieved? Glad that the relationship was over and he could finally move on with his life? Jane couldn't stomach the thought, to think of him with another woman made bile rise up through her oesophagus.

But, what if he was dating someone else already? Jane tortured her mind, imagining the many scenarios that could be occurring. Then it hit Jane. *Alessandra.* Jane only had Matthew's word for it that Alessandra was the derailed stalker desperately seeking to be with him. But, what if that was all a lie? What if Alessandra *had* been in the picture the whole time and Jane was the idiot, too blind to see what was right in front of her.

Jane tormented herself thinking of Matthew with her. She had to find out if she was right, but she knew deep down that she was. Looking back, it had been obvious, the chemistry the two had shared, the way his arm brushed against hers.

It was midday and Jane was still in her room with Jack and Ruby. Tess approached Jane's bedroom door and knocked gently.

No response.

"Jane, would you please come out and talk to me?" Tess demanded firmly.

No reply.

"You have been in that room for weeks, Grace, Beth and Josh miss you, they don't understand why their Auntie Jane doesn't want to see them." Tess wasn't ashamed to use her children as blackmail.

The door opened, Jane peered round the corner with her duvet over her shoulders and smudged mascara smeared beneath her eyes, Jack and Ruby nudged their noses round the door to try to peak a look at the visitor, too.

"Tess, I'm sorry, I'm such a terrible house guest, I just don't feel like doing anything or seeing anyone." She admitted, squinting her eyes at the blinding sun coming from the light bursting through the open door.

"I understand, Jane. You have had a lot to deal with over the last few weeks, it must be hard just getting out of bed, but, you need to at least try and get up and out of the house. This hiding away in your room isn't healthy." She urged seriously.

"I just can't face it, Tess, I hate going out at the best of times. I just want to be back at my house with my dogs and live a quiet life and not be bothered by anyone." Jane sighed heavily, closing her eyes against the strain of having to keep them open.

"I know you aren't up to doing much at the moment, Jane, but even just come downstairs and say hello to the children. You have made such progress over the last year; don't let all that hard work go to waste." She pleaded, her forehead creased in despair.

Tess was referring to Jane's antisocial behaviour and preference of being a recluse. That had all changed when she had met Matthew, he had opened a new world for her, one where she could be open and trusting of other people. That Jane was gone forever, Matthew's abandonment had shattered that Jane in to a million tiny little pieces. She had been hurt by too many important people in her life, she wouldn't be making *that* mistake again.

Jane agreed to leave her room that day and say hello to the children, she had to have a shower first as it had been a few days. She went downstairs and was greeted, very excitedly, by

Grace, Beth and Josh, who immediately ran towards Jack and Ruby. As the two dogs dashed excitedly over to the three children, Jane smiled at the warmth between her two beloved dogs and her nieces and nephew.

She embraced the children warmly, but the clutch of a child's embrace only further deepened her despair, to know that she would never cradle her own child seemed to submerge her in a sea of grief all over again. She turned away, knowing that her eyes were welling up. Tess noticed and asked the children to go in to their playroom.

The children ran off, Ruby and Jack followed them, the two dogs enjoyed the playful run a rounds of the three young children.

"Jane, how about we go out for a few drinks tonight? Get you out of the house and take your mind off things." Tess asked, cautiously, daring a glance at Jane.

"I really can't, Tess, I'd rather just stay in. I don't think I'm ready." Jane replied depressively.

"Just for an hour, Jane, we can just go in to the village, I think it would be good for you." Tess pleaded.

"What if we go and see *him*?" Him being Matthew of course, she couldn't bear the thought, what if he looked happy? What if he was with another woman? No. It was best to stay indoors and avoid that risk at all costs.

"Jane, I have been patient with you for weeks now, but this can't go on anymore. I worry about you moving back to your house on your own. I have already said to Millie, Martha and Jennifer that you are coming out tonight." This last sentence was said a little tentatively. Tess looked at Jane sheepishly, scratching at the back of her neck, waiting for the argument. Jane's eyes widened angrily with shock and anguish.

163

"You shouldn't have done that, Tess!" Jane screeched angrily. "That's not fair!"

"You forced my hand, Jane. I can't have you falling in to this rut of moping around the house, not washing or seeing anyone. You've been here before and it's a dark place and hard to crawl your way back out of again." Tess looked miserable, her face was tired and lined from the last few weeks of worry.

Jane noticed her sister's miserable guise and felt immeasurably guilty, her behaviour had affected Tess immensely, she was being selfish. Maybe going out would take her mind off everything for a while and maybe make it easier for the next time. She considered this for a moment;

"Ok, I'll go out, but only for an hour, Tess." Tess jumped up in delight.

"Oh, excellent! I'm so excited! We're going to have so much fun, I promise!" She smiled widely and started running around, fussing over Jane, discussing what they were going to wear and where they were going to go. Tess's husband, Glenn, was to stay in and mind the children and the dogs while they went out.

Jane and Tess met Millie, Martha and Jennifer outside the local pub, Penny's, at eight o'clock that evening. There was a lot of hugging and screaming much to Jane's dismay. She'd made a huge mistake. She wasn't ready for all the excitement and chatter. She wanted to leave right away, but how could she when they had only just arrived?

Jane's heart was pounding as they entered the bar; "Please don't let him be here, please don't let him be here." Jane thought anxiously to herself. Relief flooded over her when she glanced quickly around the bar, noticing no sign of Matthew.

164

They got a table in the middle of the bar which was disheartening to Jane, she would have rather hidden in a booth in the corner and pretended to be invisible.

They were approached by an attractive, male waiter who Martha eyed up ferociously like a hungry animal. Tess and the girls all ordered various, elaborate cocktails, Jane ordered a house red wine and sipped it slowly, keeping her eyes peeled for anyone coming through the entrance door. Jennifer was talking animatedly about a new love interest she had at the moment. "Great," thought Jane, "everyone is so happy getting on with their lives and I'm so miserable."

"He's called Ben and he's a policeman." Jennifer was saying. "He's thirty, so he's probably a little old for me, but what does age matter if you are just having a little fun?" The girls laughed hysterically. Jane tried to join in but she couldn't find the fun in Jennifer's promiscuity.

"Jane, that is exactly what you need," said Martha, "a fling with some handsome, hot stranger, to take your mind off everything and make you feel good for once!" Martha had a teasing look in her eye, her cleavage was exposed voluntarily and she plumped out her chest any time a man walked by. She loved to talk about men and the things you can get up to with them. It occurred to Jane that Martha had probably cheated on her husband on quite a few occasions.

"I don't need a fling, I just need back to my house and back to my normal life. *And* with no men to distract me." Jane retorted, with a teenage, sullen attitude.

"That is the last thing you need," cried Millie, "now you know what it is to be truly in love, you know what you are looking for. Of course, it will take some time, but you can't give up on true happiness because of this one bad experience.

Life is about getting hurt, it's how we respond to that hurt and grow as individuals that truly shows who we really are."

Millie was always so sensible and always had a long winded description in the back of her mind, ready and waiting for when the occasion asked for it.

"I agree with Martha and Millie." Tess announced, raising her glass.

"Tess!" Jane scolded. "I am your little sister, you can't encourage me to have casual relationships with strange men!"

"Why not? It might be a good distraction, and you never know, you might actually enjoy yourself." She giggled with a twinkle in her eye.

"Tess, you are being ridiculous!" But Jane actually laughed at her sister, she didn't often see that side to her.

"Check out the guy at the bar over there, he's really cute!" Jennifer pointed excitedly in the direction.

Jane glanced briefly over at the bar, paying no attention to the man but gave a response to pacify Jennifer; "He's ok, not really my type."

"Jane, you say that about every guy, and besides, you didn't even look properly!" Millie reproached, slapping Jane playfully on the hand.

Jane looked back over at the bar, but then... "Oh *no*."

"What is it?" Millie asked, looking concerned, wondering had Jane spotted Matthew.

"It's that doctor, James, the pompous, over confident guy." Jane said, already feeling repulsed, dreading her decision to come out. A leering man all over her was the last thing she needed, talk about staying under the radar, *that* wasn't happening.

"Oh, my! He is *hot* Jane!" Martha croaked huskily.

166

"He's vile." Retorted Jane

"He definitely isn't." Said Jennifer, who was also eyeing him up quite keenly.

Jane turned her back on him and tried to avoid drawing any attention over to their table.

Some time passed and the girls needed their drinks replenished, it was Jane's round, feeling rather tipsy and having forgotten that she had wanted to go home, she approached the bar with a silly grin on her face.

"Can I get five mojitos please?" Jane asked the attractive bar tender, slurring her words slightly.

"I think five cocktails might be too many for just one small girl like yourself." Said a strange voice behind her.

Jane spun around unsteadily, it was James. In all her drunkenness she had forgotten that he was there, but the compliment of being described as 'small' made Jane feel a little less frosty towards him.

"Ha, yes, you would think so, they are actually for my sister and friends, too." Jane said, her vision blurred, she swayed slightly on the spot.

"Jane, isn't it?" He asked. "Haven't seen you about in a long time."

"Yes, well, I have just got out of a long term relationship so I haven't been out much, and you transferred to another maternity unit didn't you?" Jane replied all in one breath. She didn't know why she had told James about her break up.

"Yes, I transferred out to another hospital about an hour away. I have been completing stints in various hospitals as part of my rotation." He explained, looking much more laid back and nowhere near as pompous as he had appeared on their last encounter.

167

"Ah, we aren't exciting enough for you in Clovelly." She stuttered.

"Well, I don't really get a choice in the matter, we have to rotate and experience all the specialities in order to progress further in our careers."

"You work very hard." She stated simply.

"You've got to work hard if you want to play hard." James said jokingly. Jane laughed too, although, she was unsure why, because a comment like that would normally have been enough to make her want to vomit in her mouth. James noticed her facade drop slightly, he moved in closer. Jane felt her heart quicken slightly, she could smell his aftershave, hints of Bergamot and Cedarwood, she liked it.

"Why do you not have a girlfriend yet, James?" Jane surprised herself with her overly blunt question, she rested her elbow on to the bar and her posture relaxed, popping her hip out, exuding confidence and what she thought might have come across as sex appeal.

"Haven't found the right person I guess." He replied sincerely, he stood, cross legged, against the bar, oozing wealth and sophistication. His fitted shirt and equally fitted slacks were drawing Jane's attention away from his face. Had he always been this good looking?

"Ah, the classic line, I guess I'm the one you have been waiting for this whole time?" She laughed teasingly, amazed by her wantonness. She had actually reached out and playfully touched his arm. James looked down at his arm and then back up to her, a smirk smeared generously across his face.

"Maybe you are, Jane." He said, standing very close and brushing his hand against hers that still remained on his arm.

Jane felt warm and fuzzy inside, she wanted to stay in James' company. Was this not repulsive, supercilious James she couldn't stand before? Next minute, he lent in to kiss her, Jane, not expecting this, stared at him uneasily, but having so much alcohol, she couldn't think of a reason as to why she shouldn't just throw caution to the wind and kiss him. It was wet but surprisingly pleasant. She forgot about the dozens of people standing around her, she forgot about everything for that one moment. Savouring the sweet licks of his tongue and the addictive scent of his skin.

Then they were abruptly interrupted by the bar tender; "Miss, your drinks are ready for you now."

Jane withdrew from James, horrified, kissing a stranger for all to see, out in the open. She quickly grabbed the tray of drinks and ran (as fast as she could with the tray) back over to her table.

"Jane! Were you just kissing James at the bar?!" Millie squealed excitedly, clapping her hands together.

"Yes. Let's not talk about it." Was Jane's only embarrassed reply. Covering her face to hide her blushing humiliation.

"Oh, you dog *you!*" Martha taunted.

"Did you give him your number?!" Jennifer asked exuberantly.

"No, we were kind of interrupted by the bar guy and I ran off." Jane wanted the world to swallow her whole.

"Jane, you *need* to go back over there and get back to where you left off!" Urged Millie encouragingly, her eyes dancing from her to James, alive with delight.

"I don't know girls, I'm quite drunk now, I don't want to do anything silly." She played about with the straw in her drink, feeling awkward and uncomfortable with the inquisition.

169

"Life is about making mistakes and not taking things too seriously, you only live once, Jane!" Millie pushed, inspiring confidence.

Jane looked over, James was still standing at the bar, alone, apparently waiting for her return because he kept glancing over his shoulder at their table. Jane pushed back from her seat. The girls all gave a "woohoo!" as they realised she was headed over to see James again.

"You go for it, sis!" Screamed Tess, Jane looked over at her sister in confusion and astonishment and gave her a 'quit it' type look.

She approached where James was patiently waiting for her;

"Sorry about the quick getaway, I don't normally kiss random guys at bars." She stood near him, feeling the warmth radiate from him, staring anywhere but at him, wanting the ground to swallow her up.

"Don't mention it. How about we get out of here?" James asked as he glanced back at the table of girls with their eyes glued to the two of them, immensely enjoying the spectacle.

He was very good looking and she had been miserable for so long, what harm would it do? To take her mind off things and maybe spend a night with someone mildly interested in her.

"I don't know." She said, unsure of what she wanted to do.

"No pressure, only if you want to." He said. Why did he look so good?

"Ok." She replied quickly, before she changed her mind.

Chapter 16

The next morning, Jane woke up in a bed that was not her own, feeling fuzzy headed and slightly nauseous. Fear grasped Jane, threatening to consume her, filling her up with dread. What had she done? What terrible mistake had she made? Most importantly, where was she? How had she got there? Then it hit her, like a slap in the face, she had gone home with James. She was in *his* house.

What an idiot. Jane had been here before. Not James' house specifically, but she had, many a night, clambered in to an unknowing bed, searching for 'love' or, well, at least some form of attention or feelings of love for the night. All in a feeble, and embarrassing, attempt to try to fill the gap in her life that her aunt and uncle had left within her. To try to feel good enough for somebody. It had never worked. The end result was highly unfulfilling. Feelings of shame and disgust permeated her soul as she permitted these men to abuse her body for the night, only because they found her faintly attractive. But, at the time, it felt good; she craved the attention, to be *wanted*.

Jane, however, severely regretted the mistake with James more than the others. Sleeping with another man, in Jane's mind, signified that it was officially and absolutely over with Matthew. She wanted very much to cry hysterically, but forced back painful tears in case James was still in the house. The realisation was too hard for Jane to come to terms with. If she had already had sex with another man, then Matthew had, absolutely, one hundred percent, had sex with another woman.

The thought made her want to throw up. Her Matthew. Her beautiful, amazing, wonderful Matthew, with some other woman's hands all over him. She cringed at the thought. She wanted to lose her mind again, to throw something across the room, to rid herself of the rage within.

Then Jane was reminded of Alessandra. Was Matthew back with her? No. She tried to shake the thought from her mind. She was the crazy stalker he couldn't get rid of. Well, that's the story *he* had told Jane. Alessandra was extremely beautiful. A mad man would have to say no to her. Jane thought about texting Matthew to challenge him on this, she even got her phone out. But, she quickly changed her mind, she wouldn't lose face and contact him. She had to maintain her self respect, which wasn't looking too high at that very moment as she lay in a stranger's bed.

What had she been thinking? James was vile. But, then again, she had been extraordinarily drunk. How had her sister and her friends allowed her to go off with a complete stranger to his house on her own? Although, Jane supposed he wasn't a complete and utter stranger, she and Millie knew that he was a doctor from work, and what doctors normally turn out to be serial killers? Not this one apparently. Where was he?

She was in his king size bed, alone. Had he made a run for it and was waiting at a friend's house until he knew the coast was clear and he could return? His room was outstanding; it almost had a feminine touch to it. Had a woman lived there before? Everything was grey and silver, the bed was a grey, crushed velvet sleigh bed. The side tables were made completely of mirror with large chandelier style lamps, on top, that looked very grand. Directly facing her were completely mirrored, built in slide robes, this room was amazing. He definitely had style and taste.

Jane got up and started to put her clothes back on from the night before. She was naked. Jane clasped her hands to her face, exasperated at another stupid mistake she had made, yet again. Had they had sex? She couldn't remember, it was still very hazy and unclear from the alcohol. She opened the door and peered round, the hallway was completely covered in expensive looking marble tiles.

"Pays well to be a doctor I suppose." Thought Jane. She walked down the large hallway and reached the stairs that were carpeted with a grey plush carpet, the same as the bedroom. She couldn't hear the TV or any voices. She had her purse and her phone so that, at least if the house was empty, she could quickly order a taxi and get home. But what was his address?

Jane was racking her brain, trying to remember anything, but she could barely remember getting a taxi there in the first place. She walked in to the kitchen and there he was, James, sitting on one of the stools in the middle of the kitchen at a very grand and expensive looking island, with a marble effect quartz worktop. He had what looked like a cappuccino in his hand, looking relaxed, reading a newspaper. Jane was flabbergasted to see him there. He hadn't noticed her yet, she remained in the doorway to the kitchen, appreciating more of the magnificent house.

The kitchen was bright and airy and mainly white, the same marble tiles were on the floor that had been in the hallway,

173

and the windows spanned nearly the size of the room letting copious amounts of natural light in. It almost had a clinical feel about it, it was so clean, and the worktops were free of clutter apart from an expensive looking coffee machine. It appeared he was excessively clean and tidy.

Jane walked in slowly, feeling like a school girl about to be told off. The 'morning afters' were always the worst; awkward, forced small talk that had to be endured for a certain amount of time until both could dash off in separate directions and get on with their lives.

"Good morning." James greeted Jane cheerfully, setting down his coffee cup and newspaper.

"Morning." Her voice croaked and she coughed slightly, not remembering when she had last used her voice. He looked great, had he showered already? He appeared very fresh and exhilarated and didn't seem to have the same lingering hangover that she had.

"Did you sleep well?"

"I can hardly remember," Jane answered honestly, "it's all a bit of a blur." She edged slowly over to him, shuffling her feet, wishing she could be anywhere but there.

"Oh dear, I mustn't have made that much of an impact on you then!" Said James, slightly disheartened.

"I'm sure my memory will return, I'm just tired." Jane replied quickly. Why was he so disappointed? What was it to him if she had a good time or not? He'd got what he had wanted.

"Can I make you some breakfast?" James asked eagerly. Jane had expected cocky, self assured James to be gloating in all his glory at conquering Jane Abbot. Instead, he was revered and polite. Jane was taken aback.

"That would be great, thanks." She answered gratefully, realising how hungry she was. She perched herself on to one of the stools carefully.

Why was he being so nice? Was this not repulsive James? His behaviour was exemplary and not once had he come across as pig headed, despite the obvious love making that would have occurred the night before, if only Jane could just remember!

"Coffee?" He asked. Jane contemplated this for a moment, she would rather have had a Darjeeling tea but she supposed James didn't have that stocked in his tidy kitchen cupboards so she answered with only a; "Sure."

"So," James started tentatively, "do you remember anything from last night all?"

"Sort of, not all of it. Sorry, I was really drunk, I probably shouldn't have come back here." She looked anxiously around for an escape exit.

"Why?" Asked James, looking disappointed, maintaining a steely gaze. "I had a great time, you didn't seem that drunk or I wouldn't have asked you back to my place. Sorry, you must think I'm a real jerk." He hung his head slightly, appearing to be plagued with disappointment and shame. He stood up and began lifting utensils out of the cupboards in order to prepare breakfast.

He was being gracious and polite, Jane was stunned by these kind manners and his nervous disposition.

"It's fine, my own mistake. As I said last night, I'm just out of a long term relationship and I guess I was just looking for something to take my mind off it." She wanted to crawl out of there on her hands and knees and never look back, the embarrassment was severe. How must she be looking? She hadn't even seen a mirror.

"Is that what I am now?" He said jokingly, trying to ease the tension.

Jane laughed awkwardly, "No, of course not, but you have to admit, last night was just a bit of one night fun, that is, when I can begin to remember it all." She bit her lip.

"Well, I would probably like to do it again some time." He turned to face her, looking at her determinedly.

"Really?" Jane's mouth parted in surprise.

"Yeah, I like you, Jane. Have done for quite a while now." He admitted, shifting nervously.

"You like my body, James. You don't even know me." Jane surprised herself with her brashness.

"Yes, I do. But, I like you, too. I'd like to take you on proper date some time, but, no pressure." He looked at her pensively, longing for her to say yes.

"Can I have a think about it?" Asked Jane, feeling overwhelmed at these turn of events. It was all so unexpected.

"Yes, of course." James replied, but he couldn't hide the intense disappointment scrawled across his face.

James made Jane coffee from his expensive and complicated looking coffee machine, made from real coffee beans that he had retrieved from a cupboard and emptied in to the top opening of the machine. The coffee was delicious, topped with frothy milk and cinnamon sprinklings. James seemed to be passionate about coffee the way Jane was about tea.

She told James she had to go back to her sister's after she had finished her coffee, poached eggs, bacon and toast, because she would be worrying about her. James offered her a lift home which she accepted.

Jane had forgotten to check her phone, she had also forgotten to tell everyone that she was safe. She was sure everyone would be incredibly worried about her. She didn't want to look at her phone, she knew there would be a bombardment of messages and missed calls from her friends and Tess, when she unlocked it. As expected, it was inundated with missed calls and text messages;

Tess – Four unread messages and six missed phone calls:

1.30am: "Are you ok, Jane?"

2.15am: "What time will you be home?"

2.30am: "Are you staying over at his house tonight?"

8am: "Jane, I'm starting to get worried, just let me know that you are ok!"

Millie – two unread messages:

1am: "Hope you're having a good night Jane, please stay safe and let us know when you are home."

9am: "Hi Jane, how did you get on last night? Are you home safe? Your sister has been texting me, I think she is quite worried. Maybe give her a call to let her know that you are alright. ☺"

Martha – One unread message:

12.30am: "Who's the slut now, you cheeky little minx ;-)"

Jennifer – One unread message:

9.30am: "Hope you had fun last night and got home safe. Need to meet up again soon to get all the goss! Love you lots, Jen xx"

Poor Tess. Jane phoned her quickly and told her she was on her way home. Tess sounded relieved to hear from her and then a little annoyed that she hadn't been contacted earlier. James dropped her off at her sister's, he gave her a quick kiss before she got out of the car. Jane jumped when he had leant in and recoiled instinctively at the breach of personal space. He looked, if possible, even further disheartened, Jane made a dash for it, apologising as she ran up the drive to her sister's front door.

"I'll text you to arrange that date." James shouted out to her from his rolled down car window, arm hanging out casually, looking suave.

"Talk to you then." She shouted from the front porch and a smile crept over his face. Poor guy.

Jane opened the front door, slowly. She was greeted by two very over excited dogs, she bent down and stroked them, as they planted wet kisses on her face. She stood up and was faced with a very grim looking Tess;

"Don't *ever* do that to me again, Jane!" Tess shouted, as Jane entered the house, standing far too close to her and emanating fury from her every pore. She screwed up her face and her shoulders tensed.

"You knew I was going back to his place, Tess, you knew where I was. What's the big deal? You were the one encouraging me last night to let my hair down and meet new people." Jane spat, shrugging her shoulders, angry at the justification when she was thirty one years old. Was this not what the girls had been encouraging her to do all night?

"I didn't expect you to go home with him, Jane! I thought maybe a snog and an exchange of numbers would be about as far as it would go! I'm hardly going to encourage my little sister to have casual sex with random men!" Tess looked scandalised and enraged as they stood battling it out in the hallway, the dogs stood patiently beside them both, heads bobbing from woman to woman.

"Well, you weren't objecting when the others were egging me on!" Yelled a dismayed Jane, blushing severely, wishing she could retreat to the safety of her room.

"I didn't expect you to just do whatever those stupid girls told you to do!" She shot back.

"Those girls are my friends, don't call them stupid!" Jane scowled, her eyes narrowed maliciously.

"Well, you have to admit yourself that they are fairly immature! Especially Jennifer and Martha!" Tess raised her eyebrows, an air of superiority radiated. Jane felt her anger bubble further, how dare Tess stand and judge her.

"Well, up until last night you always really liked them. You can't blame my friends for my decision, you were there too, you could've stopped it if you wanted to! And, by the way, I had a great time thanks for asking!" She was now feeling decidedly worse about her decision, she clutched at the anxious pain in her chest.

"You're acting like a child, Jane!" Tess screamed.

"I'm an adult, Tess, I don't need all this questioning! And, you don't need to make me feel any more terrible than I already feel!" Tess stopped in her tracks and looked at her, shocked by her statement. She didn't say anything further.

Jane looked at her with fury and resentment and stormed off to her room like a scolded child, the dogs followed their owner, loyally, wagging their tails and she slammed the door behind her when she and the dogs were in the room.

As if she didn't already feel disgusted enough with herself, she felt even further degraded and repulsed because of her sister's judgement added in to the mix. What's the big deal? It was rebound sex after the crappy few weeks she had been

179

having. It was a completely normal thing to do. But this thought did not make Jane feel any better.

Tess went up to Jane's room later that day to apologise for shouting at her;

"Jane, I'm sorry about how I reacted, I was just so worried something had happened to you. Of course you can make your own decisions, you're a grown woman." She said apologetically, sitting beside her on the bed, looking ashamed with herself.

"It's alright," sighed Jane, she lay in the bed and turned to face her sister. "I just felt rubbish about what I did last night and your response to it just confirmed how stupid I had been. What was I thinking?"

"Have you heard from him at all?" Tess asked, knowing the answer already.

"Yes." Replied Jane.

"Oh, *really?*" Tess couldn't hide her surprise, it was uncommon to hear from the guy after a one night stand.

Jane laughed at her sister's reaction.

"Well, what has he said?" She looked delighted with the new, positive turn of events.

"He wants to go out again some time." Jane maintained a poker face, giving nothing away.

"How do you feel about that?" Tess examined her carefully.

"I'll probably go, beats sitting in my room feeling sorry for myself all the time. You were right, Tess, I need to get out and distract myself. I feel as though I'm losing my mind thinking about Matthew all the time." The mere mention of his name sent daggers through her heart.

"You miss him a lot?" Tess put a comforting arm around Jane as they sat on her bed.

"More than words can say, but he was certain he wanted to end things and what am I to do about it? Dating another guy will surely distract me from the pain?" Jane looked to her sister for support, longing for the right answer to relieve her suffering.

"If you rush in to something too quickly you might just delay the grief that needs to be felt. Do you really like this guy, James?" Tess asked, knowing the truth, raising her eyebrows in a shrewd look.

"I don't know, I hardly know the guy, but he seems to like me and seems interested. What's the harm?" Jane asked curiously. A distraction from her feelings was exactly what she needed. The tightness in her chest from all the grief was hard to suffer through. Some times it got so bad she thought she was having a heart attack.

"Well, you might end up hurting the guy if he develops real feelings for you and you have admitted yourself that you are using him to deny the pain of what you have experienced, and, inevitably you will feel that pain at some stage." Tess looked at her seriously.

"When did you become so smart?" Jane smirked, nudging her sister fondly. Tess laughed and they grasped each other, Jane savoured her sister's embrace, the one person she could truly rely on.

Chapter 17

Two weeks later and Jane had moved back in to her own house, Tess was sad to see her go but was very much relieved the two dogs would no longer be staying with her. Three children, three adults and two dogs was a tough household to manage. Although the house was upside down and required a deep clean following the eviction of the tenants, Jane was overjoyed and delighted to be back in her own home again, and most of all, was pleased to be alone. As hospitable as Tess and Glenn had been, Tess had been full on; checking in on her all the time, always looking to go out somewhere or do something. At least now that Jane was home, she could do as she pleased.

Jane had been on three dates with James, he was a great improvement from the original man she had spoken to in the bar over a year previous. He was kind and attentive and seemed genuinely interested in her, but something was missing for Jane. The relationship was lacking spark or electricity. They hadn't made love since the very first time and Jane was unsure if she wanted to again, she couldn't be sure if she was even attracted to James. To look at he was obviously good looking, he was tall and broad with a very sculpted physic, he had sandy brown hair with steel, grey eyes and swarthy skin. He was very appealing to look at but Jane could not discern the attraction, he didn't have the same charm as Matthew had, she didn't feel that *tingle* or giddiness when their hands touched or when he looked at her. But, he was pleasant to be around and Jane enjoyed feeling wanted and sexy at a time where she couldn't feel anything less.

Jane felt tremendously guilty about leading James on, it was out of character. She was a kind person who always thought of the feelings of others, it was one of the reasons she was so good at her job. She had the ability to empathise with another's suffering and help them through it, it was her gift. But now, she was using James for her own gratification, merely because she was feeling rejected and insecure.

She knew she was doing something wrong, but she couldn't stop, because if she did, then she would just be on her own again, lost and lonely. Being alone had never bothered Jane, she had always preferred it, but now, the thought of having no one to love her seemed scary and unbearable because she knew that, ultimately, she was denying the feelings that were lingering beneath the surface waiting to come up for air.

Jane left the house that day to do her weekly grocery shop, she decided to do her hair and make up and put on some nice clothes in an attempt to pick herself and give herself a boost. She was tired of staring at the dark bags underneath her eyes and the dishevelled and untamed hair.

She was perusing the shopping aisles aimlessly, thinking about what her next meal would be, scolding herself for shopping whilst hungry, when she suddenly felt eyes on the back of her head. She immediately became overly self aware, her arm hairs stood to attention. Jane spun round quickly. Standing at the end of the aisle with his eyes fixed solely on her was... *Matthew*.

Jane instantly felt the palpable energy between them, she knew she had felt his eyes on her, they had a chemical energy that sent fireworks throughout her even when they weren't touching. Jane was suddenly very conscious of herself, standing out, unguarded. She felt goose bumps ripple over her, sending a shiver down her spine.

Jane stared in to those dark, seductive eyes, but they were cold and distant. The effect caused Jane to feel the all too familiar lump in the back of her throat. He was over her. The look said it all. He was disconnected and disinterested, as though the last year had never existed.

Jane tore her eyes away from him and made to change aisles to get away from him. Looking at him caused unbearable pain and mental torment. She craved him beyond measure, she remembered a time when she had the right to touch him, to kiss him, to put a hand through his hair and feel the soft strands sifting through her fingers. Now, as she walked away, she knew she could never do that again. Here he was in the same building as her, within touching distance, but she couldn't walk up to him and take his mouth in hers, couldn't take his hand and walk straight out of there as though the last few weeks had never happened.

She turned the corner in to the next aisle and let out the long breath she hadn't realised she'd been holding. Her lips trembled and tears spilled heavily down her face in an uncontrollable torrent. She knew she was in a public place and surrounded by people and she knew Matthew was in the aisle next to her, but, she couldn't stem the flow of tears.

Matthew appeared at the top of the aisle, Jane's shock and humiliation at him seeing her crumbling to pieces was

184

devastating, she wanted to be strong, to show him that she was ok. But she was *far* from ok.

He was walking towards her, sheer determination in his eyes. Jane wondered why. She wiped the tears from her face but knew her mascara must be hideously smudged everywhere. She wondered was she blocking the part of the aisle that he needed to get to, she moved to walk away again, aware of her every movement.

"Are you running away from me?" He breathed in a low, raspy voice, oozing charisma and sex appeal. Jane could feel the hairs stand up on the back of her neck. She thought about running away, she couldn't face the torment of looking at him, seeing her dream life standing before her, only to be snatched away.

"No." She answered, turning back around, feeling as though the universe was punishing her. She looked up in to his face, she couldn't read him, he showed no sign of emotion. She yearned for even a small sign of pain or regret, but it wasn't there.

"How are you, Jane?" He studied her face. He had witnessed the breakdown in the middle of the shop, the question was pointless, he could see how she was.

"I am doing *splendid!*" She joked and chuckled slightly. He smiled sadly back at her. The sorrow touched his eyes in a way Jane had never seen before, she looked in to his eyes and thought she could see right in to his soul. The look was gone in a second and his gaze had reverted to indifferent and cold again.

"I've missed you, Jane." *What?* Jane hadn't expected the bold statement. Her heart pounded rapidly against her chest, hope swelled up inside of her, thinking things might not be as over as she thought they might be.

"I've missed you, too." She whispered, lips trembling, voice shaky.

He touched her hand, electricity sparked through Jane like a current, her pulse quickened at his touch. She wished her palms weren't so sweaty.

"I'm sorry I've done this to you." He held her hand, his fingers caressing her skin, the small movement created a whirlwind of static electricity to spread through her. She caught his scent, the effect was intoxicating, she wanted her hands over him. Caressing his face, putting her hands through his hair, touching his strong, masculine frame.

"We could forget about it all, we belong together." Her voice shook outrageously as she said these words. She knew she couldn't handle the rejection that awaited, but she clung to the hope that he had given her.

He looked at her sadly with apologetic eyes and Jane knew her answer. Knew that Matthew didn't love her the same way she loved him.

"Why?" Jane asked, unashamed tears invaded her face, crashing violently to the ground.

"I can't explain it." He answered. Jane noticed tears were threatening his eyes, why was he doing this to them?

"You don't love me anymore." She squeaked, wondering had he ever loved her, staring at her feet rather than in to his magnetising stare.

There was silence. She looked up. He stared at her with heart rending sadness and she knew the answer. She reluctantly released her hand from his, knowing she would never touch that hand again, and walked away. The pain riddled through her like quick fire, threatening to buckle her knees and collapse her in to a heap in the middle of the store. She didn't look back.

A few days had passed since Jane's disastrous encounter with Matthew and she was no further on, if possible she was even more glum. Spending time with James only made her heart ache soar, it was a stark reminder that she would never even come close to finding what she had with Matthew for the rest of her life. But, she cherished the memories she had with him, reminding herself of the quote by Alfred Lord Tennyson; ''tis better to have loved and lost than never to have loved at all.'

Jane thought of herself as an old woman, looking back on the life she had lived and she was suddenly glad to have had Matthew, she could look back through her life and cherish that brief time in her life when she had experienced true love in its rawest form. Feeling grateful that she had experienced the kind of love only a few ever really find.

Jane arrived in the hospital car park the next day to start her day in work, she knew Millie was working and enjoyed spending break time with her. Millie was a fantastic midwife so they were a great team when together.

"How are things going with James?" Millie asked that morning, as they sat in the tea room before they started in to their gruelling thirteen hour shift.

"It's going ok, thanks." Jane answered, not really paying attention to the question, her thoughts permanently focused on Matthew.

"Are you guys an official item now?" Millie was being persistent.

"I'm not sure, we've only been on a few dates." Jane was non-committal to the James topic, James was a bridge to a better part of her life, a life where she could be moved on from Matthew and didn't feel excruciating pain every single moment of her waking day. She knew it was wrong of her to be this way, but she was fed up caring about others and their feelings, it had never gotten her anywhere.

"Do you think it's wise to be getting in to something so soon?" Millie continued.

"I'm not really getting in to anything, we aren't in a serious relationship, I'm just seeing where it goes and taking each day as it comes." Jane was tired of being scolded like a child every corner she turned, what was it to them? It was none of their business what she did in her personal life.

"But, what if James thinks it's serious?" Millie responded seriously, putting her mug up to her mouth and blowing on the hot liquid within.

"I have worried about that Millie, but if he becomes too emotionally involved then it's his own fault. I told him two weeks ago that I was just out of a long term relationship and wasn't looking for anything serious." Jane replied simply, as if that was a good enough excuse to continue leading someone on and toying with their emotions.

Millie was shocked at Jane's cold attitude and blatant disregard for another's feelings.

"Jane, you were both drunk that night you told him that, he probably doesn't remember, or thought you were just playing hard to get. He probably thinks he's in with a good chance now that you guys have been on a few dates."

Jane contemplated this for a moment, sipping on her hot tea. Jane had an infuser teapot and a stash of tea leaves in work also, refusing to tolerate low-grade teabags no matter where she was. Her work colleagues found this hilarious and called her 'posh', she didn't care though, tea was her thing and she wouldn't cheapen it just to fit in with other people.

She knew she was leading James on but was basing it on the knowledge that he had all the information and was entering in to the arrangement at his own risk, After a moment's silence, Millie continued;

"When are you next seeing James?"

"Tonight."

"Maybe you should have a conversation with him about where he sees this going." She wasn't giving up.

"I can't face it, Millie, I just want to relax and have fun, why does everything have to be so serious? I'm tired of this pressure." Jane asked, genuinely interested to know, plagued with fatigue of always having to explain her decisions.

"Because, there are people's feelings at stake here." Millie responded, as if this should be very obvious.

"I bumped in to Matthew yesterday." Jane blurted out, swiftly changing the topic. Millie's jaw dropped in comical shock.

"And you're only telling me *now?!*" She squealed. "Where? When? How?" She gasped, sitting up to attention, ears pricked to listen.

"Yesterday. At the supermarket." Jane replied sullenly.

"*And?!*" Millie demanded, on tenterhooks at the edge of her seat.

"I walked away, he looked so cold and distant, I couldn't bear to look at him so I moved to the next aisle and completely broke down. I was hysterical, Millie, in the middle of the supermarket in front of everyone." Jane explained, gulping down her rising emotions with sips of Earl Grey.

"I'm so sorry, sweetie." Millie walked over and sat beside Jane and put a consoling hand on her shoulder.

"But he followed me in to the next aisle." Jane continued, eyeing up her friend.

"*What?!* And you were crying at this point?" Millie gasped, her expression firm and concentrated, hanging on every word that spilled from Jane's mouth.

"Yes." Jane hung her head, Millie looked shocked, devastated for Jane. "I went to walk away again, humiliated by the situation," Millie nodded her head in understanding, "but he stopped me, asked was I running away from him," Millie looked as though she was watching her favourite television programme, eyes darting over Jane's face, tight lipped and sitting upright.

"He touched my hand and made small talk. I thought he was reconsidering things, he told me he missed me, apologised for what he had done. I said we should forget it and move on together. The look he gave me, Millie, it was earth shattering. I knew he was certain about the break up. I asked did he not love me and he couldn't even answer." Jane's lips trembled, Millie looked on, her eyes squinted in pity, her head tilted to one side in an attempt to look sympathetic.

"I've been racking my brain this few weeks wondering why he has done this when we had such a wonderful thing going on and he answered me today. He just didn't love me enough. The way I felt about him, he didn't feel towards me." The pain hit Jane hard like a stab in the chest, her breathing quickened, her pulse thudded rapidly, she could feel another panic attack looming. Not in work, she thought to herself.

190

Millie stared at her with the most pathetically solemn expression, tears brimming the edges of her eyes and her hand cupped tightly around Jane's.

"I'm so sorry, Jane, I can't imagine how you must be feeling."

Chapter 18

That evening, James was due to call over and Jane couldn't help but reminisce back to the first time Matthew had met her mother, Charlotte. Charlotte, in all her nervousness, had asked Matthew why he had chosen to become a paramedic rather than a doctor, only after, had she realised how offensive that had come across.

Jane secretly would love to have seen the look on Matthew's face when she was seen to be dating a doctor, she knew this was petty and pathetic but she wanted Matthew to feel as terrible as she did, for leaving her in this mess of misery and gloom. But, she also wanted Matthew to see her moved on, that he was ancient history to her, even though this could not have been further from the truth. Jane knew that Matthew would never find out, they didn't socialise in the same circles for the news to be delivered back to him.

James and Jane had just finished salmon and mashed potatoes with green beans and decided to tuck in to a bottle of Chianti (Jane's favourite), when James reached across and placed a wanton hand on to Jane's thigh, stroking softly in an attempt to appear seductive, Jane thought. Noticing where it was headed, Jane moved herself to the other sofa and thought of Millie's advice, she really should be honest and upfront.

"Look James, I haven't been totally honest with you." Jane started nervously, drawing her knees up to herself.

"Oh dear, this doesn't look like it's going in the direction that I wanted it to." Replied James, half jokingly, looking uncomfortable, disappointment coursed across his face.

"I know, I'm sorry, I just feel as more time passes and we are still dating that you should know that I'm not in a very good place. It's only been five weeks since my last relationship ended and it feels very sudden to be entering in to another one so quickly. I don't think it's fair on you for this to go on any longer when I'm just in a different place from you." Jane hugged her legs tightly and looked up at James apologetically.

Jane hadn't expected to break up with James when she started talking, but now that she thought about it, she didn't understand why it had even started.

"I understand, Jane, I'm not an idiot, I can see your sad expression some times and I know you are thinking of him. I was just hoping I could change that, make you forget about him and fall madly in love with me." He laughed sadly in to himself.

"Thanks for being so understanding, maybe if you are still single in six months you can call me up. God knows, I'll still be single!" She laughed, relaxing slightly.

"Look, no hard feelings, you are super hot and have a badass job with a cute personality, you're a real catch. But I know the timing isn't right. I just hope we can meet up again when the timing is right for you."

James got up to leave, he gave Jane a peck on the cheek and was away. Jane was relieved. That had felt relatively painless as far as break ups go. Maybe she had made a mistake. Maybe she should've just stayed with him and he might have grown on her? No. A feeling can't be forced just because on the

193

outside they tick all the boxes. She needed *that* feeling again the feeling only one person had ever given her.

Jane was in work the next day, her and Millie were completing their long day shift together. She felt invigorated and refreshed after breaking things off with James. She needed some time to herself, to figure her own head out. She had gone from being in a deep depression after things had ended with Matthew, to then plunging straight in to a semi serious relationship with James.

The only problem she was faced with now was that she was alone again; she didn't have a distraction from the heart wrenching pain that was the loss of Matthew and their beloved, unborn child. James had been an ideal divertissement, he had given her attention and affection, but Jane had to get to grips with herself. It wasn't the love and affection she was craving for, it was a quick fix. Tess had been right; she was only delaying the inevitable pain that would eventually raise its ugly head again.

All the same, she needed alone time, she needed quiet, she needed things to be simple and straightforward for the foreseeable future.

Jane and Millie had a very busy morning on the maternity ward; they worked specifically in the delivery suite of the maternity unit. There had been multiple natural deliveries that day that had all went fairly straightforward, and there had been two emergency caesarean sections, an unusually busy morning for only eleven o'clock. The two girls went to the break room for a well deserved cup of tea. Thankfully there was no one else around.

"How are things going with you, Jane?" Millie asked, as they sat down to cups of tea and biscuits, gifted to them by grateful, discharged patients.

"I'm actually doing ok, I'm feeling a bit better, I think. I'm just so happy to be back in my own house to some space and freedom." She sighed.

"I'm glad to hear it, Jane. How did James take the news?" She asked, gingerly taking a bite of a chocolate biscuit.

"He took it really well, he actually was a really nice guy, just bad timing." She explained, scoffing a chocolate chip cookie.

"Definitely not, you need to figure out your own head for the next few months before even considering dating anyone." She advised.

"Agreed, I'm officially off men for the foreseeable." She laughed, "how are things going with you and Oliver?" Jane asked, painfully aware that they always seemed to be talking about her and her issues.

"Yeah, really good, I really like him. It's easy and he's fun." She smiled thoughtfully.

"That's brilliant, I'm so happy for you guys." Jane meant this sincerely. "How long have you guys been going out for now?"

"Nearly two years. And no, before you ask, we don't have any plans to get engaged any time soon." She laughed and rolled her eyes melodramatically.

"Getting a lot of hassle about that?" Jane surmised.

"*A lot* of hassle! My mum can't understand why we aren't engaged yet. It's a lot of pressure, you know? If we are happy why do we need to rush anything? It hasn't even been two years as well, surely that's too quick for a proposal?" Millie begged, her brow creased in frustration.

"You and Oliver should do whatever makes you both feel happy, pressuring you both in to doing something neither of you are ready for seems like a stupid idea to me. Mother and daughter relationships can be difficult." Jane had a good relationship with her mother but she knew that Charlotte could be overbearing at times. Jane couldn't blame Charlotte, though, her worries were justified following violent and abusive visits to her aunt and uncle as a child, unknowingly facilitated by her mother and father.

"You are definitely right there!" Millie breathed in exasperation.

"Obviously!"

Millie and Jane headed back out to the delivery suite, there was a patient due in at twelve o'clock. The two girls were both setting up the room for her arrival. Valerie Thompson appeared at the door of the patient's room, sitting in a wheelchair, escorted by a porter along with a tall, kind looking man who Jane presumed was Valerie's husband.

At first glance, Jane was immediately concerned, Valerie was as white as a sheet, her eyelids were heavy with fatigue, a layer of clammy beads traced her brow and she was breathing rapidly;

"Hi Valerie, I'm Jane, I'll be your midwife today. This is my colleague, Millie." Jane pointed towards Millie.

"Hi, thank you so much." Valerie gasped through breathless words.

Jane and Millie helped Valerie up on to the bed.

"How long have been feeling unwell for, Valerie?" Jane asked, not taking her eyes off the unwell patient.

"About an hour. Around the time my contractions started." She breathed.

"Any bleeding?"

"Just some spotting."

Jane attached a sphygmomanometer on to Valerie's arm and placed a pulse oximeter on to her finger to check her blood pressure, pulse and oxygen levels. Jane placed the two prongs of a stethoscope in to her ears.

"Your blood pressure is eighty over fifty, your pulse is one hundred and twenty. I think you might be having a heavy internal bleed, it's called a haemorrhage. It's fairly common when you're in labour but I want to give you some fluids just to ensure your blood pressure doesn't drop any further. Is that ok?"

"Yes, of course. Will everything be ok?" Valerie asked anxiously, her eyes wide with terror and beads of sweat trickled down her forehead.

"Yes, we're going to take care of you and your baby here. All will be ok." Jane hated making promises, but she needed to keep Valerie calm. She couldn't see any reason to stress Valerie out any further, they had to keep mother and baby as relaxed as possible at this crucial time.

Jane quickly inserted an intravenous cannula in to Valerie's arm, Millie ran off to alert the doctor. In emergency situations, Jane knew that she would need to start a fluid resus before a prescription could be written by a doctor, in order to replace some of the already lost fluid. Jane sent urgent bloods to the lab to be cross matched for packed red cells in the event that Valerie would need a blood transfusion.

Jane attached a transducer to Valerie's abdomen in order to monitor the foetal heart beat.

"One hundred and forty beats per minute, your baby has a healthy heart." Jane explained.

"Oh, thanks goodness!" Valerie wailed through painful breaths.

Next, Jane physically examined the position of the baby by palpating Valerie's abdomen and performing an internal exam.

"Your baby appears to be in the correct position, they are head down and in the birth canal. You are six centimetres dilated, you are quite far along. So far, it is all looking good for baby. Just need to stabilise your blood pressure and all will go smoothly from then on." Jane explained, trying to come across as calm and reassuring.

Jane did not feel reassured though, Valerie had turned grey. Where was the doctor? Millie hadn't come back yet, either, she could do with some back up right at that moment.

"Are the contractions becoming painful?" Jane asked her, creating a distraction.

"They are ok, not great," she laughed, "but ok."

"There is some Entonox beside you if you ever need to use it. Sorry, I mean gas and air." Jane explained in layman terms when Valerie gave her a confused expression. "You will get the most benefit out of the gas and air if you take long, deep breaths of it, in and out, fairly slowly. If you breathe too rapidly your body won't absorb it as effectively."

Just then, Valerie's eyes rolled to the back of her head, her body flopped to one side and her husband caught her just in time as her body went limp. Jane saw the blood gushing from between her legs, she pulled the emergency buzzer and shouted for help. She then applied oxygen at fifteen litres per minute via a non-rebreather face mask. Jane was then surrounded by the staff on the ward, including the doctor that Millie had been trying to get a hold of.

Millie contacted the lab and requested an emergency dispensing of packed red cells to be sent immediately. Valerie was given multiple infusions of intravenous fluids, delivered extremely quickly via a peristaltic pump. The blood arrived, she and Millie double checked the bags, ensuring that it was the correct blood and correct blood type for the patient, Jane manually squeezed these in as fast as she could. The doctor, meanwhile, was examining for foetal movement and establishing if there was any further bleeding. Millie was reassuring Valerie's husband that everything was under control.

Valerie started to come round; she lay feebly in the bed, her husband clutched at her hand, his expression wretched, his eyes with tears. The doctor approached Jane;

"We need to go for an emergency C section, she's ten centimetres dilated, we need to go now. I don't think she would survive a natural delivery." He wiped sweat from his brow.

The doctor ran off to check the availability of the emergency theatres and to inform them that they would be transferring an emergency caesarian section right away. Jane approached Valerie;

"How are you feeling?" She stroked Valerie's hair.

"I'm ok, how's my baby? Are they ok?" She asked urgently, her voice panic stricken.

"You haven't given birth yet, you are quite far along, the doctor thinks that because you lost so much blood that it would be better to perform a caesarean section." Jane explained, trying not to stir alarm.

199

"I really wanted to deliver naturally." She cried.

"You are very weak and have lost a lot of blood, you might not survive any further blood loss. We have given you five blood transfusions already." She glared at her seriously.

Valerie looked horrified, "Ok. I trust you guys. Thank you." She squeaked. Her husband continued to squeeze her hand and kissed her face tenderly.

Jane and Millie escorted Valerie, on the hospital bed, over to the emergency theatre, they both scrubbed in and prepared for surgery. Valerie's husband, Dave, was allowed to enter the theatre despite the emergency situation. An epidural was inserted in to Valerie's back and a large barricade was placed between Valerie's head and her abdomen in order for her not to see the surgery being performed. Valerie's infusions of blood and fluid rapidly continued on either arm to try to compensate for the extensive blood loss.

It was a tense few minutes while the doctors performed the surgery. Jane and Millie passed the various, quickly demanded, instruments. The baby was lifted out of the abdomen, along with umbilical cord and placenta. But, no noise, no crying. The baby was handed over to Jane who quickly wrapped the bundle in towels and took it over to the nearest procedure table and began to rub the baby's back vigorously to try to stimulate the lungs in to breathing.

Nothing. Jane was panicking. Sweat beaded her forehead. Was she going to be handing over a stillborn baby to Valerie? Then, that sweet noise, crying. There were cries of relief all round. Jane had tears streaming down her face. Valerie begged to hold her baby. Jane gladly obliged.

An incubator had been reserved in the neonatal unit after Valerie had first taken unwell, earlier in the day, in the likelihood that the baby would be in distress during labour and birth. Jane quickly presented the new baby to Valerie but said she had to take them away for assessments.

"You have a baby girl, Valerie." Valerie was convulsing with tears, she wanted her baby in her arms.

Dave stroked her hair and cried silently with her, the pain and worry was obvious. Millie consoled them both while Jane whisked away. The doctor stitched up the open wound in Valerie's abdomen.

Valerie's baby only ended up staying in the neonatal unit for one hour, she was doing well, her lungs were working independently and she was very strong. Jane brought the little baby back to the room Valerie had been transferred to. She entered the room carrying the tiny baby and presented her to her new mum and dad.

Valerie wailed loudly with tears of happiness and exhaustion and practically clawed her baby in to her arms, holding the baby close to her with all her might.

"Jane, I don't know how to thank you. You saved us both." Valerie cried, smiling gratefully up at her.

"All in a day's work!" Jane smiled endearingly, "I'm so happy for you guys. This guy needs to look after you both for the next while; you have been through a major trauma." She pointed to Valerie's husband, Dave, and winked at him.

"She'll be back vacuuming the house from tomorrow," he joked, "don't worry, I'll take care of everything, I'm just so glad you are both ok." He cradled his wife and new baby very tenderly.

It was a beautiful scene and Jane could feel the tears prickling her eyes again. She made her excuses and left the room to start the heavy paper work that entailed.

201

"I think we deserve a cup of tea now, I would think." Millie sighed in relief.

Chapter 19

Jane returned home that evening to the dogs who bounced up and down unrestrainedly at her arrival, she greeted them with hugs and in return got a sizeable quantity of slobbery kisses to her face. Tess was a stay at home mum, therefore, if Jane was ever working long days, Tess was only too happy to mind the dogs while she was at work. Tess had reminded Jane that it was good all round for everyone as it delayed her ever having to get a dog.

"The children are too young at the moment." She had said to Jane. "It would be too much work, three small children and a puppy. At least your two keep them happy for the meantime, I'm not sure how long that will last, though."

A typical evening for Jane was spent sitting with her feet up, usually accompanied by a glass of red wine or a cup of tea and Ruby and Jack squeezed in beside her, competing for prime position on Mummy's lap. She normally liked to curl up on the sofa with a good book or sometimes a movie. Currently, she was reading a series of period drama novels, these stories had the power to whisk her off to another time and place, an escape from the current world she was living in.

She loved the romance, the heart break, the suspense and the drama. When Jane was at work she wished she was reading, often staying up late to squeeze in just one more chapter.

When she took the dogs on their daily walk she would often squeeze a book in to her coat pocket to read on the walk. On occasion she would go to the nearby forest park and just sit on the bench and read, the dogs were happy to run around and sniff the open air while Jane occasionally threw them a ball.

Jane was out for her daily walk, four months after ending things with James, she had just finished a half day in work. She never went back to *that* beach again in the fear of running in to Matthew. Instead, she regularly went to the forest park nearby, there were no painful memories there, no reminders of that fateful day when she had first laid eyes on the mysterious stranger from the bar and her world had changed forever.

No, in the forest she could admire the large trees and breathe the fresh air, it was generally very quiet as most dog walkers used the beach, which suited Jane perfectly. She enjoyed a quiet walk, just her and the dogs, where she could enjoy their playful innocence. How she longed to have so little worries as that of a dog, no cares in the world, living each day as it comes and as though it was the last, enjoying every blade of grass and every sniff of those scented flowers, it really was a dog's life.

Not a day had gone by that Jane hadn't thought of Matthew. The acute pain of the loss was now easing but had left a dull ache in the centre of her chest. She missed his smell, his magnetising charisma, his silly jokes and the way she felt utterly amazing around him. He had the ability to make her feel like the only woman in the world. But, she had forced herself to not think of Matthew, to move past and get on with her life. She *had* to. She had no other choice. Jane was sure, though, that the feeling Matthew had given her, would be like no other.

Jane was sitting on her usual bench with one eye on her book and the other on the dogs, when her thoughts were interrupted by shouting nearby;

"Hunter! Hunter!" Screamed a stranger maniacally, not within Jane's sight. *"HUNTER!"*

Jane craned her neck to see where the calamity was coming from, ousting her book away. Whoever was screaming sounded as though they were in a real panic.

Just then, dashing round the corner, came a massive Black Labrador, bounding straight towards her. Ruby, Jane's smallest dog, noticed the excitement and charged straight in to the path of the Labrador. The big dog fired on his breaks and skidded to a stop, overwhelmed and slightly concerned about the new, feisty intruder in his path.

Jane's dogs were pleasant and always eager to play with other dogs, the Labrador was not so sure of them at first, but quickly started to relax and join in. A moment later, a young man came running round the corner, obviously the culprit who had been calling for *'Hunter'*.

"Sorry about him, he's only ten months old and I can't normally let him off the lead because, well, you can see why." The stranger laughed breathlessly as he came to a stop in front of her. Jane noticed that he was tremendously attractive as he flicked his hair off his face, an act that left Jane feeling weak at the knees.

"I wouldn't worry." She squeaked nervously, trying to nonchalantly fix her hair that she hadn't even bothered brushing that morning.

"So, these are your two? How do you get them to behave?" The handsome stranger asked.

"They're a bit older, they definitely had their moments when they were puppies." Jane smirked and glanced nervously up at him.

"Oh, that's a relief." He was still trying to catch his breath after running. "One is a bit of a struggle at the minute, I don't think I could handle another."

"They're great, actually, they keep each other occupied, they're never lonely. If they were puppies now I think that might be a different story." She chuckled.

"True, puppies are a handful, as I'm experiencing with this one." He pointed toward Hunter, then smoothed his hair back again.

"He'll calm down as he gets older." She explained, she stared at him in awe, mouth gaping slightly, feeling idiotic.

"Sorry, I haven't introduced myself, I'm Theo." He showed his teeth in a breathtaking, knee quaking smile.

"I'm Jane." She blushed at the introduction.

"Nice to meet you, Jane."

"You too." She smiled. Were they flirting? Jane couldn't be sure, it had been that long since she had been in the company of a man. She shuffled nervously, was this just mere small talk or was he interested?

Their stare lingered upon one another, Jane felt her heart give a flutter. She broke the silence; "Well, hope you get on alright with the puppy training."

"Thanks." He inhaled, apparently lost for words.

"Maybe see you around." Jane made to turn away, Theo stood looking at her for a moment, she stopped, swivelled on the spot, staring at him curiously. He appeared as though he had something to say but wasn't quite sure how to word it.

"Would it be forward of me," he started hesitantly, clearing his throat, "to ask you for your number? I just don't know when we'll next bump in to each other." He looked up at her nervously, fiddling with Hunter's dog lead.

Jane smiled, she was hoping he would ask. "Of course."

"Great! I'll text you." He smiled widely.

"Bye Theo."

"Bye Jane." Jane walked away, stifling an excited scream, smiling ridiculously.

Later that day, Jane was feeling the best she had felt in a long time. "Oh, Theo." She thought to herself. How comfortable she immediately felt around him and how lovely and goofy his big dog Hunter was. She liked him. He had an allure that was compelling and mesmerising, with his bright, greyish blue eyes and irresistible, charming smile. He liked dogs too, he seemed to be the perfect package. Was she to meet all her future lovers on dog walks? Well, if that was the only public excursion she went on, then, she surmised, that it was probably her only option. A good option too, Jane thought, as having a passion for dogs was a must if anyone was going to date Jane Abbott.

Jane seemed to realise over the last couple of months that she had been feeling rather good, she had thought of Matthew but hadn't had the horrendous stabs of pain each time she did, and she had been on several nights out with the girls. They had chosen a different watering hole just outside the village in order to avoid bumping in to the ever growing list of Jane's lovers. Life was good, she had her dogs, her job, her friends, family and her home. She had recently redecorated her house, it was a much needed facelift after having it rented out to strangers, she wasn't ashamed to admit that she used James' house as inspiration for some of her changes.

The meeting with Theo had come at exactly the right time when Jane had come to terms with the miscarriage and had learnt how to live without Matthew. Theo had said he would be in contact to arrange an organised dog walk. Jane thought this was very endearing, no fancy restaurant offerings or expensive cocktails, just welly boots and dog walking – *perfect*. Theo was not Jane's usual type, in appearance, as she seemed to normally be drawn to men with dark hair and dark eyes, but Theo had a surfer style look about him that was so breathtaking that she felt she could waver from her usual 'type' just that once.

They met four days later at the same spot for their arranged dog walk. Conversation flowed well, Theo found it refreshing to find a girl who was happy to tie back her hair, stick on a pair of wellies and not be afraid to get her feet wet. He was captivated by her green eyes that lit up like emeralds when she smiled, he also admired her incredible figure and roundly backside, that he took the opportunity to glance at whenever possible. Jane noticed Theo's lingering stare and found her interest piqued, Theo had sex appeal and she was satisfied to see that the feeling was mutual.

Theo's parents had divorced when he was younger also and he had one younger sister. Jane felt as though her and Theo could relate to one another, both from broken families as young children. She had often felt twinges of envy towards Matthew's normal and pleasant upbringing. With Theo he had a damaged quality also, would he be more capable of relating to the extent of her past if she ever decided to reveal it to him?

Theo was an accountant. "Thank goodness." Thought Jane. She had dated enough medical staff to last her a lifetime.

"My parents separated when I was eleven," Jane explained, "it was horrible. They fought all the time. Home was never a happy place when they were together. Then they split up and life was much easier after that, mum was so much more relaxed and dad settled down quite quickly with his current wife, they are great match, better than my mum and dad ever were. Anyway, I'm rambling, this is probably very boring for you." She said quickly as they walked side by side along a path in the dense forest, dodging puddles and thick patches of mud. She glanced nervously at him. What had gotten in to her? To tell him so much so suddenly was incredibly out of character.

"I like learning about you, Jane. Don't be afraid to tell me *anything*. I'm sorry your childhood was rocky at the start." He replied kindly, his eyes trained seriously on her as he took long strides in knee high welly boots.

"Thanks, it's not something I talk about with too many people, *especially* on a first date." She laughed awkwardly. "It's a bit of a sore topic."

"How come?" He asked, staring at her with deep interest, his gaze was unnerving.

"Well, there was a little more that went on that I'm not really comfortable telling anyone." She said nervously, why was she saying all this? She had to stop herself, she felt herself blush outrageously.

"Well, there's no pressure from me to talk about anything right now. Have you ever spoken to anyone?" He asked, concern etched the lines in his face.

"Not really." She lied, there was no need to bring Matthew up that day. Plus, she hated the thought of having to deal with a jealous man. What if she told Theo that she had told her ex her deepest, darkest secrets but wasn't willing to tell him? It wouldn't go down well, plus, it was only their *first* date, she had to reign herself in.

"Gosh, so you keep it all to yourself? Have you ever considered counselling?"

"Well, I went as a child, but not as an adult, I'm not crazy or anything, it's just never really come up or I've never found the right words to articulate it, I also worry that whoever I tell will judge me profusely or break my trust by telling others." She explained. What was she doing? She begged with herself to change the conversation.

His brows jumped. "Must be pretty serious." Jane's throat parched, restricting her reply. "Well, your secret would be safe with me if you ever felt like revealing it." He continued, looking at her sincerely.

"Thank you, you're very sweet. Gosh, this is all very serious for a first date! I'm sorry, I don't normally get on like this." She put her face in her hands, mortified with embarrassment, attempting to hide the crimson colour spreading over her cheeks.

"No need to apologise, my upbringing wasn't exactly straightforward either so I can understand how you're feeling. We're all different and all have different life experiences, some harder than others." Jane looked at him with immense respect, this guy was incredible.

Jane got home after her date with Theo, she gave the dogs a much needed bath. She had time then to reflect on the date; she was horrified with herself. How could she have babbled on so rigorously about her parents' marriage? He probably thought she was a complete lunatic.

"Asking me if I would ever consider counselling, *jeez*, I'm such a bloody idiot!" Jane said out loud to her self, as she washed Jack in the bath. Jack was giving Jane his best subdued face, surrendering to the terrible ordeal he was having to suffer through, despite being more than happy to jump in to freezing, cold puddles and lakes. Oh, no, bath time was *torture*.

Jane was sure that she would definitely never hear back from Theo again, and if she did, she would probably be too embarrassed to ever lay on eyes on him again.

Jane was meeting up, that weekend, with her mother, Charlotte. The two spent a great deal of time together, Charlotte was always making excuses to see Jane. Jane knew that her mother worried terribly about her and wanted to know her every movement, at all times. Jane often wondered if Charlotte worried that her aunt and uncle would come back for Jane in a further attempt to hurt her. It was the only explanation for her overbearing behaviour.

Jane loved having such a strong bond with her mother, they could share their deepest, darkest secrets with each other, she felt she had a mother and a friend. Jane couldn't deny that the constant need for contact was frustrating at times, but she knew her mother meant well and had a maternal concern for her.

Jane allowed her mother to have her stalker tendencies, she wanted Charlotte to know that she didn't blame her for the time she had endured with her aunt and uncle. Jane carried around a lot of guilt, she had possessed a lot of resentment

211

towards her parents, feeling that they had allowed the abuse to go on right under their noses. Jane punished them for this by not talking to them for a long time after she had moved out of home at eighteen. Now Jane was making up for lost time.

Jane and Charlotte were meeting at Clovelly Coffee that afternoon, a coffee shop in the village, Jane tried to dress fashionably and find clothes that had a slimming affect. She knew that her mother would be looking glamorous and pristine; Jane idolised her. Jane arrived just a couple of minutes late and entered the charming coffee shop in the centre of the village, it was filled with plush grey booths, tiled white flooring and artful, pendant lights on the ceiling. The place looked warm and welcoming whilst appearing classy and expensive at the same time. Jane loved it there as they served the most delicious coffee, a faithful tea drinker, she had never found anywhere close enough to convert her to coffee apart from this place and then, of course, her brief stint with James also, his coffee creations had been incredible.

Jane's mum was sitting in a corner booth waiting for her. She was wearing a tight, navy pencil dress with killer black heels and a faux fur coat. She had dyed blonde hair tied tightly back off her face in to a neat bun, her nails were perfectly manicured and her make up was applied flawlessly. She sat with perfect posture and stared around at the goings ons surrounding her. Her eyes fell upon Jane and her face lit up in delight, smiling as she approached.

"Hi mum, sorry I'm a late." Jane said, leaning in and kissing her mother on the cheek and taking a seat opposite her.

"Hi, Jane. Not to worry." Charlotte took in all of Jane's appearance, eyeing her up from top to bottom, studying what she was wearing.

"Jane, you look positively radiant." She smiled, beaming at her proudly.

"Thanks mum." Jane giggled, appreciating the compliment. "You look well too, mum."

"Thank you, dear. I've lost four pounds, you can really notice how thin I am now, can't you?" She smoothed down her dress to highlight her slim waist.

"Yes, you look great." This was common practice; Charlotte was always trying out the latest fad diet and kept Jane up to date with her latest progress. Jane wished her mum could let her hair down and not worry about her appearance just so much.

"You look slim, Jane. Are you stressed?" Charlotte asked anxiously, tugging at Jane's loose jeans.

"No mum, I weigh just the same, but thank you." Jane smiled, who didn't want to be called thin? "How's Bob?"

"He's doing great, he's at work, trying to butter up the boss for a partner position at the estate agency." Charlotte babbled affectionately. Charlotte prided herself in the calibre of men she obtained, it pleased Charlotte that Bob was trying to climb the ladder in work. Just then, a young, female waiter approached to take their order. Charlotte ordered an Americano without milk, Jane ordered a cappuccino and a blueberry muffin.

"Are you seeing anyone at the minute?" Charlotte continued once the waitress had left, looking intrigued and excited.

"No, well... not really." She answered, already regretting giving away too much. Her mother looked at her curiously.

"What does that mean?" She commanded an answer.

"I've been on one date with a guy, Theo, he seems really nice." Jane wasn't sure if she was jumping the gun by

213

revealing Theo to other people after just one date, but she had a good feeling about him, despite her impromptu and premature outburst.

Charlotte stared at Jane anxiously, Jane knew that her mother would be irrationally concerned about future lovers after the disastrous break up and subsequent heartache that proceeded Matthew. Just then the coffees and muffin arrived, they took long, grateful sips.

"You like this guy?" Charlotte eyed her seriously as she set her cup back down, she glared enviously at the muffin Jane was picking at.

"It's probably too soon to tell, but on first impressions, he ticks all the relevant boxes." Jane blushed through mouthfuls.

"You mean he's hot?" Charlotte stated unblinkingly. The girls then burst in to fits of laughter.

"Well, you could say that." Jane chuckled excitedly, feeling immensely embarrassed having a conversation like that with her mother.

"And what does he work as?" Charlotte asked, beaming at her daughter.

"He's an accountant."

"Brilliant, a man with stable hours, that will be refreshing. Pays well to be an accountant too, bag that one while you can." Charlotte winked.

Jane was immensely proud of her career, it was extremely stressful with very long hours, often missing lunch and tea breaks but she was able to make a difference in the world. Jane knew her mother wanted her to find a man with a wealthy career, she wanted her daughter to have security and little worries in her life. Jane understood this but she wanted to be able to make a living for herself, she didn't want to be dependent on someone else for a nice house or regular holidays.

Jane made a great wage as a midwife and had a comfortable life. She had little ambition to aim for a promotion because her only move up, after midwife, was to transfer in to a managerial role, that was hell on earth in Jane's mind. Audits and meetings and staff off duty, dealing with staff dynamics, staff sickness and getting shifts covered. It wasn't for Jane, she wanted to be in the thick of it, on the front line, making a difference to people's lives. Being that go to person that families turned to when they needed help, providing a hand to hold or a shoulder to cry on. Jane loved her job and she knew she was good at it.

Jane offered her mother some muffin but Charlotte declined, Jane didn't like to overeat in front of her. They chatted happily about any recent gossip and departed with hugs and kisses. Jane left feeling even more excited about Theo, if Charlotte was happy then she was happy.

Chapter 20

Jane got home that Saturday afternoon following coffee with her mother, she instinctively made herself a cup of tea, opting for her faithful Nilgiri, before she took the dogs out for their walk, she knew the fresh air and the company of her dogs would distract her from desperately wondering why Theo hadn't been in contact with her yet.

Jane had been intermittently checking her phone throughout the day to see if she had heard from Theo; nothing, no big surprise there. It may have been the twenty first century, but Jane was a firm believer that some old traditions should stay in place, for example; a guy being the first to contact the girl after a date.

If the girl was to contact the guy first, in Jane's opinion, it came across as so horrendously desperate and needy. Jane would never do it. But she was feeling impatient, Theo was the first person who had sparked fervour within her since Matthew.

Jane's phone rang, startling her, she quickly set down her cup of tea and scrambled to retrieve it from her pocket but it was an unknown number. She didn't normally answer these.

"Hello?" She decided against her better judgement to answer.

"Hey Jane! It's Theo. Sorry, I'm using my mum's phone, I dropped mine in a puddle this morning when I was out walking Hunter." He puffed irritably. Jane skipped on the spot, she couldn't hide her delight at finally hearing from Theo, and he had a valid excuse for not contacting her until now. *Hallelujah*, he hadn't been completely put off.

"Oh, no! What a disaster! I had lunch with my mum, I'm only getting my two out now." She tried to stave the overexcitement in her tone.

"I need to get Hunter out of the house first thing; he's crazy otherwise." He sighed, half laughing, but primarily sounding exceedingly exasperated.

"The joys of the puppy stage. How's things?" She asked, trying her best to ooze confidence and coolness and all the while trying to steady the nervous shake to her voice.

"All good, was really just wanting to phone and see if you maybe wanted to go out again some time soon?" He sounded apprehensive as he asked. Jane found his nerves endearing.

"Oh, *really?* After yesterday? I didn't completely put you off?" She cringed at the thought, genuinely shocked that he would want to see her after her display of verbal diarrhoea, on a first date, too.

"Quite the opposite." Jane felt so relieved and excited at the prospect of seeing Theo again.

For their second date, Jane and Theo met at a quant pub right by the water's edge and sat outside as it was a dry evening. Jane had been nervous about meeting Theo, she still had reservations ever since Matthew had successfully trampled all over her heart and left her to scrap the pieces back together. Could she ever love like that again? Could she ever trust

217

again? She still thought of Matthew everyday and yearned for that feeling of overwhelming love and passion. But, she had learned to move on and the acute pain had mostly subsided.

Theo was equally as attractive as Matthew and she definitely got butterflies when she was around him, it would just take time to get over the sensation Matthew had given her and she had to try to stop comparing him to the other men she met. Matthew had set a standard that all future men had to live up to, Jane had to stop this in its tracks, it wasn't fair on potential suitors if Jane was perpetually stacking the odds against them, convincing herself that she would never find a love resembling that of Matthew's.

"I have to apologise, Theo, for my outburst of confessions the last day we met. It's really not like me. I think I just trusted that you were a good person." She confessed, straightening her skirt nervously. Jane had opted for a skater style skirt and a fitted blouse, with kitten heels, accessorised with a simple bracelet. Jane had always been a minimalist

"I like that you feel that way." He smiled. "And I like to think that I am." Theo was looking suave in an open collar shirt and fitted designer jeans, his hair was sleeked with gel stylishly off his face.

"Anyway, now that it's out of the way," she mocked severe embarrassment, covering her face with her hand, "how about you tell me a bit about yourself instead."

They sipped on crisp, white wine and ate pasta by the water. Jane was transfixed by Theo's face and the passionate way he spoke of life and work and family. He genuinely seemed like a pleasant and virtuous person with a killer smile and an equally amazing body; as Jane could postulate from his stature and shape. The attraction had been instantaneous.

218

Things progressed quickly between Theo and Jane over the proceeding six months, they enjoyed the out door life together. Regularly going for hikes at nearby peaks and taking long weekends to go camping with the dogs. Theo was thirty six and therefore had been clear from the start on what he wanted out of life; a family. Jane respected his honesty.

They were both out for one of their daily walks by the beach and were having a deep discussion about their future;

"I'm just not sure what I want." Jane declared one Saturday afternoon they had off together. The pain of her miscarriage always remained in the forefront of her mind, she was sure she could never go through an ordeal like that again. It was too distressing. Therefore, the thought of becoming pregnant and risking a miscarriage again was just a ridiculous concept to Jane.

"You don't want to get married?" Theo asked, his eyebrows raised in surprise. Surely all girls dream of their wedding day?

"I don't mind the idea of marriage." Jane replied candidly, throwing a ball in to the ocean for Jack. Jack sped off with all his might, racing to retrieve his treasured ball.

"So, it's children you don't want?" Theo asked in surprise. It was uncommon to come across a woman who wasn't desperate for children, especially one who was in their thirties.

"I used to not want to have children. Now I'm not so sure. Oh dear, I might as well tell you." Jane looked up at him nervously, was she really going to tell him this?

"Tell me what?" Theo's face was lined with confusion and apprehension, the wind whipped his beautiful hair away from his face, revealing his almighty handsomeness.

"I've been pregnant before." Jane stopped a moment, gulping down her nerves and glancing at Theo to gauge his reaction. He looked stunned. Jane looked away and continued, finding it easier to stare out at the ocean as she spoke;

"But I lost it, I had a miscarriage at eleven weeks." Jane swallowed back the ball in her throat, she hadn't spoke of her miscarriage in a long time. Talking about it felt good, though, she wanted the child she almost had, to be remembered.

"Oh my goodness, Jane! I'm so sorry!" Theo replied alarmingly, emotion rippled across his face and he put a consoling arm around her and eyed her up pitifully, his blue, grey eyes reflecting the depths of the ocean. She smiled sadly at him, lost for words.

"You should've told me before, I would've understood your reservation about having children."

"Really?" Jane asked in amazement.

"Of course, you must be so anxious about becoming pregnant again in case the same thing would happen." It was as though he had read her mind.

"I would be very anxious, I don't think I could go through something like that again. It destroyed the relationship I had been in before. I wouldn't want it to ruin what we have now." She felt tears threatening as she relived that horrendous chapter of her life.

"Of course, we have only started out in our relationship; there's no pressure for any decision right now." Jane was relieved by Theo's understanding of her situation, appreciative that she wouldn't feel pressured, and beyond happy that he was not put off by her past.

"I would tell you, though, that children are something that I see in my future." Theo said truthfully, glancing sideways at her. "But, not right at this moment."

"Good. I'm not ready for right this moment. Plus, as you say, we are early on in our relationship. This is heavy stuff." She puffed her cheeks in mock exasperation. Theo gently squeezed her hand and they continued their walk, confident in the knowledge that their future together was headed in the right direction.

Jennifer gave everyone a shock when she revealed the exciting news to Millie, Martha and Jane, that she was engaged. They had met at Jane's house for one of their monthly catch ups. They normally met at each others' houses or the pub when they got together. If the girls wanted a proper chat it was always easier to go to someone's house, there was less noise and no desperate men approaching them in a bid to 'get lucky.' Jane had her electric fire on, sending heat through the living room, and they had a cup of tea in hand as they all planned on driving home that evening.

Jane had prepared the girls a Phoenix Tea blend, a variety of Oolong Tea, Jane enjoyed this for its similarities to Black Tea blends but its health benefits similar to Green Tea. Millie, Martha and Jennifer enjoyed the experience of sampling Jane's many tea preferences, some of the different tea blends, however, were a bit out there for the girls, the Assam tea blend was strong and had a viscous texture, not much to the girls' likings. That night Jane had opted for one that would be sure to agree with everyone.

"Jennifer! You're engaged?!" Martha repeated in utter bewilderment, curled up on the sofa like a cat.

221

"I know! It's so exciting, isn't it!" Jennifer screeched happily, clapping her hands together.

"It's brilliant news, Jennifer. How did he do it?!" Jane shrieked in delight, her knees folded up to her chest, her eyes wide with enthusiasm, happy for her young friend.

"But you're only twenty four, Jennifer. Are you not a bit young?!" Cried Martha quickly. Martha was always jealous of others' happiness, still battling on in her loveless marriage. If it were possible, she was even more bitter and resentful.

"Well, we have been together over a year and we are happy together, what else do we need, really?" Said Jennifer, feeling a little hurt at the negative response, but not altogether surprised.

"Don't worry Jennifer, I think it's brilliant news. Shush you Martha, no need for any negativity today!" Millie admonished, throwing Martha a warning look.

"I'm sorry, Jennifer, I was just a little surprised, that's all. It's happening very fast." She reclined back in to the sofa, as though she were a scolded child.

"So, when's the big day?" Jane asked, diverting the attention away from Martha.

"Three months tomorrow!" The excitement returned to her face, lighting her up.

"My goodness, that *is* very fast!" Millie couldn't deny her shock, she glared at Jennifer seriously.

"Why the rush?" Jane asked. It wasn't a lot of time to plan a wedding, Jane wondered was there another reason she would want it to happen so fast.

"Well, we do have other news!" She said with glee, fidgeting excitedly in her seat.

"You're pregnant!" Screamed Martha, looking astonished and supercilious.

"Well... Yes! I'm pregnant!" Jennifer said somewhat defeatedly, feeling as though her big reveal had been taken from her by Martha getting to the point first.

"Oh, my goodness, Jennifer! Congratulations sweetie!" Millie screamed hysterically.

"Amazing news, Jennifer!" Jane said happily, running over and squeezing her friend in to a tight hug. "So, so happy for you!" She whispered in to Jennifer's ear.

The girls all clutched Jennifer viciously and babbled excitedly about all the exhilarating events that were to take place.

"I hope you aren't getting married just because you are pregnant! That's a one way ticket to divorce." Martha said earnestly, a crease in her brow and her arms folded, looking defensive and judgemental.

"Thank you, Martha, once again, for your kind words." Jennifer brushed off, yet again, another outspoken and unwanted comment and carried on;

"Well, to be truthful, I think it definitely did give Ben the encouragement to propose sooner." Jennifer admitted. "But, he did say he had been thinking about it for a while. He already had a ring and everything." She glanced around the room for approval.

"I took the pregnancy test and couldn't believe that it was positive, I waited until Ben got home from work, then I showed him the test. He instantly dropped to one knee and asked me to marry him. We both laughed and cried; we were so happy. I am very young to be having a child, I know, but

I'm so lucky to have Ben to share this journey with." She smiled a contented smile and looked up at the three girls.

"Oh, Jennifer! I'm so glad that you're happy and everything has worked out for you." Jane looked sincerely at her friend, grabbing her hand and squeezing it tightly. Jennifer smiled broadly, tears loomed behind gleaming eyes.

"Thank you, Jane." Jennifer appreciated that this would be arduous for Jane, there had been a time when Jane was the one announcing pregnancy news to her friends, yet, she had no baby to account for.

"How far along are you?" Millie asked, smiling widely. The three friends were sat huddled together on the one sofa, Martha was sat alone on the other.

"Three and a half months." Jane felt the tiniest surge of jealously ripple through her. Jennifer was already past the dreaded first twelve weeks of pregnancy where you are most likely to suffer from a miscarriage.

"Are you not bothered that you will be *quite* pregnant when you get married?" All three of them swivelled their heads to look round at Martha, their expressions dripping in shock.

"You're on a roll today." Jane shot an annoyed look at her friend for her lack of tact and the hurt she would be causing Jennifer on a day she should be nothing but happy.

"What is your issue?" Demanded Jennifer, now looking outraged, a deep crease forming in her brow.

"You have been nothing but callous and bitter ever since I announced my pregnancy and engagement. Are you that caught up in your own rubbish life that you can't even be a little happy for me? It's not my fault that your husband isn't interested in you anymore, maybe he would be if you weren't always looking at the negative side of every goddamn little thing!" Jennifer screeched, breathless and exasperated. Visibly angry at her friend and annoyed that her evening had been tainted by someone who was supposed to care about her.

Martha sat staring fixedly in silence, in apparent shock at the display of anger. They had never seen Jennifer lose her temper, she was always kind and warm to everyone and exceptionally laid back. Martha was ashamed of her behaviour but was unsure of how to rectify herself. It was true that she was exceedingly jealous of the new and happy relationship, but she knew it wasn't Jennifer's fault that her marriage was rapidly coming to a close. She took a moment to respond;

"I'm sorry." Martha said eventually, with her head hung low, not able to meet Jennifer's glare, with nothing else to offer other than those two words.

"Is that all you have to say?" Jennifer reprimanded, furious and saddened that her evening of delivering exciting news was well and truly bypassed at the hands of one of her closest friends.

"You couldn't just be happy for me this one time? No, of course it has to be all about you and your misery. You're going to end up alone and miserable if you keep this up." Jennifer continued, blood rising to her face, her eyes bulging in rage.

"I know." Martha squeaked quietly, swallowing back tears, staring down at her feet rather than facing the glare of the three girls.

Jennifer noticed Martha's crack in her stoney facade and felt slightly embarrassed at her outburst. She took a moment to compose herself and let her anger subside.

"I know you're having a tough time at home and I'm sure it's not easy hearing all the happy stories of others, but

225

nothing is perfect. Do you really think my dream wedding was to be fat and six months pregnant?" She said honestly, puffing her cheeks. Martha looked up at her, realising her terrible blunder, no longer able to hold back the tears.

They were soon hugging and crying, both with profuse apologies to give to each other. Soon, all would be forgotten. Meanwhile, Jane and Millie were sat silently watching the events unfold, never had they seen such an outburst from Jennifer who was normally so agreeable and placid.

"Must be the hormones." Jane said quietly to Millie and they both laughed in synchrony, joining in on the embrace their friends were sharing.

They were both equally shocked at Martha's lack of sincere happiness for their friend but were glad they were made up and rectified.

"You girls are so silly!" Millie shrieked at her friends in her mothering tone.

"Really silly." Said Martha admittedly, tears falling without restraint, staring fervently at Jennifer.

"Well, I guess I had better tell you all who I have chosen as bridesmaids!" The girls squealed with excitement and perched eagerly at the edge of their seats in expectant wait.

"Oh dear, not me anyway!" Cried Martha, feeling even more downhearted and turning away.

"Of course you are!" Jennifer screamed excitedly.

"What?! After the way I just spoke to you?" Martha jumped up, looking flabbergasted, fresh tears springing from her eyes.

"I forgive you, I know life is tough for you." Jennifer replied sweetly. Martha clutched at her friend's hand, her face contorted in tearful gratitude.

Martha's shame deepened further at the undeserving forgiveness. "Thank you." Was all Martha could say, hiccoughing through sobs.

"Actually, all three of you are going to be my bridesmaids!" Jennifer announced excitedly, waving her hands uncontrollably.

The girls jumped up and screamed in mad hysteria, violently embracing one another and deafening each other with their continuous screams of delight.

"Well, I would have been very shocked not to have made the cut when this cheeky one over here did." Jane laughed pointedly in the direction of Martha.

"I deserved that!" Cried Martha, through an unrelenting flow of tears.

They spent the rest of their evening planning and organising and deciding on colour themes for the wedding. They looked at maternity wedding dresses and decided on bridesmaid colours. As the wedding would be in September they all agreed on orange.

"Very autumnal." Said Jane.

Chapter 21

The next evening, Theo was coming over to stay. Jane had walked the dogs, cleaned the house and lit a few candles. The candles not only created an ardent ambience but they were also a great disguise for some of those not so welcoming aromas. Jane was very clean and kept her house immaculate, but there was no denying that the natural scent of two dogs was sometimes an unwanted one.

Jane poured two glasses of red wine and started enjoying her glass before Theo arrived.

The doorbell rang, Jane hurried over and allowed Theo and Jackson in through the door, Jackson greeted her with an affectionate nudge of his nose and quickly joined his canine friends.

"Hey *babe*." He drawled, kissing her in the doorway. "It's so good to see you." He smiled and picked her up, holding her tight. Jane wasn't sure how she felt about the new pet name '*babe*' but she was glad to see Theo, so she felt she could endure it for the mean time. It just felt overly cheesy.

"I have some wine poured for you." She told him as he set her down.

"You know me too well." He gratefully accepted and took a large gulp.

They sat down on the sofa nearest the fire.

"Well, anything knew with you?" He asked. "Feels as though I haven't seen you in ages." He placed a hand on her leg, squeezing her thigh affectionately.

"Yeah, I think it's been a whole week actually, how have you been able to survive this long without me?" She teased, placing her hand on his.

"Terribly, nearly lost my life." He joked.

Jane sat and admired him, taking in his striking appearance; he really was very good looking. His blonde hair was swept to one side in real surfer style, his blue eyes flecked with steel were remarkable, and he was looking effortlessly trendy in slacks, loafers and a casual shirt. Jane felt a raw, sexual magnetism towards him.

"Well, my friend Jennifer revealed some news to us last night," she started, "she's engaged to Ben."

"Ah, that's great!" He congratulated happily, "I really like Ben."

"And she's pregnant." He looked stumped.

"Oh, right, shotgun wedding then?" He scorned.

"Seems like it. Although, I think he was planning on proposing before she got pregnant." Jane defended.

"Ah, nice. So when are they getting married?"

"In three months."

"What?! My goodness! That really is a shotgun wedding. Why is she doing it while she's still pregnant?" His brow knitted in confusion.

"Not sure to be honest. I think she wants to be married before she has the baby. If it were me, I would want to have had the baby and then wait until they were old enough to be a cute flower girl or page boy." She looked pensive, picturing the scene in her mind.

"You think about getting married then?" He teased, eyeing her watchfully.

"Um, not really. I guess I have just been thinking about what I would do if I was in Jennifer's situation." She said quickly, not wanting to give Theo the wrong idea, glancing at him nervously.

"Well saved." He winked animatedly at her.

"You are so cheeky." She prodded him in the ribs.

He jumped over and began tickling her ferociously, Jane found the sensation unbearable, she lashed out and kicked viciously in all directions to try and stop the terrible torture. Theo had her pinned down, he pressed his body against hers and kissed her hard on the mouth. Jane was out of breath from all the wrestling, the kiss was passionate and breathy, she enjoyed feeling his hard body against hers. With his strong arms he gathered her up in to a fireman's lift and carried her off upstairs.

Three months later and it was the night before Jennifer's wedding, it had been a busy few months, full of organising and formalities and gatherings and excitement. None of which Jane really understood, it was all so expensive and ensued so much stress upon Jennifer. What were the point in favours? These expensive, little, pointless gifts that everyone left behind at the end of the day, anyway.

The three girls had been fitted for dresses of a burnt orange colour two weeks earlier, due to it being an Autumn wedding. Jennifer had chosen a beautiful, boutique wedding dress store, lined wall to wall with endless wedding gowns, cupboards and shelves stacked with wedding veils, tiaras, flower crowns and sparkly jewellery. The place smelt intoxicatingly of flowers and perfume.

Millie and Martha had been hysterically excited by the wedding shop and preened over the beautiful gowns and assortment of wedding paraphernalia. It was Jane's worst nightmare.

Jennifer had cried when she tried on her wedding dress, not tears of happiness, no, Jennifer's belly had grown significantly and the dress had been taken out countless times, they were now at the point where it could be taken out no more. Jennifer had gone for an A line wedding dress, her thought process had been that her bump could continue to grow and her dress would accommodate this. It, unfortunately, had not.

"I feel like a whale!" She cried as she stood on a podium facing a large mirror. It was two weeks to the wedding and this was to be the final dress fitting.

"Jennifer, you look beautiful, and you will be glowing on the day!" Millie tried to alleviate Jennifer's qualms.

"I'm bulging out of this dress and the wedding is still two weeks away! I'm going to look fat and ridiculous bursting out of this. There's nothing beautiful or glowing about me. That's just something people say to pregnant women to make them feel better about being fat!" She cried harder, looking at her reflection in disgust.

"You're worrying too much, Jennifer. You won't look fat. I agree with Millie, you will be glowing and Ben will be so happy to see his future wife and mother of his child walking up the aisle." Jane said encouragingly, nodding her head enthusiastically.

"I know, you're right. I just never pictured myself being a pregnant bride, maybe I should have waited until I had the baby." She pondered.

"Well, there is no turning back now, your wedding is in a couple of weeks, Jennifer!" Martha stated the obvious.

"Maybe I should tell Ben we should postpone it, I don't want to be a fat bride. I can't even have a glass of champagne on my wedding day!" She groaned dramatically, puffing her cheeks in indignation.

"You can't be serious?!" Martha said in disbelief, her eyes widened, putting her hand up to her mouth and staring round at the other girls.

"Yes, I am." Jennifer said frankly, staring back at Martha soberly, almost willing the challenging remark.

"Oh my god. Maybe you should think about it? Sleep on it tonight and see how you feel tomorrow?" Jane suggested, trying her best to diffuse an ever precarious situation.

"Yes, I agree. You don't want to do anything rash. Ben would be heart broken and everyone has put a lot of money and effort in to this wedding." Millie said anxiously, darting her eyes from girl to girl.

"Yes, it's really not just all about you anymore, Jennifer." Martha remarked, a little too forthright. "You have to consider other people now, too."

"Always the diplomat, Martha!" Jennifer snapped, not in the mood for Martha's arrogance.

"Well, it's true, is it not?" She asked frankly.

Jennifer thought for a moment, "I guess you're all right. But look at me!" She wailed again, melodramatically. She looked down at her huge belly and studied her swollen hands. "I'll barely get my wedding ring on at this rate!"

The three girls laughed, "Never did I picture you, Jennifer, succumbing to your emotions!" Millie breathed a sigh of relief that the situation was somewhat diffused.

"I'm being totally ridiculous?" She asked sheepishly, looking to the girls for reassurance.

"Maybe a little." Jane giggled.

"Point taken." Jennifer chuckled, a little shamefacedly.

The day before the wedding, the three bridesmaids had organised an afternoon tea party for Jennifer, along with her closest friends and family, they felt anything involving alcohol would just set Jennifer off on another hormone tangent, so they felt it best to keep to something pregnancy appropriate. Martha had been on her best behaviour over the last few weeks and apologised whenever she could to Jennifer for not being overly delighted about her very swift wedding and shock pregnancy.

They went to a patisserie, named *Délicieuse*, overlooking the seafront, it was a Parisian inspired cafe that was a sugar lover's dream, the shop was lined with every type of cake or pastry imaginable. Cream filled eclairs, chocolate gateaux, caramel squares, lemon meringue, fruit cakes, gigantic scones the size of boulders. Jane was also very fond of this patisserie because of its excellent ranges of tea, Délicieuse opted for tea leaves of many varieties depending on the customers preference. It was the one place Jane could go to for an excellent cup of tea apart from her own house.

Jennifer's mum, sister, female cousins and aunts all attended, along with some of her other close friends from work and childhood. Jennifer had relaxed significantly since the previous dress fitting fiasco and had even managed to enjoy the previous two weeks leading up to the big day. Jennifer was fixed up in comedic wedding attire during afternoon tea; donned in wedding veil, tiara and a pom pom skirt. They played hen party games and stuffed themselves full with macaroons and jam scones and screeched excitedly about the coming day ahead.

That night, Jane, Millie and Martha had arranged to stay over at Jennifer's house, along with Jennifer's mother, so as to wake up together on Jennifer's wedding morning. Ben would be staying with his mum and dad. Jane was at home getting organised and packed up to leave, Theo sat on her bed watching;

"Thanks for minding my dogs over night, Theo." She said as she neatly folded pyjamas in to her over night bag. Jack lounged by Jane's feet while Ruby and Jackson lay on the bed bedside Theo.

"Well, I near enough consider them my dogs now anyway, so it's no problem." He said happily, stroking Ruby's head.

"You've certainly been spending enough time together." She smiled at the thought of their blooming relationship.

"What will I do without you for a whole night?" Theo asked, with an over exaggerated, melodramatic flick of his arms.

"I'm sure you'll manage just fine." She chuckled, rolling her eyes and poking him in the ribs in her affectionate manner.

"Yeah, I was thinking about that arrangement," Theo began, hesitating for a moment. "We've been dating for about nine months now, right?"

"Yes." Replied Jane. Her heart stopped for a moment, was he going to ask her to move in with him? Could she go through leaving her house again and all the insecurity of being

234

homeless for a month until she got her house back off the tenant again? "No. Stop. He isn't Matthew, I need to stop being so negative, it might not go the same way." Jane thought to herself, feeling fretful.

"How would you feel if I moved in with you?" Theo asked, looking up from cautiously raised eyebrows.

"Oh. You move in with *me?*" Jane hadn't considered that. She was shocked, happily shocked. That could work, she wouldn't have to leave her lovely home and they would be making a big step forward in their relationship.

"Sorry, I'm being too presumptive and maybe you would rather move out? I just thought because your house is much better for walking the dogs, location wise, that it made sense. But, maybe it's too soon, I've probably scared you." Theo was rambling nervously.

"No! I would love that!" Jane gasped, jumping up and in to his arms.

The next day the girls had all got ready with a lot of screaming and hysterics that would be expected on a wedding morning, Martha wasn't happy with her hair and Millie responded quite abruptly;

"But you're never happy, so no real surprise there." Martha was quite hurt following this remark and remained quiet for a long time.

"Jane, can you grab my hair piece off my dresser, please? Can someone get me a drink of juice? I thought I had a coffee?" Jennifer demanded frantically, fixing her hair nervously as the hairdresser tried to pin it in place.

"Your coffee is beside you, I'll get you some juice." Said Jennifer's mother, Margaret, trying to maintain the calm.

235

Margaret was a plump, middle aged woman with a warm smile and greying hair, opting to age naturally. To Jane, she appeared to be the type of woman who was born to be a mother; patient and kind and slow to anger.

"I'll grab your hair piece now." Jane dashed quickly to deliver whatever the bride asked for.

"Now, Jennifer, you need to relax! Just enjoy your morning, everything will be fine!" Margaret said soothingly, cupping her daughter's face in her hands.

"I'm just nervous, I'm allowed to be nervous on my wedding day." Jennifer spat, turning her head away and out of her mother's embrace.

"Of course you are, dear." Her mother started, apparently not at all nonplussed by her daughter's rude comment. "But, don't forget why you are getting married. It's just one day and then you will have the rest of your life with Ben to look forward to, where every one of those days counts much more than this one, singular day." Her mother said with a wise, maternal air.

"I think I got an extra dose of pregnancy hormones today. I look huge and I feel so emotional. I'm sorry, mum." Jennifer moaned apologetically, leaning her head in to her mother's arm.

"Jennifer, you need to just enjoy this morning, no more negative thoughts, this is your happy day. The start of your life with Ben. You have so much to be grateful for, remember that." Jane implored of her friend, presenting her with the hair piece.

"I'm sorry, Jane. I'm being so insensitive." Jennifer had forgot, whilst thinking only of herself, that Jane had lost a baby only last year.

"Don't be silly, I'm not referring to that!" Jane exclaimed, "I just want you to make the most of today and not look back with regret because you were worried you may or may not look fat. And, you need to remember that you are not actually fat, you are pregnant, and you look great for it!" Jane stepped over and hugged her friend warmly.

"You're a good friend, thank you so much. I'm being such an idiot!" She shrieked loudly. "Right, let's start over, let's have a fun morning. Thank you, that's just what I needed to hear." She looked at both her mum and Jane when she said this.

"Would it be totally insensitive if I popped open the bubbly right about now?" The girls all broke out in laughter at another one of Martha's impromptu remarks.

"Perfect timing as always, Martha." Millie rolled her eyes comically.

Hair and make up was sufficiently done up and applied, the three bridesmaids had their dresses on. Margaret was leaving shortly for the church and Jennifer's dad had arrived to collect Jennifer, along with the two wedding cars. Jim, Jennifer's dad, who was still married to Margaret (an anomaly to Jane that two people, in this day and age, had remained together for so long,) was an equally plump, middle aged man with a balding head and kind, blue eyes. Jennifer glided downstairs after slipping on her wedding dress, helped by Margaret.

Jim broke down in floods of tears, unable to contain his emotion and happiness at the sight of his little girl ready to take on a new chapter in her life. This set off all four of the girls in to an excess of screaming and crying.

"Oh, Jennifer! You look amazing!" Cried Millie.

"You are so beautiful!" Jane shrieked.

"I can't cope with how amazing you look, Jennifer!" Martha squealed with happiness.

Jennifer hugged her dad first, consoling the broken man, then turned to her friends, plenty of embraces and tears were shared.

"Oh, no, our make up!" Martha darted straight for the bathroom, fanning her face with her hands as she went. The girls all seemed to roll their eyes in a synchronised fashion, laughing at Martha's dramatics.

The three bridesmaids all stepped in to the first car; it was vintage styled and cream coloured, draped generously in white ribbon. Not what Jane would've chosen, but it was nice to be chauffeured around. They were followed by Jennifer and Jim in a similar type car, and if it were possible, even more white ribbon was draped around that one.

Jennifer was getting married at the nearby church and Jane couldn't help but laugh to herself at the irony of a pregnant bride getting married in a church, but who was she to judge?

The nerves started to kick in, even though Jane knew she wasn't centre of attention, it was the first time she had been a bridesmaid. She also knew Theo would be watching and this made her even more anxious to look absolutely radiant and serene as she walked in. Did she look ok? Would she scare him off with all this wedding carry on? What if she tripped up the aisle? Was her dress tucked in to her pants? Best check before she got to the front doors.

The church was a very large and grand building, made completely of cobbled stone. It had large, mahogany double doors. The building was set slightly on a hill which gave it a castle like effect. The result was impressive, Jane had thought. It was quite beautiful.

The bride and bridesmaids had photos taken with a few of the spectators standing outside, as well as some taken by the photographer. It wasn't particularly warm and Jane wasn't sure whether she was shivering due to nerves or the cold. It was time to enter. Martha was the first bridesmaid to walk up the aisle, Jane was glad of this; she hoped this meant there would be fewer eyes on her.

Jane was the last bridesmaid to enter the church as she was Jennifer's chief bridesmaid and she would be standing by her side. She walked in, trying to maintain a slow pace and an appropriate distance between her and Millie. She slapped on a smile but she could feel her lips quivering at the strain, would everyone notice that?

She scanned the room quickly to try to spot Theo. There he was, as handsome as ever, smiling broadly at her. The rest of the crowd she didn't recognise a lot of, there were some familiar faces from the afternoon tea party. Then she caught a glimpse of a face she thought she recognised, but she had walked by and didn't want to turn her head over her shoulder to peer at the person she thought she knew.

Jane reached the front of the church and angled herself sideways like the other bridesmaids, she glanced round at the crowd and caught Theo's eye again, smiling warmly at him, he smiled back. And then she caught the face she had recognised earlier. Matthew.

Chapter 22

It couldn't be happening. What was Matthew doing at Jennifer's wedding? Why had Jennifer not told her he was coming? Was he with a girl? All of Jane's suppressed feelings for Matthew came crashing back like a tsunami, ready to drown her in a wave of heart ache, lust, confusion and adoration. Jane was overwhelmed and felt suffocated, submerged in a sea of anxiety, anger and conflict. Jennifer would have known he was coming, why was he even invited? Did he recognise her? Of course he recognised her, it wasn't as though she had gone through face transplant surgery in the last year. The day was going to be a disaster.

Jane's heart pounded loudly and she was starting to sweat. She tried to maintain a forced smile but she knew she must look as though she was stuck somewhere between constipation and the need to vomit violently. She spotted Theo and he smiled and waved again, he was sitting three rows in front of Matthew. Matthew noticed the exchange. Her eyes met with his briefly, but she looked away quickly. Crap. Where would she look now? Anywhere but at him. Jane found herself idiotically staring at the ceiling or at a random spot on the floor, all in an agonising attempt not to look in his direction again, but her eyes were being forced his way. She probably looked as though she was in some form of psychotic episode.

She glanced over again, risking a quick look. She couldn't resist. He was sitting next to a very attractive Asian girl. Who was she? Jane felt a stab of pain at the sight of them together. The girl was outrageously beautiful, Jane felt her thoughts turn sour with malice and uncontrollable jealousy. She had a strong urge to leap across the crowd and punch the pretty girlfriend right in her smug face. "What a bitch." She thought lividly.

Jennifer walked up the aisle with her father, looking the picture of health. Plump and rosy cheeked with that *glow* only pregnancy could achieve. Jane remembered that brief glow she'd had. Despite Jane's anger at her friend, she couldn't help feeling very happy for her, Jennifer looked genuinely happy and all her anxiety over the last few weeks seemed to have completely dissipated the moment she had seen Ben standing at the top of the church hall.

Jane felt overcome with emotion suddenly, tears prickled her eyes and she was shocked that she was actually crying, and at a wedding of all occasions. She momentarily forgot about Matthew and watched the exchange between Jennifer and Ben when they eventually reached each other, staring longingly in to each others' eyes and grasping at their hands. The happiness radiated from them, their faces beaming in delight at the sight of one another. That was love. Jane turned to look at her friends, both of whom had wet faces from copious amounts of tears. Martha pointed to her ruined make up and rolled her eyes and laughed silently. Jane smiled warmly at her.

The service involved an introduction from the minister followed by a couple of hymns, Jane had rarely stepped foot in a church in her life and, therefore, was unfamiliar with any hymn. As a result, she decided to just move her mouth without any sound and hoped that it would look as though she was singing along to the music. As a wedding guest it was easy to get away with this method, but she was painfully aware that she was standing front and centre in front of an enormous crowd. She could only hope, then, that all eyes would be on Jennifer and Ben.

She glanced over at Theo and made a confused face, rolling her eyes and shrugging her shoulders, she could see him laugh silently at her torture of not knowing the words. She also caught Matthew discern this exchange and she swiftly turned away. Had he look annoyed? Upset? Or was she just imagining, or hoping, that he had given away any shred of jealousy.

The vows were to follow and then the exchanging of the rings. Jane could relax slightly, the commodity would nearly be over. One more hymn, perhaps, then she would be free to runaway out of sight and become extremely intoxicated, and, in doing so, hopefully forget about Matthew altogether.

The ceremony ended, the crowd filed out of the large hall, and everyone congregated either side of the mahogany doors to allow the bride and groom to exit the building and be greeted by all their loved ones as the newly married Mr and Mrs.

Jane escaped and hid behind a tall man while Jennifer and Ben stood at the grand doors and got their photograph taken. Millie found Jane;

"What are you doing hiding over here? We need to get photos of Jennifer and Ben!" Millie looked shocked and confused at her friend's odd and disinterested behaviour.

"I'll be over in a minute." Jane whispered, ducking behind the man's large frame.

"Why are you acting so strange?" Millie looked curiously at her, tilting her head to one side.

"I'll tell you in the car." Jane was peering anxiously over the shoulder of the tall man.

"Ok." Millie gave Jane a sheepish sideways glance and stalked away.

The three girls got back in to their car, they were to be transported to the reception venue. Jennifer went in the other car with her new husband. During the drive it gave Jane the opportunity to discuss who had attended the wedding and she didn't waste a moment to begin;

"Did you girls know that Matthew was going to be at the wedding?" Jane yelled, quite accusingly, eyeing up each girl individually.

"*What?!*" Gasped Millie and Martha together.

"Matthew's at *this* wedding?! He's here *today*?!" Martha shouted loudly, her eyes wide and alive with the thought of the exciting new development.

"What the hell is he doing here?!" Millie screamed, her hands gesturing frantically, looking enraged.

"Does he know Ben? He must know Ben, I can't believe this!" Martha's head flitted between Jane and Millie.

"You didn't know he was coming, Jane?! Oh my goodness, this is crazy! Oh, how awkward! Oh, poor Jane!" Millie cried.

Clearly the girls had not known that Matthew would be attending the wedding. Her anger towards them quickly subsided.

"Do you think there's any chance Jennifer didn't know that Matthew was coming?" Martha asked sincerely. "I just can't see her double crossing you like this."

"How could she not know? She wrote the guest list and sent out the invitations!" Jane said eventually after the girls had calmed down slightly.

"What if he was a plus one, though, for another guest?" Millie urged sensibly.

"She still would've needed to have known his full name for the table settings."

"This is true. It's just so unlike Jennifer to do something like this though, she has definitely stabbed you in the back if she knew he was coming." Martha looked increasingly concerned.

"Maybe she thought if you knew he was coming that you wouldn't come to the wedding?" Millie suggested, throwing ideas out in the open.

"That is a fair point, Millie, but of course I still would have gone! That would have been so selfish of me. Plus, surely I would've been better knowing beforehand rather than having the shock of discovering it when I'm walking up the aisle with all eyes on me!" Jane shrieked, her voice rising again.

"Yes, that was a poor move if it is the case, but knowing Jennifer, I don't think she would've known that it was *your* Matthew. I don't think she has it in her to do something like that. Maybe she just thought it was someone with the same name? Or, maybe it didn't register with her at all, it has been over a year after all." Martha observed astutely.

"You're probably right." Jane admitted, contemplating to herself.

The girls continued to chat fiercely about the new turn of events all the way to the hotel. Jane didn't know what she would do or say when she had to ultimately face Matthew. How would she introduce Theo to him? Theo knew all about her past history with Matthew, having felt so comfortable to open up to him. This would not be pleasant for him either.

The car pulled up at the hotel, it was a beautiful manor house hotel set high up on a hill with endless views of greenery and trees that were absolutely breathtaking. The ocean could be viewed on the horizon. There was very little wind, due to the shelter of the high trees and this made the outside temperature feel quite pleasant.

The building itself was a very large, white, nineteenth century style structure, with intricate architraves and large pillars encircling around the outside, creating a very grand and expansive look. Around this building were various elaborate, but smaller, separate buildings that Jane presumed must house other wedding venues and reception rooms.

There were gardens surrounding the entire hotel and its buildings and they were some of the most beautifully maintained gardens Jane had ever seen. A wide and varying variety of plants, shrubs, flowers and trees, perfectly manicured. The colours were striking and uplifting, greens and purples, pinks and oranges.

Jane did not have a very keen interest in garden maintenance or flowers or plants. She had always said it was a part of her womanhood that had been omitted at birth, she could never relate to a woman's fascination with flowers because they were wilting and dying a week later. But even Jane couldn't help but admire the immense beauty of the hotel's gardens, Jennifer had chosen a wonderful location.

Jane could already feel her nerves rising again, she had exited the car and taken a few moments to appreciate the beautiful surroundings. Then she remembered... Matthew. Thankfully, she was called for bridesmaid duties as soon as she arrived and was swept off for photographs. She first went over to Theo who had waited for her outside;

"I hopefully won't be long here; I don't think they need a lot of photos of the bridesmaids." Jane said apologetically, taking his hand.

"I'll be fine, sweetie. Don't worry about me. I know a couple of the guys anyway." He kissed her on the cheek.

"Thanks, see you soon."

Theo took off and met with Martha's husband, Lucas, and Millie's boyfriend, Oliver, at the bar, he had met these men on a few occasions and was happy to wait until Jane was no longer needed by the photographer.

Meanwhile, this was Jane's first opportunity to ask Jennifer, quickly, about Matthew while they were having a bride and bridesmaid photo shoot;

"Congratulations Jen, you look absolutely beautiful, I'm so happy for you." Jane said truthfully, genuinely beaming with happiness for her friend, standing in front of an extraordinary backdrop of waterfalls and greenery.

"Jane is just being polite; she really wants to know why Matthew is here." Martha cut in abruptly.

"Always so tactful, Martha!" Groaned Jane through gritted teeth.

"I was hoping this wouldn't come up." Jennifer admitted ruefully, staring ashamedly at her feet and fidgeting her hands.

"So you knew he was coming?!" Jane asked alarmingly, unable to comprehend her friend's betraying actions.

"Well, I know his girlfriend, Tia. I invited her and she had a plus one, when I got his full name I knew it was your

Matthew, so I messaged Tia and asked her was he sure he wanted to come. She replied saying that they would both be going. Every time I saw you I wanted to say something but I didn't want you to not come to my wedding and the closer it got the harder it was to say something." She said this with profound sadness, hanging her head in shame.

"I can understand that." Said Jane. "It's not your fault that he's here, I'll just get on with it."

"I am sorry, Jane, I didn't plan this well. I should have told you." She admitted with perpetual misery.

"Don't be ruining your day thinking about it! I'll try to avoid him as much as possible. I just would have preferred a head's up; I got a bit of a shock as I was walking up the aisle! But enough of my dramatics. This is your big day!" She said, trying to feel happier about it and putting on a brave face for her friend.

"You're a good friend, Jane. I don't deserve you." Jennifer breathed a sigh of relief; she had been worried that Jane would react badly. She felt terrible blindsiding her friend.

Jane and the other bridesmaids made their way back in to the hotel while Jennifer and Ben continued on with their bride and groom photo shoot. Theo was sitting on couches in the foyer with Lucas and Oliver, all of whom seemed to be on their third pint of beer. Jane was as impressed with the interior of the hotel as much as she had been when she had first laid eyes on the exterior.

The foyer looked as though it was completely manufactured out of marble, the floors and walls were gleaming with shine. There were creative gatherings of giant vases at various points of the room making the place feel even more expensive. The

247

Chesterfield couches were a plush purple with vibrant, green cushions and gold encasings rimmed the metal arms and legs.

Theo and Oliver stood up and kissed their respective partners, Lucas did not move. There was an obvious air of tension between the two, Jane felt intense sorrow for Martha. Martha smiled and carried on as normal, pretending the cold exchange had not occurred.

They all approached the bar; it appeared to also be made of marble and spanned the length of the room. The boys ordered three more beers and the girls asked for three glasses of white wine.

They left the foyer and headed for where the reception was to be held, beside the reception room was the holding room where people waited until the main room was ready, this area was also swathed in marble and beautiful purple and green couches. They were scanning the room for empty couches and that's when Jane spotted *him*. Matthew. Tia was with him and they appeared very cosy and deep in conversation. Jane's jealousy began to rise within her, she felt her blood boil as she watched as Tia grazed her hand across Matthew's face. Jane felt her fists clench tightly in suppressed rage.

Chapter 23

Jane tried not to look directly at Matthew and the mystery girl; she wanted to avoid them for as long as possible. Theo and Matthew meeting each other was the stuff of Jane's nightmares. What should she do? Approach them and get it over and done with? Or wait for him to approach her? Or would it just be better to ignore each other altogether? He looked up and noticed her looking. Talk about being caught out.

He was getting up. He was coming over. Tia was with him, too. "Act cool." Thought Jane. Bile rose up her oesophagus, sweat prickled her brow and the palms of her hands tingled, realising that they were still clenched, her nails dug painfully in to her skin.

"Hi." Said Matthew when he approached the group, looking unswervingly at Jane.

"Hi." Jane responded quietly, a fleeting look passed between them.

Her heart was pounding, unable to meet the piercing stare that Matthew was giving her. She was disappointed to find that he still had that powerful hold over her, that all encompassing, earth shattering feeling of instinctual lust and passion. She was ashamed of her feelings towards Matthew as her current, and very lovely boyfriend, stood beside her.

Millie and Martha stared in disbelief that Matthew had, so brashly, approached them.

There was a moment of silence broken by Matthew.

"This is my girlfriend, Tia." He introduced. "Tia, this is an old friend, Jane."

"Hi Jane, nice to meet you." Tia said sweetly. Damn it, Jane already knew that this girl was a bar above the rest. Tia did not seem to recognise the significance of Jane, Matthew mustn't have told her about their history together.

"Hi." Jane smiled politely. "This is my boyfriend, Theo. Theo, this is Matthew."

Theo looked alarmed and taken aback as the realisation of who this man was, dawned on him, but he quickly recovered as he knew he had an audience. They both shook hands, Jane noticed Theo's knuckles turn white as he clutched Matthew's hand tightly, his expression was stoney. They exchanged uncomfortable pleasantries and then Jane made a move to return to her seat, hoping the rest of her party would follow suit.

"Do you want to sit with us?" Matthew asked abruptly. Theo eyed him suspiciously.

Jane was baffled by the invitation. Her stare lingered over him, wondering why he would suggest such an idea, why not just ignore each other for the rest of the night and avoid the horrific awkwardness at all costs?

"Oh, I don't know, I'm sure we would only be imposing on you both." Said Jane awkwardly, fiddling with her thumbs anxiously.

The others stood staring speechless as these events unfolded, heads bobbing between the two, quite enjoying the spectacle of it all.

"Of course not, there's plenty of room here." He replied happily. Jane was trying to read his expression but he wasn't giving anything away.

Jane had forgotten how good looking he was. Why was he so good looking? Those eyes. The deep, dark brown with hints of honey, seemed to draw her in. That piercing look that struck her deep down.

Oh dear, she had to stop that. She was there with Theo. Theo, who was sweet and kind and loving.

The group joined Matthew and Tia around their table and they all sat down together; rather uncomfortably.

After a long silence, Tia eventually said; "So, how do you two know each other?" There was a hint of an accusatory tone towards Matthew as she watched his unwavering gaze trained on Jane.

"Just friends from a long time ago, but we don't run in the same circles anymore." Matthew explained quickly, as though he had just realised he was there with another woman. Jane was glad of the lie Matthew told, she didn't want to have to get in to their dating history.

"Did you two not used to date?" Said Theo sharply, eyes narrowed and looking mean, his gaze resolutely on Matthew. Matthew's eyes jumped to Theo's in stupendous surprise, raising his eyebrows skyward. Theo was pleased with the result and smirked maliciously at him. Jane darted Theo an angry look. Why had he broadcasted that? Especially when Tia was clearly none the wiser, and it would have been better to have kept it that way.

"Well, yes, we did. A while back." Stuttered Matthew, rather shocked at this brusque outburst.

251

"You used to *date*?!" Tia cried out, looking completely furious and throwing daggers at Matthew for concealing this secret.

Jane decided to step in to alleviate the situation;

"Yes, but it ended a long time ago and we have quite clearly moved on." She said quickly. "Maybe we would be better sitting somewhere else and giving you both some privacy?"

"It's fine, honestly." Said Tia. "Please stay." She seemed to force a smile and feign politeness.

The uncomfortable atmosphere continued on for a few minutes until the bridesmaids were called over by the groom, Ben, to help Jennifer with bathroom duties. "Thank goodness!" Thought Jane as she jumped up, grateful to be getting away from the most excruciating situation of her entire life.

The three girls were walking over to meet Jennifer by the toilets;

"Well, that was a total car crash." Jane let out a sigh to the other two.

"Yeah, it was a bit." Millie admitted. "I was surprised by Theo correcting Matthew over your past, I thought Matthew did the right thing not letting on about the history between you two when his girlfriend didn't even know."

"But then why invite us to his table?" Asked Martha, hands set menacingly on her hips. She did have a point.

"I have no idea. That was the most awkward ten minutes of my life." Jane brushed a hand forebodingly over her flawless, sleeked back up do.

"Agreed." Said Millie, rolling her eyes in exasperation.

"I'm having a great time," Martha laughed. "Got to love a bit of wedding drama!" All Millie and Jane could do was stare at her in bewilderment.

Jennifer approached them, "I think this is going to be a four person job to lift this dress up to allow me to go to the toilet. It's just as well I'm not pregnant and don't have to pee every five minutes!" She laughed jollily, smiling happily at them.

"We've got you covered." Said Martha, "at the end of the day, this is probably the main reason why you have bridesmaids." Jennifer nodded in agreement.

They stepped in to the beautiful toilet facilities, Jane was pleased to see that they were gleamingly clean. The walls and floors were a granite quartz from top to bottom, wash hand basins were a glittering gold.

"Well, have you bumped in to Matthew yet?" Jennifer asked Jane, eyeing her up greedily for any gossip.

"Unfortunately, yes." Jane breathed a sigh.

"That bad?"

"Matthew's girlfriend didn't know that they had been an item previously and Theo announced it to everyone. It was super awkward. Quality viewing for us observers, though!" Martha pronounced, clearly delighted. The girls couldn't help but laugh at Martha's wicked love for drama and excitement.

"Enough about me!" Beseeched Jane, "Are you having the most amazing day?!" Already bored with the Jane, Theo, Matthew and Tia disaster scenario that was quickly unfolding.

"I really am, you really do forget about all those silly, little things that you worried about when you are standing at the bottom of the aisle looking up at your future husband." She smiled happily, tears glittering in her eyes.

"Aww, Jennifer, we're so happy for you. This place is truly incredible." Millie beamed brightly.

"We were very lucky to get this place, especially at such short notice, and it was actually significantly less expensive than a lot of other places." She said proudly. The four girls clambered awkwardly in to a toilet cubicle and began the arduous process of attempting to unravel the many layers of the dress, all the while, trying not to create too many wrinkles.

When the bride was suitably toileted, they went back to the holding room. Thankfully the group had dispersed. Matthew and Tia were sat alone at their table and the three men were back at the bar.

"I'm sorry about this," Jane said to Theo as she approached him, "I had no idea he would be here, Jennifer knew but didn't tell me."

"It's completely fine, don't worry about it." Theo replied with a kind smile, draping his arm around her and pulling her in to a one armed embrace.

"Are you sure? We can leave early if you want?" She eyed him cautiously, he was taking the Matthew situation extremely well. Jane was unsure if she would have taken to things as well, had the tables been turned.

"You can't leave your best friend's wedding early, it's not a big deal! Honestly!" Theo urged, turning back to face the group at the bar.

They all went through to the main reception room for the meal, Jane was relieved, she had just realised she hadn't had anything to eat so far that day and was exceptionally hungry. Theo was at a table with Lucas and Oliver, along with Matthew and Tia. "What was Jennifer thinking sitting them all together?" Jane spat angrily in to Millie's ear, she looked over at the table and gave Jane an 'Oh dear' type of look.

The main reception room was another show stopper, at one end there was a long wedding table for the bridal party, the rest of the room had large round tables elegantly laid out evenly around the room. Each table had an elaborate array of large, plush flowers that perfectly matched the bridal bouquet. These flowers surrounded an extremely large candelabra in the centre of each table. Each individual, beautiful, cream coloured chair had a burnt orange tulle around them to tie in with the colour of the bridesmaids' dresses.

The ceilings were covered in magnificent chandeliers and at various corners of the room were more gigantic vases. Behind the top table was a beautiful, square arch draped in autumnal coloured flowers.

Everyone took their seats, Jane could see Theo positioned between Oliver and Lucas, at least he didn't have to sit directly beside Matthew, Jane had thought. She glanced over quickly at Matthew and his eyes were in the general direction of the top table. Tia did not look overly cheerful. She sat with her arms folded, throwing looks at Matthew, with a permanent scowl on her face.

Speeches were made by the fathers of the bride and groom, the best man and the groom. The best man was met with some hostility when he could not resist covering the topic of the pregnant, expedited wedding. There were some feeble laughs but Jennifer was most surprising of all as she laughed whole heartedly.

The food was outstanding, but then again, Jane was ravenous and anything might have tasted good at that point. After the main course, Jane went over to join Theo to check to see how he was getting on. He was in the middle of a conversation with Oliver and Lucas about football. He appeared to be in good form and Jane was able to relax, she kissed him on the cheek and went to return to her table, not before noticing Matthew's lingering gaze trained upon her. Jane found it strange that he would stare so boldly at her whilst Tia sat right next to him.

They had dessert, then the crowd was asked to leave the room and step back in to the holding room while the staff set up for the dance floor. Theo and Jane found another comfortable couch with their replenished drinks;

"I can't believe she sat you with him." Jane remarked disapprovingly, "I'm sure that was so uncomfortable for you!"

"Sweetie, you are making a bigger deal out of this than is needed, it wasn't too bad, he's actually a decent enough guy." Theo looked happy and unfazed by the events.

Jane was shocked by the way Theo was handling everything, it was as though he didn't care at all. Surely he would be even slightly jealous at having to spend an entire day in the company of Jane's ex partner? Jane knew she wouldn't feel overly happy about it if it had of been one of Theo's ex girlfriends.

"I'm glad it all went ok for you, I just worried it would be terribly uncomfortable for you." Was Jane the one who was being weird about this?

"Let's forget about it and enjoy the day." It was definitely her, she was being weird about it and Theo was her mentally stable, amazing boyfriend who had just taken the whole, unfortunate situation in his stride.

The first dance was about to begin, everyone gathered back through in to the reception room and made a circle around the dance floor. Jennifer and Ben entered the room to enormous applause and cheering, they took their place in the middle of the dance floor. They looked happy as they stood with only eyes for each other. Their soft, sweet music began and they swayed from side to side in time to it. All the spectators had their phones out capturing the moment. Some guests had tears in their eyes.

After the first dance, the band started and most got up to dance. Jane was sitting at one of the free tables not feeling quite drunk enough to show off some of her renowned dance moves. She saw Tia walk off to the bathroom. Theo was over at the bar with the guys again, they all seemed to be deep in conversation. She wondered what they were talking about. Matthew maybe?

"Hi there." Said a voice behind her, making her jump. It was Matthew, he had approached the table. Jane giggled a high pitched, foreign noise and felt idiotic. Completely lost for words. What would she say to him? He was wearing *that* suit that Jane had always loved, the one that accentuated his masculine body and cute back side. Had he done that on purpose? Jane wondered to herself. She looked up in to his mystifying gaze and breathed a response barely audible;

"Hi Matthew, well, what are the chances that we would both be here tonight?" She smiled at him, fidgeting awkwardly, painfully aware of the strange way she was sitting, she was hyper aware of herself and how she was coming across. She had to pull herself together.

"Pretty high actually, we live in very close proximity and share a similar circle of friends." Matthew joked at the obviousness of this, he sat down in the chair beside her, positioning himself so that he was facing her. Jane found the closeness intimidating but also titillating. She inhaled deeply, she caught hints of Bergamot and mint, the effect was dizzying.

"This is true. I guess I'm probably surprised that we haven't bumped in to each other before now." Jane said, controlling the tremor in her hands, denying the fact that they'd had that one horrendous encounter at the supermarket where she had very publicly and devastatingly broke down over their break up in front of him.

"You've been avoiding the beach." Matthew said, looking her directly in the eye with only the confidence and sexual magnetism that he could radiate.

"I have been, you noticed?" She was finding it difficult to maintain his unfaltering eye contact, scared that she would succumb to his allure under his stare.

"I go to the beach most days and it used to be your regular spot, if you still went I would have bumped in to you by now." Was he wanting to bump in to her? Is that why he went every day?

"Guess it was just easier to go somewhere else." She explained, pausing to look at him. "Tia seems like a lovely girl. I hope you'll both be very happy."

He stared at her, his eyes boring in to her like an X-ray, did he know what she was thinking?

"She's a great girl. Theo seems pretty decent too, he really likes you."

"He said that to you?" Jane asked, all of a sudden remembering who Theo was and feeling horrendously guilty.

"Well, he talked a lot of you two planning to move in together." Had Jane sensed a brief flare of jealousy?

"Oh, did he? We have only just started discussing the idea, maybe in a few months." Jane found it strange talking about her current boyfriend with her ex boyfriend and wanted to change the conversation, or end it altogether.

"You aren't keen on the idea?" He asked, his arm leaned elegantly against the table, his aura of suave and charisma was overwhelming, she had an intense urge to smell his neck, to breath in the intoxicating pheromones.

"No, of course I am!" Jane gasped, realising he had asked a question and snapping herself back in to reality.

"Good, I'm glad to hear it. It's nice to see you happy." He looked at her sincerely... His eyes burning lust in her belly that seemed to spread like fire throughout her entire body. She felt as though she was treading on dangerous waters.

Tia arrived back from the bathroom, Matthew and Jane were still sitting at the table alone. She stormed up towards them and sat between them both, placing a firm hand over his arm. If she had been a dog it would have been less obvious that she was marking her territory than if she had just peed up against him.

"Catching up on old times?" She asked coldly, glaring tenaciously at Jane. The dirty look she threw told her it was time to leave the table.

"Matthew was just telling me how much he liked you." Jane said, trying anxiously to ease the tension.

"That's nice." She spat with heavy sarcasm, "but do you not have your own boyfriend to hang out with?" She glowered at her with loathing, keeping her hand firmly pressed against Matthew's arm, claiming what was hers.

"I'll be leaving, I'm sorry to disturb you both." Said Jane, she got up and turned away. Matthew gave her a 'I'm sorry' look as she moved away from the table. Tia noticed the exchange and her suspicious and accusatory scowl towards him was enough to make even Jane feel terrified about the repercussions that Matthew was about to face.

Tia's reaction was not surprising or unjustified; it was silly of them to be sitting alone together when Tia had only just found out about their romantic history. What was worse was that Matthew had originally tried to hide it from her, that would have already increased her suspicions, and then to find them both sitting alone. Tia's reaction was perfectly reasonable. Jane just hoped that Tia knew there was absolutely nothing going on between them, despite her feelings of quashed lust and the indecent thoughts now racing through her mind.

Jane went to the bar where Theo was standing.

"Have a good catch up for old time's sake?" Theo said, almost as coldly as Tia, not smiling or putting his arm around her like he normally did. Jane was in trouble, too. She knew nothing good would come from Matthew being there, envy and tension rippled across the room between the two couples.

"Not you as well," she whispered under her breath, "he was actually just telling me how much he liked chatting with you at the table." Jane answered honestly, trying to stem the flow of jealousy quite obviously coursing out of him.

"Do you honestly think that's what he wanted to talk to you about? That was his way in, to make you think his intentions were innocent." Theo snapped sharply, eyeing her up with suspicion, clearly trying to find any hint of infidelity.

"I don't think his intentions were anything, actually, I think he was just being polite. Why are you so jealous? There's nothing to be worried about." Jane said, a little too defensively, Theo's ears perked up at this.

"Because I know the history you have with him, I know he was the love of your life and I know you almost had a child with him, that changes things." He looked at her with a forlorn expression that tugged at Jane's heart strings, she felt terrible, that despairing look he gave her made Jane regret not just walking away from the table when Matthew had approached her. What had she been thinking? Matthew had ditched her the year previous as though she was just a piece of dirt on his shoe. Worthless. And yet, here she was, risking her current relationship for someone who treated her so horridly.

"Can you not see how much trust I placed in you by telling you all of those things? It wasn't easy for me to divulge my failed pregnancy to you, I could have easily just kept that a secret, but I chose to be open and honest, because I love you and I want you to know the real me." She implored, her emotions getting the better of her, feeling tears threaten her eyes.

Her and Theo were officially having a fight at her best friend's wedding as a result of someone who had not been in her life for over a year, she suddenly felt immense resentment towards Matthew, was she ever going to be free of his grasp? She put a hand out to touch Theo's arm, only for him to withdraw it away from her. She felt cut by his rejection, she had never experienced this cold side to Theo. All of a sudden she felt very lonely.

"Look, I don't really see why I am having to justify myself. If you are jealous and don't trust me then that is your issue and it is definitely an issue in our relationship." Jane was feeling angry now with the implied accusation, the withdrawn

261

arm and implicit allegation, he had hurt her, he was being ridiculous.

"So now you are saying we are having relationship issues?" Theo replied sharply, not able to look directly at her, his eyes distant and unwelcoming. Jane felt a shiver.

"Well, we certainly have an issue if you can't trust me." Jane said quickly, "do you trust me?" She pleaded inwardly for him to produce the correct response.

Theo looked at her. Surely this was totally unjustified just because she'd had a quick two minute conversation with Matthew about nothing particularly relevant? But, then again, Theo hadn't been present during the conversation, they could have been discussing their plan to get back together for all he knew.

"Of course I do Jane, I'm sorry. It just maddened me to see you two together, getting along so well. You are very important to me." Jane breathed a sigh of relief, Theo's hard gaze seemed to soften immediately, all was well again.

"You are important to me, too." Jane said, the threatening tears now invading her face and falling on to his chest as he embraced her tightly. She really did love him. The day had been a whirlwind of stress and suppressed emotions for the two focal men in her life.

The rest of the evening went a lot more smoothly, with no further hiccups, the three couples spent the night dancing and drinking and having fun, when they would sit down they would stare at the happy couple with happiness and a little jealousy from Martha. Matthew and Tia had left early and this seemed to ease tensions drastically. Theo appeared his normal, happy self after the bout of jealousy he had shown towards Jane and Matthew's brief encounter. They retired to their room after a busy day and fell asleep immediately.

Chapter 24

Over the next few weeks, Theo's behaviour changed significantly. The run in with Matthew at Jennifer's wedding had caused more friction than Jane had originally thought. Theo had become increasingly more edgy and suspicious. He would look over Jane's shoulder when she was texting someone or ask who she had been on the phone to. She was quite sure he had even been looking through her phone when she was in the shower too, because he would jump up when she opened the bathroom door and pretend to be doing something else.

He had become a lot more possessive towards her also; he would question her every time she wanted to go out, ask why she needed to go out to places without him and ask her why she couldn't stay in with him, was he not enough? He would offer to give her lifts to and from wherever she was going, no matter what the time or place, and even if he had work the next day. Jane knew this was all in order for him to be able to keep an eye on her.

Jane was feeling claustrophobic, she felt as though Theo was watching her every move and this created a lot of tension. One morning, when she was getting ready for work, Jane had left her phone by the bedside table while she went downstairs for breakfast. Once she had finished she decided to sneak back upstairs very quietly to see if she could catch Theo in the act, she had purposely not closed the bedroom door tight when she had left.

She opened the door a crack and there he was, swiping through her phone menacingly, he had a determined, crazed look in his eyes as they darted greedily over Jane's private information. Jane's anger bubbled rapidly, the audacity of him, she thought she might actually hurt him, she was so angry with his blatant violation of her privacy. How dare he!

"What the hell do you think you're doing?!" Jane screamed, unable to control herself and storming in to the room to face him.

"Checking to see if you're messaging Matthew." Theo replied unashamedly, with an apparent lack of interest at her presence. Jane was speechless at his reaction to being caught out, he wasn't embarrassed or guilt ridden at all. Jane felt her perpetual anger burn higher still. Who does he think he is?

"And?" She demanded, fists clenched and jaw tightened in rage.

"Not today anyway." Theo said indifferently.

"Not any day, Theo. Have you completely lost your mind?!" She snatched the phone out of his grasp and stood back. "What has gotten in to you? This isn't the Theo I fell in love with. Why are you invading my life like this?" Jane felt unexpected tears dash from her eyes, sadness now overriding her anger.

"Why do you need a private life from me, Jane? What do you have to hide?" Theo barked with an accusatory tone, eyeing her up darkly. The look sent goose bumps down her spine. He looked mad. Was she scared of him?

Jane was astounded at his response, it took her a moment to get her thoughts in order to produce a comeback. "I have absolutely nothing to hide from you, but to have my privacy invaded against my will is abusive and controlling. Can you not see that?" She pleaded, her lips trembling, her tears falling rapidly.

"If you don't have anything to hide then you shouldn't mind me looking at your phone." Theo replied simply, his voice low and measured, sending further chills through Jane. He was crazy.

"If you trusted me then you wouldn't have to look at my phone." Jane barked back, her mouth curved slightly, pleased with her counter argument.

"Well, whenever you are cuddling up to your ex boyfriend right before my eyes then it is hard to trust you, wouldn't you agree?" The malevolence in his voice was almost tangible, the harsh look in his eye was unnerving.

"Look, maybe we should postpone moving in together," she glanced quickly at him then down to her feet, "this checking my phone carry on has got to stop, I won't tolerate it, and I don't think we can move forward if we aren't in a good place." Jane was trembling with fear, Theo appeared unhinged, unpredictable. She was almost scared to look up.

"So, you're the boss now? Is that the case? And you threaten to break up with me when things don't go your way?" He spat at her with malice.

"I didn't say that, you are twisting my words!" Anger was back with a vengeance; Jane was flooded with emotions of frustration, upset and anger. Who was this person she thought she knew?

266

"It's what you are implying though, isn't it?" Theo raised his voice and jerked out of bed, making Jane jump back with fear of what he might do.

"If this were to continue I don't know what else we could do." Jane replied honestly, feigning bravery, barely able to see now, her eyes flooded with tears.

"I knew it." He growled, his hands placed menacingly on his hips and his shoulders hunched, looking large and dangerous.

"Knew what?" Whispered Jane, feeling scared and intimidated.

"That you were seeing him behind my back." Theo's anger radiated out of him, his eyes looked deranged. Did he have it in him to hurt her? He was much bigger and stronger, he towered over her loomingly, she would have no way of defending herself.

"Is that seriously what you have taken from this whole conversation? You're going to push me away if you continue this. I don't know what more you want from me, you have looked through my phone and there are no messages from Matthew and I am outright telling you that I'm not talking to him, and I'm definitely not seeing him for that matter." Jane replied, proud of her brave response, despite her ever rising fear. She puffed out her chest in defiance to his attempts at intimidation.

"You probably deleted his messages so I couldn't see them." Theo knew he had gone too far once he made this comment, his posture slackened, he reclined away and sat down. Jane could breathe for a moment. Fear no longer clouding her mind. She looked at the pathetic person sitting on the bed.

Her confidence renewed, she said; "Do you know what, I think you're right, I think I am breaking up with you." She watched him carefully, almost expecting him to jump up and thump her in the face. Jane's childhood had her conditioned to believe that anyone who got angry was almost certainly going to react with violence towards her, she expected it, feared it.

"Jane, please, no, I didn't mean it. I take it all back. I'm such an idiot. I love you." Jane was relieved that he had not reacted violently, her heart was thudding against her chest, she was sure Theo could hear it too. The desperation in Theo's voice ensued disgust and pity towards him. She couldn't look at him.

"Look, I'm going to work, I need to think things over in my head, on my *own*." Jane ordered coldly, still not looking at him, dreading the day ahead in work after the exhausting morning.

"What do you need to think about? We aren't breaking up so there's nothing to think about. Everything is fine. Let's move on, please." He begged pitiably, he stood up and stepped over to Jane, clutching at her hand desperately.

"I can't just forget about you looking at my phone without my permission and all of these accusations you have made against me, it's hard to move on in a relationship if there is no trust." Jane said truthfully, looking at him with revulsion, pulling her hand out of his grasp.

"Of course I trust you, don't be silly." Theo exclaimed, as though the preceding argument had not just happened, trying to take her hand again, but Jane stepped back, forbidding the touch.

"Your actions five minutes ago did not suggest that." She snapped at him, becoming impatient and repugnant to his begging. "Anyway, I have to go to work, maybe stay at your own place tonight and I'll call you later." Jane said this with an air of disconnect. Theo did not say anything; he merely stared at her in disbelief.

Whilst Jane was at work, she had time to reflect on the earlier conversation, or fight, between her and Theo. She couldn't believe Theo's behaviour, he had totally lost it. Why did she always attract the control freaks and stalkers? It had to end, how could it go on? Jane was very distressed and upset, she really had loved Theo, she'd had high hopes for the relationship and now it was all crumbling away.

Theo had been this warm, loving, breath of fresh air for Jane just when she was ready for a new start. Who was this person she was now faced with? Controlling and jealous and worst of all; terrifying. Jane had feared for her safety at certain stages of the morning. Last week Jane would have laughed at anyone who told her that Theo had a violent streak; today, she would have outright believed them.

Jane couldn't concentrate in work, she was tearful and distracted. Her manager noticed;

"What's up today, Jane? You don't seem yourself." Pauline asked, her brow creased with concern, as Jane sat at a desk completing paper work.

"Awk, I had a stupid fight with my boyfriend this morning." Jane said depressingly. "I think we've broke up." Jane felt her throat tighten and tears loomed behind her eyes in waiting. She set down her pen and turned to face Pauline.

"Oh, goodness, I'm so sorry to hear that, Jane. Do you want to head home now? Get your head showered?" Her voice was soft and soothing and understanding. She was a great ward manager, Jane had always felt supported by her.

"I'll be leaving the place short staffed!" Jane beseeched, "I'm fine, I can stay on and finish my shift."

"Jane, it's fine, we aren't too busy today anyway and you only have a couple of hours left of your shift. We will manage, just finish what you are doing and head on." She urged.

"Thank you, Pauline. You're the best."

Jane was walking to her car and decided to check her phone, she hadn't looked at it for a few hours. She was dreading what she might find, the anxious pain in her chest told her to prepare for unlimited messages and missed calls from Theo. He did not disappoint. Approximately twenty messages and too many missed calls were sitting waiting. Desperate pleas of reconsidering. But, there was another text message... From Matthew. Jane's head buzzed with confusion.

Jane rapidly unlocked her phone and dashed her fingers quickly to the message from Matthew, bypassing all of Theo's ridiculous attempts at reconciliation. Did he really think that desperately begging for her to forgive him was the way to her heart? "Just give me some space!" She thought angrily to herself.

Jane's heart pounded at the anticipation of opening Matthew's message and she couldn't get at it quickly enough. She was ashamed to admit to herself that she felt excited nervousness as she started to read his message, she knew deep down that she was absolutely delighted to be hearing from him, she craved his love, his touch, that magical feeling only he could ensue;

"Hey Jane, I'm sorry, I know I shouldn't really be texting you but I haven't been able to stop thinking about you ever since I saw you at Jennifer and Ben's wedding. Hope you are well. Matt x"

"Oh god, oh god, oh god! He's thinking about me! Does he still love me?!" Jane thought excitedly to herself, butterflies did back flips in her tummy. Her excitement came to an abrupt halt, was he not dating Tia? Why was he texting her whilst he was with someone else? Jane's delight took a rapid nose dive, why was she excited to hear from him anyway? She had promised herself that she would never go there again.

She would never have classed Matthew as the cheating type. Was he looking a hook up? Her head was so confused, she decided to snap herself out of the ridiculous notion that Matthew was interested in starting things up again. So, she ignored the message and went home.

Jane pulled in to the drive and felt her stomach lurch, immediate nausea instantly overwhelmed her when she saw Theo's car was still there. He was waiting for her at home. She knew that his flashy sports car hadn't left the drive all day; he had waited for her, despite her requesting some time alone. She felt her chest tighten, anxiety rising up inside, threatening to pull her down. She couldn't handle this. Was she ever going to get any peace?

Jane walked tentatively in to the house, hoping that she could diffuse the situation and ask him kindly to leave her property. Theo was sitting in the living room, with his feet up, as though he owned the place. She couldn't believe the nerve of him. She could feel herself shaking with anger, this guy was certifiably insane.

"I thought I told you to go home and I would talk to you later." She barked through clenched teeth, trying her damnedest to control her anger. "I need some space. You're pushing me in to a corner here."

271

She walked through the hallway, the dogs greeted her happily, she petted al three individually, feeling slightly cheered up by their warm presence.

"You can't just leave me on tenterhooks wondering whether we are together or not, that's not fair." Theo protested, looking hurt and dejected.

"And I said you were making me feel claustrophobic, so by being here you are not doing your case any justice." She retorted angrily, throwing her coat over the banister and dumping her bag on the ground. She stood in the doorway with her hands on her hips, demonstrating strength and determination.

"So you want me to just sit at home waiting for you to make up your mind? I'm not some kind of puppet you can control." He barked back, continuing to sit leisurely sprawled on the sofa.

"What was your plan then? Desperately beg for my forgiveness like some pathetic nut job? Have you totally lost it, Theo? Where has my sweet, caring boyfriend gone? You sound like a lunatic. I haven't given you any reason to mistrust me, this is all in your own head, you have destroyed our relationship all by yourself!" Jane screamed, unable to contain the emotions she had been keeping at bay all day.

"Well, if I'm so out of order then let me see your phone." Theo replied coolly, his upset demeanour was quickly replaced by malice. It was unnerving to watch.

"Are you *completely* mental? You checking my phone is what started all this in the first place! There is nothing on my phone!" Jane shrieked, losing her temper and feeling completely irate. Her throat stung from the screaming.

Oh, wait. There was the text message from Matthew that day! She didn't need to show Theo her phone though, the relationship was over anyway. And besides, she hadn't even responded to it, it wasn't her fault that out of all the days Matthew would randomly text her it would be the day she was breaking up with Theo.

"If you have nothing to hide then there's no reason to keep your phone from me." He said with an air of calmness that was terrifying.

"You already checked my phone this morning without my permission, you bloody nut case! Get out of my house and leave the key! Now!" She yelled wildly, so loudly that her voice cracked and her throat felt raw. Jane's anger had overflowed and she looked for things to throw at him, reverting to her old habits of destruction when she felt trapped and scared with no way out. The dogs barked anxiously, jumping up and down at Jane in deep concern, Jane barely noticed them.

"You can't be serious, Jane? You're throwing me out? After all we have been through together?" He lifted his legs down from the sofa, resting his elbows on his knees, looking pitiful and sad again, Jane couldn't keep up with his constant alternating emotions.

"Theo, we have been dating for nine months, it's not exactly a lifetime, and now you are acting like some kind of a crazed lunatic. How could you imagine we would ever have a future together with you checking my phone and continuously accusing me of cheating behind your back and stalking my every movement?" Jane shook violently, her mind racing wildly as she tried to plan a way out of this nightmare.

Jane couldn't see an end to it, he wasn't going to leave without a fight. She wanted him out of her house but she didn't know how to make him do this. Should she phone the police? They would make him leave. Ruby and Jack were becoming edgy and nervous, they pawed at Jane, Ruby was whimpering softly. It broke Jane's heart; the dogs had been through a lot, too.

"It's been the best nine months of my life, you can't just throw this away." Theo looked at her feebly, he weeped pathetically, Jane screwed her face up in revolt. He stood up and strode over to Jane unexpectedly, she sprung back in fear and put out defensive arms in front of her, but he only reached out to grab at her hands, Jane pulled away and stepped back, creating a safe distance between the two of them. Her thudding heart slowed again slightly. He was completely unpredictable.

"I was having the best time too, until Jen's wedding, then you just seemed to lose it," cried Jane, "I don't know why you had to do that, I have never been unfaithful. But now, too much has happened and it can't be reversed. I can't trust you anymore to give me freedom and let me live my own life. It just can't work. I'm really sorry, Theo, but you have to be able to see that?" She implored, studying his face for some sense of reason.

"No, I can't see that Jane, can't we just go back to normal? I'll be good, I promise. Please don't do this." Theo sobbed and begged. Jane felt repulsed by his desperate begging, she wanted to get as far away from him as possible.

"It's too late now, Theo, I have seen a side of you that I don't want to see again. I'm sorry, but you need to leave." Jane said quietly, pleading with him to go peacefully.

274

Theo went from sad to angry quicker than lightning, he closed the distance between himself and Jane. Jane thought he was going to hit her, she raised her arms over her head to protect herself from the inevitable blow, in her right hand was her phone, Theo got to Jane and grabbed her phone out of her hand and ran in to the downstairs bathroom, locking himself in. Opening her eyes slowly and looking out from her outstretched arms, Jane realised what his motive had been; to get her phone and look through it again.

"Theo! Have you completely lost your mind?!" Jane bellowed. "Give me back my phone and get out of my house!" She demanded, feeling totally frantic and deranged. There was silence. Jane was banging on the door repeatedly to get him to come out and reason with her. The dogs were jumping at the bathroom door and Ruby was barking at the confusion of it all.

The silence persisted. Had he jumped out the window? Then, the door opened slowly, Theo looked chilling, his eyelids were lowered and he peered at her curiously, with an evil twist to his mouth. Jane felt fear spread through her like quick fire. Her fight or flight hormones kicking in, attempting to guide her in to survival mode.

"You *lied* to me." Were his only quiet, low words. The dogs were jumping up and down on Theo. He raised a clenched fist, threatening to hit one of them, but he refrained. Theo wouldn't hit Jackson, his own dog, surely?

"Don't you *dare* lay a finger on any of my dogs!" Jane screamed, anger pulsing through her veins again. Fearing for their safety, she closed them in to the living room, leaving her and Theo in the small hallway. She could hear the scratching and crying at the door, the dogs were distressed and worried about their owner; bewildered by the screams and cries.

"What did I lie to you about?" Jane demanded, but she knew what he was referring to – the message from Matthew that day.

"You've been talking to *him*. You told me you hadn't been, but, here it is, in black and white, that you have." Theo was talking very slowly and quietly and with purpose in his voice, it was unnerving.

"He sent me that text message, coincidentally, today. Completely out of the blue, and as you can see, I haven't responded to it. And I hadn't planned on it either." Jane said, fear rising, feeling as though he might become violent, she tried to diffuse his anger, tried to make him see sense.

"You expect me to believe that?" He said with the continued, ominous tone, not taking his eyes off her. Jane shuddered at the thought of him ever having touched her.

"I don't really care anymore, Theo, do you really think this is a good basis for a relationship? You have just stolen my phone off me, locked yourself in my bathroom and invaded my privacy – again. And now you won't get off my property. Give me my phone back." She demanded, feeling brave and determined.

He threw it on the ground and she heard the smash. "Are you being serious right now?!" Jane screeched at him, he didn't flinch, the smirk at the side of his mouth persisted.

Jane snatched up her phone, the screen was smashed but thankfully it was still working. She quickly dialled '999' and let the phone hang by her side. She let it ring, trying not to make it obvious to Theo that she was making any kind of phone call. She slowly backed her way towards the front door.

Theo noticed her movement and ran to the front door to barricade her in. "So, you're trying to run away from me now?" He screamed in a complete frenzy, his senses completely disengaged, his eyes looking wild and feral.

"I'm just trying to get some fresh air." She lied, tears streaming down her face, terrified for her safety, he was completely unhinged. She wanted to make a run for it, save herself from this mad man, but there was no way out. She only hoped the call had gone through and someone would come to rescue her before it was too late. She would bide her time, keep Theo distracted and his temper down.

But then Jane heard it, the sound of the operator on the end of her phone; talking, Jane felt panic stricken, she could feel vomit rising up her oesophagus, the fear was crippling her. Theo looked at her unrestrainedly, evidently aware of the voice coming from her phone too.

"Have you rang someone?!" He howled ferociously, making Jane jump on the spot, she cowered away from him.

"No, I haven't!" She lied desperately through her sobs, crouched down, feeling small and pathetic.

"Then who is that talking at the end of the phone you stupid idiot? Give me that phone you stupid, little bitch!" His eyes were dancing around his head madly, he looked disturbed.

This was Jane's only chance, heart pounding, hands shaking uncontrollably, blinded by tears, she quickly put the phone to her mouth and as fast as she could get the words out she screamed at the top of her voice; "My partner has me trapped in my house and he seems dangerous! Please send help!"

Knowing that they would be able to trace her address from the phone call she threw the phone across the room without hanging up.

Theo looked terrifying. "What have you done?!" He said in his low, quiet tone, his voice shaking through his anger. And in a flash he was on top of her. He was too quick for Jane to respond, no time to move her hands up to protect herself. *Smack.*

Theo had punched her in the face, she was on the ground, she felt dazed and dizzy and pain was shooting like lightning through her nose and cheekbone, temporarily blinded by excruciating pain. She could feel a warm liquid trickling from her nose down in to her mouth, and she could hear the dogs barking manically in the background.

"Please don't hurt the dogs." She thought. She tried to get up but he kicked her as she lay there, multiple blows to her stomach and her head, Jane was badly winded, she could barely breathe between each blow. She thought he would never stop. Jane forced her mind to drift off to another place, a safe place, to block out what was happening. A technique she had used regularly when her uncle had given her merciless and savage beatings as a child.

And then it stopped, Jane's ears were ringing, she didn't dare move or look up. Was Theo still there? Was she even conscious? She lay there in a heap in her hallway, too scared to move; the taste of blood in her mouth. The dogs were still barking and clawing at the kitchen door.

She could hear the sirens nearby. The police were coming. She could relax now. She could drift off.

Chapter 25

The police arrived at Jane's house, the door had been left ajar and they found her lying in the middle of the hallway bunched up in a tight ball in the foetal position.

Two kind looking police officers approached Jane, one male and one female. "Michael," the female police officer was saying, "check to see if anyone is still in the house, it's unlikely with the door lying open but we should really check." She had a kind voice, Jane thought. The male police officer ran off to check the house. The police woman knelt herself down beside Jane, she still had her eyes closed.

"Hello, miss? I'm Constable Neill, you're safe now. Are you ok? Where are you hurt?"

Jane tried to open her eyes but they were swollen almost shut, she peered through the slits of her eyelids, her vision blurred. Jane saw the hazy shape of a woman with swarthy skin and dark hair. Jane blinked and tried to focus her vision. Constable Neill smiled sadly down at her with kind eyes. Jane was relieved that the female officer had chosen to stay with her, the thought of another man being near her at that exact moment ensued panic. Constable Neill radiated a kind, soothing presence that was reassuring to her.

"Everywhere." Jane answered, spitting blood.

"Do you think you could sit up?" She asked her softly.

Jane felt stiff, she didn't want to move, she just wanted to lie there forever and forget about everything. She stretched out her arms and legs, testing her movements, and made to move.

"Ouch, oh! Ouch, ouch! *Ah!*" She cried, new tears replacing the old.

It was excruciating to move in any direction. She felt stabbing pains in her chest and stomach. Constable Neill helped her to slowly sit round, the dizziness made her want to be sick and fall back over. Jane was helped in to the standing position, *very* slowly.

She staggered on her feet and was blinded by a splitting headache, she could see white dots clouding her vision, her knees weakened and went from beneath her. Constable Neill caught her and helped her slowly over to the couch where she lay down. Her dizziness subsided but the headache persisted.

And then, it all hit her at once, what had all happened. The argument, the beating, the accusations, the end of the relationship. She went in to convulsions. She couldn't breathe through the sobbing, her body shook, she started to wail and scream. The pain in her ribs was unbearable but she couldn't stop crying, the heaves of emotion came in uncontrollable waves. She couldn't handle the pain the deep sobs caused upon her broken body.

The kind police woman put her arm round Jane to try to comfort her, "Jane, you are in shock, you need to breathe through it-"

Jane, not expecting the stranger to touch her, lashed out in a panicked bid for freedom and safety. "Don't touch me! Leave me alone! DON'T TOUCH ME!" She screamed, flailing her arms in various directions, her eyes wild with unrestrained fear.

The other police officer, Michael, came firing down the stairs at the sound of the screaming, yelling; "Is everything ok?! What's going on?!" Michael was an attractive, young, blonde haired man who couldn't have been more than twenty five years old.

"Everything's fine, Michael, she's just in a bit of shock." She turned to Jane, "Miss, you have experienced a severe trauma, it seems, but know that you are safe now. Try to take deep, calming breaths, it should help." Jane stared at her in total bewilderment, her ribs were aching from the kicking and the heavy sobbing. She was terrified, acting instinctually, all she wanted to do was run. The nice police man was talking to her. "Your name is Jane, isn't that right? Jane Abbott?"

"Yes, that's right." She said nervously, eyeing up the strange man in her house, she wanted the woman to only be with her. She sank back in to the sofa.

"We are here to keep you safe and we are going to do everything we can to find the perpetrator who did this to you." He said seriously, his eyes alive with concern and determination. Jane felt instantly comforted by Michael's words.

"I need to check you over for any serious injuries. Can you move all of your limbs?" Constable Neill asked. Jane turned her attention back to the kind police woman, grateful that she was still with her.

Jane lifted her arms and moved her legs, they were stiff and sore, she felt a sharpness in her side with any movement at all, but she could move them.

"Good, where do you feel the most pain?" She asked earnestly, keeping her eyes focused on her.

"My head and my stomach and the right side of my ribs." She explained, pointing to the areas she had described.

"I need to check your pupil reaction in light of the head injury, if that's ok?"

"Yes, that's fine." Jane wondered how she would see her pupils, her eyelids were swollen to the size of golf balls.

She shone a bright torch directly in to her eyes. "Seems to be ok. There is an ambulance on its way also, it was dispatched at the same time as us when you phoned the emergency line. They'll check you over properly. Are you bleeding from anywhere other than your nose and head?" She asked gently, sitting next to her on the sofa.

Jane lifted her top to reveal her tummy; there was already a lot of extensive bruising there but no outward bleeding. "No, I don't think so." She answered. Jane was shocked at the sight of her abdomen, had Theo *really* done this to her? A few days ago she could never have imagined he would have had it in him to do something as vicious and cruel as to beat her so violently.

Constable Neill then lifted out a notepad and a pen from her pocket. "I'm sorry, Jane, but I need you to try and tell me everything that happened. I know it's hard and you probably don't want to have to re-live the entire ordeal but you need to tell me everything so that we can find the person who did this and get justice for you." She said sympathetically but with an urgency to her voice.

Jane explained, as best she could, what had happened. She had to stop at regular intervals to allow the pain in her ribs to subside slightly from the strain of talking and to let her crying cease temporarily. It was painful to talk and breathe at the same time. "It was my boyfriend, well, my ex boyfriend

282

now." She sniffed, "we had an argument. He was jealous and possessive and he thought I was cheating on him. He was going crazy after he found a message on my phone from an ex boyfriend, so I told him I wanted to end things.

"He got nasty, he didn't want to end it. I asked him to leave but he wouldn't, he blocked the doorway for me to get out. He was scaring me and that's when I phoned you guys. He heard the operator from the emergency line talking from my phone, that's when he completely lost it.

"He punched me in the face, he hit me so hard I fell to the ground, then he started kicking me, all over, everywhere. I don't know how long it went on for, I kind of blocked it out. Then I just lay on the floor for a while until you guys arrived." Jane breathed a sigh of relief, through her weeping, that the horrific account of events was over.

Constable Neill mopped some of the blood up from her face using gauze from a first aid kit that had been kept in the car. Jane could hear more sirens.

"Thanks, Jane, for telling me all that. It mustn't have been easy. What is Theo's full name?" She looked at her seriously, compassion evident in her eyes.

"Theo Reid."

"Do you have a photo of him or can you give me a description of his appearance, please?"

"Yes, I have photos of him on my phone."

"Thank you. I also need Theo's address and any addresses of the people he might stay with instead of at his own home. Parents or friends." She asked.

Jane told Constable Neill the addresses of Theo's parents and his closest friend, Mark. The ambulance then arrived and two paramedics jumped out of the van and walked quickly over to Jane and Constable Neill.

Constable Neill filled the two paramedics in on what had occurred. Jane was grateful for this, she couldn't bear to talk through it all again. The two paramedics were male, one looked to be around forty, balding and with a bit of middle age spread. The other couldn't have been older than twenty two, slim and athletic and full of enthusiasm for his job.

The older paramedic approached Jane, while the younger continued to talk to the police officers. "Hi Jane, I'm Charlie." He had serious eyes and a concerned expression, his eyes darted quickly over Jane's injuries, assessing and scanning the situation in his quick mind.

"Hi Charlie." She squeaked.

"How are you feeling?" He asked. He had kind, brown eyes and sat on the other sofa, with a distance between them so as not to come across as intimidating.

"Very sore." She admitted, tears slowly gliding from her swollen eyes, disturbing her vision even further.

"I can get you some analgesia for that now." He explained. "I'm so sorry about what has happened to you." He said, genuinely sad for her. "Do you mind if I check your vital signs and check you over?"

"Yes, that's no problem." Charlie turned to the sizeable equipment bag he had with him and began rummaging through for the items he would need.

Michael, Constable Neill and the young paramedic were all chatting in the corner, no doubt about Jane, as they kept glancing over in her direction with serious expressions on their faces and creases in their brows.

"Jane, all seems to be ok, but I'm just a bit concerned that you have sustained a bad head injury. I think it would be best if we took you in to hospital to get you checked over more thoroughly, just to be safe." He said solemnly, sympathy riddled his appearance. He packed up his equipment bag and sat down opposite Jane again.

"Do you think I'm badly injured?" She asked nervously.

"We can never be too careful when it comes to a head injury, but all your preliminary examinations all point in the right direction. We also need to rule out any injuries to your ribs, chest wall and abdomen. Sometimes you can sustain what is called; a pneumothorax, when you have a broken rib, this is when your broken rib breaks through the chest wall and collapses the lung on that side."

"I know what a pnuemothorax is," she explained, "I'm a midwife."

"Ah, very good, I'm teaching my granny how to suck eggs then." He laughed, Jane tried to laugh too, but it hurt too much.

The other three approached Jane. "Is there anyone you would like us to phone for you?" Michael asked, he had a kind face and a soft smile and despite his attractive looks, he had a hardness to his eyes that came with the job, the ability to remain detached and indifferent was essential in their line of work.

"Yes, I'll phone my mum and dad. I can do that myself. Thank you. Probably better if they hear it from me." The anxiety began to rise again, adding to the pain in her chest. How would her parents take it? Her dad would be uncontrollable, he would lose his mind. Her mother's anxiety would be overwhelming, she would blame herself and her sister for the partners Jane had chose as an adult.

Jane phoned her parents separately, telling them quickly what had happened, she explained she was being taken to hospital and would most likely be taken to the Main City Hospital outside of the village. She phoned Tess also, and asked her to collect the dogs and take them to her house while she was in hospital.

Her dad had been weepy on the phone, she could sense the anger, she could hear the rage bubbling away inside of him, threatening to break the surface. Her mother was, as she suspected, completely inconsolable, screaming and panicking and generally creating alarm and discontent, Jane tried to keep herself calm whilst speaking to her, she made it brief in order to escape the inquisition.

Tess had been worried and upset, but promised to be there for her whenever she needed her. Tess was her rock, her stability when she needed it.

Chapter 26

J ane arrived, via ambulance, to the very busy emergency
department of the Main City Hospital. She was
overwhelmed, scared and alone, she didn't want to be there,
she wanted to go home and stay in her bed forever. The
emergency department was bright and loud and very busy.
Nurses and doctors ran around frantically, never finishing one
job as another emergency came through the door, creating
another new and challenging task.

Jane felt guilty taking up the time of the extremely busy
staff, she was sure that she was fine. The paramedics had
insisted though. She was wheeled through on a wheelchair,
Charlie left to go and handover to the emergency staff. The
young paramedic stayed with Jane, he didn't make a lot of
conversation and Jane was glad of it.

Charlie was speaking to a very beautiful, young nurse. Jane
surmised that this was the triage nurse as she was pushed
forwards when the young nurse gestured for her to come
forward. The attractive paramedic couldn't take his eyes off
the nurse and nearly ran Jane's legs in to the side of her.

"Oh! Sorry about that!" He chuckled nervously, unable to
drag his eyes away from the beautiful nurse.

"No problem." She smiled at him. She turned to Charlie, "I
can take it from here, I'm sure you guys are probably very
busy." Paramedics and emergency room staff had a mutual

understanding of each others' job roles, bonded by pressured work environments and desperately long hours and boorish clientele.

"Thanks Samantha, I'm sure we'll see you around. Bye Jane, it was lovely to meet you. I hope everything works out for you." Charlie said with a wave and a smile.

"Thank you both so much for everything." She managed a weak smile.

"Hi Jane, I'm Samantha, I'm the triage nurse. You have been through quite an ordeal tonight. I'm sorry to hear about all this." She said sadly. Jane couldn't get over the nurse's beauty. She was of medium height and slim build, she had long, blonde hair tied back in to a ponytail. She had porcelain, smooth skin with minimal make up and beautiful, enormous blue eyes with extremely long eyelashes.

"Thank you." Said Jane, beautiful, kind *and* smart, this nurse had it all. Jane automatically felt safe in her care. Samantha wheeled Jane in to the triage room and sat down at her desk. She turned to face Jane directly. Jane felt swamped, was she going to have to re-live her nightmare all over again?

"I'm sorry, but I'm probably going to be repeating a lot of the questions you have already been asked tonight. Charlie has filled me in on the attack but I do need to know if you think the perpetrator is likely to come to this hospital in attempt to get at you?" She asked seriously, with a concerned expression, a line formed in her brow as she stared Jane down.

"I'm really not sure." Jane answered honestly. "His entire behaviour tonight is completely out of character."

"I'm just wondering whether we need to alert security that you might be at risk?" The nurse urged for an answer.

288

"Would the police not have stayed with me if they were concerned for my safety?" Jane asked, becoming increasingly more worried again.

"The police service is quite stretched, as you can imagine, they wouldn't have the resources to stay with all the victims in this hospital. But our security guards would be able to stay nearby so that you feel more protected?" She suggested.

"Yes, that would probably be a good idea." Jane replied, tears slowly ran down her face.

"I'm so sorry to worry you," said Samantha, "but your safety and wellbeing is my main priority at the moment." She looked serious, almost cross. Was Jane causing them a massive inconvenience? She wished she could go home.

"Of course, it's fine, I'm ok." Jane wiped away her tears with a tissue Samantha handed her, carefully avoiding the bruised areas.

"Now, I need to check you over again, something similar to what the paramedic would have done and you can tell me where you are sore." She explained and she stood up and brought over a portable observation machine, fully equipped with stethoscope, sphygmomanometer, thermometer and pulse oximeter.

"My face, stomach and the right side of my ribcage are the most painful." Jane said, pointing to the various areas, wincing as she moved her arms to direct her to the tender areas.

"Did you lose consciousness at any point?" Samantha asked earnestly, as she placed the two ends of the stethoscope in to her ears.

"That part is a bit of a blur, I kind of tried to block the whole ordeal out, what was real at that time and what wasn't, is hard to differentiate at this point." Jane explained gravely.

"I understand."

Jane's vital signs and reaction of her pupils were checked again. Samantha performed auscultation, listening to sounds within Jane's lungs by pressing the metal, flat end of the stethoscope to various areas of Jane's back.

Jane had to squeeze both of her hands and push her legs down against Samantha's arms. Jane knew that Samantha was checking her Glasgow Coma Scale, a clinical scale used to measure the level of consciousness of a brain injury victim, based on their eye movements, speech and ability to move their body.

"That's good, your GCS is fifteen out of fifteen." She explained. "Your oxygen levels are slightly on the low side at 94%, I think a chest X-ray would be advisable to rule out any broken ribs or a pneumothorax, sorry, I mean a collapsed lung." Jane didn't have the energy to tell any more people that she was a midwife and that she understood the medical jargon.

"Ok, thank you." Jane peeped.

"I'm going to move you to the ward where you can await your scans, the doctor will see you and decide whether a CT brain is recommended, I feel that it will be but I don't have the authority to order these." She explained. "But based on your GCS, they might not want to carry this out."

"Thank you for all your help." Jane managed. Jane was exhausted, the sound of moving to a ward was like music to her ears, it meant she could lie down in a bed.

Jane was then moved to the observation ward of the emergency department, she felt this was a good sign because the other departments in the accident and emergency room were 'Majors' or 'Resus', neither of which she wanted to be a patient.

She lay in the hospital bed for a short time until she was approached by a plump, middle aged nurse who reminded Jane of one of the old fashioned matrons, she barked orders at the others and seemed to be running the place. She was kind and courteous to Jane and gave her an encouraging squeeze of the hand, Jane immediately liked her.

She placed an intravenous cannula in to Jane's right arm and administered Morphine Sulphate, she was extremely grateful of this, she was becoming increasingly more achy and sore as time went on. When she had spoken to her mum and dad they had both been frantic about what had happened, they had both said that they were on their way to the hospital. She wondered where they were. The effects of the morphine were almost instantaneous, the pain subsided rapidly and sleep quickly followed.

Jane was woken abruptly by a young doctor who had approached her bed, it took a moment for Jane's eyes to gain focus again; she was feeling foggy from the morphine. She blinked at him through the small slits for eyelids, he was so young looking. He was probably an F1, straight out of university in to the chaos. He was only about twenty three, just a child,

"Hi Jane, I'm Dr Smith, I believe you have had a bit of a dramatic evening." He announced confidently, clearly delighted with himself. A dramatic evening was a bit of understatement, she thought.

"Yeah, I have." She said defensively, eyeing up the junior doctor with ill feeling.

"I'm really sorry to hear that. If it's ok with you, Jane, I'm going to carry out a range of neurological tests to check to see if I feel there is any evidence of brain injury. It will involve you having to get up and walk around, would that be ok?" He asked kindly. Jane was warming to Dr Smith, she felt guilty that she had made a snap judgement about him, assuming his age, good looks and doctor status would make him an arrogant idiot.

"Yes, that's fine." She answered in an anguished manner, worn out from the day's events, the morphine hangover and the ever increasing, raging headache.

Dr Smith ordered Jane to stick her tongue out straight, touch her nose and then touch his finger multiple times, she had to walk in a straight line, he checked all her reflexes with a reflex hammer, he checked her pupils and he made her squeeze his hands and move her legs against his pressure, again.

"All seems ok here." He said reassuringly. "I think because of the nature of the injury it would be better to get your head checked out with a CT scan of your brain. I'm also going to send you for a chest X-ray to check for any broken ribs." He explained in a clinical tone, staring at her notes rather than at her directly. This irritated Jane.

"OK, thank you." Was all she could muster.

"Do you have any questions for me, Jane?" He asked, looking up at her with a soft, understanding expression.

"I don't think so." Her mind was a blank, she felt numb. She longed for further sleep, not only because her body craved it, but because she wanted to forget everything for a while.

"Ok, well I will leave you to it. Hopefully we will have a bed on a ward in the main hospital for you soon and your scans should be tonight." He elucidated.

Jane woke up a bit and sat up straighter, wincing at the pain in her side. "I have to stay over night?" She asked anxiously, begging for release from this place, longing for her own bed.

"Yes, it would be advisable until we know you are in a fit enough state to go home. You have been through a major ordeal. I would say at least two nights of observation would be required due to the head injury. You can never be too careful when it comes to trauma to the head. We would then need to assess things further after we have the scan results, depending on those results it may shorten or extend your stay." This did not fill Jane with confidence.

"Ok." She managed, feeling her throat constrict, trying to swallow back the urge to cry hysterically.

Jane was very disappointed, she didn't want to stay in hospital for two days, she wanted to go home to her own bed and her dogs. She thought she would have just been getting a quick check over and then back home again.

An hour later and Jane was transferred to a medical ward in the main hospital building attached to the emergency department. It was a spacious, single side room with a large window and an en suite. It was dark outside by the time Jane got to her room so she couldn't see what kind of view she had out the window. The room was clean, modern and very stylish, it had a very large television mounted on the wall. It was like a hotel.

"Not too shabby." She thought as she seated herself in the large, blue chair beside the bed, she sank in to it. Thanking it profusely for relieving the strain on her painful limbs.

Jane was greeted by one of the ward nurses called Barbara; a kind, friendly, middle aged woman. Jane was offered further pain relief and accepted Co-codamol, thinking she would worry about laxatives in the morning. Her vital signs were checked again and more questions were asked. Her head pounded against her skull painfully, she could feel her pulse in her temple. Jane was informed by Barbara that she would be back to check on her at around two o'clock in the morning. Jane got in to the bed, slowly lowering her sore and bruised body gently on to it. Sinking in to the mattress, she fell asleep almost immediately.

Jane was woken unexpectedly at around midnight, she felt exceedingly disorientated, it took her a moment to remember where she was. Then the pain in her ribs and the pounding headache reminded her.

Barbara was standing over her, "I'm so sorry to wake you, Jane, but the porter is here to take you for your CT scan and X-ray."

Jane saw a tall man with a wheelchair standing by the door waiting to take her to the X-ray department.

"That's ok, I'm getting up now." Jane was still in her blood stained clothes from the day before, having not seen any of her family, she hadn't been able to get any clean clothes or pyjamas.

"Have you seen or heard from any of my family?" Jane asked the nurse, sitting herself round on the bed, rubbing her sore side and waiting for her light headedness to pass.

"Yes, they phoned to ask about you. I said you were doing ok, a little shaken, but ok." She explained, trying to hurry Jane along in to the porter's chair, clearly anxious to get back to her other duties.

"How come they haven't come up to see me?" She asked, feeling quite hurt and dejected. Had they not bothered to come to see her? Jane couldn't imagine it.

"Our visiting times were over by the time you got here." She stated quite plainly, her voice completely devoid of emotion and persisted to anxiously hurry her along.

"And you didn't feel you could make an exception considering my circumstances?" Jane snapped, staying firmly put on the bed, punishing the busy nurse.

"Rules are rules." Barbara snapped back. "Now let's get you in to the chair, the CT department might not wait for you, they are very busy."

"Well, why don't you try getting beaten to a pulp and see how you feel when you are denied your family when you need them more than ever because '*rules are rules*'." Jane's voice rose, anger coursing through her veins. How dare this nurse deny her the comfort of her family when she had just been through one of the most horrific ordeals of her entire life.

"I understand how you are feeling; it's a very stressful time-"

"Have you ever been beaten up by somebody?" She bored her eyes maliciously into Barbara's.

"Well, no-"

"Then how can you *possibly* understand how I am feeling?" Jane demanded, aware that she was creating a scene but not caring about it.

"I will not tolerate this shouting, you got here very late and you fell asleep very quickly, I felt it wasn't appropriate to have your family here when you quite clearly needed your rest. I can certainly call your family to come up now if it would make you feel better? It was not my intention to deny you your family at this critical time." Barbara said, angrily and emotionally, trying desperately to justify her decision to the weakened victim.

"It's fine, just leave it, I'll be ok on my own until morning. I'm sorry for shouting at you; I just need to have someone here who loves me." Jane accepted the nurse's reasoning but still felt angry about it. She was feeling scared and lonely, her tears came again. She needed a big, bear hug from her dad. She sat on the bed, weeping silently.

Barbara walked over and pulled her in to a rib cracking hug, Jane winced but accepted. "I'm sorry." The nurse started. "It was silly of me not to get your family up here right away, bad judgement call on my part."

"It's ok, I'm sorry again for shouting; it's not like me to be so rude." She conceded. Barbara smiled warmly at her and placed a consoling hand on her shoulder.

Jane went for her chest X-ray and then her CT brain, it was nearly two o'clock in the morning by the time she was getting back in to bed. The nurse she had shouted at came back to check her vital signs again. She checked them quickly and then let Jane go back to sleep.

Chapter 27

Jane awoke early the next morning to see Barbara standing over her; she gave a jump, not expecting to see someone hovering over her. The pain in her side gave her a huge wake up call, stabbing her violently with pain.

Jane sensed someone else in the room and looked round and saw her dad. She wailed audibly at the sight of him, he ran over to her and hugged her as tight as he could, without hurting her. Jane could have remained in her dad's safe embrace forever.

She whimpered in to his shoulder. He stroked her hair and shushed her softly. He had always been Jane's protector, but today, he looked vulnerable and debilitated. His eyes were red and puffy. She looked up at the defeated man.

"My little princess, what has he done to you?" He cried, staring at her bruised face and gently stroking her hair.

"I'm ok dad, honestly." She attempted a brave voice, wanting to be strong for him.

Gary, Jane's dad, then stood up quickly and looked filled to the brim with rage. He allowed Barbara to check Jane's vital signs again and leave.

"I'm going to kill him, Jane, I can't let him get away with this." He was pacing about the room, clenching his fists menacingly with his jaw tightened.

"Don't be silly, dad," Jane tried to reason, "The police are out looking for him, they will find him soon and then hopefully he will go to prison. There's no point you going to jail, too! How would I cope without you then?!" Gary seemed to consider this.

"I'm just so angry, Jane, what was he thinking? How could he do this to my sweet Jane?" He demanded lividly, his face was turning purple with contained rage.

"I have no idea; I never would have suspected he would have ever been capable of doing something like this. He turned sour after Jennifer's wedding when Matthew was there. He was totally consumed by jealousy." She explained solemnly. She really didn't want to have to relive it all again.

"I'm surprised with this too, Jane. Disappointed in myself that I didn't read the signs, he was obsessed with you. I just thought he was really in love, but now I can see, in hindsight, that it was all possession and control. I'm so annoyed with myself. I failed to protect you, Jane." A tear streamed down his face, his anger turning to inconsolable misery.

Seeing her dad cry crushed Jane, her dad never cried, he was strong and indestructible. "Dad, it's not your fault!" She yelled. "If anyone is to blame, it's him and him alone. I didn't see the signs either and I was the one who spent all my time with him!" She gestured to her dad to sit down beside her rather than pacing the room.

He plonked himself in the chair, fidgeting between his hands. Jane rested a hand on them.

"You are so strong, Jane." His tears flowed easily now, silent trickles of pain seeping rapidly along his cheeks. Jane felt helpless to console him. She held his hands tightly and he squeezed back.

"Are you staying for a while, dad?" She asked, hoping he would stay for the duration of her admission.

"I'll stay for as long as you want me to." He reassured her, attempting a small smile, putting his other hand on top of hers.

"That would be great, thank you." And Jane relaxed back in to bed. "Where is Agnes?"

"She thought it best to let me come alone; we didn't want to overwhelm you. She can come up later if you are feeling up to it." He explained.

"Of course!"

Jane's dad was her knight in shining armour, he would never know how much comfort it brought Jane to have him there, knowing that no harm could come to her while he was around. Gary had always made her feel that way, especially as she had grown up. He had provided a sanctuary for her where she could runaway from her abusive aunt and controlling mother.

He was her confidante and someone always with a level head when times were hard. He provided her with so much love and support after her miscarriage and subsequent break up from Matthew, and now he was there again, to take all her troubles away. She went in to a very comfortable, deep sleep knowing that he was nearby.

Jane woke up an hour later, her dad was gone but her mum and Tess were there;

"Oh Jane! I've been so worried about you! How could this have happened? Why did he do this? What is happening to him? How are you feeling?!" Charlotte asked all at once, the moment Jane had opened her grossly swollen eyes. She was clearly stressed and upset, Jane knew her anxiety would be off the Richter scale, but Jane's head was too sore to answer all the questions at once, never mind not knowing most of the answers herself.

"Mum, I'm fine." Jane replied calmly. "The police are looking for Theo and I'm sure they will find him soon."

"So, what you are telling is that at this very moment that monster is still at large?! You aren't safe?!" She screamed frantically.

"Mum, they will find him, don't worry." Charlotte looked at Jane in dismay then her expression dramatically changed to wretchedness.

"I'm so sorry, Jane, here I am trying to make sure you're ok and I'm making you feel even more worried!" Charlotte ran over and embraced Jane tightly. Jane screamed out in pain under the firm clasp. "Oh, I'm so stupid, I'm so sorry!" Charlotte cried, releasing Jane, deep worry lines were permanently formed over he face.

"It's ok, mum. I'm just so glad you are both here." Jane managed a smile at her mother and sister.

"How are you feeling, Jane?" Tess asked softy, sitting down in the chair beside her while her mother stood up and stared worriedly out the window.

"A bit sore but otherwise I'm ok." She lied. Tess gave her a warm hug. Her mother stood fidgeting nervously in the corner. Jane felt sorry for her and asked her to come in for a hug too. The three women sat clutched together for a few moments, tears spilling copiously.

"How are the dogs?" Jane asked Tess, longing to see them again.

"They're doing great, the kids are so happy to have them over to stay again. They are trying to persuade us to get a dog." She laughed.

"You really should, there's nothing better than a dog. I've never been hurt by a dog." Jane said wistfully, her eyes gleaming with tears and sadness.

"Matthew was here, Jane." Tess informed her abruptly, swiftly changing the topic.

"What?!" Jane wheezed, unable to grasp this new reality. Her head spun in confusion, causing her to feel more nauseous than she already did.

"Yes, when you were sleeping. He brought a card and those toffee sweets you like." She explained, a knowing sparkle in her eye.

"How did he know I was here?" Jane asked in alarm. Was Matthew another psychotic stalker?

"I can only assume Jennifer told Ben and Ben has told Matthew." Tess replied, studying Jane's reactions. Ben and Matthew were friends? Had they grown close after the wedding?

"He messaged me yesterday, out of the blue, I never responded, Theo had seen the message and that's when he really lost it. He was convinced I was having an affair." Jane explained, feeling her chest tighten at the thought of it all, "but I haven't spoken to him since the wedding."

"Oh, so he messaged you yesterday, I wonder why? I thought he was seeing that Tia girl?' Tess asked curiously, wariness in her face.

"I thought so too, my initial thought was that he was looking for a hook up and he didn't mind cheating on Tia." Jane admitted, hoping that it wasn't true. The aching loss of Matthew had never left her after all this time. The trauma caused by Theo and the reappearance of Matthew deepened her longing for him. She needed him, in the most desperately

301

needy way imaginable. She longed for his touch, those lips, those arms; lifting her to heights she thought she would never reach.

"They must've broken up, I couldn't imagine Matthew cheating." Tess pondered, breaking Jane's reverie.

"Well, we have all learnt today that we can never truly know what a person is capable of." Said Charlotte, quite wisely.

"That is very true." Admitted Jane, raising her eyebrows in agreement.

"I just never could have suspected Theo of being capable of doing something like this; he always came across as so friendly and cheerful and not at all the jealous or violent type." Tess said, tears brimming her eyes, Jane noted a glint of rage also.

"My thoughts exactly." Jane said honestly. Jane loved being in the company of her sister, if there wasn't a two year age difference between them Jane would have said they were twins. Always thinking along the same lines and finishing each others' sentences. Jane could truly be herself around Tess.

Tess and Charlotte left Jane to allow her to get more rest, they said they would be back later on to see her. Thankfully, her mum had left her some clean clothes, pyjamas and a wash bag. She was grateful of this. She jumped in to the much needed shower; it was a painful ordeal. Every movement she made was an agonising struggle. She had a lot of dried blood on her face and all throughout her hair, which took a few tentative washes to get out.

After showering and getting in to a new set of pyjamas she was feeling refreshed and a little better for it. The doctors came round on their ward round a little after nine o'clock in the morning. The medical consultant was a tall, African man with a friendly disposition. He introduced himself as Mr Abebe. He was accompanied by an entourage of doctors, the last doctor stepped in and closed the door behind himself, as he turned to face Jane, she looked up. It was *James*. Jane's stomach lurched, the palms of her hands became slick with sweat. It was the worst possible time to bump in to an ex boyfriend, it was mortifying that the next man she had decided to date following him, subsequently had chosen to beat her senseless.

James looked at her, recognition flooded his face, he studied her grotesque injuries briefly, pity in his expression and then quickly looked down at his clipboard, frantically making notes, ensuring not to look back up again.

"Jane, your CT brain was completely normal which is reassuring news. I believe you have a mild concussion which will resolve over the next few weeks." The consultant explained.

"Your chest X-ray, unfortunately, does show two fractured ribs, seven and eight, on the right side. Thankfully, there is no evidence of a pneumothorax noted on the scan. For fractured ribs, as you probably know, there is no treatment for, just rest and plenty of breathing exercises at home. The nurses have assured me that you have already been referred to the physiotherapist." The ward sister standing at the back of the room gave him an approving nod that confirmed this.

"Thank you so much, Mr Abebe. Does that mean that I can go home today?" She asked desperately, delivering him her most pleading look.

"I think it would be best if you remained as an inpatient for one more night, just to keep an eye on you considering that you did sustain a head injury. It would also be good to monitor your lung function as well. A collapsed lung can still occur a period of time after the fracture." He explained apologetically.

"Ok, I understand." Jane felt defeated; she desperately wanted to go home.

The ward round then swept off quickly on to their next patient. James was the first to make a very swift exit out the door. After the disappointment of having to stay in hospital another night had worn off, Jane's mind drifted off to Matthew and his recent text. And now, even more surprisingly, his recent arrival to the hospital to check on her.

Jane's head was swimming, Theo had landed her in hospital, James was one of the doctors in charge of her care and Matthew was visiting and texting. It was the worst kind of reunion Jane could imagine.

What did it all mean? Did Matthew want to start things up again? Was he just looking a quick hook up? Where was Tia in all of this?

Jane was exhausted again, the visit from her mother and sister, the shower and then the ward round made her feel as though she had completed a day's heavy labour. Her body was aching again, she wondered when the nurse would come by to give her more pain relief.

Jane lay on the bed watching television, wondering how she would pass the day other than sleeping, scrolling social media on her phone and drinking really bad tea. She then realised that she actually hadn't even responded to Matthew's text message. She picked up her phone to draft a reply;

"Hi Matthew, thank you so much for the card and the sweets, it was very thoughtful. Sorry that I'm only getting back to you now, I've been a bit preoccupied. Jane."

That was a simple, non committal text message, acknowledging his kind behaviour but not opening up the channel of communication. *Bing!*

A message from Matthew. That was fast. Jane snatched excitedly at her phone. Feeling that familiar heart flutter, the cadence in sequence with her breath;

"How are you feeling? I can't believe Theo did this to you, if I could get my hands on him I would kill him."

Matthew was worried about her, Jane was ashamed to admit to herself that it gave her a lot of pleasure. Love and affection were what she yearned for right now when she was feeling her most vulnerable. She decided to reply to his text straight away, she wasn't playing hard to get, she wasn't playing *any* games for that matter, this was a purely platonic conversation;

"I'm feeling ok, just a bit sore but otherwise fine. How are you?"

"I'm doing ok. Do you think it would be alright if I visited you at some stage?"

What was his game? There was no messing about there. Was he not still with Tia? Surely he wouldn't still be looking a hook up whilst she was in such a terrible state? Her view on men was somewhat tainted at the moment, she didn't know what degree a man would stoop to now.

"I'm getting out of hospital tomorrow, but I'm still feeling quite tired, so I'll probably just chill on the sofa with a movie and the dogs tomorrow night." He'd probably take the hint that she needed some alone time.

"I can come round tomorrow and keep you safe?" Clearly not. This enticed Jane to want to agree, she felt bereft of comfort and attention, the thought of his protective embrace was all too tempting right then. She wanted to snuggle her head in to his chest, breathing in the drug that was his natural scent, captivated by his pheromones.

He was persistent, she would give him that much. She knew she would enjoy the distraction, and ever since she had started thinking about Matthew it was hard to stop. Did she really want to get in to that, though? Was it not *completely* ridiculous to have one man over to her house immediately after she had literally just been assaulted by another?

Jane agreed to him coming over against her better judgement. She couldn't resist, she was too curious to know what he wanted her for. She had longed for a moment when Matthew would come running back and sweep her off her feet and confess his undying love for her, and now the timing of it all was too significant to ignore.

"Ok, but be warned, I look a mess and the house probably isn't too tidy either."

"I don't care. I'll give you a call tomorrow x"

Jane was ashamed to admit that her heart gave a jump and she felt butterflies in her stomach at the thought of Matthew coming over to see her the next day. She had craved his warm, loving touch for as long as she could remember. Despite her traumatic ordeal and the pain literally all over her body, Matthew was still able to ignite that fire within her. That primal, sexual desire for him was intensely strong. But she had to snap out of it, her behaviour was absolutely ludicrous.

"This is probably a terrible idea." She thought out loud to herself. She was having her enigmatic, masculine, earth shatteringly handsome ex boyfriend over to her house straight after she had been assaulted. "Am I crazy?" Was Matthew preying on her at her most vulnerable moment?

Chapter 28

Jane didn't cancel her plans with Matthew, and the next day, as she was getting discharged home, she still hadn't contacted him to cancel. She knew she wanted to see him despite her better judgement. Her excitement rose at the thought of seeing him again, those dark eyes igniting that spark of lust inside of her. To feel his skin against hers. The overriding emotion of desire was defeating her sense of reason.

She would have to try to fix her face. She looked at her reflection in the mirror in the hospital en suite. She had a weeping gash on the top of her nose, covered with a dressing, and two swollen, black eyes. Her hair was everywhere and she still had traces of dry blood in it that the shower hadn't managed to wash out. She would need to attempt another shower when she got home.

Despite Jane's exhilaration, she had to admit to herself that Matthew's reappearance was unbelievably poor timing, she was just out of a very serious and volatile relationship and Jane was feeling particularly vulnerable. Was he attempting to deceive her? To gain her trust whilst she was weak and helpless just to take advantage? Or, was he trying to start things up with her again? Surely not after after such a traumatic ordeal? He was also probably still dating Tia.

And surely he wouldn't try anything on with her right after the assault, her body was too bruised and sore to do anything anyway. She could barely take a deep breath let alone have sex. She wasn't exactly feeling sexy right at that moment. Maybe he was just being kind and friendly? "Yeah right!" Thought Jane with scepticism, laughing at her own joke. Jane was always dubious of other peoples' kindness – there must be an ulterior motive, she always thought.

Jane's mum, dad and Tess all came to the hospital to take her home. Jane was discharged from the hospital with a head injury advice leaflet and a concoction of analgesia and advised to stay off alcohol and work until her headaches had eased and she had full range of movements following her rib fractures. She was given breathing exercises and movements to do everyday, by the physiotherapist, to reduce the risk of developing community acquired pneumonia as she may not expand her lungs properly due to the increased pain on inhalation. She was told she would need to take a minimum of six weeks off work for her ribs to heal properly and to even attempt driving again.

When Jane's parents and Tess had delivered her home, she was delighted to see the dogs were awaiting her arrival. This was the nicest welcome home that she could have imagined. She hugged them both firmly. They were all desperately excited to see her again, they hadn't seen Jane since the stressful activities of two days previous. She had to calm them down because the jumping up and down was excruciating on her ribs.

Her family got her settled in and started making cups of tea and lunch. Jane headed upstairs for a shower, she had to gingerly wash herself again and try to avoid touching all the tender, bruised areas, but the second shower was easier than the first. The idea of putting on any normal clothes was a major inconvenience so she opted for another fresh pair of pyjamas. Matthew would understand, and if he didn't, well, that was his issue. He had seen her in pyjamas enough times anyway.

Jane arrived downstairs to sandwiches, prepared by her mum, she ate them gratefully. Along with the sandwiches was a cup of tea, Jane could've cried, she felt so silly getting emotional over a cup of tea but it symbolised home and warmth and familiarity. She drank it gladly. Charlotte had made a Jasmine Tea blend as Jane had been advised to avoid caffeine for the first few days. It was wonderful.

Millie, Martha and Jennifer arrived on her doorstep, irate and anxious and full of questions of how it had all happened and how they never would have suspected Theo.

Millie hugged her friendly tightly. "Ouch!" Jane gasped in pain.

"Oh, I'm so sorry, Jane." She pulled away and clasped Jane's hands tightly, her face was stricken with heartache and pain as she studied Jane's features, her tears falling unceremoniously. "I can't believe he did this to you, Jane!" The three girls huddled round Jane, squeezing in tightly on to the one sofa.

"The bastard, I'll have him killed for you." Martha shouted, rage and determination in her face.

Jennifer, so sweet and kind, just stroked Jane's hair soothingly and said; "We are all here for you, Jane. No matter what you need."

"You are all too sweet, you have no idea how good it is to see you guys, thank you so much." She smiled warmly at them.

"We'll obviously spend the night with you tonight so that you feel safe. As long as your family haven't already offered?" Millie looked towards Jane's parents and Tess for approval.

"I was going to suggest she come and stay with me so she's not at the place where it all happened, but if you would prefer the girls to stay with you, Jane, then that's ok too. You could stay with me a couple of nights next week or I can move in with you for a while, so you feel safe?" Tess suggested, wanting to show Jane she had a huge support network. Jane felt massively grateful for her friends and family, their love was invaluable to her.

Jane felt uncomfortable, she felt guilty having already agreed to see Matthew. Was she really going to ditch her family and friends for a man she hadn't been with for over a year? No. She wouldn't be that girl. She would cancel Matthew, it was a really stupid idea that she should never have agreed to when she had been feeling needy and lonely and intensely vulnerable and likely to succumb immediately to his charms.

"Whoever wants to stay with me I'm happy with any of you." Jane said blissfully, feeling like the wealthiest woman in the world, with so much to be grateful for. "I would be happy for you all to stay." And she looked to her mum and dad when she said this; she knew she needed her parents more than ever at this time.

"Well, sweetie. I think you are well cared for with the girls here," Gary said, "I wouldn't want to impose on a girly night." He laughed, his warm eyes filled with love and admiration.

"Agreed." Said Charlotte. "You girls all enjoy yourselves, take Jane's mind off everything that's happened. And honey, I'll be round to see you tomorrow." Charlotte kissed her daughter on the cheek, Jane noted the tears in her eyes and her heart ached for her mother. She knew her mother loved her with all her might.

"Thank you, mum. I love you."

"I love you too, so, *so* much. Bye girls. *Gary*." Charlotte addressed her ex husband, smiling at him. Jane couldn't deny the small current that passed between the divorced couple, and in a flash, it was gone.

"Bye Charlotte." He said, smiling warmly at her and waving her off.

"I'll head now, too." He said, hugging Jane and kissing her on the cheek, also. "I'll see you tomorrow. Love you."

"Thanks dad, love you, too." And Gary was away as well. Jane missed her parents as soon as they had left. Despite her mother's imperiousness, she craved that maternal love and protection you can only get from a mother.

"Right girls! We are going to have some fun tonight! I've got the wine and a few good movies we can watch!" Martha said excitedly, her eyes alight with enthusiasm. Jane appreciated her efforts to try to cheer up and take her mind off things.

"Oh, Martha, I'm not allowed to drink alcohol, it's bad for concussion." Jane didn't feel much like drinking anyway, her headaches were bad in the morning and she didn't need a hangover to add to it.

"I can't drink either," said Jennifer, "preggers over here!" She laughed, pointing at her large belly.

"Oh, yes, of course. No worries. Well, Millie, Tess and I can have some wine and we will spend the night fetching for you, Jane, whatever you need, just name it. Tea, biscuits, food. And we'll look after the mutts for you, too." Martha glanced displeasingly towards the dogs, she was not much of a dog person so Jane knew that offering to do this was a big deal.

"Thank you, Martha. But really, just your company is all I need tonight. I can still walk, sort of." She laughed gingerly, clutching at her side.

"Of course you can." Said Jennifer, "but why walk when your friends can do that for you?" They all laughed.

"I wonder did Jack miss you at all?" Millie mocked at Jack's apparent disinterest in his owner.

Ruby, the loving and needy Cavalier King Charles, hadn't left Jane's side, she was curled up on Jane's lap and didn't appear to have any intention of moving any time soon. But Jack, her normally overly affectionate Cocker Spaniel, was standing guard looking out the window for any intruders.

"I think he's trying to protect me," said Jane, "he's probably annoyed that he allowed Theo to hurt me like that. This has been traumatic for them, too." She looked at them, feeling immensely guilty, to think that they could have potentially come to harm as a result of her choices was terrifying. She was very grateful that they hadn't been injured during the attack, she couldn't have coped mentally if she had to deal with a wounded dog as well, or worse.

"Do you really think dogs have thoughts as deep as that?" Martha asked incredulously, staring Jane down as though she had lost her mind in the assault.

313

"I think they would both risk their lives to try to protect me." Jane answered honestly. "You aren't a dog lover, so you wouldn't understand how incredibly intelligent they are. Their ability to love and forgive is so far advanced than that of a human. Most humans are jealous and resentful and slow to forgive, we could learn a lot from them, if we paid enough attention." Jane absentmindedly stroked Ruby's head and Ruby leaned in to her, savouring the moment of affection as though it were the most amazing feeling in the world.

Martha looked slightly embarrassed and conscious of the fact that she was renowned for being jealous and resentful of others' fortune.

Jane suddenly remembered that she hadn't text Matthew to cancel their plans that night, disappointment swelled up inside her and she quickly pushed the feeling back down, her friends and sister were more important, they had been solid figures in her life for many years now. Tess, her entire life. She wasn't going to ditch them for someone who had kicked her to curb the moment things got a little rough.

Feeling more determined now, Jane drafted a text message to Matthew and read it before sending to check for any spelling mistakes;

"Hi Matthew, I'm really sorry that I'm texting so last minute but I'm going to have to take a rain check on tonight. My sister and friends are staying with me tonight to keep me company and I really can't turn them away. Maybe we can get together some other time. J"

Jane hit send and turned back to her friends who were babbling enthusiastically about Jennifer's expectant baby;

"I know, it's crazy, I only have two months to go. Ben and I are super excited and now that we are married we actually feel

314

even more bonded." She jabbered on happily, looking dewy eyed and joyful. There had been a time when Jane would have performed retching gestures at these mawkish sentiments, but rather than feeling doubtful and cynical of these emotions, she felt elated for her friend. Jane was starting to thaw, her capacity to love had grown and, perhaps, strengthened.

"How lovely," said Millie, "I can't wait to be an auntie!"

"You're not going to be an auntie!" Martha exclaimed. "You guys aren't sisters!"

They all darted scandalised looks at her because of her outrageous statement, Martha shrugged, apparently unaware of what she had said wrong this time.

But Jennifer laughed, "I'm an only child, I want my children to have aunties and uncles. I would be so glad if they called all of you auntie." She smiled affectionately at the four of them.

"Oh. Right. Always sticking my foot in it, aren't I?" Martha laughed uneasily, feeling a fool.

"Easy mistake." Said Millie, reassuringly squeezing her friend's hand, Martha gave her a thankful smile in return.

Jane was vaguely listening to the conversation. Her thoughts were well and truly in the land of Matthew, she pictured him kissing her, touching her, caressing her cheek in that way he did. She looked at her phone and there was a message sitting there from him, Jane's heart leapt at the sight of it, she knew she was treading on dangerous waters;

"What about tomorrow night?"

Jane stared at the message in astonishment. He was obviously desperate to see her. But why? Jane couldn't deny that she was craving to see him too, now that he had opened this channel of communication, and he clearly longed to see her also. The only problem Jane felt was that it was a long time until tomorrow, how would she pass the time until she could see him? Jane replied, trying to feign elusiveness;

"What's the rush?"

He replied immediately;

"I want to check you are ok, I'm just sorry this has happened and I know I haven't been there for you." He wanted to be there for her. Like a friend? Or more? Jane wondered, hoping for the latter but in need of an answer as to why he would choose such an inappropriate time to get back in contact with her.

"It wasn't your fault. I'll be fine. I'm sure Tia wouldn't be happy about you making arrangements to meet up with me anyway." Jane had to know if Tia was still in the picture, this would definitely help her indecisiveness over the circumstance.

"We broke up." Right. *That* changed things.

"Ah, so I'm your rebound then?" She knew she was being overly brash and difficult.

"Definitely not, I'm worried about you. I still care about you, Jane. That never stopped." Wow. Jane stared at the message, savouring the words. Letting them fill her up and set her high atop a cloud, high on ecstasy. She desired his love, needed it to feel alive again.

How would she respond? She wanted to keep her cool, to not come across as desperate for him, as though she had been lying in wait for when he would come out of the wood work.

"Ok, we can meet tomorrow. Are you ok to come to me?"

"Definitely. Is seven o'clock ok?"

"Perfect."

Jane's heart gave a little leap of excitement, she was going to see Matthew again. Beautiful, handsome, irresistibly sexy Matthew. And, although she had many looming doubts about the arrangement, she chose to ignore them. Mainly because she was curious as to why Matthew wanted to see her so urgently, but also because she was still in love with him, always had been, it had never stopped. She had just sat on that part of her, hoping that it would stay hidden and out of the way, but it was eating her alive, from the inside out. She had to see him, she felt as though her sanity depended on it.

"Who are you texting away at?" Martha asked, eyeing up her friend curiously. Jane jumped at the interruption of her thoughts, she winced at the pain this caused in her side.

"Just my mum, she's asking how I am." She lied, hoping that Martha couldn't see right through her.

Jane felt she seemed convincing. Martha continued to stare at her suspiciously though. The problem with long term friends was they got to know you and they got to know when you were telling the truth or when you were lying through your teeth.

"Are you *sure* you are just texting your mum?" Implored Martha with a knowing twinkle in her eye.

Jane gathered her thoughts for a moment, Martha could see right through her story for the lie that it was. She thought about maintaining the charade but to what end? These people were her friends and she could trust them, surely?

"Ok, you caught me." She started, raising her hands in the air in an act of surrender. She gave them a sparkling smile that would have been much more effective if her face hadn't looked like mince meat. "I was texting Matthew." She couldn't hide the smile, she stared at them shamelessly, excited about the prospect of Matthew potentially being a part of her life again.

"I knew it!" Martha wailed excitedly. "I knew you would reply to him! Well? What's he saying?" Martha lived for the latest gossip, she edged forward in anticipation of the exciting revelation.

The four girls were on tenterhooks, leaning forward so as not to miss a word, waiting for Jane's response.

"He wants to come over tomorrow night."

"What!"

"I hope you said no!"

"He has some nerve!"

"Why does he want to come over? He knows what you've been through. What does he want with you?" Tess asked angrily. Protective sister mode had kicked in, she looked ruffled and her cheeks puffed as she spoke.

The girls babbled over one another excitedly, wondering what Matthew would want with Jane so soon after the assault and having not heard a word from him since the break up, bar the two occasions that they had accidentally bumped in to each other. Their voices were laced with anger and uncertainty.

"He actually wanted to call over tonight, but I said no, *obviously*. I wanted to be with you guys." The girls stared at Jane in disbelief.

"And he knew you were just out of hospital?" Millie asked, wide eyed, looking astounded.

"Well, yeah."

"Is he crazy?!" Cried Jennifer.

"Sounds like bad news, Jane. Predators prey on vulnerable girls and you couldn't be any more vulnerable. I don't like the sound of it." Tess said firmly, a deep crease in her brow, her eyes narrowed and lips pursed.

"He says he's worried about me." Jane said defensively, crossing her arms. She regretted telling the girls, they were bursting her happy bubble.

"Well, of course he's going to say that. He's hardly going to say, 'Jane, I know you are very vulnerable at the moment so I want to take full advantage of that.'" Martha replied with thick smugness as though Jane were completely stupid, eyeing her up with a 'know it all' expression which wound Jane up exponentially.

"No, I guess not." Jane whispered, the stark reality slowly settling in. She was an idiot; she had set herself up to be taken advantage of by predatory men. Her aunt and uncle had set the precipice for her entire life, she subconsciously chose men who would hurt her because she was conditioned, as a child, to believe that the people who loved you unconditionally, ultimately hurt you in the worst possible way.

That's why David, her psychotic and stalker ex boyfriend, had been attracted to her and that's why Theo had been drawn to her, they could sense her intense vulnerability, she was insecure and easily manipulated and she was a prime target for pathetic men who hadn't grown a set of balls, having to control and manipulate abused women.

"I'm telling you, Jane, him wanting to come over so soon is bad news. I know I am outspoken a lot of the time and some times don't always get it right, but I'm serious about this. It's weird that he wants to come over right now, to what end would he want to spend the night with an abused victim? It *screams* exploitation all over." Martha exhorted her opinion strongly upon Jane. She sat with her elbows rested on her knees and her hands gripped together tightly, staring intently at Jane, imploring her to see sense.

Jane considered her friends' comments. She couldn't help but agree with what they were saying. It all made sense, and Jane definitely wasn't thinking straight. She was desperately in need of love and comfort and safety at that moment, and Matthew's offer of affection and company was so very tempting. Should she just cancel altogether? Was he a predator looking to take further advantage of her? She couldn't imagine Matthew being like that but she also could never have imagined that he would leave her, abandon her in her darkest hour when she needed him the most; after the death of their unborn child.

Jane was torn. The sensible thing to do would be to cancel on Matthew and just forget about him, move on with her life, she had survived this long without him. The alternative was... Well, a very sexy man would be in her house tomorrow night, he was like a drug, the fire that had been dormant inside her for a year was finally beginning to rekindle. This was what Matthew did to her, gave her a reason to live, reaffirmed her faith in happiness and a happy ending. It was just too incredibly enticing to refuse. She wanted him with her so badly, to touch his hard, sculpted body, to feel those strong arms embrace her entirely. To transport her off to another world, free from Theo and life and worry.

She wanted to look deep in to those dark, piercing eyes. To feel that incredibly, magical tingle again. The feeling only Matthew Carson could give her. To stir up that ferocious, sexy woman inside of her again.

The girls ordered pizza that evening and chatted about nothing in particular, Jane was happy. This was what she needed, to have her most dearest friends near to her to take her mind off everything. She didn't need a man to distract her. She had her friends and family.

Jane was trying to decide in her head how she was going to turn down Matthew, again. Her mind was toing and froing like a seesaw, one minute she was completely certain that she wanted Matthew, the next, she was telling herself that she was crazy to have even considered it. Tess seemed to read her thoughts when she asked;

"Well, Jane. Have you thought about tomorrow night? What you are going to do about Matthew?" Her eyes scanned her face, searching for the answer before she spoke it.

"Honestly? I'm not sure. I can see where you guys are coming from and it makes a lot of sense. But that doesn't help the fact that I *really* want to see him. I've missed him so much." She felt the ache in her chest return; she was in love with him.

"Look, Jane, tonight was supposed to be about getting some rest and we were to lift and lay whatever you needed and take your mind off everything. Now Matthew has confused your head and you're even more stressed and confused. I say leave it a few weeks or months, until you have all this mess behind you, and then see where things are with him." Millie urged, looking angry and impatient. She made a good point.

"But what if he has got a girlfriend by then?" Jane asked, knowing how desperate she sounded.

"Then he wasn't willing to wait for you, so, therefore, you are better off without him." Millie retorted quickly, fire in her eyes as they blazed at her. Millie meant business.

"Fair enough." Said Jane, finding it hard to argue with such an accurate statement. She stared at her feet, feeling lost and ashamed.

"Millie's right, Jane. It's a crazy idea and I don't even know why Matthew has suggested this out of all the times in the world that he could have chosen to meet up with you! It's totally ridiculous!" Jennifer cried, instinctively rubbing her belly as though it would reassure her.

"You're all right; I'm an idiot for considering it. I won't meet up with him." Jane's heart plummeted in to her stomach, the disappointment etched across her face and she felt tears threaten once again.

"You are *not* an idiot, Jane. Don't ever think that. It's these scumbags for men who won't give you a break." Millie yelled in indignation.

Jane yawned widely, she was completely exhausted. It was only eight o'clock in the evening, but Jane was craving her bed. Her mind was a jumble of racing thoughts and emotions.

"I think I'm going to call it a night. I'm sorry I'm leaving you guys so early." She said apologetically, smiling warmly at the four of them.

"Good, you need to get plenty of rest." Said Tess. "Everyday you will feel a little bit better." She promised, kissing her sister softly on the cheek.

"Night Jane, have a good sleep. Love you lots."

"Night Jane, call us if you need anything, any time."

"Thanks girls, you're the best. And thank you for being so honest with me, that couldn't have been easy." She blew them all kisses.

Jane took a cup of Jasmine tea with her and headed to bed, Ruby came with her for some company and cuddles. Jane climbed in to bed, the exhaustion swept over her, the claws of sleep creeping rapidly over her. But before she let herself slip over, she grabbed her phone quickly and sent a very last minute text;

"See you tomorrow, Matthew x"

Chapter 29

The next morning, Jane woke to the sound of her phone ringing, her head was a blur and her entire body screamed out in agony;

"Hullo?" She croaked, her roaring headache throbbing, her brain threatening to burst out of her skull.

"Hi Jane, this is Constable Neill, the police officer tasked to your house three nights ago." She said in a military, no nonsense tone.

"Yes, I remember." How could she forget?

"I'm phoning you to update you on your case."

"What's happened?!" Jane asked as anxiety rippled through her, was he going to get away with it?

"Theo Reid was arrested last night and has been interviewed this morning. He has been charged with assault and released on Police bail and is due to appear in court within twenty eight days." She sounded as though she was reading all this from her police manual on how to talk to people, excessively serious and rigid.

"But, what does this mean?! Where was he when he was arrested?" She screeched.

"He was arrested at his mother's house-"

"Did he admit to it?!" Jane bluntly interrupted.

"He has made no admissions, he said no comment to all of our questions." Constable Neil remained calm and conformed.

"Why has he been allowed to be released on bail? Am I safe while he is allowed to be out?!" She screamed accusingly, did they not understand that she wasn't safe with him prowling the streets. What if he came back?

"Theo's bail conditions are that he cannot be within five hundred metres of your home, your family's home, or your place of work. He also has a curfew of nine o'clock each evening."

Jane considered this, the thought of Theo being allowed to roam freely did not sit well with her, what if he came back for her regardless of the bail conditions?

"Ok, thanks for all your help." Jane held back her reservations, there was nothing she could do to change it.

"You can expect a letter from the Crown Prosecution Service about your case and, also, from Victim Services who support victims of crime attending court." She explained seriously.

Jesus. A court case. Her dirty laundry aired out to dry for all to see. She could understand why a lot of rape victims didn't go to the police the majority of the time. She felt overwhelmed, suffocated, terrified. The thought of facing Theo in court and battling against him was enough to make her want to drop the charges and let him go free. But, she could never let him get away with this, he would go on to abuse countless other women the same way, it had to stop with her.

"Ok, thank you." Jane terminated the call, her head brimming with thoughts of confusion and fear, where was Theo now?

Jane was fully awake, pumped with adrenaline, anxiety, and most of all, optimism. Theo had been charged with assault, she would be safe soon. Jane's headache still felt like throbbing stabs of sharp metal rattling around her head, but, she had to admit that it was slightly better than the day before. Her ribs were still gut-wrenchingly painful and she now had a continuous ache as well as the sharp, shooting pain when she coughed or took a deep breath.

Jane made her way downstairs as quickly as she could to tell the girls the good news.

"He's been charged!" Millie cried excitedly when Jane had broke the news, she stood in the kitchen where they had all congregated, sipping on an Espresso.

"Oh, he's going down big time." Said Martha, in a low, breathy voice, sounding almost sadistic.

"Thank heavens for that!" Jennifer rolled her eyes relievedly and blew on her tea.

"Jane, this is fantastic news! That scumbag is going to get everything he deserves." Said Tess through tears, grabbing her sister in to another rib crunching hug causing Jane to cry out in pain.

"Oh, I'm sorry, Jane." Tess freed her.

"I know, I'm so glad they caught him so quickly. But, I think he will be in court soon, I'm not entirely sure what the full procedure is going forward, it's all a bit intimidating." Jane said worriedly, twirling strands of hair anxiously through her fingers, looking to the girls for reassurance.

"Well, you know one thing is for definite, we will all be here with you every step of the way." Millie explained, all four girls nodded their heads vigorously in agreement.

The girls had tea, coffee and toast for breakfast and chattered excitedly about the recent developments. They left to let Jane spend the day by herself, not without many more

326

tight hugs, though, that made Jane's ribs ache further more. Jane phoned her mum then her dad to tell them the news about Theo's arrest.

They both cried with relief. Jane knew this was killing them both, to see their youngest child battered and bruised. She knew it would bring back those all too familiar memories of when she would return home, black and blue at the hands of her aunt and uncle. This time, though, they had been powerless to stop it.

Jane felt somewhat guilty when she thought of her parents and all their worry, knowing that they would disapprove profusely when she already had made plans that evening to meet with a different man altogether. Matthew was due to call at seven o'clock that evening. Jane felt flappy and panicky about it and at one point had the text message poised, ready to cancel. She couldn't forget what the girls had said to her the night before and how opposed they were to the idea. Was she being absurd?

Jane tried her best to get the house in some sort of decent shape. Thankfully her parents and Tess had cleaned up the mess from the assault but dog hairs gathered in the house quicker than moths to a flame.

It was currently half past six in the evening, should she put on a bit of make up? Should she try to fix her hair in to a nicer style? Jane stood up quickly to have a look at herself in the mirror but black dots appeared in her vision and she lost her footing, so she sat back down, with a thud, until the dizzy episode had settled. Matthew would understand her unkempt appearance.

She got up again, slowly this time, and studied her appearance in the large mirror above her fireplace. It was not

327

a pretty sight; the gash on her nose no longer had a dressing on it, a layer of curdled blood was smeared thickly on top and had a shining purple bruise around the perimeter of it. It looked completely grotesque. Her eyes were both purple and puffy and her entire face had a bruised sheen to it.

She felt absolutely mental. She had officially lost her mind. She was having her ex boyfriend, '*The One That Got Away*', over to her house that night to discuss... To discuss what? Whilst her face looked like she'd had a run in with the local butcher. What was she doing?

It was five past seven, no time to turn back. But also no sign of Matthew, he was only five minutes late, that was ok. But it was making her nervous, the apprehension and suspense. What could he be coming over to talk to her about? Surely not to get back together? He had been so certain that he wanted the relationship to end over a year ago and he had made no attempt at contacting her until two days previous when he was obviously feeling lonely and upset over his break up with Tia. Jane felt like a total idiot allowing him to come over, when; *Ding!*

The doorbell rang. Ruby barked at the apparent intruder. Jane jumped at the sound, the sharp pain in her ribs personified, not helped by the churning butterflies in her stomach. Too late to change her mind, he had already arrived. Jane's mouth all of a sudden felt like sandpaper, where was a glass of water when she needed one? It wasn't Matthew at the door though. To Jane's monumental surprise, it was Theo's mother. Jane opened the door slowly, shock and fear ransacked her entire body as Theo's mother looked wild with rage.

"What the hell is wrong with you, Jane?! Why has my son been charged with assault?!" Veronica demanded fiercely. Ruby and Jack howled defensively at the rude trespasser.

"Veronica, as you can see, my face is the work of *your* son. He deserves to be where he is right now. Get away from my house or I will phone the police on you, too. How dare you come to my house after everything your son has subjected me to!" Jane's heart was pounding with nerves; she was shaking with rage and fear.

"I highly doubt my sweet boy did that! You probably fell on purpose and then blamed it on him. I always knew you were bad news!" Veronica snapped, looking unhinged as she stood on the porch, threatening to move in.

Jane was shaking with anger, she was ready to explode with fury at the audacity of this woman.

"Is there a problem here?" Veronica spun round. It was Matthew, and he had a bunch of flowers in hand. Jane's heart sank, she knew how this would look.

"So, my son is accused of assault and you are only out of hospital and *already* you have another man coming to the house! I told Theo from the start that you were nothing more than a common skank!" Veronica screamed, her face turning puce with frustration and vexation.

"You need to leave," Matthew demanded firmly, "your son is a low life, scumbag who beats women for pleasure!" Jane wanted to high five Matthew for this tremendous retort.

"How dare you speak to *me* like that!" Veronica's voice was shrill, her fists were clenched, she struggled to contain herself.

"How dare you attack my friend after all she has been through. Now, you are trespassing on Jane's property and she has asked you politely to leave. I suggest you do so or would

329

you like me to also phone the police?" Matthew shot back. Jane stared at him with a primal lust, seeing him standing there, strong and sturdy, fighting her battles made her want to claw at his clothes.

Veronica gave Jane a dirty look that would have singed her eyebrows if tangible, and then she stormed off, apparently knowing when she was outnumbered.

"I don't think I've seen the last of her." Said Jane sadly, turning to face Matthew, her heart pounding, not with nerves at seeing him but with anger at Theo's mother. Jane was outraged and distraught. Was she safe in her house with another lunatic after her? Veronica could see how badly injured she was but still took the side of Theo. Jane's face and side hurt from the strain of shouting. Veronica had always been so kind to her, she had got on so well with her, it hurt Jane to see her acting so vicious. But Matthew was right, that's exactly where Theo had picked up on the behaviour.

She let Matthew in and they stood in the hallway quite speechless at the previously unfolded event, he handed her the flowers. The dogs were very excited to see him, jumping up and down and giving him intrusive kisses on his mouth.

"They've missed you. Thank you for the flowers." She set the flowers on the console table underneath the mirror. She couldn't help but smile at her lovable dogs.

"You have been through such an ordeal, Jane."

He approached her very slowly. Jane could feel her insides melting under his smouldering gaze. Only Matthew could have this profound effect on her. To render her speechless and turn her in to a quivering mess.

He put his arms around her gently, as though she were a fragile, porcelain doll, and kissed her on the cheek. Jane savoured the luxurious moment, touching his hard back and toned arms. His scent transported her back to that first time in the bar when they had kissed in secret booths. She felt the fluttering tingle again and treasured every moment of the embrace. How she had missed everything about this man.

She could smell his aftershave as he hugged her; a delectable mixture of citrus and sandalwood and his own sweet scent. It was like a drug, like ecstasy to her brain. She felt floaty and care free, forgetting all her troubles. How she had missed him so terribly. But then, like a smack in the face, reality set in. He wasn't hers anymore, he had dumped her over a year ago and never looked back.

He withdrew from the embrace and studied her damaged profile, worry and anger etched in the creases marking his face. He traced the back of his hand gently across her cheek. Jane closed her eyes and leaned in to the affectionate touch, feeling that spark of chemistry spread through her veins, feeling the hairs rise on the back of her neck.

"Why are you crying?" He asked gently, taking her chin between his thumb and index finger and tilting her head to look him in the eye.

"Just so much has happened and now you are here and I don't really know why you are here so I'm just feeling a little confused." She said quickly, withdrawing from his embrace and moving in to the living room and sitting on the sofa, feeling as though she was having an out of body experience, Matthew was there. He had touched her, cared about her, but she wasn't sure how she felt. What were his intentions?

"I wanted to make sure you were ok and I didn't want you to be on your own." He replied softly, sitting on the opposite

331

sofa, Jane appreciated the distance, she couldn't focus when he was so close to her. Pheromones clouding her brain.

"Why care for me now after so much time has passed?" She asked, more eagerly than she had intended.

"I have always cared for you. After we broke up I felt so guilty about what I had done to you, I wanted to change things and make it right but I also knew we both needed time to clear our heads.

"When I finally thought about getting back in contact with you, you were already seeing Theo and I knew I had missed my chance. So then I met Tia and I tried to move on with her. It just so happened that Tia was friendly with Jennifer, I encouraged Tia to try to get an invite to the wedding, I knew you would be there." Matthew said, staring down at his feet. Jane stared at him in alarm, her mouth half open, utterly speechless.

"So, em, so, you planned that meeting at the wedding even though you knew we both had partners?" Jane stuttered in mock disbelief, revolted at the thought of him touching another woman apart from her.

"I wanted to see you again. I also wanted to see if you and Theo were the real thing, if you were both serious then I would leave you well alone, if not, then I knew I might stand a chance in the future." He answered honestly, staring her directly in the eye, he wasn't joking. Jane gulped, taking her eyes off him, his gaze was smouldering and she had a feeling she was going to get burned.

"But can you not see how awful that was to do that to Tia? You basically used her to get to me." Jane scolded furiously, was he always using and ditching women at his convenience?

332

"I know, it definitely wasn't right and I did feel guilty, but we both knew deep down that it wasn't working out between us. And then the way she behaved towards you at the wedding, I knew she wasn't the one for me." He clarified formally.

"You could hardly blame her, Matthew! She had every right to be annoyed. Especially if she was to now find out that you had set the whole thing up to accidentally on purpose bump in to me!" Jane was even more confused and angry at Matthew's blatant disregard for Tia's feelings.

"I wanted to see you; I've missed you so much. I regret all my actions. I was cold and heartless towards you after the miscarriage. If I couldn't have you romantically I thought I could at least try at having a friendship with you. So, of course, I saw you and Theo together and you both looked very happy so I was sure I had missed out.

"Then I decided to text you, going against my better judgement, because I missed you too much." His eyes averted to the ground, was he crying? "When I didn't hear back from you I thought you were just moved on, but then I heard from Ben that you were in hospital following an assault, I was sick with worry about you. I was so angry with myself for not being there to protect you. I had to find out what happened and make sure you were ok. So Ben told me what hospital you were in and I decided to visit you to see how you were, but, when I arrived you were sleeping so I left the gifts. I was shocked when I saw you; Theo really did a number on you."

His fists clenched angrily. Jane felt self conscious, knowing that her injuries must be hideous to him. She brushed her hair across one half of her face to at least try to hide some of it.

"Your mum and Tess were surprised to see me." He continued, laughing.

"I'm sure they were, I'm surprised my poor mother didn't have a coronary!" She laughed as well, making sure she kept a lot of her face hidden by her hair. "What did you say to them?"

"I told them I had heard about what happened and wanted to check you were ok. Your mother had many questions." He chuckled.

"I'm sure she did." Jane rolled her eyes at the thought.

"I feel so guilty, Jane. If I had never left you then this never would have happened. I'm a complete idiot. I knew as soon as I broke things off with you that I had made a terrible mistake, but I didn't know how to go back to fix everything. I was sure you would never even look at me again let alone take me back." Tears pooled in his eyes, he looked at her intently, his eyes ablaze with lust and compassion, as though he was aching for her, craving to be near her. Jane shuffled in her seat, excruciatingly aware that she wanted to be near him too, all too aware of the magnetic connection between them.

"So, why are you here now?" She asked bluntly, bringing herself to her senses slightly, trying to stifle the yearning girl inside of her, telling her to be reasonable and discover some answers. "Two days after I got out of hospital after a vicious assault? Did you not think that was maybe bad timing?" Anger laced her voice unintentionally, but she had been hurt by so many men in her life, she was tired and fed up.

"If you are angry at my timing then why did you agree to it?" He asked defensively, the blaze in his eyes dimmed slightly, clearly shocked at Jane's swift change in tone.

"Because I was curious, I wanted to know why you were at the hospital and why you wanted to see me. And, don't forget, you were very persistent. I could hardly say no." She replied, equally as defensive.

"Well, you could have." He said, with a cheeky smirk, trying to lighten the ever increasingly tense atmosphere.

"Well, yes, I could have." She felt her icy exterior thaw slightly and she grinned back at him, it was impossible to stay mad at him. She also didn't want to scare him away, she wanted to get to the bottom of the visit, she couldn't lie to herself that she wanted him. She looked up at him from hooded eyelids, attempting to appear seductive and irresistible when she remembered her battered face and knew she probably looked like some kind of constipated ogre.

"Can I get you anything? Wine, water, tea?" He asked, standing up.

"A tea would be lovely, thanks. Help yourself to anything in the kitchen."

He returned with two cups of Chamomile Tea, handing one to Jane and sitting down on the opposite sofa.

"Thanks. So, you still haven't told me why you are here." She implored again, knowing she was being bold but feeling as though she had nothing to lose by finding out the truth.

"I told you, I wanted to check how you were after everything." He breathed exasperatedly.

"Well, you can see that I'm doing fine, so why are you still here?" Jane knew she was being unbearable and all over the place but she was confused and angry, she was hardly going to open her arms out to him again after the way he had treated her.

335

"I want you back." He said simply. Jane spat her tea out and choked violently, her injured ribs cried out in protest, she struggled to catch her breath. She was caught completely unawares. She glanced at him, he was staring at her confidently. He hadn't shuddered, he didn't appear nervous or scared to admit this. Jane was lost for words, they sat in silence for a moment, Jane considered her thoughts, trying to gather an appropriate response. Did she want to get back with him? Could she trust him if they did?

"Just like that?" She eventually said. "After a year apart with no contact and after the way you treated me?"

"I know, Jane. What I did was unforgivable. But you can't forget that I was hurt, too, I had lost a baby as well. I felt suffocated in a world of misery and I didn't have you for support, I needed you, Jane, and you shut me out. I couldn't go on like that anymore, I had to break free and grieve my own way." He stifled tears, gulping them down, looking down at his feet as he spoke and back up at Jane to try to decipher her body language.

Jane was repressing tears also, "You told me you were relieved that we had lost the baby." She burst in to tears at those words, unable to contain herself for any longer. The tears stung the painful abrasions on her face. The past year's struggles finally overwhelming her in one fell swoop.

"I'm disgusted with myself, I didn't mean that, you must know that?" He begged, leaning forward, his elbows rested on his knees, his face strained with remorse and sorrow.

"How would we ever survive as a couple when the first difficult hurdle we came across you were gone with the wind?" She snapped, looking at him accusingly. Condemning him for what he had done to their relationship.

"I've thought about that, I shouldn't have bailed so quickly. But I didn't know what else to do. But now that I know that I don't want to live my life without you, I know that we could face anything together, with a different perspective." He pleaded his case, his brow creased and tears filling his eyes. Jane couldn't look at him, it was too difficult, she had longed for a moment like this for so long and now that it had arrived she didn't know what to do with it.

"I'm so confused, I don't know how to think or feel. So much has happened." Jane was perplexed as to what to say.

"I know, I've bombarded you when you already have so much going on. You don't have to answer right now, have a think about it." As he said this he looked dejected and dismayed. The disappointment at Jane not accepting his offer with open arms was overwhelmingly poignant and devastating.

"Thanks."

Jane and Matthew then chatted for a long time, filling each other in on the past year. Jane couldn't deny that it was like an adrenaline hit to see him again, he ignited life back in to her, stoking a fire that had been lying dormant for some time. She felt alive.

Jane also felt extremely safe in his company, but it was painful to see him again. The pain of losing him had been devastating to her, she had never loved anyone as much, she knew she would never experience another feeling like that again.

And now, here he was, with her but not actually with her. It was torture, how she had ached for him for so long. To feel his strong arms embrace her and take her off to another world, just the two of them. But she had to be sensible, she couldn't start anything back up with him, it had been too painful to get over him the first time.

Jane was feeling sleepy. "I can sleep in the spare room so you have someone with you tonight?" Matthew suggested innocently. Jane looked at him suspiciously. "I would be a perfect gentleman!" He tittered, raising his hands, yielding to her suspicions.

"No, honestly, it's ok. You go on home, thank you for being so nice to me." Jane replied, smiling at him warmly but her eyes heavy with fatigue. The truth was, she didn't want him to go, when would she see him again if he left?

"Are you sure? I'm worried about you." He urged.

"You go home. I don't think it's wise for you to stay the night." Jane had to have some boundaries, staying over would be ridiculous.

"Ok, no problem. As long as you'll be ok. I'll call you tomorrow."

Jane walked him to the door, the closeness the two of them shared sparked electricity inside of her. She wondered if Matthew could feel it too, that magnetic pull to be close to him, to be touching him.

Jane thanked him again and looked up at him longingly. Why was he so incredibly good looking? It was hard to look him directly in the eye because she felt she might spontaneously self combust from the fire that crept up within her.

As they stood facing each other at the doorway, Jane was painfully aware that she probably looked a wreck. She looked down at her feet, feeling excruciatingly aware that he was studying every crevice and curve of her face. He must be disgusted by her appearance.

But then, Matthew raised his right hand and using his index finger he propped it under her chin and lifted her face so that she was looking directly at him. Jane gulped at the intensity at which his dark eyes bore right in to her soul. She saw beautiful flecks of honey throughout those mesmerising, coffee coloured eyes.

Matthew leaned in, but he merely hugged her goodbye, Jane's heart was pounding, she thought he was going to kiss her, how she wanted to kiss him so passionately. She squeezed him tightly. She felt severely disappointed, she yearned to kiss him. Then he pulled away and looked at her again, he must have read the expression on her face because, just then, he slowly leaned his head towards hers. He kissed her softly, barely brushing her lips, careful of her sore face. Jane savoured every single moment of those incredibly soft lips. They stood there kissing for what felt like a lifetime, Jane couldn't bear to separate from the embrace, she knew she shouldn't be doing it but it was too unbearably hard to resist.

Jane eventually broke off the kiss, her legs felt like they could have gone from beneath her. She couldn't be sure if her light head was from the concussion or the breathtaking kiss.

"I never stopped loving you." She told him.

"Me neither." He replied.

And he was gone.

Chapter 30

Jane woke the next morning with a painful ribcage and an even more painful headache, but she couldn't help but smile at the thoughts of Matthew. Being with him had transported her off in to another world, as though she were walking on clouds in irrefutable ecstasy. Jane wanted to do nothing more than just live in the bubble of her and Matthew.

Jane had to remember, though, that they definitely were not back together, as much as she wanted that to happen, and this pained her even more than the headache. Last night felt like a form of torture to her, to dangle Matthew right in front of her and then take him away again. She felt as though she was spiralling down a dangerous path and yet her overriding emotion was that she wanted to see him again and she wanted to see him soon. Could they make it as a couple again after so much had happened between them and such a lot of time had passed?

Matthew had been quite clear about his intentions, he wanted her back. But, was it too soon after Theo and Tia? Jane was also trying to recover from the recent assault she had received from her ex boyfriend. Not ideal timing for another ex boyfriend to rise up out of the wood work.

Jane's head felt like it had been scrambled, she was overwhelmed and she knew she had enough to be dealing with at the present moment, never mind dramatic proposals of undying love from someone she hadn't seen in a year.

Jane checked her phone and wasn't surprised to see messages from Millie, Martha, Jennifer, Tess, mum, dad and... *Matthew*. The girls were texting Jane frantically in a bid to find out if she actually did get together with Matthew the night before. Jane poised a generic message and copied and pasted it and sent it to all four of the girls;

"Yes, I saw Matthew last night. I can fill you guys in later if you want to call over after lunch? X"

Jane knew she had to tell the girls what went on, she wanted their advice on what to do next. She also wanted to fill them in on Veronica trespassing and verbally attacking her.

Jane read the message from Matthew next;

"Good morning, was lovely spending the evening with you last night. I hope you're ok and hopefully I didn't make you feel too pressured in to a decision x"

Jane replied quickly: "Morning, thank you for keeping me company last night, it was a real comfort. No, I didn't feel pressured, but we maybe should take things slowly. Hope you understand x"

"Of course I do, just take your time and whatever you decide is fine. Fancy doing something tonight? ;-)"

Jane read the last message and laughed, assuming it was a joke, but she read and re-read the message and against every single ounce of her better judgement, she replied;

"Ok."

"Oh right, really?" He answered back quickly.

Oh, shit. Maybe he actually *was* joking and she looked like the desperate idiot.

"Never mind, forget it." She texted back, feeling idiotic and throwing her phone down. She heard it *bing* again, she grabbed for it; anxious for a positive response this time.

"Why?"

"Probably a bad idea."

"You agreed to it before." Maybe he did want to see her? She felt so confused, why was he sending her mixed signals?

"Well, yeah. It's hard to refuse a direct offer but then I thought you were maybe joking."

"I would never joke about seeing you, I'd love to do something. I can come over to you again? As long as you're sure?"

Jane contemplated, letting him suffer in wait for a moment. Excitement rose through her, she replied manically; "Is seven ok?"

"Perfect."

Jane felt her pulse quicken and her temperature rise, the tingle was back and spreading through her. How she craved for his body, to feel his breath on her skin.

She knew the decision to see Matthew, once again, was unwise but her elated excitement and impatience to see him again was overpowering, and she just couldn't resist.

Jane was also feeling nervous in her house on her own; and lonely, and when she thought about it; what harm would it do really? Jane knew the answer to this deep down – heart shattering disappointment and heart break all over again if it didn't work out and she lost him again.

Millie, Martha, Jennifer and Tess arrived over after lunch, excitedly talking and screeching as they entered the house;

342

"Jane! You need to tell us everything!" Martha bellowed as she threw off her coat.

"Did you kiss?"

"Are you back together?"

"Did he stay the night?" Jennifer, Tess and Millie all screamed over one another.

"Guys, guys! Calm down!" Jane squealed. "No, he didn't stay the night, and no, we aren't back together."

"So you guys kissed!" Martha screeched, giggling and jumping up and down in a teenage, girly delight as they plunged unceremoniously on to the sofas, sitting in waiting, ears pricked to attention.

Jane looked at her feet. "Yes." She looked up and smirked at them with a devilishly, happy grin.

"Oh, you little hussy!" Millie wailed excitedly.

"What does this mean, Jane?!" Tess asked.

"Never mind that silly question." Said Martha, brushing off Tess. "What was it like? How did it happen?"

"You are so nosy!" Said Jennifer, Martha threw her a '*so what?*' kind of look.

"It was absolutely magical, it was scary and sexy and passionate." Martha stuck her index and middle fingers in to her mouth, pretending to make herself wretch.

"Hey! You said you wanted to hear about it!" Jane laughed, rolling her eyes.

"Why was it scary?" Millie asked seriously.

"Because I felt foolish doing it. What if I get hurt again? God knows I've had enough hurt this year to last me a lifetime!" She appealed to the girls for support.

"Maybe it's just a little bit too soon after everything that has gone on the last few days?" Said Jennifer sensibly. "Maybe you need a bit of breathing space."

"Maybe." Jane thought out loud, looking pensive.

Jane contemplated everything in her head later that day, she felt so confused that she decided to forget it all and just spend a romantic night with Matthew, she needed it badly. She needed a distraction.

Matthew arrived punctually. Jane was waiting for him at the door with palpable apprehension. He looked effortlessly dapper in a T shirt and tight blue jeans and his dark hair swept off his face. The curve of his butt in those jeans was enough to send her over the edge.

They kissed straight away as she opened the door. Jane felt a hunger for him, she couldn't get enough. They kissed fiercely as though they had craved for each other the entire time they had been apart. Her hands covered his back and arms and neck and face, she wanted to feel it all, to memorise every curve and crevice. She would never take it for granted again.

Jane had forgotten about the pain in her side and face, too distracted and excited to have him back with her again. She didn't want to lose out on this chance.

Matthew spent the night.

Jane felt euphoric and exhilarated. She felt safe and secure and had, for the night, forgotten about everything else that was going on. She was with him, he was hers. How she had earnestly wished for a moment like this for so long.

"Good morning." Matthew said as Jane woke up from her reverie.

"Good morning." Jane smiled, turning on to her side to face him in bed, he lay there with only the duvet to cover him. Jane's eyes traced hungrily over his masculine physique.

"How do you feel?" He asked, studying her expressions, looking apprehensive.

"A bit sore, but ok, thanks. How are you?" Jane asked with a cheeky, seductive look in her eye.

"I'm really good." He relaxed and smiled and stroked her face softly. "I have to go, though. I have to go to work." He explained.

"Oh, I didn't realise you were working today." She said sadly, her bubble of happiness was rapidly bursting. "We could have done this another time when we were both off the next day so that you didn't have to rush off." Had this just been some kind of sick attempt at a booty call?

"I'm only on a half day until one, I'll call round after if that suits you?" He tried to reassure her.

Phew! Panic over, he still wanted to see her. "Yes, that would be lovely." Her pulse slowed again.

Jane spent the morning pining after Matthew, what was wrong with her? "You're an adult woman, you need to relax yourself. You're supposed to be taking things slow with him." She tried to reason with herself.

As most girls do when they are in need, she phoned her best friend, Millie, who was always able to see sense. Millie, Jennifer and Martha had been a great support network since the 'incident' as they called it now. Bringing round prepared meals, baking cakes and just generally being there. Phoning her at every opportunity to make sure she was ok. Her friends had been the one steady constant in her life who had never let her down.

"Hey Jane, is everything ok?" Said Millie, sounding anxious, worried about her friend's welfare.

"Matthew stayed over last night." Jane stated in a matter of fact way.

"I'm coming over." And Millie hung up.

Millie, only living five minutes away, arrived shortly after.

"How did this happen, Jane?!" She exclaimed excitedly as she clambered through the door in to the hallway. Jane was stood in the living room, biting her nails anxiously.

"He came over again last night." Jane couldn't take the smile off her face. "And then one thing just kind of led to another. I was so desperate to see him again after the day before."

"Oh, Jane, you little minx! And to think that us girls thought you were going to be sensible last night and just stay in on your own." She grinned, sitting herself down on to the sofa.

"When he asked to come over again last night I couldn't even pretend that I didn't want him to. I wanted to see him again so badly." Jane smiled, gingerly lowering herself down on to the same sofa.

"Were you not sore though, I mean, when you were doing it?" Millie asked, as a devilish grin spread across her face.

"Well, we didn't actually get that far, I'm so sore it just wouldn't have been possible. But it was so wonderful, having him here, I feel as though we connected again." She turned to face Millie.

"Jane, I would be absolutely delighted if you and Matthew got back together, I really would. I always liked him, but you were so hurt the last time, you need to be careful. And things

346

are different this time, I'm not altogether sure I am happy about him coming over and taking advantage of you when you have been through such an ordeal. *And*, you will still have more to go through, there will be the court case and everything." Millie said seriously, eyeing up her friend with caution.

"Burst my bubble why don't you." Jane retorted, feeling despondent.

"I know, I'm sorry. I am excited for you but I just worry about you as well. Maybe taking it slow wouldn't be so bad?" Millie suggested timidly.

"I know, you're right. You're definitely right. I've just got completely caught up with him. I missed him so much, you know?"

Jane's happy little bubble was well and truly burst but they were probably the wise words she needed to hear.

"Please don't cry, sweetie. I'm sorry, I didn't mean to upset you. When are you seeing Matthew again?" Millie asked soothingly, squeezing Jane's arm.

"He's coming round after work today." Jane answered, no longer feeling as excited as she had been, her eyes glistened. Why had she invited Millie round? But she couldn't think like that, Millie was her closest friend and only had her best interests at heart.

"Maybe chat to him about how you are feeling and where you are at the moment. But do what is right for you, Jane. Don't let me or Matthew make you feel pressured in to a decision." Millie said, staring at her earnestly.

"Ok, thanks, you're a good friend, Millie."

Matthew kept his word and was over at Jane's house for two o'clock, Jane was unsure of what she wanted to say or do. How could she turn him away when all she wanted was for him to stay with her forever?

"Hi, again." He said as he entered Jane's house for the third day in a row. He smiled at her warmly, his eyes had lit up when he saw her. He bent down and kissed her softly on the lips. The brush of skin caused sparks to fly throughout Jane's body. No. Stop. She had to think sensibly. Keep a level head. She couldn't let his good looks and charisma cloud her mind again.

"Hi."

"You look worried." He said nervously as they stood in the hallway.

"I'm just wondering are we rushing in to things too quickly?" She decided not to mess around and just face the problem head on. She couldn't meet his gaze, she fidgeted nervously.

"If we are happy, then what is stopping us?" He asked seriously, worry lines chiseled in to his face.

"I have so much going on in my head. There will be the court case coming up in the next few weeks and Theo's family will be unbearable I'm sure. I'm sorry I have messed you about this last few days.

"I really have missed you so much and would love for things to work out between us, but I don't think the timing could be any worse. I don't expect you to wait for me but if you can I'm sure this will all be blown over in a few months." Jane continued to stare at her feet, tears rolling down her face. Unable to look at him, unable to face the broken expression she knew would be all over his face.

Matthew was speechless. He hadn't expected this when he had left to go to work that morning. Jane had been so happy to see him when she had woken up. What had changed in that short space of time?

"Jane, we spent the night together last night and now you are telling me that I can't see you for months? That's not fair." Matthew fidgeted agitatedly, he was furious and upset. "You're firing mixed messages at me everywhere, if I'm being honest I feel completely used." He folded his arms, eyeing her up for some kind of explanation.

"I'm so sorry, Matthew. It wasn't my intention to make you feel that way. You knew I had just gone through this massive trauma and wouldn't be ready to dive straight in to something new. I just feel like we are getting in to something too quickly that will ultimately end in hurt again. I can't go through what I went through last year, it was too hard." She cried, imploring him to reason with her.

"I already feel hurt." He snorted derisively. "I understand what you are saying, I just don't understand why you agreed to have me over if this was going to be the outcome."

"*Matthew*... You were so persistent with me, I turned you down the first day you wanted to come over and you persisted the next day as well. You knew I had trepidations about this, so you knew nothing was set in stone. We hadn't decided on anything." She tried to reason with him through gasps of exasperation, her ribs ached from the strain. They were both crying now.

"You've been talking to someone? Getting someone's advice on this?" He asked quietly, feeling defeated and devastated.

"Well, yes." She was shocked he knew this.

"Your mother?" He guessed, rolling his eyes in understanding. Charlotte had a strong and controlling hand in Jane's life that some times Jane wasn't even aware of.

"No, Millie, actually." She admitted, noting the disdain he felt towards her mother.

"I'm surprised." He admitted, looking crestfallen. "I thought Millie would have actually been on my side. I always liked her." He looked beat, tears tracked down his cheeks. The pain in Jane's chest heightened and she rubbed it, trying to ease it away.

"Millie really likes you too, but, she is also uncommonly logical and sensible. She made a good point about me not being in a good place and having so much coming up."

"And, forgetting what everyone else is telling you, what do *you* want, Jane?" He asked earnestly.

"I want you. I have always wanted you. But I don't want to rekindle our relationship while I am battered and bruised and I'm being dragged through court cases." She cried, allowing her tears to fall heavily on to the ground. "What if I got you back but the stress of having to relive my previous relationship and all that will be coming with that would be too stressful for you? I just can't go through losing you again. It's too much."

"I wouldn't runaway again. I promise." He pleaded desperately. "I could support you through it all, look after you, protect you." He cried, begging her, stroking her hand gently. Jane had never seen him looking so low. Was she making a terrible mistake? Could they make it work after all?

"I know you think you would but I think I need to do this on my own, I can't deal with all of this at once. I'm sorry. I hope you will wait for me." Jane's mind was made up, she kicked herself for not taking more time over it, but she had to clear her head after everything that happened in the few short days.

He stood and cried, looking pathetic. Jane's heart was broken. She couldn't believe she was dumping Matthew, maybe to never be seen again, but she knew she was doing the right thing. She couldn't mentally cope with worrying about Matthew and dealing with everything to do with Theo as well, her head was already fit to burst and it had only been three days. She needed breathing space.

She walked over and hugged him; they stood in their embrace for a long time. Both shoulders wet from their tears. Jane could have stayed there for the rest of her life. She breathed in his intoxicating aroma. She ran her hands along his strong back, memorising every groove because it might just be the last time she touched him again.

And he left. Just like that. Just like that he was out of her life again. She was on her own. Jane broke down and fell to the floor, no longer able to carry her legs, her chest heaving in painful, uncontrollable sobs. The stabbing in her ribs intensified with each shudder of her breath. She clutched painfully at her side. Had she made a terrible mistake? Should she call him to come back? Jane's mind was in over drive. She thought she was having a panic attack. She couldn't breathe. Why had she let him leave? "Get him back." She thought desperately.

Chapter 31

Jane had ended things with Matthew in a bid to not get hurt again. But Jane was hurting. She wished she'd never agreed to meet up with him. Such a stupid, idiotic thing to do. Of course it was always going to end in heartache. What had she expected?

Jane felt as though she had delved back in time to one year ago when the fresh memory of the break up was so crisp and clear in her mind. The pain was absolutely unbearable. She would take another fractured rib over this agonising pain any day.

To make matters worse, Jane was informed by Constable Neill that there was a date set for Theo's first appearance in court in two weeks time. She was relieved that things were moving forward in the case but the reality of what was facing her in the future was stark and horrifying.

Constable Neill informed Jane that she could be present in court if she wished, as court hearings are open to the public, with the exception of juvenile cases. She also explained that Jane's Prosecutor would be presenting a case to have Theo remanded in prison until the date of his trial was confirmed.

This brought Jane some comfort, she had been extremely anxious over the last few days, knowing that Theo was out there, somewhere, potentially ready to attack again. Even though she knew he had a curfew and a restraining order, what was stopping him from breaking it? Yes, he would go straight to jail but maybe the risk of jail was worth it to come back and finish her off? Jane's parents and friends vowed to stay with her round the clock to ease her trepidations.

Jane wished Matthew had been there as well to stay with her and keep her safe. Jane's closest friends were very supportive, spending days and nights with her, making meals and generally creating a distraction from her thoughts. She was grateful of this. Jane was also very thankful for her dogs; they provided the love and comfort a lot of adults wouldn't have the capacity to fathom.

Over the coming days, Jane was painfully aware that the court hearing for Theo's first appearance was looming. Jane's father provided her with a great deal of support; researching court processes and the likely sentence Theo might receive. It pained Jane to discover that Theo would not be taken to trial and sentenced for many months. She could only hope, then, that he would be remanded in prison at the upcoming court date, and she could move on with her life for a time.

It was the night before the court hearing and Jane felt sick with nerves and stress, she paced up and down her room, fidgeting and fixing things that had already been fixed and readjusted multiple times before. Why was she putting herself through this? She didn't even have to be there, really. She could just sit it out and wait to hear from Constable Neil as to what the outcome had been.

Jane had considered this over the last two weeks, but, she didn't think she could live with herself if she didn't have the courage to look him in eye, for him to know that she wasn't

353

scared to put up a fight. To make a statement, that she wouldn't allow him to do this to another woman. He deserved to go to prison and that's what she would aim for.

Jane spent the evening with her mum and dad. Her dad had such a calming effect on her. Charlotte vowed to be on her best behaviour and would keep her anxiety levels to a minimum and would just be supportive. Jane wasn't mentally equipped right at that moment to deal with her mother's consternation along with the stress and pressure of the impending court appearance.

Jane and her dad sat at the kitchen table, while Charlotte made a pot of tea;

"Jane, you have nothing to worry about. You are going to burn yourself out overthinking this." Her father was saying. "You need to try and get a good night's sleep."

"What if he gets released on bail and I have to worry for months about whether he is going to come after me or not?!" Jane felt as though she was losing it, she was on edge, pacing around the kitchen faster than ever, she pulled anxiously at her hair and had bitten all her nails down to the quick.

Charlotte presented them with Lavender Tea, to try to calm the steadily rising nerves, she gave Jane a tight hug. Jane found it strange spending time with both her mum and dad together, she wondered were they horrendously uncomfortable, if they were, they hadn't shown it.

Jane's dad drew towards her, he held her by the shoulders and stared at her seriously from an arm's length, "Jane, it is all going to work out. The judge and the jury will be given all the evidence, they will have photos of your injuries, details of the hospital admission, they have the police statements and they have your statement. It's basically a closed case before it has

354

even started. Today is also just a formality, you really have no need to get yourself so stressed out, we will all be here to protect you if Theo doesn't get remanded." Charlotte nodded in agreement.

"Dad, what would I do without you? You are amazing." He pulled her in to a tight hug and she weeped in to his chest.

Jane slept poorly that night, she logged maybe three hours sleep. She got out of bed at six o'clock as she could lie there no more. She made herself a pot of Assam Tea, she needed the caffeine and she needed the bitter, malty flavour to give her the boost and awakening she would need for the day ahead. She couldn't face eating anything. The nerves in her stomach were making her feel sick. She took one sip of tea and thought she might actually spew over her kitchen counter. How was she going to keep her cool in court?

Jane got showered and dressed, her headache and the pain in her ribs were still very much present, her whole body ached and she still felt a sharp stab when she breathed in. She put on a smart, grey pant suit that covered her up well. She didn't want to reveal her legs or cleavage, it wouldn't send a great message.

"How are you feeling, Jane?" Charlotte asked tentatively as Jane crept downstairs, nervously straightening her clothes. Charlotte's eyes were wide with fright.

"Terrible." Jane replied coolly.

Charlotte looked as though her repressed anxiety was breaking the surface, ready to explode at any moment, her face glistened with tears. She ran over and grabbed Jane in to a rib cracking hug. Letting out huge, heaving sobs and breathing rapidly with angst.

"It will all be ok, my darling. Your dad and I will be here for you every step of the way!" She breathed, gaining control of herself again. Charlotte's momentary breakdown was enough to send Jane in to hysterics of panic, she didn't want to go through with it.

"Thank you," was all Jane managed. Taking deep breaths, her lips trembled uncontrollably on the exhale.

Jane arrived, an hour early, at the court house, along with her mum and dad, she spoke to a security guard who directed her to Victim Services who were situated in a side room off the foyer. Her mum went off to find the tea and coffee vending machine but her dad went with with her to meet with Victim Services. The room was cold and unwelcoming which added to Jane's terror. She was met by a kind, stout lady, Jane guessed she must have been around sixty years old.

"Hi Jane, my name is Patricia. I'm a volunteer for Victim Services. I can help answer some of the questions that I know must be buzzing around your head." Jane instantly warmed to Patricia, she was kind and reassuring and she was also a volunteer, Jane was in awe. Who would take time out of their own day to do a job like that?

"Thank you, Patricia. How did you end up becoming a volunteer?" Jane had to know. Patricia ambled around the room, there was a mini kitchen in the room and Patricia hurried along and made three cups of tea. Jane eyed the teabags but refrained from saying anything.

"I was a victim once, *too*, Jane." Patricia eyed her seriously, Jane noted a glint of sadness and fear in her eyes.

"That's amazing." Jane stated. Patricia's mouth curved in to a warm smile.

Patricia was a god send, she filled Jane in on a lot of the process surrounding court hearings and made clear the difference between family hearings and criminal hearings. Theo would eventually be tried in the Crown Court as he had committed a criminal offence. But, because today was only his first appearance, they were attending the Magistrate's Court. Jane's head swelled with the abundance of new information, it was a whole new world to her.

She met, shortly after, with the Prosecutor who introduced himself as Charles Malcolm. A tall man in his mid forties, Jane had guessed. He had dark brown hair that was greying only slightly at the sides. He had bright, blue eyes and a kind smile. Jane felt more reassured as soon as she saw him. This didn't stop her hands from trembling in her lap though. Her dad placed one of his large hands over both of hers to try to still the shaking, Jane squeezed his hand tightly.

Charles Malcolm quickly dashed away after their brief introduction, Patricia informed them that Prosecutors had a monumental work load and being able to introduce himself to her was impressive.

Jane's whole body was trembling, she was not sure she would be able to hold up in court when she had to face Theo. Her dad put an arm around her and gave her a reassuring squeeze, she started to cry.

"I don't want to do this, dad." She cried pitiably.

"I know, honey and you don't have to, you can back out now." He caressed her face softly. Gary looked riddled with concern and anxiety for his daughter. His anger rose inwardly towards the man who was subjecting her to all this suffering.

At these words Jane found strength within, she would not back down to Theo as though she were some weak, little victim. She would stand tall and proud in defiance of the man who had tried to beat her down.

"I will be with you every step of the way. It will all be over soon." Her dad continued.

"I hope so," was all she could say, wiping her eyes and grabbing the compact from her bag to try to camouflage the tear stains that had sneaked through her make up.

They entered the gallery of the courtroom, it was a large, dull room lined with wooden stalls that reminded Jane of a church. In front of the stalls there were two long desks, one in front of the other. Jane noticed that Charles Malcolm was already sitting at the desk furthest away.

In front of these two desks was another that seemed to be up on a platform, raised above ground level, there were a couple of serious looking officials sitting there. And, behind that platform was the Judge's podium, it was a thick, wooden, intricate structure that was raised high up far above the rest, it dominated over the room intimidatingly. Jane felt terrified and overwhelmed by the cold officialness of the room.

There were a few observers in the stalls. Her mother, Bob and Tess were amongst them along with Millie, Martha, Jennifer and Jane's stepmother, Agnes. The sight of them gave her strength.

On the other side of the room, Jane spotted Veronica, Theo's mother. She shot Jane the dirtiest look she could muster. The sight of Veronica filled Jane with drive and determination to get Theo thrown in to jail for a long time. Jane's fear was replaced by anger and strength of mind to do what needed to be done. Theo was going down. Also present, were Theo's father and younger sister, who she had met on multiple occasions. They seemed to not even fathom her existence and merely looked directly through her, to imagine that she had known these people and previously had such a close relationship with them was hard for Jane to comprehend.

Gary and Jane sat down beside Agnes in the stalls. Jane's friends and family gave her encouraging nods and thumbs up, she smiled weakly back at them. She felt tears press the back of her eyes, she gulped them down.

Theo entered the room, head down, appearing subdued, along with his solicitor. He sat in the stalls, beside his mother. He quickly traced the room and his gaze landed upon Jane, his eyes grew wide with stumped shock, Jane smirked inwardly, Theo had obviously not expected her to make an appearance.

Jane thought he looked tired, there were dark circles under his eyes. She could only imagine that he had not slept very much over the last two weeks.

Jane read from the name tag that Theo's solicitor was called Andrea Gibb; she was a tall, thin woman with long, blonde hair. She was very attractive but with a stern, no nonsense face, she had an air of confidence that made her intimidation even more profound. She sat herself at the desk closest to the gallery and produced a large wad of documents from her briefcase that she neatly laid out in to organised piles.

Before the Judge entered, one of the court staff stood up and announced; "All stand!"

The Judge then entered, he did not make eye contact with the crowd, he sat down and shuffled through his papers. It disappointed Jane that the Judge was male, would he be less likely to vote in her favour? He looked to be approximately fifty five with salt and pepper hair and a thick, bushy moustache the same colour as his hair. From the plaque sitting

359

on the desk, Jane could read that his name was 'Judge R.J. Johnson'.

Charles Malcolm then announced; "Good morning, Your Worship, case thirteen, first appearance of Mr Theo Reid."

"Is the defendant in court today?" The Judge asked.

At this point, Andrea Gibb stood up and spoke in a severe voice that could have cut through glass; "Good morning, Your Worship. This is Mr Theo Reid." She gestured in the direction of Theo who was sitting behind her.

The Magistrate then said; "Stand up Mr Reid and take the box."

A member of court staff then ushered Theo in to a windowed, boxed off area which was occupied by a prison guard.

The court clerk began; "Theo Reid, you are charged with the offence of grievous bodily harm with intent. How do you plead?"

Theo stared down at the floor awkwardly and mumbled; "Not guilty."

Jane stared in disbelief. *Not guilty?* How could he? How could he deny what he had put her through? How would he explain the injuries and the hospital admission?

The Prosecutor then turned to Constable Neill and asked; "Constable, can you please take the stand."

At this point, Constable Neill, who had been sitting at the front of the gallery, went and sat in the witness box. A court official turned to the police officer and asked her to take the oath. The officer held a Bible in her right hand and stated; "I swear to tell the truth, the whole truth, and nothing but the truth, so help me God."

"Constable, can you connect the defendant with the charges?" Malcolm asked.

Constable Neill then replied, directing her answer to the Judge; "Yes, Your Worship."

"Constable, do you have any objections to bail?"

"Yes, Your Worship. The Police object to bail on the grounds that we suspect the defendant is responsible for inflicting injuries that left the victim, in this case, hospitalised for three days, and we believe that it's in the best interests of her safety that this man be remanded in custody." Jane was feeling hopeful, she could finally sleep if she knew he was in prison.

The Prosecutor then declared that he had no further questions for the Constable. The defence solicitor repeated these words to the Magistrate and Constable Neill left the witness box and took a seat in the public area again.

Gibb then said to the Magistrate; "Your Worship, my client is not guilty, he merely defended himself on the night that he was attacked by his *so-called* victim. He has no previous criminal convictions. He is an upstanding, employed member of the community. He has no previous history of breaching bail conditions and as we can see from the last fourteen days, this man can be trusted to honour bail."

Jane was completely dumbfounded, she wanted to jump up and scream at the audacity of this comment. She looked at Theo but he continued to stare resolutely ahead. "This guy's a psychopath." She thought. He was claiming that she attacked him!

The Judge then proclaimed loudly; "Bail granted, the terms of this bail are to remain the same as previously stated. Court dismissed."

Jane darted her glances frantically to her family and friends, reaching out for support. They all sported mixed expressions of concern and trepidation.

"Don't worry, Jane," said Martha, "that Malcolm guy seems bad ass, he'll pull through with the right result. He *has* to." Jane bit her lip anxiously.

"He made bail. God knows when his trial will be, I have to live knowing that he could be anywhere?" Jane's eyes were swimming with tears, she darted her head nervously around the room. Theo was making his way out, with Veronica by his side.

"Jane," Agnes approached, "I have quite a few bottles of Champagne in the house, I was hoping that we would all be able to celebrate tonight. We could pop them tonight anyway? Take your mind off everything?"

Jane smiled at Agnes, "Yes, that would be lovely."

Chapter 32

The plan that evening was to have everyone round to Jane's house for a party. Jane was feeling optimistic, although Theo had no previous convictions, all the odds were stacked against him. She decided to relax and let her hair down and believe that a good outcome would be waiting for her at the end of this long and winding journey.

Jane also had other burning issues on her mind, she couldn't stop thinking of Matthew and how she would have loved to have had him there with her for support and encouragement. Matthew consumed her thoughts every moment of every day, she longed for his touch. She missed everything about him, his unforgivable good looks, his powerful charisma, his ability to make her feel weak at the knees, his kindness and the way she felt adored by him.

She checked her phone but Matthew had been true to his word. He was giving her space. She didn't want space anymore, though, she wanted *him*.

Jane decided to take the chance, she took out her phone and started typing a message;

"Hi Matthew, my first court case was today, not the result we were hoping for but hopefully all will work out. Just thought I would let you know. Also, I have been thinking about you a lot lately x"

Jane sent it. As soon as the message had been delivered she immediately doubted her decision, overwhelming feelings of self doubt and self destruction began to fill her up. What if he was over her? What if he thought she was desperate and needy for messaging him out of the blue? What if he just didn't want her anymore?

Jane didn't know if she could handle that, the absolute rejection all over again. "He doesn't want you. He doesn't love you." No. She couldn't start falling in to that deep, dark hole again, she needed to be positive, if he'd changed his mind then she would find a way to move on.

Jane's friends and family were coming over to her house at six o'clock that evening, it was currently four, there was plenty of time to get showered and dressed and get the house looking half presentable. Tess's husband, Glenn, had kindly walked Jack and Ruby for Jane whilst she had been at court. They were both looking suitably burnt out and snoozed peacefully on the sofa. Jane periodically checked her phone, hoping for a reply. An hour passed, but nothing. Had she pushed him away for good? Her stomach somersaulted nauseously. She yearned for the reply.

Everyone arrived shortly after six, it was one of the rare occasions where Jane's parents were seen in the same room together. They were old enough that this wasn't made in to an issue, although Jane felt sympathy for Bob and Agnes, it was probably highly uncomfortable for them; their married partners in the same room as their ex partner. This caused Jane to reflect back to Jennifer's wedding when Theo and Tia were swept up with jealousy over Matthew and Jane being in the same room together. Bob and Agnes appeared completely unperturbed by the fact. Jane inwardly applauded them.

Jane's three best friends were also there; Millie, Jennifer and Martha along with their partners; Oliver, Ben and Lucas. Tess and her husband Glenn were there along with their three children; Grace, Beth and Josh. Jane adored these children. They came running in and all three did a leap jump in to their Auntie Jane's arms. Jane was pretty sure she had sustained another broken rib, she squeezed them warmly. Jane couldn't help paralleling children with dogs, their loving innocence, finding the fun in every single activity, not taking life seriously. Although, dogs were a blessing in that you were guaranteed not to have any temper tantrums.

The music was started and the champagne was popped, Jane was feeling fortunate in that moment to have all her favourite people around her. Her mood had picked up already. Millie, Martha, Jennifer and Tess had planned to stay overnight.

"We can sleep on the sofa, we don't care!" Martha declared happily when Jane had pointed out that five people staying in a two bedroom house could be a rather difficult conundrum.

"It'll be so much fun, Jane, like being a child again and having sleepovers!" Jennifer giggled excitedly, breathless from carrying around an incredibly pregnant belly.

Jane checked her phone again after about an hour in to the party, but still no response from Matthew, she was feeling distracted and irritable. Why had he not replied? Did she not even deserve that courtesy? Jane decided to give up on waiting for a reply from him. "Why should I ruin my night?" She thought. Jane carried on with her celebrations, trying to get the handsome, unassailable man out of her head.

Jane mingled through the house, checking that everyone had topped up drinks and that there were enough snacks on the tables. Her mother and father were in the kitchen talking, Bob and Agnes were in the living room, clearly unaware of the transaction of words between the ex lovers. Jane watched the two of them. Jane was ashamed to notice that her mother was being an insatiable flirt. Charlotte continuously kept touching Gary's forearm and bicep with her hand and giggled girlishly at everything he said. It was painful to watch. Jane overheard part of their conversation;

"Gary, we really did create wonderful girls between us, didn't we?" Charlotte slurred slightly. Jane appreciated the compliment but knew her mother's behaviour could be slightly unpredictable with alcohol on board.

"We sure did." Gary agreed blithely, standing awkwardly, darting sideways glances at Charlotte as she swayed slightly.

"I'm sorry it just couldn't work out between us. You seem so happy with Agnes now." Charlotte breathed, her eyelids hooded heavily.

"I am, Charlotte. Anyway, I best get back to her." He smiled, grabbing his drink and leaving for Agnes.

Jane approached her mother and put an arm around her.

"You doing ok, mum?" Jane asked.

"When you have children some day, protect them, never let any harm come to them. They will be the most precious thing in the world to you." Charlotte said wistfully, almost to herself.

"Of course, mum." Jane wondered was this an apology from her mum, for not protecting her as a child from the wrath of her aunt and uncle.

"Your dad will always be special to me; he gave me you and Tess, that creates a bond, you know? I hope I didn't make him feel uncomfortable just now." She took a long sip of her champagne.

"I don't think you did." Jane lied. "I'm sure he just didn't want Agnes to feel uncomfortable." Charlotte smiled fondly at her.

"You're a good girl, Jane. I'm so happy this nightmare is nearly all behind you. I fear I may never take my eye off you again." Jane looked at her scoldingly.

"You have to let me be free, mum. I have to make my own mistakes and learn from them." Jane said earnestly.

"But, your mistakes ended you up in the emergency department, I cannot cope with the worry I face every day for you. What if this happens to you again? And, what if I'm not there to protect you, again?" Charlotte was becoming slightly frantic. Jane put an arm around her again to soothe her agitation.

"Mum, it's all going to be ok. This was just a one off, really terrible situation. It won't happen again." Charlotte looked at Jane with a solemn expression. Jane hated that her mum was so disturbed because of her decisions in life, Jane would have to do better in order to protect her mother. Her mother was fragile, delicate, she needed protection from life's horrors as much as Jane did.

Jane left her mum with Bob to go to the bathroom. She looked at her phone, but still, there was no response from Matthew. Maybe her aunt had been right all those years ago, maybe there would never be a man willing to be bothered with her, maybe she would just be alone forever because of her own detestable personality. But, despite her aunt's determination to beat Jane down and rid her of any self worth or self esteem, Jane knew deep down that she was a good person and had great qualities to offer. Going against her better judgement and feeling excessively vulnerable and needy and heavily intoxicated from champagne, she clicked on Matthew's number and began ringing.

"Hello?"

"Hey, Matthew."

"Hey, Jane, are you ok?" His voice was unreadable.

"I was just phoning you because I see you haven't responded to my message and I was just checking that you were definitely completely over me and now have just reverted to ignoring me." Jane tripped over her words slightly.

"I'm in work Jane, I've been at a car accident all evening." He explained coldly.

Oh, dear. Oh, no, what had she done? She was lost for words, how could she rectify the situation? Her inebriated brain could not figure out how to get her out of this one.

"Hello?" Jane had been silent for a long time.

"I'm still here." She said. "Sorry, I shouldn't have phoned you. I'll let you get back to work." She was disconcerted and mortified, she wanted the ground to swallow her up.

"Look, I'm finishing my shift soon, can I call you after?" He asked.

"I'm having a party." She stated simply.

"Ok, well, I'll call you tomorrow then."

"Ok, bye." And she hung up.

What a car crash. Literally. Why had she phoned him? Phoning exes when drunk was never ever a good idea. He probably thought she was a complete idiot. Jane felt even worse than before. She had stooped to a whole new level of low. The one good thing, she thought, was that he hadn't just been ignoring her. He was just busy at work. Hallelujah. Unless that was a lie and he was brushing her off. Oh, the confusion.

Jane returned to the party and tried to forget about the hideous phone call, she poured another glass of champagne and swayed unsteadily to the music. Everyone was either deep in conversation or dancing excitedly. Jane didn't feel much like doing either, she plonked herself firmly on to the sofa. She desperately craved Matthew, she regretted her choice to send him away weeks ago.

Jane knew deep down that the couple of weeks she hadn't seen Matthew were just what she needed to get her head in a better place, but now Matthew had apparently moved on and Jane knew she had lost her chance. She felt tearful all over again, it was really over with him, he didn't want her, *again*. She sat down on the sofa, predicting a severe hangover in the morning already. Her dad moved over and joined her on the sofa.

"Are you ok, sweetie?" He asked, putting a supportive arm around her and squeezing her tightly.

"I'm fine." Jane lied, staring fixedly in to space, trying to block out her demonising thoughts. Her dad wasn't to know what was really on her mind.

"Your mum is very worried about you." He looked at her sombrely.

"I know, she worries an awful lot. I feel terrible having put you guys through so much stress." Jane admitted, staring feebly down at her hands.

"Parents are supposed to be stressed out and worried about their kids, it's part of what you sign up for. But, what happened to you was serious, your mum and I are riddled with concern about you. We have a suggestion to make." He explained, no longer looking at Jane. She wondered anxiously as to what the suggestion might be.

369

"Ok?" Jane said tentatively, nodding for him to continue.

"Your mum and I have discussed the possibility of you coming to live with one of us," Jane darted him a scandalised look, Gary continued before Jane could interrupt. "It would just be in the short term until the whole court process is over and that scumbag is officially out of your life."

"You know I can't do that, dad. I appreciate the concern you and mum both have but I won't be able to move on from this if I'm living under the watchful gaze of you both. I'll lose my freedom altogether." Jane yawped, feeling suffocated and trapped, moving away, creating distance between herself and her father.

"But at least we could protect you, and we would know you were safe." He pleaded, looking disheartened.

"But, what if I go out with my friends? Are you going to follow me to make sure I'm safe there, too?" Jane demanded, slightly more angrily than she had intended. Gary's expression was forlorn and hurt. Jane felt immensely guilty for being so harsh.

"No, Jane, it was just a suggestion. In case it would make *you* feel safer, also?" He looked down at her with sad eyes.

"I'm sorry I snapped, dad. I just really need my own space and freedom at the minute. I can completely get where you guys are coming from, but it would set me back a lot. I need to try to get back to my old life and my own routine, I think that is best for everyone." She explained determinedly, she needed her independence, her own space, that was essential. Living with her parents would be a step in the wrong direction. She looked up at her dad, imploring him not to pursue the topic any longer.

"I understand, sweetie. Just know that your mum and dad are always here for you. I know that there may have been a time in your life when we weren't, but we want to make up for that." Jane looked slowly round at him, was he also referring to what her mother had suggested earlier? Had they both been in cahoots recently about the goings on with her aunt and uncle all those years ago?

The doorbell rang. Jane dragged her eyes off her dad, she heard the door open. She wondered who it could be, for a moment she panicked that her aunt might make an appearance like she had after the miscarriage. But then, she heard Jennifer's excited voice;

"Oh. Hi Matthew!"

Matthew! It couldn't be *her* Matthew?! What was he doing there! She spun round quickly and there he was, stepping forward in to the living room with his natural air of self assurance and good posture, she was taken aback by his appearance, as she always was, she could never get used to the intense, intimate gaze he gave her. Everyone was staring at him, in mesmerised shock.

"What are you doing here?" Jane asked clumsily.

Matthew did not seem perturbed by this blunt welcome, he spoke in front of everyone but directly to Jane, those eyes boring in to her, reaching a part of her soul that made her warm from the inside out, making her feel like the only girl in the world.

"I finished my shift and realised I probably sounded abrupt on the phone and didn't want you to think I had cut you off." He explained, standing confidently with his hands in his pockets, looking effortlessly sexy in slacks and a T shirt.

371

"Well, I probably shouldn't have phoned you in my current state." She rubbed at her neck, feeling intensely vulnerable and self aware.

"I'm glad you did." He said. Everyone's eyes were still on them. Neither of them seemed to notice.

"You are?" Jane asked, looking puzzled. She thought Matthew was over her, moved on.

"Of course." Matthew then turned, seemingly only just noticing that he was the centre of everyone's attention. He looked slightly sheepish in his sexy, boyish way and announced to the party; "I'm sorry for gate crashing, I heard there was a party and I didn't want to miss out." He laughed, it was a feeble attempt at an excuse but everyone joined in on the laughter and they all seemed to disperse to various other parts of the house. He placed a hand at the small of Jane's back and directed her in to the kitchen where no one else was standing.

He turned to face her, Jane felt her legs go to jelly. "I'm so glad the first court case is behind you." He said, almost in a whisper, his eyes bright with pride.

"Thanks, it's a relief to have one part of it over. Unfortunately, that was the easy bit." She scowled at the thought. "So, how come you are here?" She asked again, feeling warmth course through her veins as his presence radiated towards her.

"I told you already."

"You don't just turn up at someone's house because you are worried if you sounded offensive or not on the phone." She teased.

He laughed as though he had been caught out; "It was a good excuse though?" He smirk and pushed his hand through his hair, looking vaguely embarrassed but not all together ashamed.

Jane laughed, "It was a feeble excuse but I'm glad to see you."

"It's good to see you." He confessed, his expressive eyes giving away a momentary glimpse of sadness.

Their gaze lingered on one another. Jane could feel her heart rate rising and the hairs stand up on the back of her neck despite feeling very warm.

Jane felt hunger for him, his powerful gaze and his strong demeanour made her feel like putty in his hands. She harboured a strong urge to touch him, even just to feel his arm, to feel the warmth spread through her like fire. Jane suddenly became aware of herself and looked around.

"Ever feel like you're being watched?" She chuckled.

Standing in the kitchen door peering in at them were Millie, Jennifer, Martha and Tess.

"Want to go for a walk?" He asked.

"Everyone is kind of here for me." She explained sheepishly, desperately wanting to go for the walk with him. She bit her lip. Matthew seemed to notice this and his eyes narrowed and burned harder for her.

"Sorry, yeah, you're right. I can't just gatecrash and then take you away from the party." He smiled down at her.

"It's fine. I'm glad to see you. Tonight was a bit of a train wreck anyway." She admitted.

"How come?" He implored, his brow creased with concern.

"My mother was here earlier." She said simply with no other explanation.

"Ah, ok, point taken. You probably need a drink then?" He said, noticing her empty hand.

"Wouldn't be such a bad idea. What's the worst that could happen? I've already drunk dialled an ex boyfriend." They both giggled, Matthew's hand swept across hers, their eyes met briefly.

Jane's friends and her dad chatted to Matthew through the course of his stay. Gary looked wary, he was on high alert for his daughter who had suffered a stressful enough time over the last few weeks.

"Well, I think I have well and truly overstayed my welcome." He turned to face Jane in the living room. "Are you free over the weekend?"

"Do you want to call over tomorrow night?" Jane asked quickly, hoping that she had hid the eager desperation in her voice. Matthew looked at her and his lips curved in to a smile.

"I'll be there." His eyes lit up like torches, passion exploded within Jane. She had a sudden spontaneous urge to tell everyone to get out of her house and just leave her and Matthew to it.

"Anyway, I will leave you to enjoy your party." Matthew was saying, Jane had realised she was day dreaming. A terrible habit of hers she could never get rid of, much to the displeasure of her mother. "I have stolen you away for long enough."

Jane walked him to the door and he kissed her on the cheek goodbye. Jane's mood had flipped suddenly, she had felt beyond depressed earlier in the evening when her mother and father couldn't hide their concern, but now, she couldn't be happier. She had one ex boyfriend hopefully awaiting a prison cell and another hopefully ready to make a permanent reappearance back in to her life. And her mother and father's suggestion of living with them, well, that was just something she would have to put to the back of her mind.

The girls approached Jane;

"That looked promising." Martha teased enthusiastically, squeezing her arm.

"Are you guys dating again?!" Jennifer demanded excitedly.

"Of course not, Jane has only just got rid of one man! She needs to take these things slowly!" Urged Tess, her eyes bore holes in to Jane's.

"No, we are not going out again but he is coming over here tomorrow night." She said, trying hard to contain her delight.

"So, why was he here tonight?" Millie asked concernedly.

"Because I drunk dialled him and he was worried about me." Jane admitted, putting her head in her hands.

"That's got to be the first ever successful drunk dial I have ever heard of!" Millie chortled.

"We don't know if it's a success, *yet*." Jane said, trying not to get her hopes up too much.

"Jane, he looked as though he could've picked you up and carried you right out the front door when he saw you." Said an excited Martha.

"I'm sure he was just being polite." Said Jane, but deep down she was hoping and praying that Martha was right. Jane was invested in the hope that things were rekindling with Matthew, and this made her feel fearful and insecure.

For so many years, she had remained single in order to not become dependent on another human being, and now, here she was, the fate of her own happiness resting on one single, solitary man. She felt idiotic, but she couldn't help it. Now that she knew what she wanted. She had to have him.

The next evening Matthew was due over, it had been the longest day of Jane's life. Why had she not asked him to come over in the morning and then she wouldn't have had to wait so long. But now the time had come and Jane was terrified, she thought she might vomit with the amount of back flips her stomach was doing.

Jane knew why she was so scared, she was going to ask Matthew to be with her again, she *had* to. She could be without him no longer, she had to find out if he felt the same way.

Jane thought positively to herself that surely that was the reason why he was coming over again? The reason that he turned up the night before, uninvited?

Then again, Jane's pessimistic mind set came in to play once more and she began to self destruct like she always did. He was only coming over for a quickie in the sack, she was easy meat and she was serving it to him on a plate.

Seven o'clock came around too fast and Matthew was punctual when she heard the knock on the door, Jane thought she might not make it to the door she was shaking that badly. What if he ended it forever?

Jane opened the front door to him; he looked effortlessly debonair in loafers, chinos and a shirt, his hands tucked in to his pockets giving the impression of a model. Jane's breath was taken from her, all she could do was stare at him.

"Can I come in?" He scoffed.

"What? Oh. Yes. Sorry, come in." She felt mortified, staring at him like a gormless idiot.

"I'm glad I still have that effect on you." He said playfully, delight warmed his eyes at this greeting. Jane remained lost for words.

"You look pretty great, too." He poked fun at Jane's continued silence. Jane blushed at the compliment and her eyes burned just from looking at him. Time to talk.

"Sorry, you look amazing, it kind of takes my breath away every time." She admitted, shaking herself back in to reality.

"I love that.' He approached her and ran the back of his hand against her cheek, it sent a shiver down her spine. She wondered did he feel it too, the invisible connection of energy between them.

Just then, Matthew unexpectedly closed the gap between the two of them, his warm, hard body pressed against hers. Ever so softly, he pressed his lips against hers, then, in a matter of seconds they were ravenous for each other, clawing at hair and clothes, breathy through unrestrained desire.

Tearing themselves away from one another, feeling flushed and lightheaded, Jane asked; "Can I get you a drink?" They both giggled as though teenagers.

"Sure." He answered.

Jane poured two glasses of red wine and thought wistfully of hers and Matthew's future ahead. Would they make it work? Could they survive their wounded past and Jane's multicoloured baggage?

Jane sat down beside him and offered him the glass. He accepted it gratefully, turning his face to align with her, in a swift moment his lips were on hers again, soft and passionate. She caressed his neck, he ran his fingers through her hair. Banishing the demons in their closets, they came up for air.

Matthew stared at her sincerely with those lustrous eyes. "We can do this."

Acknowledgements

To my husband, Peter, for being my very own editor and counsellor through the late night writing splurges and many moments of self doubt and confidence in my abilities to achieve this goal. I could not have done this without you. To my four dogs; Jasper, Maisie, Samson and Milly, you four truly are the masters of mindfulness, life is so much better with your happy innocence around me. To my family and friends who had no idea that I was creating this project, thank you for moulding me in to the person I am today, without her I never would have been able to create Jane.

Printed in Great Britain
by Amazon